IN TO WRITE MY EPITAPH

LET NO MAN WRITE MY EPITAPH

books by Willard Motley

LET NO MAN WRITE MY EPITAPH

WE FISHED ALL NIGHT

KNOCK ON ANY DOOR

LET NO MAN WRITE MY EPITAPH

Willard Motley

RANDOM HOUSE   NEW YORK

FIRST PRINTING

Excerpts from *Knock on Any Door*, by Willard Motley (pages 10-13, 98, 99, 100-103, 245-249, 259, 327, 328, 350-352, 396, 397). Copyright, 1947, by Willard Motley. Reprinted by permission of the publishers, Appleton-Century-Crofts, Inc.

The following songs were reprinted by permission, as noted:
"Mood Indigo," by Duke Ellington, Irving Mills and Albany Bigard (pages 14, 26, 32, 38, 41, 448, 449, 450, 451). Copyright, 1931, by Gotham Music Service, Inc. Used by permission of the copyright owner.
"One for My Baby," by Johnny Mercer and Harold Arlen (pages 464, 465, 466). Copyright, 1943, by Edwin H. Morris and Company, Inc. Used by permission of the copyright owner.
"I Can See Everybody's Baby," by Kirkland and Thomas (pages 125, 126, 129, 130). © Copyright, 1955, by Progressive Music Publishing Co., Inc. Used by permission.
"As Long as I'm Moving," by Charles Calhoun (pages 96, 97, 98, 277). © Copyright, 1955, by Progressive Music Publishing Co., Inc. Used by permission.
"Make Believe," by Jerome Kern and Oscar Hammerstein II (page 382). Copyright, 1927, by T. B. Harms Company, New York. Copyright renewed.
"A.B.C. Boogie," by Al Russel and Max Spickol (pages 435, 436, 437, 438, 439). Copyright, 1954, by Myers Music, Inc. Used by permission.

Manufactured in the United States of America by H. Wolff, New York

FOR MY SON SERGIO

Let there be no inscriptions upon my tomb, let no man write my epitaph. No man can write my epitaph. I am here to die. I am not allowed to vindicate my character; and when I am prevented from vindicating myself, let no man dare to calumniate me. Let my character and motives repose in obscurity and peace, till other times and other men can do them justice.

ROBERT EMMETT, speech on his
conviction for treason,
September, 1803

Let no man write my epitaph; let my grave be uninscribed
and let my memory rest
Till other times are come, and other men
Who then may do me justice.

SOUTHEY, written after reading
the speech of Robert Emmett

1 *a stranger and afraid*

1

Dandelions were in yellow circles. He stood on the hillock on his small, thin legs, with long fingers of grass tickling his bare legs, sunshine all over him, and the sky was big and wide and open, blue, bluer than his blue crayon, with the sound of a bird off somewhere and his ear pointing to catch the notes somewhere in the pine trees that were straight on the hills like the arrows Indians used, and he could smell with his little pinch of a nose the good smells from the kitchen and already taste the cookies they would have with milk after dinner that were sweet and crunchy and brown and good and afterwards you licked your fingers for all the little left crumbs, with your fingers gentle you picked them off the floor and put them in your mouth.

This was a *nice* place! It wasn't like the city at all. Mother told him this was the country. And there was a room with a lot of books with pictures in them and little tables and chairs that fit him and the other kids. You could even take the picture books and lie on your belly in the grass with all the little dandelion faces looking at you and turn the pages with pictures on them of cows and horses and chickens and ducks just like they had here. There was a pool for little kids his age where you took steps in the water and it was cold at first even if it was summer because Mother said this was a northern part of the country. There was a young man in red swimming trunks who sat all day long between this little pool and the bigger one for bigger kids, all day long as if he were sleeping. There were letters in red on the back of his white chair, and if he could read he would know what they said. Each mother and her child or children had a little house all their own, just like his. Mother put a dandelion under his chin. He had never seen one before. And she said let's see if you like butter. It tickled and he laughed. Every day they played that game. Every day he laughed and Mother said he liked butter because it was yellow under his chin. He did too! Mother told him about the silver ones. She said that just like people all the dandelions got gray hair when they were old. "But, Mother, your hair isn't gray."—"But I'm not old yet." Only, Mother said, they looked like crowns that kings in stories wear. And you blow them. Hundreds of little silver people would then float out across the sunlight and the blue of sky and wherever they touched there in the grass next year other dandelions would grow with shining little yellow faces. And he started to ask her to play the game of butter again when a rainbow came out like all his crayons scratching across the paper and he had never seen one before. His mother held his hand as they watched it (but why did she cry?) and then she pulled him close until his forehead was down against her shoulder and hurting a little and she was humming to him; then it faded out as soon as it had been there and it had never been there and his mother said something about milk.

"Yes, Mother?"

"Let me show you where the milk comes from."

She took him to where there was a cow in the barn and wiggled him under it. He opened his mouth in obedience and squinted his eyes shut. It was hot and milk was always cold and he spat it out—

"Nicky!" she called. "Nicky!"

He came running on his short legs. She knelt down on the grass and took him into her arms. She was crying. But so that he could not see: They took him away from me and I gave him back.

"I love you!" Nick said, hugging her fiercely with his thin arms.

"I love you too, honey, and we're going home tomorrow."

blue, bluer than his blue crayon . . .

She had told him the story in the dark. He had finally fallen asleep and now she sat in the darkness of the little cabin. This was the first time she had been in the country since she was fifteen. She thought

4

of her uncle's farm and of her uncle. There were stars in an irregular pattern at the cabin window and outside the frogs made their night sounds. This charitable organization had offered two weeks' vacation to working and widowed mothers and (it implied) unwed mothers. She had signed up and been accepted. She was an unwed mother and they had accepted her. The woman director of the program had smiled at her kindly, as if she knew and understood and was glad that she could take this vacation. "What a cute little boy!" she had said, patting Nick on the head. "What is his name—what is your name, sonny?"

. . . In the darkness in the little cabin. Thoughts coming and going. And then her mind was numb because there were things she didn't want to think about. Even through the closed door she could smell the clover. She could see their purples. Things she didn't want to think about. She listened to her son's breathing. Her eyes edged up to tears. She put the back of one hand up, first to one eye and then to the other. Her son moved in his sleep. My son! My son! She must see him, look at him. Quietly she turned on the light, shielding it from his face, and she smiled a bit as she looked at him. Gently her hand touched his face, caressingly, palm then fearfully on his forehead for fever, fingers across his cheek, into his hair, palm in a kiss across his nose. My son. He moved again and mumbled in his sleep. Gently she put her hand across his lips. Automatically his mouth opened, searching for her thumb. "No, no," she whispered, smiling. And looking at him: The book said that you mustn't spoil them. That at five they are becoming independent and you should respect them as individuals. Quietly she tucked the woolly gray blanket securely about his feet, lay down in the bed with him, pulled the blankets up until only his pinch of a nose was out from under the covers.

On the morning you left, you did not need to go to the big dining room; an attendant, an underprivileged high school girl getting a vacation too, brought your breakfast to you so that you could eat, pack, do any number of personal things by way of getting ready for the trip home.

After they had eaten, Nellie, as any good waitress always does, cleared the table and cleaned it, washed and stacked the dishes. Then, first seeing that the seams of her cheap silk stockings were straight, she picked up the pasteboard suitcase and, taking Nick by the hand, went to the office. The superintendent was smiling when they came in, and stood to greet them. She held out her hand to Nellie. "I hope you have enjoyed yourself, Mrs. Watkins, and I hope we have you with us again next year."

Nellie averted her eyes a moment: she had only written Nellie Watkins on the application. "Yes, ma'am. We—we had a real nice time. Especially Nick—and thanks a lot." She straightened the collar of Nick's jacket and gave his hair a final pat in place.

" 'Bye, Nicky!" the superintendent said cheerfully. She had a small toy for him. "That's so you won't forget us."

He held his mother's hand on the bus and looked up into her face. Then his head was down on her lap, the fuzzy quality of her skirt tickling his nose . . . asleep . . . awake . . . Past his eyes ran the trees and the hills, the wide greenness of it all. The bus going up and down, over the hills of Wisconsin and he inside the bus, up and down like when his mother took him sometimes to the kiddie amusement park and he sat on a horse on the merry-go-round . . . asleep . . . awake . . . and houses once again with lights turned on inside, and streetcars, automobiles like his toy automobiles. Then the bus making noise like a cat when it is mad and the bus driver saying: "*Chicago!*"

In the big bus depot people patted his head and said, "What a cute little boy!" and though she couldn't afford it Nellie took a taxi and gave the direction.

Nick was half asleep when they got there and, struggling with him and her suitcase, Nellie paid the fare and he clung with his arms around her neck, his legs tight about her waist like a baby monkey clinging to its mother as she stood on the sidewalk under a lamppost.

It was a hot summer night. Hoboes stumbled along the sidewalk. Drunks staggered into them. Bums sat on curbings. Men stood against store fronts and in doorways letting their water as unconcerned as horses. This was West Madison Street and it was her street. Most of her adult life had been spent here.

She moved toward the darkened door. Nick slept with his head on her shoulder. Bar smells hung over the sidewalk, damp-sweet and sickening. Juke boxes smacked their high-pitched, falsely hilarious songs out across the sidewalk and halfway across the street in shrill blasts. Inside the tavern window the upper half of a woman, silver-dyed hair, smear of red lips singing into a microphone. The puff-pouted red and black lips of a Negro on a trumpet, red where the blackness of the lips stopped. The tinny jazz notes of out-of-tune pianos banging against the street noises, the hunched back of the player crouched, as over a victim, over the chipped and yellowed keys. Up and down the street. Both ways. Both sides.

Nellie came to the black, weather-eaten door and pushed it open with her foot. Dank staleness and heavy darkness emptied down the long flight of steps at her. She felt her way up the stairs, holding onto the sagging banister and stumbling on old newspapers that drifted down. At the door at the top of the first landing she dropped her suitcase and fitted a key into the lock, then stepped inside. She laid Nick on the bed, and her searching hand found the cord and the light went on: a naked bulb on a long cord, like the dead head of a chicken hanging down.

It was a high-ceilinged, grim, frowning room.

Nellie went immediately to a small end table and turned on the dime-store table lamp. Above it was a framed photograph, from a newspaper, of a young man. From behind the glass he smiled at her. She looked up at him. His eyes met hers. They were brown, friendly, innocent.

She went to the tall windows and opened them to the heavy summer night. The two windows were set close together, reaching almost from the floor to the ceiling. As she pushed them open, straining to do so, the ragged shroudlike curtains (by courtesy of the landlord) stirred slowly back and forth. She had moved the bed against one of the windows because she had been afraid Nick might fall out. Against the other she had placed a small dresser on top of which was an electric one-burner plate. Next to it was an orange crate into which she had inexpertly nailed two shelves. On top of it were several books: *Baby Care, Child Care, The Child Between Two and Seven, Our Children*. On the dresser, too, was a washbasin, filled in the bathroom down the hall to keep Nick's face and hands clean. Near the foot of the bed was a rack for clothes, which sagged like a scarecrow in a field and which she had made out of two-by-fours. The rack was empty; all her belongings were in the pasteboard suitcase sitting on the warped and uncarpeted softwood floor. Through the cracks in the boards, like a multitude of strange beings, had seeped lint and dust, balling together and rolling occasionally like living things. At one place near the foot of the bed, the plaster had fallen from the ceiling. The walls had been painted many times, but not at all for a long time. They had no definable color. For this front room in a once desirable apartment building Nellie paid twelve dollars a week because she had two windows and the view and noise of West Madison Street. The other rooms, windowless, were two dollars less.

Nellie undressed Nick and put him to bed. She glanced at the smiling young man on the wall.

I need a drink.

She sat smoking a cigarette, two, watching Nick and making sure that he was asleep.

I need a drink.

She tiptoed out of the room and went down the steps, slightly twisting her ankle on one of the alive-like, eel-like newspapers that loitered like bums along the staircase.

Ghosts, particularly one, followed her down the broken steps. Followed her into the bar.

She pushed into Levin's. A bar went down one end of the room. Schooners of beer and shots of whiskey, different-colored ambers, were set on its brown top. On the other side of the uneven floor were tables with chairs pushed up to them and middle-aged and elderly men and women, hard-looking, coarse-looking, drunk-looking, sitting at them.

Nellie sat at a table. "Hello, Jack," she said to the bartender. "A shot." He brought it. Automatically she tossed it down. Lit a cigarette. "Another," she told the bartender. The Ghost sat in the chair facing her across the table. She turned her face away and stared at the bar. Familiar odors began to come back. The place was crowded and reeked with the smell of foul, damp bodies. Cigarette smoke hung foggily. A one-legged man leaned against the bar catching peanuts in his mouth, both crutches propped under one arm. A man in a dirty straw hat with the band missing was saying to the woman in a wrinkled dress who smiled at him through sleepy eyelids, "You know all the tricks—keep the dog hungry." At a table behind Nellie a woman slept with her head in her arms, her straight gray hair sticking out from the brim of a shapeless hat.

Nellie sipped the second shot: I hope Nick is all right. I hope he's asleep. She looked back across the table and into the face of the Ghost. Drank all the whiskey. Called to the waiter for another.

At the table next to Nellie's an elderly woman, fat, sloppily dressed, and an old woman, drinking too much, poked their heads together to tell dirty jokes, giggling and pushing each other with their hands, laughing loudly, vulgarly. And now the fat woman nodded her head in a sharp gesture over her enormous shoulder. "Country girl is back," she said. The old woman sitting with her said, her mouth revealing no teeth, "First stop, the tavern." She cackled it.

Nellie turned dully. "Hello, Bertha. Hello, Pearl."

"What you think about all them cows?" the fat woman asked.

"I seen some around here worse."

"Going back to slinging hash tomorrow?"

"What else?"

A skinny man, unshaven for a week, his eyes bloodshot, the front of his dirty white shirt torn from its pocket down to his belt and showing dirty skin underneath, stopped by Nellie's table. "Glad to be back on West Madison, Nellie?" he asked.

Nellie shrugged her shoulders.

"How's that boy of yours?" he asked.

"Oh, wonderful! Wonderful!"

A man and a woman stood, drunk, in the middle of the floor. He held his cigarette to give her a light. She couldn't hit the cigarette with hers.

This time Nellie asked for a glass of beer. Then she sat, her gray-blue eyes looking into its brownness: If she could just stop thinking about it.

She thought about it. And suddenly she grew panicky. Frightened, leaving the rest of her beer and her purse on the table, she rushed up to see if the boy was all right.

The boy was not in bed. He was kneeling on the floor under the light from the table lamp, with his crayons spread out and a piece of drawing paper between his small elbows. He was drawing, the colors coming off the crayons onto the paper. His tongue was stuck out of his mouth and reaching up for his nose in concentration. His little pajama-ed behind pointed up.

Nellie stood a moment in the door: The book said your child might get up in the middle of the night when everyone is in bed and wander around the house. He might want to go to the toilet, or to the cookie jar. He may want to look at a book. He should be allowed these excursions.

"Hello, honey. Why aren't you in bed?"

"I'm not sleepy."

"All right, honey. When you get sleepy you go to bed."

She locked the door and went back down to the tavern.

She was getting drunk now. And still she couldn't stop thinking. A woman's voice, drunken and shrill, broke across the tavern, laughing and cursing. The juke box blared, beating down the street noises. An old man with a drooping hat and a generous beard spread out on a swollen chest shared a bottle of wine with a beggar who sat with his dark glasses on the bar and stared vacantly with socket-empty eyes that receded into dark, narrowing hollows in his head.

Again Nellie went back to the room to see if her son was all right.

She opened the door. First she looked at him and then she looked up at the picture.

She looked fondly at her son. He lay asleep on the floor, his cheek across his crayon drawing. She looked at the photograph. The boy in the photograph met her gaze. They took him away from me and I gave him back.

The boy in the photograph looked at her, smiled at her. He was handsome. His hair was dark and curly and smoothly combed. His eyes were a clear, clean brown. His teeth were white, his dimples firm. She looked at his broad, square face, his wide cheekbones. He smiled and yet he had a haunted look in his eyes.

The boy in the picture was about twenty years old. The boy asleep across his crayon drawing is named Nick Romano. The boy in the photograph was named Nick Romano. A little over five years ago the headline over that smiling photograph had said:

PRETTY BOY ROMANO

DIES IN ELECTRIC CHAIR

2

She went down for another drink. She lived it again . . .

Fearfully she came into the packed courtroom looking for him, looking for Nick, trying to find him with her eyes.

The courtroom was staring eyes. Trembling she moved to where she was being led. Frightened she stood in front of the witness chair.

"Take the stand, please—" the bailiff said. "Kindly raise your right hand . . ."

She did so.

"Do you solemnly swear before the ever-living God that the testimony you are about to give in this case shall be the truth, the whole truth and nothing but the truth?" the bailiff said in his monotone.

Seated, she was staring over the rail of the witness box at Nick. He looked at her. Then he lowered his eyes and hung his head.

Andrew Morton, the defense attorney, said to Nellie, his first witness, "Are you employed, Miss Watkins?" Her voice trembled as she said no. "Do you remember the night of November seventh, last year?"

"Yes, sir," she said timidly.

"Did you see Nick Romano that night?"

"No, sir." Her voice was weak. She clutched her coat about her breast with a black-gloved hand, two of the fingers sticking through where the cheap material and the inexpert darning had given way.

"Do you know Mr. Kerman"—Morton motioned to him with his hand—"the distinguished gentleman on the other side of the table?"

"Yes, sir." Her blond strings of hair stuck out from under her hat where they had come loose from their curl.

"Did you ever talk to him about this case?"

"Yes, sir." Her eyes looked at Kerman fearfully, then at Morton. "I was picked up by the police when I was quitting work at two o'clock in the morning just after the policeman was killed."

"And were you taken to the women's quarters at State Street?"

"No, sir . . . I was kept in a jail until the next morning when they took me"—she looked fearfully at Kerman again—"to Mr. Kerman's office."

"Did you have a conversation with Mr. Kerman and, if so, relate it to the jury."

"Mr. Kerman asked me if I hadn't been Nick Romano's sweetheart and I said yes." She wiped one cheek with the back of her gloved hand. "And then he said well you know he killed the police officer don't you and I said no I don't and I don't believe it and he said you saw Romano on the street at about eleven-thirty didn't you and I said no and he said you did." Her weak blue eyes were wide and tear-filled. "I said no I didn't and he told me well, you're—you're going to testify that you did or I'll find a way to send you away for a long time as an accessory to the murder."

Morton said, "Miss Simpson, please read that back to the jury," getting it in twice. "Is that all, Miss Watkins?" he asked Nellie.

"Yes, sir—only he said I'd have to come to court and testify. Then he said I could go home."

"How is it, Miss Watkins, that you weren't subpoenaed to appear in court?"

"I got scared and quit my job and went away and hid because I didn't know what he would do to me if I didn't testify the way he wanted me to." She tried to hide her holey gloves in her lap. "Then when Nick had to come to court I came to see you and I told you that we had been sweethearts and I didn't believe he'd do anything like that." It all came out in a rush and she was crying.

"Excused, cross-examination," Morton said gently.

"How much of your story is true?" Kerman shouted.

"All of it," Nellie sobbed.

Kerman frowned at her. "Do you know what perjury is, Miss Watkins?" He slurred the "Miss" at her.

With her head and eyes drawn in she looked at him. "Yes, sir—it means that you haven't told the truth."

"You know, then, that you have deliberately perjured yourself before God, this court and these intelligent ladies and gentlemen of the jury—don't you!"

"No, I didn't." *Again she tried to hide her holey gloves in her lap.*

"Who was the officer with me when you alleged I talked to you?"

"No one."

"Who brought you to my office?"

"A policeman."

"Did he bring you in a patrol wagon?"

"In a taxi."

"Was there a policewoman with you?"

"No."

"What became of these policemen after they brought you to my office?"

"I don't know."

"What time in the day was this?"

"Ten o'clock."

"How many times have you been convicted of crime?"

"Never."

Kerman lifted his brows. "How many?"

"Never."

"Have you ever talked to Mr. Morton about this case?"

"I went to Mr. Morton's office and—"

"No!— No!— Answer that yes or no."

"Yes."

"And did Mr. Morton tell you what to testify here?"

"No. I went there to see if I could do anything for Nick and I told him we had been sweethearts and I didn't believe he'd do anything like that and he told me that he—"

"Just answer the question!"

"—that he didn't believe that Nick had done it and that he would do his best for Nick and said good-bye—and I went away." *Again it all came out in a rush and again she was crying.*

"How much of your story is true?" *Kerman shouted harshly.*

"All of it," *she sobbed.*

"Didn't you know that the defendant was going to hold up that bartender?"

"All I know is that you had me picked up and I had to quit my job." *The tears ran down her cheeks and her lips twisted with the words. Her hands, in their torn gloves, clutched the rail of the witness stand as if she wanted to rise and run from the courtroom.*

"Didn't you know? Didn't you?"

"No—I don't think he did it."

"Just answer the question! Wasn't he at your room! Didn't he plan this with you!"

"No—no—no." *It was almost a wail, trailing into a half-sob.*

"Didn't he live with you—Miss—Watkins? Didn't you support him half the time—? Didn't you give him money?" Nellie's scared eyes stared at Kerman from under the crushed felt hat. "No . . . no . . ." A tear fell in her lap.

Morton spoke up. "Object. These questions are incompetent for the reason that they seek to have the witness give testimony against herself as having lived in an immoral state with the defendant. I further state, if it please the Court, that the only purpose, in my opinion, of this questioning is to influence the prejudices of the jury against the defendant, that it is not good practice and the act of a shyster!"

Judge Drake looked down. "Sustained by reason of the first part of the objection."

"If it please the Court," Kerman said, standing up, "I object to the term applied to the State's representative by counsel for the defense."

"I guess, after all, Mr. Kerman, that's a matter between you and Mr. Morton." And Judge Drake leaned his cheek against his fingers.

Kerman looked at Nellie angrily. "How much of your story is true?"

"All of it," Nellie said.

"You're in love with the defendant, aren't you?"

Nellie stopped the tears that were rolling down her cheek with the fingers of her holey glove. She nodded her head yes.

"You want him to get out of this, don't you?"

Nellie was standing in the box. "Yes—because I don't think he did it!"

"The jury will decide on that— That's all!"

Kerman turned to Judge Drake. "I would ask at this time that your Honor hold the witness on a charge of perjury to be filed upon my complaint!"

"There is absolutely no warrant for that remark," Judge Drake said, "save to prejudice the jury, Mr. Kerman, and the witness is now under the protection of this Court and will neither be intimidated nor arrested . . . Have you any questions, Mr. Morton?"

"None, your Honor."

"The witness is excused," Judge Drake said.

Nellie half stumbled from the witness box and walked across the courtroom toward a seat in the audience, still stopping the tears with the fingers of her gloves. As she neared the counsel table her large and tear-filled eyes looked at Nick. Her head turned, still looking at him as she passed by. Nick smiled at her, saying something to her with his eyes . . .

Nellie's tear-filled eyes stared at the bar. He was trying to tell me he loved me.

She called for another beer, still staring vacantly.

She had been pregnant when she was on the stand, but nobody had known it. Hope revived and lost again with each succeeding headline . . . ROMANO TO DIE SEPTEMBER 16TH . . . PRETTY BOY GETS STAY . . . Nellie drank deeply of her beer . . . ROMANO TO DIE JANUARY 8TH . . . NO REPRIEVE: PRETTY BOY ROMANO DIES FRIDAY . . .

That Friday . . .

That Friday at midnight she feared that she was going to lose the baby. That night, when he died, she sat in her room, her hands on the arms of the chair as if she herself were going to the electric chair, her large stomach bunched up in front of her. She bit her hands and her lips until they bled. But nothing could halt or slow the seconds ticking away into eternity, eating time, numbering his life by minutes . . .

The newspaper headlines next day said PRETTY BOY ROMANO . . . and the pain started in her stomach . . .

She was crying miserably, her elbows on the table, her hands up to her eyes, the tears lashing her wrists and arms like torrential rain suddenly falling.

The man with the dirty and torn white shirt, in strips like parts of a destroyed kite, was back and wavering over Nellie's chair, his blond hair dirty in a tumble over his forehead. "Can I buy you a drink, Nellie?" He didn't notice that she was crying.

"All right. Just don't talk to me. Please."

"Okay, kid."

She drank his shot and forgot that he was there.

"Okay, kid," he said again, and walked away.

The juke box said:

> Yoooouuu ain't—been bluuueee
> Nooo—Nooo—Nooo—
> Till you've had thaaaat
> Mooooood In–di–go
> That feeeelin'
> Goes steeeeeeaalin' . . .

. . . She went into the medicine-smelling clinic and sat on one of the chairs there with the many other women in all stages of pregnancy, still seeing the morning headlines, sure that the time was near.

Some of the women didn't show yet, some were just getting paunches, some looked as if they had watermelons stuck up under their dresses. They sat in little groups of two and three, with their chairs turned toward each other, talking about their condition. There was an impatient, waiting look in their eyes. Their bodies were languid, their hands in their laps or crossed over their stomachs in protective positions.

"Ain't you scared?"

"Of course I'm scared. It ain't no picnic!"

"When I was eighteen, I had a cute little figure then. That's what got me into this."

"A cute little figure? You could never tell it!"

A titter of laughs.

"Gosh, kid! You're big. Are you sure it ain't gonna be twins?"

"How long have you got to go?"

"Do you want a boy or a girl?"

"Does it hurt—an *awful* lot?"

"This is my fifth one. I don't know why I'm so careless."

"Well, just so you got a husband."

A titter of laughs.

"I got a husband, all right, but I had to chase him to get him. Now I can't keep him out of bed with me. But I bet I won't have another one after this." And proudly, "People say wherever he puts his eyes he puts a baby."

The women sat, sizing each other up, deciding who was going to have a boy and who was going to have a girl.

The doctor, in his white uniform, came into the room and stood talking to a woman in front of Nellie. "Well," he said, kidding the woman, "do you still think it's a tumor, Mrs. Wells?" Mrs. Wells smiled and shook her head incredulously. "I just can't believe it, Doctor! After all these years and me nearly forty!"

"Yes, you're going to have a tumor all right," the doctor kidded, "but it's going to be one of those two-legged tumors— Oh, hello, Mrs. Jones—" He turned to the big Negro woman who came laboriously down the aisle. "How are you?"

"Ain't he cute!" a girl in the seat behind Nellie whispered to another expectant mother. "I hope I have him!"

"Only tol'able, Doctor," Mrs. Jones said; she grinned good-naturedly and put her hand against the side of her stomach. "Ah'm powerful ti'ed of carryin' all this weight around with me!"

"Well, it won't be long," the doctor said. "I'll see you as soon as I finish with Mrs. Wells." He reached out and pinched her cheek loosely. "Take it easy— Oh!— Remember Annabelle Parkins? She had her baby last week." He let his voice get loud and joking so that all the women could hear. "When she was having it she kept yelling, 'Oh, Mama! Mama!' I told her that her mother didn't get her in that fix and she better yell for her husband." He tossed his head back, grinning. "All right, Mrs. Wells." He sauntered off toward the inner office, Mrs. Wells, large, swollen, awkward-footed, following him.

The woman next to Nellie asked, "Is this your first one?" Nellie nodded yes. "How long have you got to go?"

"I don't know. But soon I think."

"What do you want?"

"Oh, a boy!"

If she had a boy—

The woman turned her head, closely examining Nellie's stomach, leaning way over with her head close to the swollen-out hard balloon of it, looking first at one side and then the other, prodding it with her fingers. Nellie watched the slow examination the woman's eyes made.

"You're going to have a girl," the woman said.

If she had a boy she would name him—

A few days later the boy came.

She put out her hand.

"Hello, Nicky—"

They took his life and she gave it back.

3

Home from the hospital she hugged the baby weepily in her room on West Madison Street. It wouldn't happen to her son. Nothing bad. She would give him everything and protect him against everything. It wouldn't be like her life.

Pieces of the past came back to her.

Her mother's hand was rough and cold. She kissed it and cried and clung to her mother and didn't want to stay there. "You have to for a couple of months." No more than that, her mother said with an expressionless face.

She was seven and afraid of the dark, afraid to be away from her mother, afraid of the man who cursed and beat her mother, and she was here alone with all her fear and thirty other girls about her age. The bigger kids told her that her mother was never coming back, and she cried. They were right. Her mother never came back. She never saw her mother again. She was to find out that it was a place where parents dropped their unwanted kids and left them. A juvenile detention home in Iowa, for both juvenile delinquents and unwanted children.

Nellie sat at the tavern table, her drink in front of her, her hand against her forehead, her fingers up into roots of her hair that fell long and blond and slightly curled about her wrist: Dropping from this today to those yesterdays the mind goes backward in time . . .

She had met Nick on West Madison Street. There had been sex for the first time in the detention home. She could remember little of the early days there. Just crying and beatings from the matrons, wetting the bed and about twenty girls her age all sleeping in the same long room on all-alike iron beds . . . And a few years later, she guessed, there were whispers of sex and then innocent, childish experiments among themselves. How old was I? Nine? Ten? Maybe even twelve. One or two of the matrons even did things to the girls, but she wasn't pretty and they never did them to her. The girls were afraid to tell or didn't care or, knowing nothing, thought this was right. It made you special and showed that you were liked and the girls told each other even if the matrons told them they better not.

After six years in a place like that you got wised up. With brains you can get places. They came down looking for workers to wash dishes. All the kids knew that if you worked in the kitchen you got more to eat and didn't have to go to school six hours a day. All the girls had their hands up in the air, waving them; a couple even shouted, "Me! Me!" I used what I had between my ears. I slumped down on the bench in a corner pretending that I didn't want to work and, just like I thought, they chose me. "Come on, you!" So I worked in the cafeteria and was eating all I wanted—and stuff the guards and matrons ate.

    . . . Nellie turned the glass round and round, making wet circles on the table top. She lit another cigarette, the smoke curling up into her hair . . .

On the other side of the large, glass-partitioned-off kitchen were the boys who also worked peeling potatoes, cutting up vegetables and washing dishes. You could look at them if you were real careful and none of the matrons caught you. On the other side of the glass there was a red-headed boy maybe fifteen or sixteen years old and she often sneaked looks at him. He always grinned at her and a couple of times got hit across the head, hard! when he was caught by the guards. Sometimes when the red-headed boy caught her eye he'd wave to her, grinning all the time. She giggled; and she knew what he meant.

Those girls in juvenile were horny as they could be. They were locked away from the boys but when a boy went along the hall they could see him through the bars. They'd yell at the boys and throw kisses and shout dirty things like, "I'd like to have you screw me"— "Oh, look at that good-looking one with the blond hair! I bet he knows how to do it!" The girls would even yell at the colored boys.

The minister there said that they mustn't think about boys, that they must pray. . . . Nellie, in the tavern, smiled sadly, bitterly, at such useless advice given so sincerely; smiled bitterly at all her days and nights there. She drank again from her frothy glass . . .

Getting smokes was the toughest part. Sometimes one of the girls would have a cigarette, sneaked in somehow. They'd stand together, smoking, at the end of a long hall. They'd stand looking around out of the corners of their eyes; one set of eyes looking one way, another the other way. They passed the cigarette on. They didn't waste any of it.

If the matron came along the hall someone yelled jiggers! and they ditched the butt. The matron came sniff, sniff, sniff, "All right! Somebody's been smoking. All right! All right!" The kids' hands and Nellie's hands all slipped out from their sides, empty, and were held out in a gesture of we ain't got any, honest!

Alice, her only friend in the place, fooled her mother. Alice told her mother she wanted a package of cigarettes. "I want to give them to one of the matrons. She treats me nice."

"Will I get in trouble?"

"Aw no—you're on the outside."

Alice had her smuggle them in.

. . . Nellie looked up out of the past and into the noisy bar, drew deep on her cigarette, looked back ten years into the past . . .

Boys were what you thought about.

One day in the cafeteria the matron went through to the boys' section with a stack of dirty dishes. The red-headed boy was on the other side. She yelled, "Yoo-hoo!" not too loud. With the matron way at the other end of the room with her back turned to them they ran toward each other.

The red-headed boy said, "What are you in for?"

At the same time she said, "What are you in for?"

They stood grinning at each other. He was only a foot from her. The matron had turned around and started back. The boy moved away. Nellie ran back from the door. She waved at the boy just at the moment when the matron got to the door. The woman saw the boy ducking away. She looked over at Nellie quickly. Nellie dropped her waving hand to her hair as if she were smoothing it away from her forehead. The matron smiled, amusedly, for a moment, and then her face set in a hard official frown.

The red-headed boy and some other fellows used to stick their eyes to the crack in the toilet door. On the other side they could see the girls in there. Once she and Alice had been in there when the boys called out excitedly, "Hey, babe! Hey, sweets!" She and Alice looked at each other, smiling. They moved closer to the door and Alice said, "What do you want?"

"Give me some of that stuff!" the boys said vulgarly, enticingly.

"Sure! Here!" Alice said. Far enough away from the crack in the door for them to see, she wiggled. "You want it?" She ran her hands over her legs and up to where her legs came together, bringing the skirt up with them.

"A little bit higher!" the boys yelled.

Nellie watched. Shamed. Excited. Fascinated.

But she didn't do what Alice was doing.

Curious, she spent a lot of time in the toilet after that, and often looked through the keyhole when none of the other girls were there. A couple of times there were boys on the other side at the urinal. And she could see! *That* was what they had!

In church the matrons said, "Don't look at the boys," and if you did, whack! right in church they'd let you have it! Those matrons were like men.

Boys were what you thought about.

All the older girls ganged up together whenever they could, talking and bragging. It was nothing like not going to school. That was baby stuff. Telling about shoplifting, smoking marijuana, getting caught with boys in the school assembly hall during the day, the school yard at night, and in the park, and being brought there, about being here for prostitution. "Taking money," they said, "for what comes naturally." The one girl who impressed all of them was a big fat girl fifteen years old, who was in for murder. She had killed her mother and stepfather while they were sleeping in bed.

. . . Nellie ordered still another drink and again slipped ten years back . . .

His voice said softly, "Pssssttt! Come here." She didn't know yet how he had got over the high brick wall that separated the boys from the girls. But there he was, red-headed and handsome and big in the early dark evening of the juvenile grounds when the boys and girls had half an hour free period before they were locked up in their dormitories for the night.

She went over to him. "How did you get here?" It was a whisper.

He didn't say anything. He just grabbed her and kissed her hard and his hands were fumbling roughly with her clothes, almost tearing them. He pulled her into the bushes, and she went half eagerly. He pulled her down on the ground beside him and she went with apprehension. But he put his arms around her and pulled her arms around him and it seemed better then. Someone was being nice to her for the first time in her life. No one had ever put his arms around her before, and he had his arms around her. She felt like crying. And then pain came. And she didn't like it and wanted to get free. But couldn't. And then she did like it and it was the only affection she had ever had.

When they had finished he did and said something that she would never forget. Rusty, who was sixteen and who was in juvenile for stealing cars and knifing a man, took her chin under the palm of his hand and then slipped his arm around her and patted her on the shoulder. "I'm sorry," he said.

"I don't care," she said. "And I think I liked it."

"Tomorrow?" he whispered. "Right here?"

"Yes," she whispered. And it was a defiance to all of her life that had been empty and ugly and without anything.

Many times after that they were there together. And later she brought Alice and another girl. He brought other boys. Several of them. She had no thought of guilt nor of shame. It was kindness you could give and kindness you could receive. It was love. Yes, it was love she had never had from anyone. A kiss. A gentle pat on the back. A connecting of two bodies that made you feel wanted.

. . . Nellie looked up into the tavern again. Her out-of-focus eyes came back to the present. She stared at the bar and the back bar with its many bottles standing stiffly. Yes, she had long learned that sex was a gift. You gave it to people who were kind to you, or who were sad and unhappy, or who needed warmth and kindness . . . it was such a little thing.

She drank the shot that one of the customers from the restaurant where she worked had bought for her. Time bent her back to the days in the juvenile home . . .

She had been abandoned by her parents. This would never happen to her child. All those years alone at the juvenile home. Then one day they told her she had visitors. My mother! She has come to get me! She must love me after all! She had never been happier before or after in her life. My mother! I'm going to get out! She walked toward the office. She didn't even know what her mother looked like. She just remembered the cold, unfriendly hand. But her mother had come for her and she was going home! She had never had a home. And that was the most beautiful word in the language. My mother! Home!

In the office two people waited for her, sitting side by side on the hard bench. They both had blue eyes and freckled red skin, skin that was taut and dry. They looked like people who had stood unshaded against sun and wind and rain. Their knees, their elbows and their wrists were knotty. The woman said, without standing up, "I am your Aunt Martha and this is your Uncle Clarence." Her voice held no small note of cheerfulness. It was neither soft nor harsh. Only matter-of-fact. "We have come to take you with us. We live on a farm in Missouri." She straightened her skirt and looked penetratingly at the girl. The man got to his big feet and stood in his blue denims with his hand stuck out. "Hello, Nellie." His voice gave the first warmth to the interview. The woman said, "We can give you a home and you can help us work."

Papers were signed and Nellie went out into the free world for the first time since she was seven. The free world right now was a finely kept model-T Ford parked along the driveway.

They started out for the farm. Her uncle and aunt seemed neither curious about her nor anxious to welcome her. They sat the long hours in silence. Only once Uncle Clarence had dug into his blue jeans and brought out a candy bar.

"For you," he said, pushing it awkwardly at her.

"Clarence, you will spoil her," the woman said.

"Thank you, Uncle—Uncle Clarence," Nellie said.

The farm was a poor one on poor Missouri soil and flat, monotonous land that stretched in four directions without even the relieving break of a hill, like the uninteresting palm of a hand. The farmhouse was a plain building with a stone foundation and rough wooden sidings in need of paint. There was a cellar where the summer potatoes and the apples of fall, red and shiny, were kept against the snowy days of winter. In the front room there was a pot-bellied stove with a chimney going upstairs to keep the room warm up there. It was there that her uncle and aunt slept; a rough cot had been placed in the front room for her. There was no running water in the house. In the yard was a well with a hand pump, and far beyond that, almost where the cornfield began, was the outhouse with a quarter-moon cut in the door. They had five cows —they sold milk—a few calves, enough chickens for eggs and a very occasional meal, and two pigs because Aunt Martha said pigs eat anything. The farm was a cornfield and a vegetable garden for their own use.

Nellie and her aunt and uncle were like strangers, and it stayed that way a long time. She was seldom spoken to by her aunt unless it was to be told to do something. Her uncle and aunt seldom spoke to each other. When they did it was quietly and like two acquaintances not yet accustomed to each other; or like two old friends so used to each other that they were bored. Still there seemed to be love and understanding, comradeship between them. But there was seldom laughter between them or in that house.

Nellie milked the cows at seven in the morning and again at six in the evening. She took care of the calves and the chickens and did the washing and cooked on a wood stove in the kitchen, chopping wood in the yard and carrying armloads to keep the fire alive. There was no joy in her life and no one her age living nearby. She worked and ate and slept. Her aunt wouldn't let her eat all she wanted. When Uncle Clarence added an extra helping of the infrequent chicken to her plate, even the neck, or gave her part of his apple pie, saying he couldn't eat it all, Aunt Martha would say sharply, "Clarence, you're spoiling that girl!"

Uncle Clarence always looked guilty. He was used to obeying Aunt Martha.

Nellie grew more depressed and frustrated. She had brought, after the detention home, her hopes and dreams here, a child, dreaming of the world outside, and they were dropped, like very small pebbles, into a deep well. This was no different from the world inside. It was of bars and hard words. The hard words of her Aunt Martha.

Only Uncle Clarence showed any compassion for her. Once when he went to town he brought two paper-backed books for her and a tiny box of candy, saying, "Don't tell Aunt Martha." He let her help him gather the apples and, far out of sight and sound of Aunt Martha, let her eat all she wanted. That day, too, he said, "Come, Nellie, I want to show you something." It was a dandelion with a silver crown the color of some of the hair that had begun creeping into his blond hair, and he said, gently for this big, awkward man, holding the stem of the dandelion gently, "The dandelion is so delicate that you always get some back on your nose and if you get some back on your nose the dream comes true." Then he said, "Blow and blink." She blew and blinked . . .

She had no great ambition. The dream was maybe just to be a typist in a building in a big city like in one of the movies they had at the detention home once a month if all of the kids were good.

One other nice thing happened in those first weeks on the farm. Once, way out by the outhouse, when she was bringing a pail of water for the calves, Uncle Clarence had been coming from the other field. He said, "Put the pail down, Nellie." Then he said in unusual tenderness, putting his arms around her and kissing her, "Your Uncle Clarence thinks you're a nice girl."

He carried the pail for her.

He thinks I'm nice!

She cried.

Somebody cared about her.

It took her a long time to ask, but when she got nerve up, one day when she was coming into the kitchen with the chicken she had to kill and clean for dinner because the township minister was coming to eat, she looked into the sunlight and across the room at her aunt. She said it quickly, gulping it out while she still had courage, "Aunt Martha, what was my mother like?"

The taut, freckled skin went tighter, especially around the mouth, and the blue eyes narrowed. Her mother's sister said, "Don't ever mention that woman's name to me again!"

Winter came. Aunt Martha's voice, in command or complaint and directed at either of them, was like the hot roar of the fire going up the chimney when it first caught, like the creak of heavy-soled shoes in the thick, frozen snow outside. Nellie stayed silent. Uncle Clarence watched her with gentle affection. If their eyes met he would smile sadly with just the corner of his lips and maybe wink and she would hang her head, afraid that she might start crying.

During the days, with the cold and the wind tight against the rough board sidings of the house, Uncle Clarence fingered the calendar as if it were his holy beads. Spring and summer were on the pages of the calendar. And better times. The soil breathing again. Blooming again with crop.

During the days Aunt Martha complained of the bad weather, of bad times, and of how much Nellie ate.

Nights, all that long winter, she lay on her hard cot in the front room, not going to sleep for a long time, good smells still coming from the kitchen, with supper long finished and a little ache of hunger still in her stomach. The stove would be glowing dimly, like an old person napping. She could hear the crack of frozen branches in the wind, twigs snapping and breaking and falling away like her hopes, even the smallest ones. Then Uncle Clarence, as on many nights, making some excuse, would come through the down-stairs in his long underwear and on his bare feet and he would sneak her food and sit on the side of her cot a few minutes patting her head or her shoulder while she stuffed the food in.

This night: "I forgot the pot."

Aunt Martha's cold but peeved voice. Uncle Clarence's long legs and knotty knees coming down the steps in the long underwear, the only light from the sleeping stove and the nude moonlight on cold snow.

And Uncle Clarence—

"Nellie," he whispered.

He sneaked her the pieces of roughly sawed ham he had cut and the cold, cold glass of milk, like the weather outside.

He sat beside her. His hand touched her forehead, then his whole palm over her head twice. "Martha ain't a bad woman," he said in a whisper. "But stingy. Stingy with everything. Try to understand her. She likes you. It's just that—" His long-underweared shoulders came up in a long, grotesquely hunched shrug and fell back in place like a sigh. Then he quietly took the empty glass back to the kitchen to wash, and put it back in its place on the shelf while Nellie could hear from above Aunt Martha calling crankily, "Clarence—what's taking you so long? What if I wanted to use that pot right now?" Then she could see the big white pot with the big white handle going through the dark at the knotty knees of the long-underweared, bony figure. And she lay staring in the dark at the things of a house, table and chair, stove, edge of a sink, that were only recently familiar to her . . . listening to the creak of the frozen window and bringing her eyes to its sound to see there the forest of pines that were etched in ice and that sometimes, childishly, during the day she liked to stick her tongue against. Then, the cold, like desire creeping down her spine inside the blankets. Maybe to be a typist in some office building. That's all I ask . . . And sleep . . . and in the morning the unbroken, unspoiled view of snow as far as you could see over the flat plains of Missouri.

The days on the calendar that Uncle Clarence had fingered came. The sweet-smelling days of spring, of black, healthy soil and of seeds, fondled by Uncle Clarence like jewels, and the leafing out of green things. But in her everything was dead and began to sear under the hot summer sun. Nights, though dead tired from the work of the farm, she could not sleep and sat in the long, wide wooden swing on the low front porch, listening to its creaking on its linked chains and feeling the warped porch boards under her feet. She stared across the flat plains. The world was empty. She thought of the red-headed boy. If she could even have that again.

Uncle Clarence watched her with gentle affection all that spring and into summer, with compassion. And one summer night late when Aunt Martha had long been asleep, he came to the front porch still dressed as for the day.

"Nellie?"

"Yes, Uncle Clarence?"

He sat next to her.

He sat down heavily. The swing complained back and forth on its chains. Lightning bugs gave their light near the swing. She could smell the clover. He said, "It's warm tonight."

"Yes, Uncle Clarence."

There was a long silence, with only the night sounds. The cornstalks rustling together. The frogs in their beds.

"Nellie—" he said, and stopped. Then he said, "Me and Martha's been married for thirty-one years." It said something or nothing.

There was another silence and the next sound was not words. It was the swing as he moved closer to her and took her gently into his arms. His calloused fingers softly patted her hair. "Oh, Uncle! Uncle!" Her tears of tenderness and gratitude couldn't soak the blue cloth of his overalls but they shook him with responding gentleness, tenderness. He kissed the palms of her hands in gratitude. "Nellie—"

Then his arms were about her again.

"Nellie—"

His hands were on her girl-garters. She knew what he wanted. She strained toward him and her young, moist lips met his hard, cracked, chapped lips and she was glad to take some of the tautness from them. The brass buttons of his overalls scratched her skin and his big farm shoes made horse-hoof sounds on the boards of the porch in his almost clumsy first effort. The sky gave some stars.

Almost every night, late at night, in the lonesomeness of the night when Aunt Martha was snoring upstairs, he spent an hour or two on the swing with her in the quiet, peaceful, unwatching night. If they were happy nights for her, they must have been the best to remember for him. Their lips held and clung and their arms held and clung. It didn't seem bad to her. Even now it didn't seem wrong. It was something nice you could do for people. By giving, you can be loved. It was such a little thing to give for warmth and love and smiles.

And so her life had been colored . . .

4

The juke box said with sad horns and melancholy-blue voice:

> *That feeeeelin'*
> *Goes steeeeeeealin'*
> *Doooooown to my shooooooes*
> *While IIII sit and siiiiiigh . . .*

Nellie rubbed her fingers under her high cheekbones, trying to take away memory, take away thought.

> *Goooooo 'loooooong, bluuuuuues . . .*

I can't drink any more. I'll be sick and won't be able to go to work tomorrow night.

But she drank more . . .

She was to be sent away again. Again she wasn't wanted. In her sadness she was surprised that her aunt cried. And her aunt said it wasn't that they didn't like her. They liked her very much but times were hard and they had to struggle just to feed themselves. They couldn't afford the food for her. Uncle Clarence was used to obeying his wife even if his own pleasure was involved. He sat, hedged in, unable to say, "My hands gave us this living, little as it is. We can feed another"; but only able to let those calloused hands hang between the blue denim of his long pant legs, his face sober and sad and like one who had no will of his own. By this and by Aunt Martha's tears, Nellie knew that her aunt did not suspect her. And by the words, "You have cousins in Detroit. We are sending you to them. They have a big house of seven rooms and you can help them for your keep. I am sending a letter by you to our cousins. Clarence will take you to the bus in the morning."

Her aunt cried a little more, dryly, and blew her nose on her apron. It was as if she cried for this girl because she had nobody, no love, no future, nothing—but they had to look out for themselves. They couldn't be burdened with another adult, and, after all, no more than her evil sister's awful mistake. "Isn't that right, Clarence?" she had perhaps said in the bed the night before. And Clarence, empty and miserable, had probably nodded yes.

"Well, no more nonsense, now," Aunt Martha said, blowing her nose again. "What has to be has to be. Let's get them supper dishes washed."

Nellie complied. Her hot tears ran down her cheeks and popped onto the dirty dishes and into the suds. Nobody ever wanted me. Nobody ever will.

She took a long time washing the dishes, and late that night, long past midnight when she was still staring from the rough couch out into the dark and at the unfamiliar things, table and chairs, sink, that for a while had become familiar and meant home, Uncle Clarence came and lay beside her. He just lay there, comforting her, his arms around her for those long hours until daylight touched the window sill and it was the awful tomorrow of uncertainty, of being again sent away.

At breakfast, Aunt Martha, in comfort, or guilt, or shame, fried a spring chicken and made hot biscuits, giving her two helpings and filling her glass a third time with milk. She could hardly swallow the good food but had to smile and do so.

Then it was good-bye time and Aunt Martha shook her hand. She had no clothes to carry in a suitcase, so in the clothes she had worn from the detention home, she walked out to the model-T where Uncle Clarence was waiting.

Uncle Clarence sat stiff and upright, driving to the little township nearby, and she sat next to him trembling in fear. When they were far enough away from the farm, he stopped the car. He had a spray of flowers for her and pushed them at her awkwardly. They weren't real flowers. They were just clover blossoms and dandelions. But she held them tightly on her lap in her two hands and squeezed her eyes shut, but still the slow tears got through and ran off her chin.

For a long, long time they sat like this in silence as the old model-T churned surely on toward the township, with the grain elevator already sticking up in the flat distance. Then a couple of times, her uncle cleared his throat. But he said nothing. Yet once again he cleared his throat and then said, "Your mother—"

Again it was just the sound of the car motor like a long-distance runner breaking for the tape. But after a while, after the last farmhouses, before you entered the township, slowly passed them, he said, as if there had been no interruption, "She was just a young girl —just a kid—" His hand came up off the steering wheel for a moment. "—and she got into trouble—"

They bumped over the first street of the little town. And Uncle Clarence said, his eyes meeting hers for a moment, "Don't blame your mother. There is things some people have to do and they can't help it."

He would say no more about her mother and she didn't ask. She was afraid to know too much. And they came to the bus depot in a general store on the only main street of the town.

She kissed him good-bye. He took her hand and kissed it. "Nellie —Nellie—" he said.

She sat in the bus, trembling, afraid of these new people, her cousins. Unhappy in her fifteen years of unhappiness, but young and after a while, between unhappiness, pretending that she was an important young college lady going to visit her mother. She had expensive leather bags full of clothes, and she patted the imaginary luggage where it was propped near her silk stockings and high-heeled shoes. Her hair was piled on top of her head and she wore a fur coat. Now her fear came back to her. In her coat pocket was the letter being sent to her cousins. She took it out and fingered it, turned it over and over in her hands. It, too, was a part of her fear. Mrs. Katherine Walsh it said, and the address was written below. The heat and the weather had curled the sealed flap back a little. She put her fingernail under it, and bit by bit, it rolled back. Her heart beat fast and for a long time she was afraid to read what was inside. But at last she did:

> Dear Cousin Kate:
> We are sending this girl, Nellie, our cousin, to you. Without mentioning the name you know who her mother is, and the disgrace brought on the family. But the girl is a good girl and she works hard. We are sending her to you because we are, unlike you, poor country people and can't afford to feed her. She's skinny but she can pack it away. As I said, she is a good girl and honest but eats too much. But we feel that you will be able to feed her. She is not too smart and will never be but maybe you can train her. You have a big house with seven rooms and she can be a servant girl for you.
> Please forgive us for not letting you know ahead of time but this idea just came to me yesterday. Clarence and me send you love, and by the girl, a box of twelve apples which must be very expensive where you are. With family love,
>   Your Cousin Martha

Nellie sat with her face twisted against the bus window, her tears running down her cheeks, the glass cold, then hot against her forehead. She wouldn't eat hardly anything and then maybe they would like her. I won't eat any breakfast.

She was afraid of the city. She had never been in a city before. But she had to go into a drug store and buy gum, chew it real fast and seal the envelope with part of it. Then, as Aunt Martha had instructed her, she asked a policeman how to get to the address on the envelope. With part of the quarter Aunt Martha had given her for the purpose, she paid the carfare and, asking the motorman, standing close to him as if he were her only friend, she got off at the right stop. Then she had to walk, and losing herself a half-dozen times, asking a lot of people the way, she got to the right street and then, counting house numbers, finally stood in front of her cousins' house.

It was already dark and Nellie stood in front of the door wetting her lips and getting up courage to push her lifted finger against the bell. Overhead the porch dome-light was turned on, putting dullish color on her blond hair. Lace curtains were at the windows.

A woman came to the door. She was a plump, bosomy woman with marceled hair and rimless glasses. Nellie, unable to say anything, looked down at the woman's sensible low-heeled black oxfords and pushed the letter out at her. The woman looked at the girl, then at the envelope and took it. "Come inside," she said, and in the light of the hall read the letter. "Well—well—" she said as she read, her lips tightening several times. "Denny," she called. A male voice answered "Yeah?" It didn't sound pleased, but it was followed by a man in his stockinged feet and a roll of stomach and a tired red face. The woman said, "Martha Wallace has sent her sister's child to us." The red face had a mouth that fell open as if it were yawning. But it was the reaction of shock. They both stood regarding the girl for a moment. Then the woman said, "Come in, child." The voice was irritated, almost angry. But the woman tapped the girl lightly on the shoulder. The tap had something of pity in it.

Nellie followed them into a dining room that had a round table in it. The woman motioned her to sit on a chair against the wall; there was a crucifix attached to the floral wallpaper. She pulled a chair around and sat facing the girl. The man was reading the letter and frowning.

"Are you hungry, child?" the woman asked.

Nellie looked down into her lap. "No, ma'am."

The woman said, "I'm Mrs. Walsh. I'm your cousin. This is Mr. Walsh."

Nellie stood up and held out her hand to each of them in turn, as they had taught her to do in the detention home. She couldn't look at them and one tear fell on the floral pattern of the rug. Mrs. Walsh saw that. She patted Nellie on the shoulder and sort of hugged her over toward her bosom. "Now, now, that's not necessary."

The three of them sat down again, facing each other. And all were uncomfortable. "Well, I don't know where we're going to put her up," Mrs. Walsh said. Mr. Walsh only shrugged his shoulders as if it were her problem. "I know, dear," she said to Nellie, "you can sleep on the couch in Bridget's room. Bridget is my daughter—your third cousin. Come, I'll show you the room!"

And it was suppertime and they all sat at the round table with their heads bowed and hands together while Mr. Walsh said the blessing. He didn't put on his shoes.

Besides Mr. and Mrs. Walsh there were the two girls at the table, their daughters. Jane was sixteen and had buck teeth and wore glasses and was only in the second year of the Catholic high school. Bridget was almost beautiful, with big green eyes and black hair, and her mother and father called her Briddie when they weren't calling her darling. It was on the couch in her room that Nellie was to sleep. And now at the round table there was the best meal she had ever eaten but she kept trying not to eat much, even if she hadn't eaten since that morning on the farm, and kept shaking her head no even when Mrs. Walsh put more on her plate. She didn't speak during dinner. And right after dinner she went to the kitchen and took the dishpan and turned on the hot water. Mrs. Walsh came out into the kitchen with a stack of dirty dishes. "Now, isn't that sweet!" she exclaimed, going behind Nellie, and, putting her arms around her, kissed her on the cheek. That only made Nellie feel even more like crying.

Jane came out to dry the dishes, hustled there by her mother. "Where you from?"

"The country."

"What country?" That was funny and was followed by a squeal of laughter.

"From—from Missouri."

"Misery." That was funny too. But the dark eyes behind the heavy glasses stared at her steadily.

Nellie put some washed plates on the drainboard. Jane said, "Ma tells me we're cousins—some sort of cousins far distant."

Nellie nodded.

"I don't like you," Jane said. "And I don't think you're my cousin."

Mrs. Walsh came out into the kitchen. "Now, Jane," she said, "you mustn't talk like that. We're all going to be one family." She hugged Jane. Then she hugged Nellie.

Briddie Darling was in the front room reading a movie magazine.

30

The big house of seven rooms was a modest frame house on the west side of Detroit off Dix Avenue and near Holy Redeemer Church. Every room had holy pictures on the walls and every bedroom had a crucifix over the bed. The front room was furnished with once-fashionable overstuffed furniture—two chairs and a couch. They had crocheted doilies on the headrests and arms. There were end tables with glass tops and more doilies under them. And an upright piano that Jane had failed to learn to play but Briddie Darling would conquer. It was Nellie's job to scrub the bedrooms, dust the holy pictures and statues, scrub the margin of varnished hardwood boards around the rugs in the parlor and dining room, vacuum the rugs and wash the windows. Once a week she had to take the burners off the stove and boil them in lye water. Mrs. Walsh petted and kissed everyone. Even her friends, women as old and fat as she was. She hugged and patted Nellie. Her commands were given with kisses and hugs. "Nellie, honey." A hug against the enormous breast. "How would you like to cut the lawn? It's such a nice day and the exercise would do you good. Afterwards, honey, you and I will clean the pantry. I saw a cockroach there last night. You haven't been leaving garbage in the kitchen overnight, have you, dear? No, I know Nellie wouldn't do that!" A peck on the forehead. "Now get along with the lawn, dear!"

Mr. Walsh sat with his stockinged feet propped up on the banister of the front porch reading *The Michigan Catholic* while the lawn mower went back and forth.

Mr. Walsh worked for Graham-Paige, and he and his wife were all the time telling her that she, a girl from a non-Catholic orphanage, should behave herself and go to Holy Redeemer Church every Sunday. She went with them on Sundays to please them and all the time she tried not to eat much so that they would like her.

She lasted only a week in Briddie Darling's room. The favorite daughter came storming down from her room one afternoon, screaming, "I won't sleep with her! She's always mooning around like a cow! I won't have her in my room! She cleaned it and she changed everything around! I can't even find my lipstick!"

Mr. Walsh had a tool room in the basement. It was sectioned off away from the boiler and coalbin and even had a wooden floor. There was a long workbench with a lathe and tools all hung up in order. It smelled good of oil and wood shavings and sawdust. Her cot was moved down there and Mrs. Walsh hugged her and said, "You will be able to be by yourself here. When I was your age I always wanted a room of my own and I never had one." Nellie's head bounced against the mastlike breast, almost hurting as she was hugged, and Mrs. Walsh, in compensation, gave her two hand-me-down dresses that Jane had outgrown. But when Mrs. Walsh and her daughters went to the bingo at the Catholic church twice a week, she had to stay home and cook dinner for Mr. Walsh and hear him complain about the food and how hard he worked or tell her to always go to Holy Redeemer and some day she would become a Catholic.

Once Jane lost a schoolbook and accused her of stealing it. That was another time when she cried. But the worst time of all was one night when she couldn't sleep and crept out of the basement and lay on the lawn thinking even the farm was sometimes better than this. On the front porch sat Mr. and Mrs. Walsh. The swing made the same complaining sounds as the one in the country. There were no lightning bugs.

Mrs. Walsh was saying, "But it's our Christian duty—"

"Yes, I know all about that. But do you know that they're laying off out there at Paige?"

"Our Christian duty."

"The girls don't like her."

"If we are really good Catholics—"

"Somebody else's kid—somebody else's trouble—"

They were talking about her and it was one of the first times she didn't cry. She just listened, and the next late afternoon when Mrs. Walsh and the girls went to a church benefit, she wrote a note and quietly let herself out of the house:

> I took five dollars and thirty-three cents from Cousin Briddie's jewel box from on top of her dresser. I'll pay it back when I can. I'm not a thief. I just can't stay here. You were nice to me, Mrs. (cousin) Walsh.

. . . Nellie looked back into the tavern . . . she had sent the money back . . .

> YOU AIIIIINNNNN'T BEEN BLUUUUUUE
> NO NO NO NO NO NO NO NO NO NO NO NO NO NO
> You ain't been bluuuuue . . .

From her cousins' house she had walked down Michigan Avenue and under the viaduct where the railroad tracks cross the avenue near the Cadillac plant. She huddled there two hours, three. Sometimes she tried to hitchhike a ride, lifting her thumb at cars and trucks, but most of the time she was scared and just stood there with traffic roaring past her. But finally a man and a woman stopped. "My mother is sick in Chicago and I have to go there," she said in a rush.

"Hop in, kid."

They took her a way, then she had to get off. It was dark now. After a long time, a woman in a pickup truck stopped for her. The woman wore a scarf over her head and had sacks of potatoes and onions and cartons of canned goods in the back. Nellie told her the same thing, fast. And she kept having to lie because the woman asked questions. The woman said she was going to White Pigeon, which was about halfway, where she owned a restaurant. Nellie was sorry she had lied and wished that she could ask the woman for a job. But now she couldn't.

White Pigeon was a dead place on the highway just before the road crossed into Indiana. It was a stopping place for truck drivers who broke the long journey with hot coffee and sandwiches or bowls of chili.

Nellie bought a hamburger in the restaurant owned by the woman who had befriended her. Then she hung around outside in the dark. The truck drivers, big-behinded and broad-shouldered, moving their legs, working the cramps out of them, walked past her into the restaurant and out, back toward their trucks and the long journey that linked Detroit and Chicago.

Nellie approached the truck drivers. They looked straight ahead without answering, toothpicks stuck in their mouths, or grimly shook their heads no. A couple looked at her face and then her body, but still, with squinting eyes, shook their heads no.

When with shoulders sagging and head held down she thought she wasn't going to get a ride, another truck driver, crunching gravel under his big feet, came along. "Mister, can you give me a ride to Chicago?— My mother—"

The truck driver grinned out of his big face. "I can't take you," he said. "You better walk across the state line or pick up another truck. There's the Mann Act waiting for anybody who does."

"If I walk—" she said, "then will you take me? My mother's sick and—"

He grinned at her lie. "Start walking," he said. He turned back over the gravel road and went into the restaurant for a beer.

She walked until her feet hurt; many cars and trucks passed her in the night, flashing their lights in warning. Then after a long stretch of blackness, headlights beamed the highway and the truck came slow. He leaned out of the cab window. "It ain't far now," he yelled. And he went slow, lighting the way for her. Then the metal highway sign, black on white, said INDIANA, and he motioned her across the state line.

He pulled off the highway and turned off his lights while she crawled in.

She watched him drive. They didn't say anything for a long time. Then, holding the steering wheel with his big forearm, he lit two cigarettes. He handed one to her and when she took it he looked at her approvingly. He was a young man about thirty-five, but even in the light from the dashboard she could tell he had grown so bald that his blond hair was like the yellow grass under a rock you had just picked up. He sweated a lot and wiped it from his forehead onto the yellow hairs of his brawny forearms. His cigarette sparked amber-blue in the dark and he said, "What's this stuff about your mother?"

"I was lying," she said, knowing she was caught; and lied some more. "I'm running away from a reform school."

"Oh," he said, probably believing her, and then didn't say any more. They drove on through the night for over an hour. Then he pulled the truck off onto an embankment and turned off the motor, switched out the lights. He sort of rubbed his hands together. "Well, baby, are you going to give me any?" It wasn't a question.

"All right."

When they got to Illinois, she had to get out and walk across again.

She said, "I was in reform school because I was caught as a prostitute." She was remembering the talk of the girls in the detention home and she didn't know why she told him that. Maybe so that later he wouldn't feel bad because she was so young.

He said, "The best place for you is to hit West Madison or North Clark Street and look for a job as a waitress. Tell 'em you're seventeen."

He let her out at the dead end of a car line where there was no traffic, and told her how to get to those streets.

"Thanks, mister! For giving me a lift!" She waved a friendly, cordial hand, waving good-bye frantically as he drove off, as if he had done her a favor. He drove off fast.

And she stood alone, then, in the great beast of a city. It was at the moment eating its young and its old. They went, stooped and over cobblestones, to and from their jobs, weary and broken on the same benches of the streetcar she rode. It was like a blue-black beast in the night. Its eyes, neon, were cat eyes in the dark. And its heart beat. She could feel the throb and glut of it. Its muscles moved, shifting from one buttock to the other, head sunk between heavy, heaving shoulders. Its bare feet in the mud, toenails black and broken. And the heavy breathing of an animal asleep but its cat eyes open.

It frightened her.

5

A young girl, a country girl, alone in the big city she stood, at night, on West Madison Street. Fearfully she slipped from lighted shop window to lighted shop window. She was a frightened wraith, a shadow, slipping from shadow to light and back again.

The street looked at her with its thousand neon animal eyes.

Her timid feet propelled her on, and bums and drunks stumbled past her, staggered aimlessly toward the curb and away from it. Her big eyes, gray with fright, stared, and pulling her shoulders in tensely, she withdrew against the fronts of buildings and shop windows.

She walked a long way down one side of the street and then the other. She was hungry. She was sleepy. Her young stomach began to ache for food. She wished, almost tearfully, that she was back washing dishes for Cousin Mrs. Walsh, with the security of holy pictures even in the kitchen and her room in the basement.

She found herself with her hand against the doorknob of a cheap restaurant and her heart beat fast but she forced herself to go inside and the smell of chili and hamburgers frying brown made her stomach ache more. With her head down, afraid of this place, of these people sitting eating, she moved to a back booth. She unknotted the handkerchief and took out one of the dollars she had taken from Cousin Briddie's jewel box, carefully knotted the rest of the money back into the handkerchief.

The banging of a heavy water glass slopping water on the porcelain table top and the knife and fork jangling together made her jump.

"Yeah? What's yours, sister?" the man in a dirty blue shirt with the sleeves rolled up said, almost as if he were mad at her about something.

"A—a hamburger. And—and chili."

"Chili's all gone. We got spaghetti."

35

"All right."

She ate it all, rubbing the hard-crusted French bread in the plate to sop up all the spaghetti sauce.

Then she sat, afraid to leave, not knowing where to go. Outside the restaurant window blank, black night stood like a wall . . .

A big rough hand shook her and she woke up.

"What are you doing here, kid?"

"I—I was eating."

"We're closin'. It's three in the morning."

She started seesawing down the seat of the bench so that she could get up.

"Maude," the man called.

A fat woman came from the back. They both stood looking down at her. "Heavenly days!" the woman said. "Heavenly days!" And they both went on staring at her as if they had found something they couldn't identify.

"Where do you live, kid?" the man asked.

Quickly, while the cheap cloth of her dress moved up and down to the beating of her heart, she said, "I just got to Chicago. My mother is sick and I—I—"

The man and woman looked at each other meaningfully.

"Come on in the back," the woman said. "You can sleep."

In the morning the man said, "Wanna work?"

She nodded yes.

"How old are you?" the woman asked.

"Seventeen."

"You don't look a day over fifteen."

They let her work. Washing dishes in the greasy, dirty kitchen where rats sometimes came even in the daytime. They let her sleep. They paid her nothing and fed her only what they couldn't sell.

She stayed with them four months, and then when she was smart enough and knew she could be paid for what she was doing for nothing, she got a job as a counter girl at another restaurant.

And after that she had many jobs. Always as a waitress or a counter girl or cleaning dirty dishes off sticky, coffee-spilled tables. She worked at a German restaurant on North Avenue, at a hash house on North Clark, at a chili and hot-dog joint on West Madison, at Thompson's, at the Marquis. At first she was often fired because she had no experience and dropped things or spilled things. Then she learned her trade and these were her streets of employment, West Madison Street and North Clark Street.

The city ate away at her.

The animal brushed her with its arched back. It clawed at her and bared its fangs. Its claws were always partially withdrawn from their dark, silky pads. It blinked its sleepy eyes and regarded her.

The blue-black animal was always there, lying in the tall grass of skyscrapers.

Nellie looked down at her fingers twisted together on the tavern table. The man in the torn shirt stood over her, weaving so drunkenly that beer spilled out of the glass he was holding and thudded brown and white on the table, then rolled in a quick, liquid stream down into her lap. "Here, Nellie."

"Thanks, Slim," she said.

Dabbing the beer off her skirt with a handkerchief, Nellie smiled, remembering . . .

After a year and a half she had learned her trade as a waitress and could get a job in any of the cheap places on the North Side because she *was* a good waitress and she knew how to kid with the customers and make them feel good. She smiled again. And after this year and a half, she had learned how to pluck her eyebrows and put black on her blond eyelashes to make her eyes look good. And, yes, she did have pretty eyes. She was working in a place on North Clark which was both a tavern and a restaurant. The windows had strips of paper pasted to them that advertised shots of whiskey, glasses of wine, schooners of beer, chili and hamburgers, Irish stew. The entire stock inside and the price of each item was plastered there on the window in venetian-blind effect. Nobody could see inside very well either, which was what the proprietor also had in mind.

She and two other girls worked at the steam table, carried plates to the customers and drinks from the bar. They also had to sit with the customers if they wanted them to, have a drink with them if they were asked.

Her feet were aching and she was dead tired when he walked in. She looked up over the steam table at him, up over the pork chops in grease, the watery cabbage, the lumpy mashed potatoes in their stainless steel limousine, the round pots of blood-red chili and spaghetti and baseball-hard meat balls. And her mouth fell open a little; there was a catch in her throat. And the steam arising obliterated his face momentarily, again took more of the curl from her long blond hair. Then the steam rose up to the ceiling and he was, in profile, walking square-shouldered, broad-chested, thin-hipped past her.

He was the best-looking fellow she had ever seen. Her eyes followed him to the bar stool where he sat, his mouth showing white teeth as he laughed with the bartender. She stared at his wide cheekbones, the hair that fell curly over his forehead. His deep, innocent-looking eyes. She kept staring at him. He looked like a movie star to her.

He began hanging out around the place, coming in every night or so for an hour or two. Sometimes he came with girls. Sometimes with a Mexican and a Negro fellow. Sometimes he was drunk.

She had been working here only a short time; everybody else knew him and called him Nick. Some people said he was tough and a jackroller. He never noticed her. Why should he? She felt herself plain and unattractive. Waitresses look the same everywhere. Generally they are skinny and unattractive and in the background. She was one of them. That's the way she had it figured out why he never noticed her.

She had seen him maybe fifty times. Each time she would have the same feeling of awe because he was so good-looking. And each time she felt bad to see him on the street because he didn't look like he belonged down there. But if he didn't come in then she wouldn't see him, so she was glad that he came to their place. She always looked at him when he came in and then secretly stared at him as long as he was there. But he didn't even know she was alive . . .

> *In the eeeeevenin'*
> *When lights are looow*
> *I'm so lonesome I could cccrrrrryyy*
> *'Cause there's nobody who cares a-bout me . . .*

Nellie's deep gray-blue eyes looked across the tavern without seeing Slim slip off his chair to the floor and sit stupidly there in a drunken haze.

. . . That night it had been different. She hadn't even noticed that Nick had come in. Hopping around alone on the sawdust floor, holding her coat open and sawing back and forth with her body in a dance motion, though there was no music, was an old drunken woman, gray hair streaming down her back and over her face, half hiding it. She staggered into a table and flopped down, out of breath and laughing. She put her head down on her arms in their dirty, raveled sweater; then lifted it. Laughter, but not real laughter, came from her loose, liquor-sagged mouth. An elderly man, bald and heavy-jowled, went over to the woman and, leaning over, talked angrily to her. He put his hand on her shoulder and shook her. She looked up. He showed her his fist.

Nellie came out from behind the steam table and from around the end of the bar. She picked up one of the tin trays with *Pabst* BLUE RIBBON BEER stamped on its outer rim. Approaching the man and holding the tray like a weapon, she shouted in the man's face, "That woman's crazy! You touch her again and I'll—I'll kill you!"

The man looked at her and at the tray held menacingly in front of his face. Mumbling, he walked off toward the bar.

Nellie moved between tables back toward the steam table swinging the tray in her anger. A blue serge pant leg was suddenly thrust out, blocking her path. She looked down into Nick's smiling face, his body slumped loosely, gracefully across the chair in a long, muscular angle. His smile showed strong white teeth and dimples. His brown-black hair curled over his forehead and over his ears.

"Say, you got spunk!" he said.

She just stood there with her mouth open. And she almost dropped the tray. Then he moved his leg so that she could get by.

She went into the toilet and sat down and cried.

When she could come out, first dabbing powder on her face and trying, with her fingers, to put curl back into her hair where the steam had taken it out, she went back on duty.

Now she was afraid to look at him. He might catch her. And once, when she had to take a tray of beer mugs past his table to a table behind him, he said loud enough for her to hear, "Good-looking legs too!"

Her face colored but she was pleased.

Every time he came in after that he'd stop by the steam table, drunk or sober, and say, "Well, how's Joe Louis tonight?" Once he even stuck his hand down into the limousine in which the hot dogs rode in weak red water and lifted one out, bit down on it with his strong white teeth before moving to the bar. He was smart and cute and wonderful.

One night he came in very drunk. He staggered to the steam table, weaving there, his brown eyes hazy through the steam. "Hi, Joe Louis!" Then he said, "Bring me something to drink. Anything at all. Surprise me."

He reeled over to a table. She carried a small glass of beer on a tray and the bar rag to clean the table top.

When she stood alongside him, Nick pushed out a chair with his foot. "Sit down," he said; then, "Hey"—leaning toward her—"when are you going to give me a chance?" He half grabbed hold of her arm. She pulled it away. "Aw, go on!" she said. Surprised, embarrassed, in love, she slapped at him playfully with the bar cloth.

"I'll buy you a beer," Nick said.

"I don't want a beer."

"Sit down." He half pulled her into the chair and she sat obediently. Then, feeling her face go red looking at him, being so near him, she wanted to get up.

"Please, Nick."

"Oh, you know my name!" Then, "Everybody on the street knows my name."

He leaned on the table with his elbows to steady himself. She saw his broad, square face, his wide cheekbones with their touches of tan, his cheeks not heavy yet with any beard but smooth and soft. And he looked up at her. She saw the innocent brown eyes. "I'm a little drunk," he said, "but I think I like you."

She was trembling. She said, "This street is no good for you, Nick. You're too—too—" She couldn't find the word and she couldn't say good-looking.

Nick leaned back in his chair and looked up at the ceiling. Bored.

"Honest, I mean it," Nellie said.

"I'll buy you a beer," Nick said.

"Look—what would your folks say to you? What would your father say if he caught you down here?"

"He's dead," Nick said. His eyes seemed to harden, not sorry.

"Clear out while you can," Nellie said; and to herself: I can't. I can't.

"What do you want me to do? Join Moody Bible Institute? Come on, I'll buy you a beer."

"I don't want a beer."

"That's the way you make your living. If we don't buy, you don't eat." He had her by the arm again. "Come on, baby."

"I don't want a beer.

She wouldn't take one.

The next night he was standing with his back against the plate-glass window waiting for her when she got off from work. He took her arm. He didn't say anything. He didn't have to . . .

Nellie looked up into the tavern into this moment of this night. She said, almost aloud: Sure he had other girls. He was good-looking. Sure I gave him money. I loved him. Sure he had other girls. But he loved me. He used to stay at my room nights. Of course I loved him. Of course he lived with me. Of course I gave him money. I would have lied, I would have said anything on the stand to save his life.

At the table in the West Madison Street bar Nellie was weeping softly, despairingly.

He loved me. He loved me.

She had to believe that.

YOU AIIIINNN'T BEEN BLUUUEEE
NO NO NO NO NO NO NO NO NO NO NO NO NO
You ain't been bluuuee
Till you've had that Mooood In-di-go
That feeeeelllin' goes stealin'
  dooooowwwwn
Down to my shoes
Whiiiillleee IIIiiii sit and sigh
GGGGGOOOO 'LLLOOOONG, BLLUUUUES . . .

The last time she saw him before she sat on the witness chair in court was a night on West Madison Street. He was drunker than she had ever seen him. He was alone on the long, long lonely street. He was steadying himself with one hand against buildings as he walked.

She caught up with him. "Nick."

"What do you want?" Mean.

"Nick—please—"

"Go on—beat it—"

"Please—Nick—"

"Beat it—do you hear me—?"

"Come on with me, Nick."

He stood weaving, facing her, weaving horribly, eyes glazed. Like a boxer in the ring just before he goes down to take the count. She put her hand on the sleeve of his coat. The city crouched around them blackly.

"Go on—beat it—before I slap you in the mouth."

"Please come with me, Nick."

Resistance went out of him. "Okay. Okay." It was like a child speaking.

He leaned heavily against her and she supported him. He followed her blindly.

The city was a blue-black panther that slunk along beside them. The tall, skyscraper night-grass hemmed them in. The thousand neon animal eyes watched their going.

In her room he pushed her gently but drunkenly into a chair, his fingers pleading with her to sit down.

Then he knelt on the floor in front of her and put his head into her lap.

"Nellie . . . Nellie . . ."

A trolley pole on the streetcar wire went by in a wild screech.

"Nellie . . ." he said.

He was quiet for a while.

"Live fast, die young and have a good-looking corpse. Hahahah," he said.

She fondled his hair, tousled in blackness there on her lap. She rocked him back and forth.

"I'm no good. I'm no good," he said.

At last, gently, she got him to lie across the bed. Then she lay down with him, both fully clothed. She put her arms around him. She started to, but did not tell him that she was pregnant by him. She held him all night long as one holds a child.

Pairs of neon animal eyes stared into the window. Night waited outside. The wind went in an animal howl.

Two weeks later the police officer was killed.

The owner of the tavern now brought Nellie a drink and set it before her. "This is on the house," he said. "Take it easy, Nellie. Make it your last." And patting her on the shoulder, "Remember the kid."

. . . the kid.

Her son . . .

6

She had been a good mother. Home to her one room over the West Madison Street car tracks with her baby, and still weak, she had to go to work. It was a hash house run by a Greek, Mike Manos, and he was nice. She worked for him from six in the evening until three or four in the morning depending on business, but she never got there before six-fifteen because the baby had to eat at six o'clock.

That was something she worried about. Nick was supposed to eat every four hours. The hours were six A.M., ten A.M., two P.M., six P.M., and two A.M., around the clock. She had to take so many ounces of milk and water, carefully measured, though her hands trembled every time she did it, and mix them a certain way and put exactly three and a half ounces into each of the six bottles for that day. She worried making sure that they were exactly right. And she was so frightened that she wouldn't feed the baby one minute before or after the time she was supposed to. She checked her cheap wrist watch and, when she could, called on the telephone to find out the exact time. Even if Nick was asleep, she awakened him on the exact minute to feed him. She set her clock after work so that she would wake up half an hour before each feeding.

Mike Manos had known Nick. Mike Manos was bald and fifty and unmarried and let her keep the baby in the back of the restaurant when she was at work. They had rigged up a big, unused dishpan for a crib, putting blankets in it, and there the baby slept while she waited on tables.

She had bought all the books on baby care that she could find, and when she wasn't working out front, when business was slow, she sat on a stool in the kitchen at the vegetable and meat chopping table biting her lip, scratching her head and reading about how a baby should be brought up. It said that a child needs love and not to be afraid to respond to its needs, that a mother can make funny noises and faces when she is changing his diapers so that he won't start yelling and will feel secure. She made all kinds of strange and weird faces and noises at these times, like the book said. It told exactly how to bathe him, and she and Mike Manos together, laughing and pleased, bathed the baby using one of the sinks in the kitchen that was generally used for pots and pans.

She jumped up from reading the baby book and, first consulting her watch, rushed to the wall phone in front, dialed the number.

". . . is exactly one-forty-two P.M. and twenty-three seconds," the precise voice said.

She went back to the restaurant kitchen after adjusting her watch and put the nursing bottle into a pan of warm water on the stove. Biting her lips, she kept watching the second hand. Then she took the little form into her arms and began coaxingly awakening the pudgy, wrinkled, red, almost bald little senator-like face into awareness. She held him tenderly in her arms while he drew the white liquid from the bottle. He wouldn't call her Ma. He would call her Mother, like the rich children did in the movies.

Then, when he was four months old, she bought him applesauce and bananas—but, feeling them with her fingers, rejecting many, she bought black-flecked, ripe bananas—like the book said, and mashed them fine with a fork, but two more times than the book said, pushing her blond hair off her forehead and working away at them, making sure.

And Mike Manos took part in all her activities with the baby. It was almost as if it were his child. He made strange noises and faces at the baby in his dishpan, bending his bald head near while his fat finger waggled back and forth before the hypnotized eyes.

It was all she had to offer Mike Manos for his kindness. She said, "You can have me if you want me."

He patted her shoulder. "You good girl, Nellie. When I want I go where girls no are nice. You be mother now."

Before work, she had nowhere to go but to the tavern. These

were the only people she knew. The tavern was a club. The men and women living in rooms on West Madison and its nearby streets went to the tavern in the same manner that people in better neighborhoods visited each other's houses. It was their meeting place. Nellie went there. She took Nick with her. On the tavern floor he learned to crawl; across its cigarette-butt-strewn surface, he took his first steps. And he was loved by all of them. Drunkard. Bum. Prostitute. They all fussed over him. He might just stand and solemnly gaze at a stranger or hand him his toy and then take it back, or pile everything on an old tramp's lap, everything he could find—soda caps, empty beer bottles from nearby tables, the bar rag, coke glasses, a cigarette package, match books. And Nellie, sitting here with the only friends she had, would watch him with loving eyes and exclaim, "Ain't that cute! Ain't that cute!"

They all agreed with her.

She was making two dollars a day, meals and tips. And tips weren't anything in the place she worked. She slept with a man to get the money to buy Nick's high chair. She slept with a man to pay for Nick's play pen. The baby got sick. She faced a child that was crying. She took him to a clinic. The doctor said he needed a special formula. It meant more money. It meant more men.

Nellie looked up into the tavern.

Her need was desperate to see and be with her child.

She stood up, forgetful of the liquor that still remained in her glass. She moved toward the door. Staggering at the tavern door were drunkards taking drunkards home. The beast of night crouched outside.

Nellie went up the long, grimy flight of stairs toward her room. Old newspapers at her ankles whispered sad things of the past.

Nellie opened the door and stepped into the shadow of life and death.

Her son still lay asleep across his crayon drawing, his cheek down on the blue and yellow scrawlings.

My son! She looked at him and moved toward him. Then she looked up at the boy in the photograph on the wall. Their eyes met. His eyes said: I didn't do it. I'm innocent.

Nellie gathered her son up off the floor and into her arms, undressed him and put him to bed.

And she sat, trembling.

"Nick. Nick."

And she was talking to the boy's father. Needing the sound of his name in the room. Knowing that he had done it. Learning late in the trial, long after her testimony, that he was guilty. She looked again at the picture. I'm innocent, his eyes said. He had always had that look of innocence, about everything.

She closed down her thoughts. She didn't want to think of him as guilty.

"Nick. Nick," she said.

And now she was speaking to her son.

7

She didn't have to work until the next night after they returned from the country. She had a hangover and needed a drink. Having fed Nick and left him with a crayon book, she walked down the flight of steps and into the harsh sunlight of West Madison Street. As she stepped out onto the sidewalk, an elderly man approached her. The sleeves and trouser cuffs of his suit were threadbare and the collar of the white shirt was badly raveled, but a cheap satin tie flourished like a flower down its front and his shoes were shined. He lifted his battered felt hat to Nellie and bowed with dignity. "Good morning, young lady," he said, and held his hat over his chest in a courtly gesture. "I am a merchant, young lady," he said, and exhibited a shoebox he carried under his arm. Quickly the hat went back on his head, and he lifted the lid of the box. "The usual items, of course." And he named them: "Razor blades, pencils, fountain pens—cheap ones, I will agree; hair nets—blond ones for you; handkerchiefs, bobby pins, brooches—not really very good, I must admit. Oh yes, and shoe polish. I have purchased a box of polish myself, out of my earnings and at wholesale price. I always keep my shoes shined, shining them myself. It adds an air of respectability, don't you think?"

Nellie stood smiling up at him, almost grinning in delight; and he went on in his rather broad English accent, "Indeed, young lady, if fortune shines on me and I sell to you, it shall be my first sale of the day, though I am assured that selling to you, it shan't be my last, for to have someone as lovely as you purchase from me would assure me of a very good day."

He held the box out to her temptingly. But his hands were shaking. Nellie saw that. She looked up into his bloodshot eyes. She said, "You're hung over too, huh?"

For a moment his eyes twinkled. He said, "Well, indeed, if you so happen to have a small drop in the house, I must be shameless and

say that I would most sincerely appreciate it. You see"—coughing—
"I suffer from a little touch of—"

Nellie was grinning at him. When he saw that, he laughed. "To tell you the truth, I'm afraid I'm caught." He laughed again, loudly, and said, "Yes. Hung over."

"There ain't anything at my place," Nellie said, "but—" She nodded toward the tavern. "And I need one too. That's what I came down for."

"Young lady, this embarrasses me to say, but I do not, as yet, my day just starting, have the price—however, if you will accept one of the brooches in exchange—"

"Aw, come on," Nellie said, leading the way toward the tavern.

"—As I mentioned earlier, they're not very good brooches. I purchase them for nineteen cents and sell them for half a dollar. You would honor it to wear it."

"It's my treat," Nellie said.

He escorted her into the low-down tavern, pulled out a chair for her and helped her settle herself into it. Then, removing his hat, he sat down facing her. He was a dignified-looking man, perhaps sixty, and his graying hair, wavy, needing cutting, was also artistic-looking in the way it flowed back from his wide forehead. His eyes were twinkling and they were mischievous. His voice sounded like a college professor's and his English accent was attractive because it was real. His nose was large, perpetually red, and crisscrossed with many blue veins.

"Allow me to introduce myself," he said. "Judge Edward Joseph Sullivan, formerly in the circuit court of the State of New Jersey—"

"I'm Nellie," she said, and he arose gracefully in acknowledgment, his hand stretched out to her.

Seated again, he continued his own summary: "University of Pennsylvania, 1899. Yale Law School. Track team at Pennsylvania, where I set a record for the hundred-yard dash. Right end on the football team for three years." He smiled across the table at her. "So you see, young lady, we are not all bums here on West Madison Street."

The bartender stood at the table and Nellie ordered two shots of whiskey. "Best for a hangover," she said. Judge Sullivan looked at her appreciatively.

They drank them down in a swallow and smiled we needed that at each other across the table.

Nellie called to the bartender. "No, no." Judge Sullivan half rose. "I must not overextend your hospitality."

"Please, Judge," she said.

He hurriedly reseated himself.

The new shots came. Judge Sullivan rolled a cigarette. His fingers still shook with his hangover. He lit the ragged edge, and his heavy mustache, the white edge stained yellow from tobacco, fastened over it. Then he looked up. "I *beg* your pardon!" He offered her the sack of tobacco and they both laughed as she tried to roll one. Then he rolled one for her, instructing her to run her tongue along the edge so that she could secure it.

Nellie bought still a third shot of whiskey for them above Judge Sullivan's protests, and when he had finished it, he arose, shook her hand, bowed once again, thanked her with the hope that they would meet again when he could reciprocate.

Nellie watched him go, his shoebox of merchandise under his arm, his erect, almost proud bearing taking him under the day-blinded eyes of the neon signs. Nick! She had been here too long! Running on her low-heeled shoes, she hurried to her door and up the flight of steps.

Nick had squeezed behind the bed and stood at the window with his chin on the sill. He liked the sky that color blue. He liked the clouds.

Nellie looked at him. His ears were slightly pointed, and that always made her smile, thinking of a baby rabbit.

Without moving his chin, he turned his eyes toward her and they were the color of an autumn leaf, like his hair that stood bushed and straight above his small forehead. "Mother," he asked, looking at her, "what are clouds made of?"

"Oh, honey!" she said, and coaxed him to her. She didn't know what to tell him. "Honey," she said, hugging him, "don't go behind the bed any more. I'm afraid you'll fall out." She lifted his chin. "Do you want to go outside with me?"

He nodded yes.

Nellie sat on one of the stools in the front of the restaurant so that she could look out the window and keep an eye on Nick. She sipped coffee, feeling better now, the whiskey easing her tension. The restaurant had a juke box near the door and she had put in a nickel. It was the song she spent a lot of her tip money on:

> You are my sunshine
> My only sunshine . . .

And that's what Nick was to her. Her sunshine. That's why she loved that song.

Nick stood outside the plate-glass window. He wasn't allowed to go away further than the length of the window when he was out there alone. He loved this street. It was a wonderful world. Like the circus his mother had taken him to once. It was always exciting, with noise and people and movement. Some of the men, and the women, too, who walked out by the curb and then way over by the fronts of the buildings looked like they were dancing. The crippled men on crutches looked like those people at the circus who walked way over your head in the air. He wished the man on skates would come by. The skates made nice, busy sounds. He had a low little roller-skate platform and let himself down the curb with it. He wore a red sweater. In his hands he had little long things something like Nick's play blocks. He put them out in front of him on the cobblestones and pulled himself forward. The skates bumped over the car tracks. In the red sweater, with his rounded shoulders, his long arms swinging in front of him, he looked like an animal his mother once showed him at the zoo. The skates whirred softly against the cobblestones, and when the water was falling a little and the sky was not blue, the skates left damp marks behind them. The pads left dry-wiped spots on either side of the tracks the skates made. The legless man crossed the cobblestones and the streetcar tracks. He hoisted himself and his attached framework up to the other curb. He always says hello to me:

"Hi, kid!"

"Hello."

He has a big, heavy voice for such a little short man. Once he had some candy in his pocket for me. Then he went running away, lower and faster than all the other people. I made a drawing of him once but Mother said it only looked like scratches of color. But that's the way he goes. And I like colors. That's what I like best. Colors. All kinds. Especially blue. I bet it's *fun* to go riding like that. A couple of times, I wanted to ask him to take me riding with him but I didn't. Mother would get mad.

And I like the organ grinder when he comes by. Sometimes he lets me turn the handle and beautiful music comes out. The organ has only one leg. The organ grinder even gave me a nickel once to give to the monkey and I did. It would be nice to have a little cap like that with a rubber band under your chin. And I like beggars. When I get big, I'm going to be a beggar. You talk to everybody and people are nice and they help you. I like the women who sell flowers in the tavern. He seldom saw flowers. But one lady has a red one in a can on the fire escape outside her window. One woman who sells flowers had white, round ones, real soft white ones and they smelled *good!* That must be the way heaven smells. That colored man who blows that yellow horn in the tavern window, he looks like he's blowing a big yellow flower up the way I do with balloons. But the lady that sings, I don't like her because she is real fat in front and wears hardly no clothes. I told Mother that that colored man's mother didn't make him wash and Mother got real mad with me and said I should never say that again. Mother said he can't help it. But she's always washing me.

"You Are My Sunshine" was playing on the juke box.

And this was three days later. It was a dull afternoon in the restaurant. Mike Manos was changing the filter in the coffee urn. Nellie sat with her head propped between her elbows. On the counter in front of her, its pages open, was a copy of *The Child Between Two and Seven.*

The record ended. Nellie jumped up, put in a dime and pushed the same button twice.

"Jesus, Nellie!" Mike Manos said.

Nellie didn't hear him. She liked that song and she could read and listen at the same time.

When the juke box again went silent, Nellie searched in her apron pocket for change. It was then that she saw Judge Sullivan walking past the window. Grabbing the book, she ran out of the restaurant and after him. "Judge! Judge!" she called, and at last he saw her and stopped. She caught up with him. Breathless, she said, "I bet you haven't had a woman run after you so fast in a long time."

Already Judge Sullivan had his hat off and was bowing to her. "Oh yes, I have," he answered. "When I've had her pocketbook."

Nellie stood smiling and still breathless. "Would—would you come over some time?" she asked. "You see it says—it says right here in this book—wait—"

She started thumbing through the book and at length came to a section. "—It says, well, that a boy—that my son needs male company—that, that all fatherless kids do. That they have to know that there are men too—and—well, would you come over? It says that the boy needs to pattern himself after a man or some older boy he likes."

Judge Sullivan stood tall, straight, and smiling. "Well, I wouldn't suggest that he pattern himself after me, though he could find worse examples." Then he patted her on the shoulder. "Of all the women I have known, you are the finest example of a mother to my knowledge. I must, in the near future, meet this offspring of yours."

"Oh, thank you, Judge!" Tears of gratitude were in her eyes. Impulsively she leaned over and kissed his cheek.

"I am sure," Judge Sullivan said, "that after this running after me and this generous kiss, that I, an old man, will break my leg sprinting up to your apartment tomorrow or the next day." He bowed extravagantly and turned away.

Under his arm, with his shoebox, he carried a brown paper sack. It hadn't been a good day. He crossed the streetcar tracks and turned into Levin's bar. Stopping at the bar, he pulled one of his used but clean shirts out of the bag, and asked the proprietor, "Sir, may I have your permission to sell a good shirt in here?"

"Sure."

Judge Sullivan walked down along the bar speaking to several men who sat there, "Well, here goes a good shirt and a tie for half a dollar. Size sixteen and a half."

He had no takers.

At the door, he said to the proprietor, "Thank you kindly, sir, for the permission. If I sell it, I will spend the money in your place."

Nellie turned away from Judge Sullivan and back toward the restaurant. A streetcar thundered down West Madison and two pigeons lifted from the trolley wire in its wild passing. They were gray and hung in the air for a moment. A few feathers fluttered loose and slowly descended to the street. On the sidewalk in a half-circle stood three ragged boys. Their shoeshine boxes had been left under a lamppost. In a grimy doorway, half in shadow, stood the figure of a man. You could see the tips of his shoes and his hand held in a loose fist. He was jiggling some coins in his hand, pennies and nickels. "Okay," he said, "get ready. And don't let anybody get them too easy. If you have to slug somebody—slug him."

The coins danced a moment in the hot July sunlight, then fell to the dirty sidewalk and rolled away, one into the gutter, the other to the curb. The boys scrambled after them, scuffing their knees and elbows, wrestling each other for the pennies, one boy even kicking out at another as they rolled off the curb into the street. The man in the doorway laughed.

Dirty hands went into pockets with what had been gained. They lined up again.

"Hey, mister! Throw them this way!"

"Hey, mister! Mister!"

The man's voice said, "Okay—there's two dimes with the pennies this time." And then, "Hey, nigger, I bet you ain't tough enough to get them from the white boys. Okay!"

The coins somersaulted through stuffy air and clanged against the concrete.

"Yah! I got a dime!" the colored boy said.

"Me too!" one of the white kids said.

The man had another jingling of coins in his hands, but looked out of the doorway just as Nellie was approaching. Not even looking in the direction of the kids, he threw the coins across the sidewalk and stepped out of the doorway.

The boys ran, scrambling after them. A streetcar came to a screeching halt just in time.

The man stepped out directly in front of Nellie. Only he wasn't a man. He was a youth about twenty-two years old. Nellie glanced up at him. His eyes were cold, almost insolent. And they looked her up and down. His waist was thin and his shoulders square.

Nellie stepped around him and continued on her way.

"Hey! Wait a minute!" he called.

Nellie turned around and walked up to him. "What do you want?" Cold. Angry. What does this guy think I am?

"Hello."

"What do you want?"

"Don't you want to know me?" he asked.

"Shove off!" she said.

She stood directly in front of him, her hands now on her hips, and he reached around, and laughingly slapped her hard but playfully across the behind.

She swung at him with the book. He ducked. She swung again, but, laughing, he had moved out of reach. Now he turned and walked down the street.

"You dago pig!" she yelled after him.

He laughed at her.

The kids followed him down the street, the straps of their home-made shoeshine kits over their shoulders.

"Hey, mister, throw us some more!"

"Beat it, you punks!"

8

Nick was playing with some stones on the sidewalk, piling them together and then scattering them, when he saw the shadow of the legs that stood directly in front of him. He looked up curiously. An elderly man, with friendly eyes and a big mustache brown and gray and yellow, stood there. The man was smiling and he said, "I used to play that game when I was your age."

"You *did?*"

"Yes."

"Do you want to play now?"

"Well—" Judge Sullivan felt around in his pocket. "And every boy I see playing my old game gets—here it is right here!—a peppermint stick!"

Nick stood up, small beside the man, and took the red and white striped candy like a barber's pole. "Thank you."

"I see that you are an extremely polite young man," Judge Sullivan said.

Nick had the candy in his mouth and his eyes looked up at the man. Judge Sullivan took off his hat and gently scratched his gray-mixed hair as if to bring back memory. Then he said, "I think I know a friend of yours, young man. She's a beautiful woman with blue eyes and blond hair and she works in a restaurant."

"Why, that's my mother!"

"Let's go see her."

The man took the boy's hand and the boy tugged him along, calling, at the door, "Mother! Mother!"

Mother stood at the open door and she was beautiful and wonderful as the man said and he hugged her around the knees. "I love you! I love you!" And Mother and the man shook hands. The man acted and talked like they do in the movies. The man said, with the upper part of his body bowing down and then up, "You see, young lady, the idea of being a guest in your home compelled me to wait no longer than one day, and your delightful son has escorted me here. In fact, we came so swiftly at his urging that my prediction of broken limbs was almost fulfilled."

"Please come in and sit down, Judge," Nellie said gratefully, her eyes filling. She brought the only chair in the one room for him and he, bowing again, said, "If I may," and sat down. Nellie sat on the bed. Nick said, "Mother, he plays the same games I do!" And Nick went and stood beside him, half leaning against his leg. "I like you," Nick said. Judge Sullivan said, "The feeling is mutual, young man," and, seeming to know how to handle children, first rumpled Nick's hair, then lifted him, grunt-sighing as if the boy weighed a lot, up onto his knee. "What say if we be pals?" Judge Sullivan asked.

"Gee, I'd like that!" Nick said.

"By the way, young man, what is your name?"

"Nick Romano."

"Nick Romano, that's a nice name!"

"His father is d-e-a-d," Nellie said.

"I've got crayons," Nick said.

Nellie put a pot of coffee on the electric plate. The man and the boy were talking. Nellie sat on the edge of the bed looking at them and twisting her fingers together, almost unable to keep from crying. The boy brought all his toys to show to the man. The coffee boiled and Nellie rushed down to the restaurant to get cuts of pie. When she returned, the man and the boy were kneeling side by side on the warped, uncarpeted floor and Nick was drawing while Judge Sullivan said, "It may be only a minor point—take it as you wish—but my suggestion is this—that you make the grass green."

"But I like blue."

"Ahhhh!" Judge Sullivan said. "I am pleased to see that you have an independence about your art. And"—nodding—"you have an excellent example in one Pablo Picasso."

"What makes the grass grow?"

"Son, it's all a matter of life locked up neatly and securely in separate little houses and it has to do with the sun and soil and rain. Look—" He searched in his shoebox. He had magic there. From the box he drew out a package of flower seeds. "From my spring stock," he said to Nellie; then to Nick, "These are for you. These will grow just as the grass does. You put them in a hole in the ground—oh—about as deep as the first joint of your little finger —give me your finger and I will show you—see? . . . Then you cover them over and every day you water them and one day you will have flowers like the picture on this package." His eyes twinkled first at Nellie and then at Nick. "But be sure and plant them under the porch where the sun won't shine on them."

Filling Judge Sullivan's cup a second time, Nellie said, "I hope you will come over again soon. Come over any time you want to. You don't know how—how—"

Judge Sullivan's eyes twinkled under their shaggy brows. "Does that include tomorrow? I would be honored—and, on occasion, may I take the boy for a walk?"

"Any time, Judge. Any time at all." Nellie looked at her son and then turned her eyes back to Judge Sullivan. "I like to be honest," she said. She tapped her ringless wedding-ring finger. "I wasn't m-a-r-r-i-e-d to him," she said, spelling the word. "I loved him. I don't make any pretensions."

"Young lady," Judge said, "there should be more mothers as concerned about their children as you are about yours. Already I feel like a member of this family, through your love and concern for your son." And he stood. "Call on me in any and all emergencies, and you will find me as, no doubt, your own father was."

That made her want to cry.

"Why isn't grass white like water if you put water on it to make it grow?" Nick asked.

When Judge Sullivan had gone, Nick asked his mother, "Is he my father? Is he coming here to live?"

"No, Nicky, he's not your father," Nellie said. She lifted her son up in her arms and, carrying him to the end table, stood him on it where his eyes were level with the framed photograph from the newspaper. "This is your father," she said. "His picture was in the paper because"—her voice broke—"because he won a scholarship for college."

Judge Sullivan came every day to see the boy, or took him for walks. Sometimes he was drunk and laughed loudly and staggered but he never failed to come to see Nick. On their walks he always managed to have enough change for a chocolate ice cream cone, a popsicle, sometimes a hot dog, wiping the boy's mouth when he had gulped it all down. Then he would again take the boy's hand and they would move on down the street.

When the need came, and it sometimes did on these walks, Judge Sullivan would make Nick promise to stand right there without moving away and Judge would go into the tavern for a nickel glass of beer or a dime glass of red wine, drinking it near the window where he could see the boy.

And Nick loved him. The walks they went on. The stories he told. They were better stories than any his mother had read from books. Judge made them up about anything. The beggar who walked past. The old lady feeding pigeons. The shoeshine boy who was really a prince.

Nick loved him. He had gentle hands and a soft voice and Nick didn't notice that he was sometimes dirty and smelled of alcohol and was almost a bum.

9

And now fall had come to Chicago. It did not come to West Madison the way it came to other parts of the city where there are houses and families. Here, alongside the curbs in front of houses, there were no piles of autumn leaves sending their lavender smoke upward in an incense that perfumed whole neighborhoods. No tall, clear blueness of sky between the branches of trees. Nor children's voices calling. Nor the sound of footballs off the shoes of young boys. Nor four-o'clocks coming to seed, the little beads gathered and set away in mason jars for next spring's planting.

Here the bums huddled. Here the drunks filled the taverns, needing even more alcohol to take the cold from their bones. Here even the sidewalks and the buildings seemed to chill. And the water towers, the smokestacks frowned down. And the sky was a menace. Any day now, if Indian summer did not come, it might snow. The hawk of winter was on the wing and wheeling this way. The disinherited of this street, this neighborhood, waited.

Nellie waited with them. She had to buy herself a coat against the winter, and heavy shoes for Nick, save money to buy him a snow suit. Her tips grew thinner, for her customers like herself had to plan for winter. But it was a happy period for Nellie. Her son was growing and becoming more lovable every day. Judge Sullivan had become almost a father to her, a grandfather to the boy. She had no problems; her work was hard, but she didn't mind because it meant she could provide for her son.

There was only one irritation. The young Italian, who had thrown the pennies to the boys and had slapped her across the behind, was often on the street. Several times he had passed her and glanced at her. She didn't like his eyes. And twice he had turned and followed her several blocks, whistling tonelessly. Then he had begun coming into the restaurant and she had to wait on him. He was good-looking and well built but she didn't like his eyes. They were cold and seemed to stare through you. And his mouth. There was something suggestively mean about it. He always left a quarter tip and this made her mad because she didn't want a big tip from him, she didn't want him to come into the restaurant. She became rude. She became the kind of waitress she had been before she knew her trade. She slammed things down in front of him. He'd just smile. A sort of cold smile. She was peeved when he came in and surprised when he didn't. Almost disappointed. He tried to talk to her. He tried to get familiar. She never heard him. Then he knew her name. "Nellie, bring me another cup of coffee." She'd flush and bring it and slam it down.

One day she took Nick walking, to the little park, Jefferson Park, one street off West Madison. The park was bare and ugly. Only a few trees grew there. They were ragged because their leaves were leaving. They were like gaunt scarecrows and like the bums you saw walking along West Madison. On the benches under them sat old men. They leaned over on the benches in their age. Withered leaves rustled down around them, sometimes touching their shoulders in a whisper of something ominous before settling to the ground at their feet. The old men, bundled in their coats, picked at the leaves with their canes, or stabbed them through, cruelly, in a sort of revenge or distaste. Their old bodies, stooped, leaned toward the ground as if soon it would claim them.

Nick and Nellie walked into the park. The grass was shaggy, getting ready to die too, and there were bare-scraped places where bums and drunks had walked, had slept at night when there was nowhere else to sleep. There were empty wine bottles thrown into the bushes.

Then Nellie saw the patch of dandelions, old too, now, each with its little silver head of age. She quickened her step toward them, tightening her hand on Nick's. She thought of her Uncle Clarence. And when she came to the dandelions, she knelt down before them and drew Nick down with her. "Look, honey! Remember I told you that the dandelions get gray hair when they get old?"

She plucked one, some of its milky juice staining her fingers as she held it for Nick to blow.

Then she said, as Uncle Clarence had said to her, "Blink and blow! . . . Blow and blink! . . ."

He blew and blinked. The little silver parts were on his nose, tickling it, and dancing against his closed eyelids.

She plucked another, saying, "A child will always, always blink and blow," and again Nick, laughing delightedly, blew and, blinking his eyes open this time, saw all the little silky people go dancing out onto the air and then slowly settle to the ground where Mother said next year they would be shining little yellow faces.

Mother held still another for him to blow. Mother said, "The dandelion is so delicate that you always get some back on your nose. If you get some back, the dream comes true . . . blow and blink . . . a wish and a dream . . . and the dream is more important than the wish . . ."

Nellie, laughing with Nick and brushing dandelion fuzz off his hair, looked across the park. She stopped smiling immediately and, arising, lifted Nick to his feet.

He sat on a bench watching them, the fellow who came into the restaurant and bothered her. His long, muscular body was sort of sprawled out across the bench. His shoulders were broad and he held a roll-your-own cigarette between his lips. The lips were tight on the cigarette. The lips were smiling, tautly, at her. The eyes regarded her coldly.

Nellie turned and, holding Nick by the hand, walked out of the park.

10

That night Judge Sullivan came up the steps and to Nellie's room with a half-gallon bottle of red wine hooked in his index finger. He uncorked the bottle and into coffee cups poured a drink for Nellie and himself. "I came to ask," he said, "aside from returning your hospitality on our original meeting, if I may take Nick to the Field Museum tomorrow. Indeed, this wine was brought along to induce you to say yes. But perhaps I should put the question after we have consumed the bottle."

Nellie smiled and said yes, but there was a strange quietness about her tonight that Judge Sullivan sensed and he poured her cup full of the red wine before it was quite empty. Nick came over and crawled into his lap, snuggled there close. "Listen to this, boy!" Judge Sullivan said, and began reciting poetry. His voice filled the room, sometimes lusty, sometimes whispering:

> "I celebrate myself, and sing myself,
> And what I assume you shall assume,
> For every atom belonging to me as good belongs to you."

He laughed. "That's Walt Whitman, boy! God, how that man could write!" he said, and fitted Nick more securely in his arms, the red wine almost slopping from his white, cracked cup. His face grew reverent. "When I was a young boy, no older than you, my father took me to one of his Lincoln lectures in New York City. He had a beautiful face and a long white beard, long white hair. Listen to this:

> "I have heard what the talkers were talking, the talk of the
>   beginning and the end.
> But I do not talk of the beginning or the end.
> There was never any more inception than there is now,
> Nor any more youth or age than there is now . . ."

He paused a moment, then, whispering into the silence of the room, quoted:

> "Not I, not anyone can travel that road for you,
> You must travel it for yourself."

57

And drinking his wine, with his mustache suddenly dyed red, he went to other words, smoothly, without faltering, without hesitation:

> "Tell zeal, it wants devotion;
> Tell love, it is but lust:
> Tell time, it is but motion;
> Tell flesh, it is but dust:
> And wish them not reply,
> For thou must give the lie."

And, laughing, "That's Sir Walter Raleigh, English explorer, statesman, courtier, historian and poet. It is not known whether he was born in 1552 but it is definitely known that he died in 1618. Do you know why? Because he was beheaded. Listen to this and you will know why:

> "Say to the court, it glows
> And shines like rotten wood;
> Say to the church, it shows
> What's good, and doth no good:
> If church and court reply,
> Then give them both the lie."

Nick's boy-eyes looked up into Judge Sullivan's face. "Tell another one."

Nellie sipped her wine, tense and nervous, and suddenly held her cup for Judge Sullivan to refill.

Now Judge Sullivan was silent and sad, his eyes far away. Suddenly he said, "I've never told you, Nellie, but it's my fault." He waved at the window and West Madison Street below. "I drink. I drink. I have a beautiful and wonderful wife almost twenty years younger than I am and two fine children, a boy and a girl, eighteen and twenty years old. They live here in Chicago." He glanced into Nellie's eyes. "So, you see, we all have our troubles." He put his arms gently around Nick. "Take good care of our boy."

Nellie stared into Judge Sullivan's eyes and slowly nodded yes. Then she glanced up at the framed newspaper photograph and filled Judge Sullivan's cup, filled her own. Then she sat on the floor beside his chair and put her hand in his, her cheek down against his knee.

For a long time they sat in silence. Then Judge Sullivan chuckled. "You ought to be like this boy here," he said. "He's sitting here asleep. You—you're wide awake."

"Thinking."

Judge Sullivan got up slowly and quietly and laid Nick across the bed, covering him with a blanket. Then he returned to the chair. "Thinking what?"

Nellie still sat on the floor at his feet. She set the cup down as a child would and twisted her fingers together with her head lowered. "Will you do something for me, Judge?"

"If I can, I shall."

"I ain't smart. I didn't go much to school."

"Many nincompoops are turned out of our great universities annually," Judge Sullivan said.

Nellie looked up at him pleadingly. "I want to talk good English in front of my kid. I want him to be smart. I want him to get an education. Can you teach me to talk right?"

Judge Sullivan was moved. He stood and walked to the window, looked down on the car tracks. Nellie came and stood behind him. "Will you? Please."

"Yes, Nellie."

And when the old man turned back toward the room, there were tears on his cheeks.

"Will you give me lessons every day?"

"Yes, Nellie."

"I'll wash your shirts and socks and underwear and I'll iron them."

He stood facing her. "Hohoho! Dear lady, I propose an occasional bottle of wine such as this in lieu of the manual labor." But the tears were on his cheeks and she saw them. He wiped them away. He said, "I must be drunk." He filled their cracked cups again.

For two more hours they sat drinking and then there was no more in the bottle and he was going home, saying he would take Nick to the Field Museum tomorrow afternoon, and he paused in the open doorway, his battered felt hat on at a rakish angle and recited:

> "Tell fortune of her blindness;
> Tell nature of decay,
> Tell friendship of unkindness;
> Tell justice of delay:
> And if they will reply,
> Then give them all the lie."

The boy and the old man walked down West Madison Street. The old man held the boy's hand walking under stretches of neon: BEER   ROOMS
GOLDMAN'S
          Since 1904
WINES
LIQUORS
     ROOMS 20¢ MONARCH BEER

The smell of taverns floated out across the sidewalk. Canes and crutches and men with black eyes stumbled along.
Rheingold

R
O
O
M
S

25¢ BUDWEISER OTTAWA HOTEL *Kelley Beer.*
Jackrollers and pimps walked wise-eyed. Drunks stumbled.

Down this street and past these people the old man and the boy walked hand in hand. And Judge Sullivan, accustomed to talking to the boy as if he were his own age and his equal, said, "Look around you, Nick. You don't see an intelligent face. You see some stolid faces, some rough faces, some vicious faces. You see some splendid physiques. And anemic individuals and disease-ridden people. They wander drunk, sober, drunk again. But they are not all getting up the next morning looking for another drink. They're thinking, 'My God! My God! My God!'"

Staring straight ahead Judge Sullivan continued down the street and across the urine-stained sidewalk holding the boy's hand. JESUS SAVES. And next door—BUDWEISER ON TAP. "Yes, son, you have to look far past this street to see the stars." HOUSE-OF-ALL-NATIONS. FIREBALL TAVERN *Rheingold Beer.* From the other direction, approaching them, came three young fellows. One wore blue jeans and a white turtle-neck sweater. MILLER HIGH LIFE BEER. One was a young Mexican perhaps twenty-two years old, with wavy hair and a slice of a grin in his light-tan face that took and reflected many highlights from the early afternoon sun. CHILI CON CARNE. The third fellow SCHLITZ—THE BEER THAT MADE MILWAUKEE FAMOUS was slim and short and wore a plaid jacket. He was rather effeminate-looking.

The three came abreast of Judge Sullivan, and the Mexican boy, grinning, stepped directly in front of him.

Judge Sullivan looked up in surprise and then matched the Mexican's smile. "Good afternoon, gentlemen," Judge Sullivan said, bowing; then added, his eyes twinkling, "And what are you hooligans doing off North Clark Street?"

"Hi, Judge!" the Mexican boy said.

"Hi, Judge!" the boy in the turtle-neck sweater said.

And Judge Sullivan, his eyes moving in mischief to the third of the three boys, "And who in Christ's name are you?"

The third boy flushed a little but smiled when the old man held out his hand and said, "I am Judge Sullivan, not at present practicing my profession, but at your service."

"My name is Norman Vance," the boy said, shaking hands. He was blond, with long wavy hair straight at the edges; he wore a stub collar and there was a neat Windsor knot in his tie.

Judge Sullivan asked him, "How did you get mixed up with these safe-crackers?— But, mind you—they are friends of mine though I seldom admit it."

Norman said, "I came to West Madison with Max and Phil to view the bodies. I'm just a visiting tourist." He laughed a little.

"Hi, kid," the Mexican boy was saying to Nick.

"This is Nick," Judge Sullivan said. "Shake hands, Nick, with Max—"

Nick and the Mexican boy shook hands.

"And Phil—"

Phil was tall and slim but well built, wore his brown-blond hair in a short crew cut and had clear blue eyes and thin-chiseled features.

"And Norman—" Judge Sullivan said.

Judge Sullivan had brought his shoebox along, telling Nick that he might find some customers along the way. Max now tapped it with a fingernail while a warm Mexican grin hid his eyes in slits. "You got any of those little things, Judge?"

Judge Sullivan drew himself up straight in mock severity and, while a smile played around his graying and weedy mustache, said, "As well you know, that type of merchandise is beneath my dignity —and I'd appreciate it if you would not speak like that in front of my young friend, even though he does not know what you mean." He took the cigarette Phil offered and cupped his hand over the lighted match Max held. "Furthermore," he said, "the proper word for such devices is contraceptive or prophylactic."

"Well," Phil said kiddingly, "let's ungoof long enough to see the merchandise."

Obligingly Judge Sullivan displayed his wares, and Max bought something he didn't need, Norman bought a handkerchief, Phil purchased razor blades, and all of them pushed their change into Nick's hand.

"Well," Judge Sullivan said, "my young friend and I are going to the Field Museum. I assume that none of you young gentlemen care for the better things in life, the educational, though perhaps useless, paraphernalia that constitutes an educated person."

"Score us in on what you're talking about, Judge," Phil said, his hand affectionately on the old man's shoulder. "In other words, ungoof, man."

Nick had his finger against the blue and red drawing he had seen on Phil's wrist. "Oh," Phil said, laughing, "that's a tattoo." He squatted on his heels so that Nick could see it. There was another one up further on his arm and he pushed up his sweater sleeve so that Nick could see that—a floral design with a name inside of it. He pushed his sleeve up still further, then stopped suddenly when the nude legs of a girl began to appear. "No, you can't see that one but I got three on my other arm." And he showed those to Nick—one a tombstone with the word MOTHER on it, another an anchor and the third a heart with a girl's name on it.

Toward the other end of the street, Nellie came down the flight of steps from her room and started along the sidewalk. She was slim in a cheap, wrinkled cloth coat. She was hatless; blond hair lay in a coil on her neck. One hand, the red polish chipped from her nails, held her purse.

She started across the street. Then she saw him ahead of her. She hurried. She caught up with him. "Wait a minute!" she said angrily.

He turned. The smile went slowly across the lower part of his face as the lips stretched out tautly. "Yeah?"

His eyes were as she remembered them. Cold. Blank. Not really seeing you.

They stood on the sidewalk facing each other.

"You been following me. I don't like it. You been coming into the restaurant just to make trouble. I don't like it."

"Yeah, you like it, all right."

He was insolently rolling a cigarette from a Bull Durham sack. He looked across the paper at her.

She went cold inside. She knew now that she had been attracted to him from the beginning.

"Okay, you win," she said.

He sneer-smiled.

"What do you want?" she asked.

Smiling, he licked the paper and rolled the cigarette between strong fingers.

"What do you want? To sleep with me?"

"Yeah," he said.

She lowered her head, shamed.

After all, I'm a woman. I have to sleep with somebody.

But she was ashamed.

11

He was putting on his shirt. His chest was completely covered with black hair. He buttoned his shirt and Nellie said, "You gotta get out now. My son will be here soon." She unbolted the door.

He said, "My name is Frank. Get used to it." He struck a match to the roll-your-own cigarette. "Frank Ramponi." He stood tightening his belt. He had a beautifully slim waistline and his shoulders were enormous. He had wavy black hair. And those staring eyes.

"If you come back," Nellie said, opening the door, "nothing's going to happen while my kid's here. I don't want him to see nothing." The strange, acrid smell of the tobacco he smoked burned her nose.

"I'll see you," he said, stepping out into the hall.

And he did come back, many times. She grew used to him. He was, she guessed, if people have types, her type. All of her boy friends, when she had a choice, were always dark and Italian-looking: remembrances of Nick.

So now it was Frank. She didn't love him. He filled up an empty spot.

One day Nick was in the room with his mother when Frank came, walking in without knocking. Nellie looked up, her face grim, and shook her head no, nothing doing.

"Frank, this is my son Nick."

"Hi, kid!" Frank handed him a quarter. "You wanna go out and play?"

"He ain't going nowhere," Nellie said.

"Okay," Frank said, and walked out.

"Mother, I don't like him," Nick said.

Frank didn't show up again for a week. She didn't care very much.

Judge Sullivan, true to his word, began giving Nellie English lessons, coming each day at the same time, drunk or sober, with a little notebook in which he had lessons for her to memorize. Each day he would start the lesson with "Now we ain't gonna speak no bad English today," his eyes twinkling and his large, red, blue-veined nose almost wiggling in amusement. Ain't and gonna had almost become sins to Nellie. She never used them when she remembered.

Today he continued, "Well, young lady, have you committed to memory the lesson of yesterday—the proper pronunciation of the ten words we selected from common everyday English—but first"—slipping his hand into his pocket and bringing out a half-pint bottle of wine—"I brought along a small sampling of dago red—now there's a word that should never be used and is used only by ignorant and prejudiced persons to vilify another race, a race of people, by the way, more ancient than we Anglo-Saxons. You see, I brought the wine to illustrate a language point but don't you think we should drink it too?" He put back his head and laughed loudly in that way he did when he was a little drunk.

Every day they had their lessons and Nellie tried pitifully to speak good English in front of her son. Bit by bit she was learning.

Autumn gave a few more good days and for Nick these were the most wonderful days of his life. Every day Judge took him for walks while his mother was at work and almost every day Max and Phil and sometimes Norman would meet them on the street. They called him Our Boy and Max sometimes put him on his shoulders and carried him down the street that way. They always had things for him. Candy. Maybe a balloon or a little tin truck. They came to the restaurant where his mother worked and talked to her and played with him. When they found out that he liked to draw, they brought crayons and even water colors. He liked to think of them as his three uncles. Mother even let them take him for walks at *night*, and sometimes when they went to see Judge, he would be asleep in his room with his clothes on, even his shoes, and a couple of wine bottles turned over on the floor near the bed. In Judge's room there was just a bed and one chair, and after the boards went up a little way, there was chicken wire that went up the rest of the way to the ceiling. He loved Judge. And he loved his three uncles.

Tonight Judge was sleeping on his cot, so Nick went along West Madison walking between Max and Phil and each of them held one of his hands. He liked the colors the neon lights made on the sidewalk and now a little bit of rain was falling. That was nice, too, because it made little brown dots on the gray sidewalk. He could do that with his water-color brush if he threw the water.

"You want an ice cream cone, kid?"

"No, Max," and, remembering what Mother said, "thank you."

"Your mother said we could keep you out for two hours, so how'd you like to go to the show?" Phil asked.

Nick's eyes lit up.

Max said, "Christ, I can't take another cowboy picture!"

Phil said, "You want to take him to the burlesque?" and they both laughed.

Nick looked up at them admiringly. He liked the tattoos on Phil's arms and he liked Max's brownish face that was always grinning.

While Max sat wincing at the cowboy movie, Nellie sat in her room with Frank. "Look—" she said, "it still goes—you ain't going to let Nick find out anything about us. And he ain't—isn't—going to call you Father. He's got a father. There he is"—she nodded toward the framed photograph—"my son's father. He'll call you Uncle, if you want."

Frank held his roll-your-own cigarette to Nellie's lips and she drew in. He said, "I don't want him to call me anything but Frank."

Two days later, when Judge Sullivan came at the appointed time for the English lesson, Nellie said, "Please, Judge, can we skip it today? And would you take Nicky for a walk." Then she introduced him to the stranger: "Judge Sullivan, this is Frank Ramponi."

"Come, boy!" Judge Sullivan said to Nick. "Let's take a long walk and I'll tell you a story. Two stories!"

Nick looked as if he had been crying, and he got up quickly, came to Judge Sullivan and took his hand. "Good-bye, Mother."

When Judge Sullivan and Nick left, Nellie came and stood in front of Frank, her hands on her hips. She said, "You dago bastard— and I'm not supposed to say that but I will—what do you mean by yelling at my kid?"

As when she had confronted him on their first meeting, he reached around and slapped her across the behind.

"Don't—" she said, moving back.

He smiled his thin smile. "Come on and have a drink."

"No," she said. She flung away from him and sat on the edge of the bed, throwing her blond hair off her forehead. "Let's get something straight," she said. "I don't love you. I never will. Don't get the idea you can come here and boss my kid around. And don't get the idea I'm a whore you can flop with any time you want."

He carried a drink to her. She slapped it away. "No, I'm no whore." Tears were standing in her eyes. "Sure, I've slept with fellows. But it wasn't just any guy. It had to be a guy who respected me and wanted me."

He turned from her and went back to his chair. She said to his back, "And when luck was bad, when I wasn't working, what else can a woman do to get by?"

He sat watching her with that stare of his, his long arms hanging between his long legs, the smoke from his cigarette curling up.

"I don't love you," she said again. "I went with a fellow some people might say was bad. I loved him. Yeah—" Again, with a snap of her head, she tossed the blond hair back over her shoulders. "I loved him. He's the father of my child. It's as simple as that. I don't love you. I never loved you. I can't love anybody but him. Give me a drink— Sure, I sleep with you and like it. But you can leave any time you want." She took the glass and drank swiftly, saying, "If you ever hit me—or my kid—or my kid—do you hear that?—that's all. That's quits. There are a lot of guys to sleep with."

"Okay, kid," he said, patting her on the back.

She lowered her head and some few tears fell on her wrists.

He patted her shoulder again. "Come on, kid, it ain't that bad. I'll even say I'm sorry."

That didn't cheer her up. With her head down and the hair hanging long and loose at her temples she said, "You got to have some affection. Otherwise it's all screwed up."

"I know, kid." He stood with his big-palmed hand on her shoulder. There were a lot of guys to sleep with; he knew that. He treated her with respect. He had never treated his mother with respect. He liked to sleep with Nellie.

In a bar downstairs a man on a tavern stool said, "This is West Madison Street. This is Skid Row." He said it proudly.

12

Now the Salvation Army Santa Claus was on the corner with his iron kettle and clanging bell. And now shoppers every evening boarded streetcars with armloads of packages. And now the store-front decorations appeared in the windows of tavern and drug store, huge cardboard signs advertising a brand of whiskey or soft drink and made seasonal with gaily colored Christmas wreaths and chiming bells.

And each evening at the Nickel Plate, Max, Norman, Phil and Judge Sullivan happily counted out the money that was being saved for Nick's electric train. Into a worn envelope Judge Sullivan placed it, noting in pencil on the outside the amount of money they now had. And each morning Judge Sullivan, going onto the street from his room with his shoebox of wares, used a little of the funds for the drink or two he needed: he would pay it back tonight when he had sold some things from his shoebox.

The sad signs of Christmas appeared along West Madison Street. The bums and drunks moved as before, up and down the street. But there was a knowledge in them of the season and the day to come. Sadness sat upon them. Drunk or sober they knew of the houses in other neighborhoods and the preparations. They each remembered a home. Sadness ate upon them.

The day came closer. The look of Christmas was not a happy look on this street, in this neighborhood. But the bars were filled. The juke boxes played.

And it was Christmas Eve. And Max had won a turkey in a raffle and carried it under his arm. And Judge Sullivan, Phil, Max and Norman went downtown to buy the electric train.

Snow came to cheer their way back from the Loop to this street, and happy with the happiness they would bring the boy tomorrow they laughed and joked and stopped only once in a tavern for a drink, for they were going up to Judge Sullivan's room to try the train out, to see if it really worked.

Going past drunks and coughed-up phlegm, going past tramps who slept or only sat, staring, in the flophouse lobby, even going past the twenty-five-cents-a-night hotel bar, they climbed the stairs to Judge Sullivan's room.

In the room, so small that they had to crowd up against the walls, the dusty chicken wire above them complaining of their crowding, they took the engine and the cars, the railroad tracks from their neatly packed boxes and, Max having to go down for a double socket, they watched with the eyes of a boy, the same eyes a boy would tomorrow use, the little electric train move in its oval around the tiny rails. They laughed and they uncoupled the cars with a switch, and they made the train back up to pick the cars up again, and they laughed.

Outside, streetcars screeched and lampposts leered and all the neon signs down the length of the street looked, unblinking, at the Christmas Eve.

And now it was eleven o'clock and they were not yet tired of playing with the train and Norm brought a bottle of wine which they drank while the train went around, occasionally throwing little sparks, and they laughed and were good inside, clean inside because they were doing something for a small boy.

Then it was twelve o'clock. It was Christmas. They must take the train now so the boy would see it the first thing in the morning. Happily they put it back into its several boxes, happily descended the stairs and started down West Madison toward Nellie's room.

The blue-black panther of a city watched their going. The unblinking neon animal eyes watched their going. Thousands of neon signs lit their way. In an alley behind West Madison Street half an hour before, a bum, drunk, had frozen to death lying in the back doorway of a pawnshop. The blue-black panther crouched over him.

The four of them, carrying a train and a turkey and a shoebox because Christmas is a day when people are generous, happier than they had been in a long time, and especially Judge Sullivan, walked, perhaps a little unevenly from drink, down West Madison and came to an empty lot.

The man there was huddled over a small oil burner in a little hut, his hands under his armpits to keep them warm. He wore earmuffs and his nose was iced with a small frozen icicle. Where there had been a forest of pines there were now only a few, straggly and picked over.

He came from the stove unwillingly (for business had been good and he was not a greedy man) when the four of them came onto the empty lot and stood among the Christmas trees.

But he came out and Judge Sullivan said, "A Merry Christmas to you—"

"Merry Christmas," sleepy, tired, chilled.

"—We wish to purchase a small tree for a small boy."

"A small tree for a small boy?"

He had none, no table trees, but he cut the top off one of the big ones and held it in his gloved hands, asking, "Will this do for the small boy?"

"Indeed, sir, it is what we wish and what will delight this boy. What is the price of this tree?" Judge Sullivan said.

"Well—is ten cents too much?"

"A most fair price," Judge Sullivan said, drawing a dime from his pocket and paying for it.

They moved away from the empty lot. The man lifted his hand in a wave and said, no longer tired, sleepy, chilled, "Merry Christmas!" and went back into his little hut, warmed, with the four figures moving toward the happiness of a boy.

The four figures walked under neon, past tavern fronts, flophouses, pawnshops, carrying a train, a turkey, a tree.

They walked, burdened, steadying themselves against the wall, up the steps to Nellie's door and there gently tapped.

Sleepily Nellie said, "Just a minute"; and then, sleepy, standing inside the door, "Who is it?"

"Judge and the boys," Judge Sullivan said.

She opened the door and stood so that they could enter but with her finger against her lips in a gesture of silence, indicating that Nick was asleep.

They brought in their packages and Nellie put a towel over the light so that Nick would not be awakened. Then they showed her what they had. Tears sprang to her eyes. "Oh, you shouldn't of—have."

"Ah, dear lady," Judge Sullivan said, "it is already Christmas Day," and embraced her.

She kissed each of them.

They set the train on its tracks. And there was a tavern still open and to it Phil went to lug two gallons of red wine up the steps. The cups were filled and clicked, cracked side against cracked side, and Merry Christmas said all around. There was no Christmas tree stand. But there was an empty gallon wine bottle that had lasted through a week of English lessons. Into this they stuck the tree.

"Oh my God!" Judge Sullivan said. "There are no ornaments for the tree!"

But they were inventive. Judge Sullivan put his shoebox on his knees. Inside were packages of razor blades, some women's paste-pearl earrings, paper clips, a couple of fountain pens. And they gathered beer bottle caps, punched holes into them and threaded them into Christmas tree decorations with thread from Judge Sullivan's shoebox. All would give a touch of color. And one rhinestone brooch for a star.

They set the tree on the small end table under the photograph of the boy's father. They decorated it. They clicked the cracked cups again. "Oh!" Max said, having forgotten. "Look, Nellie!" He unpeeled the turkey from its paper. And Norman found five empty one-service corn-flake boxes. With a razor blade he carefully cut them into small houses and barns with doors and windows. These he placed under the tree in a little village. And Phil discovered a package of gum on the dresser. He took the silver-like foil off the sticks of gum and twisted the foil to the green branches of the tree.

Hooked to the radiator cap was a stocking filled with candy and nuts, one bump showing the form of an orange. On the floor under it was a box, a Christmas present to Nick from Mike Manos, who had gone out of town to spend Christmas with his married brothers.

All stood admiring the tree. Again the cups were filled and clicked together. Again all voices said Merry Christmas.

There was no sleep that night. Nellie went into the bathroom down the hall and dressed. They all sat, smiling at the sleeping boy, talking in whispers so that he wouldn't awaken but wishing he would, drinking wine.

In that neighborhood morning comes up bleak and sooty, smudged over. So it came. And it was Christmas Day. And Christmas was a sad face on West Madison Street, like the colors painted on the circus clown.

First the creak of ice as an automobile goes by. Then the frown into your room of the red brick building across the street, its windows frosted over like cold, unfriendly eyes. Then a bum stumbling along trying to keep warm. Now a drunk, unevenly. And the wind like the howling voice of the blue-black panther, hunting, finding. And the clanging of impersonal streetcars. And each bar of neon, cold, dead. No message. The clown takes his bow and it is Christmas Day.

On the sidewalk below, the panhandlers, the beggars, the memories of the bums and drunks. Home! Home! A sad time for them. Home! But this was home now. The only home and the grave. Turn time, backward if you can. Give us back the tears of childhood. The dreams of youth. The hopes of young manhood. Distantly, from the Loop, the skyscraper church sounds its chimes.

Nick's eyes came open largely. His mother flung herself across the bed and hugged him, then carried him to the tree to see it and, underneath, the snow suit and a few toys that were her Christmas presents to him. "But look, honey!" she then said, and carried him to the train on the floor by the window. "This is your Christmas present from Judge, Phil, Max and Norman! Isn't it wonderful, honey!"

And Nick went then, as a well-mannered boy, from the train to Judge first and then the others and put his small, thin arms around the neck of each of them, kissed each of them.

"Merry Christmas! Merry Christmas!" they said, and then they all knelt on the floor around the electric train, Nick in his blue and white pajamas.

They showed him how to work it, and Judge Sullivan on his knees on the floor for the next hour simulated the train whistle, the ticket taker moving through the cars, the dining-car chimes, the waiters and porters, people getting on and off, saying hello and good-bye to friends and relatives.

Meanwhile Norm and Phil had gone out to find a store open and returned with sage, bread, celery and onions for the turkey dressing. And Nellie took the only pot into which the turkey would fit, the basin she had used to bathe Nick in when he was a baby, and scrubbed it with soap in the bathroom and brought it back. The turkey was put into it.

"I don't know how to fix the dressing," Nellie said.

"I can fix it," Norm said, and set to work.

Nellie sat watching him. She sat looking from face to face of the four of them. She had never had a Christmas. The others had to plan it for her. This, her first Christmas. The tears came and went from the surface of her eyes. But none fell.

Norm had cut the celery and onions, and now, his arms up almost to his elbows in the bread dressing, he kneaded the ingredients together. Meanwhile the others were improving the tree. Max and Phil were scratching the paint off the beer caps with razor blades so that their metal would shine. And Judge Sullivan, wine slopping out of his cup, came across the room, shouting, "Maximiliano Moreno!—an *abrazo* as in your country and a very, very Merry Christmas to you!" They fell into each other's arms and slapped each other resoundingly across the back in the Mexican custom of greeting.

And the turkey was finally put on the electric-plate burner. And they all toasted it in wine, cups clicking. And the day went beautifully. The day went toward darkness.

The turkey smelled good but wouldn't get tender and they had to add so much water to keep it from burning on the bottom that they were almost boiling it. And the first star showed its light over the streetcar tracks, over bum and drunk and tavern front. The first star was at the window. A large, unfalling snowflake.

Now the turkey needed one hour more, maybe two. And now Judge Sullivan stood with his finger crooked into the stem of the gallon wine bottle, the bottle over his shoulder, the wine spilling in maroon liquid from spout to cup. And Judge Sullivan said, "I have a suggestion. In that we have so much to eat, let us each invite someone to share this Christmas repast. Somebody from the street. But we must invite only the beaten, the lost, the forgotten and the forsaken."

They all fell in with the idea and discussed it eagerly. Judge Sullivan said, his eyes twinkling, "I know just the lady I will bring. A little dice girl from the Long Bar."

"Oh, cheating on me, huh?" Nellie said.

"I am faithful to all the ladies," Judge Sullivan said, "for an hour and a day."

They got into their coats, Judge Sullivan, Max, Norm and Phil, and went down onto the street to give their invitations.

Judge Sullivan walked into the Long Bar and up to the 26-table. "Hello, Helen," he said, "I have come to extend a Christmas invitation to you."

In the bar you wouldn't know that it was Christmas. They were doing the same thing they did every day. They stood at the bar drinking. They sat at the tables drinking, laughing coarsely, putting coins in the juke box.

"Oh, I'd love to go!" Helen said. She was a large girl, almost plump, with full lips, red-painted, large eyes, plucked eyebrows and an artificial gardenia at each temple. Her large nose was sprinkled generously with freckles over which powder had been drawn. Her bushy brown hair stood out in a full crop about her head and gave her an even plumper appearance. She got into her cheap cloth coat and, taking Judge Sullivan by the arm, went with him to Nellie's room.

"Nellie, this is Helen Kosinski," Judge Sullivan said, and Christmas greetings were given. Helen hugged the little boy and looked at the Christmas tree and suddenly her eyes were filled with tears: it was another Christmas a long time ago when she was a little girl. Her mother had baked two pounds of hamburger and stuck a turkey feather in it on Christmas Day. "We have turkey too. Just like everybody else we have turkey," her mother had said, laughing though the tears were running down her cheeks.

Helen turned back into the room and impulsively walked to Nellie, hugged her. Then she said she'd be right back.

When she came back she had a box of candy for Nellie and the boy and she had brought her dice cup which she turned upside down and set among the corn-flake houses and barns, saying it was a silo.

Max walked into the Nickel Plate. He would be philosophical and wise in his choice. He'd take somebody who would really be made happy. He sat at a table with a cup of coffee and looked around. The bums were there, out of the cold, the drunks were there. A radio over the cash register played Christmas music.

Squint was cursing his luck. Kid Fingers laughed through his nose. At the table against the other wall there was a youth of about seventeen. He had pulled off his shoes and, with his legs stretched out, wiggled his toes in holey socks, bringing them close to the hissing radiator. He came now across the floor toward them in a torn jacket. He was brown from sun. Crisped light-brown hair, smoky from dirt, crinkled straight up on his head. He carried his old pair of shoes in his hand and limped slightly. He was singing the hill-billy line of a cowboy song. He flopped down at the large table where Squint and Kid Fingers sat, shoving the chair way out from the table and spreading his legs out. The song had stopped. He just sat. Then after they had gotten used to him sitting there, he said, "Can you-all give me a cup of coffee?"

No answer.

"What part of Chicago is this here?" the tramp kid asked.

"Skid Row," Kid Fingers said.

"West Madison—did you ever hear of it?" Squint asked.

"Don't reckon as how I did."

Squint's eyes and Kid Fingers' eyes lit on him like flies on sugar. They exchanged mocking glances.

"Boy, where you-all from? Texas?" Fingers asked, imitating the southern drawl.

"No."

"Jo-jah?"

"Guess again," the southern kid said good-naturedly.

"Kaintucky?" Squint asked.

"You's comin' close—Tennessee." His hand went down and scratched his crotch.

"How do you-all like Chicago compared to Tennessee?" Fingers asked.

"One's heaven and one's hell."

"Which is hell?"

"This is heaven." He scratched again.

Another fellow came and leaned over the boy's chair, kidding him too. "Man, how'd you-all git here?"

"Ah grabbed a freight and Ah thumb-snagged."

They all laughed. Fingers said, "How'd you-all eat?"

"Ah managed. Who's going to buy me a coffee?"

Squint said, "Ah bet you-all can really eat."

"Man, you buy and Ah'll break you—even if you got a hundred dollars."

Max, listening, thought: That's my guest.

Fingers said, "You's broken-down and Ah'm broken-down too. We's all broke, man."

"You-all ever pick cotton?" Squint asked.

The southern kid had an itch again. All over. He scratched, first with one hand, then the other, at the small of his back, then one leg; and his stomach.

"Look at that boy go!" Fingers said; then to him, "You been sleeping with a dog?"

And Squint, "Stop by a flea circus and you'll get a job."

Tennessee scratched below his belt with his hand inside his shirt. All the fellows laughed.

"What's the score?" Squint asked.

"New York—two," the southerner said.

Fingers said, "Boy, you sure got crabs."

The radio over the cash register was playing "I'm Dreaming of a

White Christmas." The tramp kid said, "Boy, Ah'd sure like to dance!" He wiggled in the chair. "Anybody got a gi-tah? Ah'll show you-all some real music!" He scratched again.

"What's the score?" Fingers asked.

"Chicago Cubs—three," Tennessee said.

Whitey, who had walked over, said, "I've got a guitar down the street—locked up in the pawnshop."

The kid was scratching inside his shirt again. He grinned and said, "I think the Cubs got a home run."

Max walked over. "You want coffee?"

Max bought it for him and they started talking.

In Nellie's room Phil had arrived with his guest. Phil brought a prostitute and she went all to pieces when she saw Nick. She cried and hugged him and poured more wine into her already heavily liquor-scented mouth. She stood looking at the Christmas tree. "Now ain't that sweet! Ain't that just too sweet!" She added her lipstick as an additional decoration.

And Max walked in with Tennessee.

In the tavern the panhandler selected a stool far from the front window. From an inner pocket somewhere in his ragged clothes he produced a half-dollar and slapped it on the bar. He lifted two fingers. The bartender pushed the foaming steins along the mahogany. The panhandler pushed one over in front of Norm. "On me," he said, "It's Christmas." The panhandler threw his suds off in one long-drawn gulp. "Rotten night," he said, "but good for business."

Norm drank slowly, watched the hard faces that lined the bar, that leaned over tables. Everyone drank heavily. There was no joy in their drinking. They were only sad, or noisy, or sick.

Norm's partner at the bar wanted to talk. "I been a panhandler for ten years," he said. "It's a good racket. I work a regular beat here in Chicago. Been to both coasts a couple of times. Oh, I get around." The rim of the glass and the bronze liquor pouring in hid his lips for a moment. "I like good old Chicago though. Food's cheap. Booze's cheap. And"—chuckling—"sometimes those Gold Coast guys you try to bum are pretty damn cheap too." He pushed both glasses at the bartender and nodded. "Portland, Oregon's a good town to stem. I can size my customers up pretty good. Know just about how much I'll get out of a guy. Sometimes I make as much as ten dollars a day when I work it right. Could do better if I had a leg off or an eye out. But hell, I ain't kicking. I do all right."

The door pushed open and a boy, dirty-blond, rough-speaking, strode into the tavern and sat next to the panhandler. He spun the nickel on the bar, shouted, "One beer, matey, and easy on the suds!" Screwing around on the stool he slapped a big hand across the pan-handler's back. "What-da-ya-say, Weepy!" he shouted, then let his voice drop to an undertone. "What was the take today?"

"Only four-sixty, kid. And this Christmas too. I swear some of them got rocks where their heart should be," Weepy answered and, turning to Norm, "The kid here is one of the guild. They call me Weepy because I got such a good line."

"Oh hell! I did better than that, Weepy!" The kid laughed deri-sively. "The beer's on me. Know what happened tonight? Some old dame stopped me and without me askin' her nothin' she hands me half a rock. See—it pays to be young and good-lookin'!" He rattled off part of his beer. "The world owes me a livin' and I don't give a damn who I collects it off of." He finished the beer. "Well, drink up, bums!"

Weepy said, "Yeah, but let me pop for it. One more'n I'm blowin'."

The kid said, laughing, "You know, this panhandlin' is a funny business. Once I stemmed a cop in Omaha and he said, 'We'll have to put ribbons on you guys or you'll be bummin' each other.'"

The kid had still another beer, pulled the cheek of a middle-aged woman bar fly and bought her a drink.

Weepy said so-long and sauntered out into the night.

"He's a good egg," the kid told Norm. "Crooked though. Who the hell ain't in this damn crooked world?"

Norman said, "How would you like to go somewhere with me for a Christmas dinner?"

"Jesus! It is Christmas!" the kid said.

In Nellie's room now they were all sitting on the floor because there was only one chair. Nellie gave Nick a tiny taste of the wine with water and sugar in it. Max brought two more gallons of wine. The men had to drink out of the bottle because there weren't enough cups to go around. The young panhandler wasn't tough any more. His voice was soft and his eyes fell away from Nellie, from Helen, when they looked at him, and he half blushed for these were decent people. And Helen sat thinking about her kid brother Chet. He could never appreciate this and this was real. These were the real people. He was even ashamed of his family. But they didn't mean him no good. It *would* be better if he just cleared out. He was a sweet kid and a smart kid. I hope he gets somewhere. He's in plays, ain't he? Yeah, and he changed his name from Kosinski to Lockwood. Well, I love him. I wish he was here.

And the prostitute was saying, loudly, "Ain't this a Christmas! Ain't it!" And Judge Sullivan said to Helen, "Why so pensive?"

She smiled at him and, holding her cup in salute, said, "Smialo!— In Polish that means be of good cheer."

And Tennessee said, "Ah sure wish Ah had a gi-tah. Ah'd entertain you-all."

Max sat with one arm around Judge Sullivan's shoulders and the other around the prostitute.

Nick knelt by his train, right where the curve of the tracks was, and his cheek was down against the floor as he watched the train come and take the curve, come and take the curve, some little yellow and blue sparks flying.

Again the red wine was poured.

Then the turkey was ready and Judge Sullivan insisted on doing the carving. Then he came with it in the basin Nick had been bathed in as a baby. He came singing, " 'God rest ye merry, gentlemen! let nothing you dismay,' " as he passed the turkey around. His face was as red as Santa Claus's.

And they were eating turkey with their fingers because there were no plates, knives or forks. And they sucked their fingers of the juice. And the turkey was burned or boiled, half done or almost raw, depending upon what part you happened to get.

"Ain't this a Christmas! Ain't it!"

And quietly, unseen in a corner, Nellie sat crying. Crying with joy. These kind people. She looked at the invited guests. Then she looked at Judge Sullivan, Max, Phil and Norman. The feeling of a family. The first real family she had ever had.

The young panhandler noticed her and secretly slipped her his handkerchief. "I'm just happy," she told him.

"Ah sure wish Ah had a gi-tah!"

And they sat on the floor, leaning against the bed and the wall in a circle, all getting drunk and singing Christmas carols together.

And Judge Sullivan holding Nick on his lap and telling him about his boyhood at Christmastime and riding in the big, horse-drawn sleigh and the bells that jingled.

And Nick's head nodding and Nellie, gathering him into her arms, saying, "My little monster is sleepy."

She undressed him and put him to bed.

His eyes opened a little bit and he saw the window. And a single snowflake, falling. Then more. And many more.

His eyes began to close a little. These wonderful people. He loved them. And he loved the train they brought him. But most of all he loved them.

He heard, going to sleep, the words they said, then only the mumble of their voices. And he didn't understand. And he was asleep.

The prostitute was saying, "All I want to do is to live up there and be by her— I told you I had a daughter. You think this is a good life, Chicago? What have you got? Taverns. If you're going to be a leech then stay here and suck it. I'm tired. I want to go home. I'm so tired of kissing asses and saying yes to things you know are no."

Judge Sullivan cleared his throat. "Shall we sing another carol?"

"This is the nicest Christmas I've ever had," Helen Kosinski said.

"Any of us has ever had," Judge Sullivan said.

"Ain't it!" the prostitute said.

And the red wine coming from the bottle. The talk. The laughter.

"Imagine laying a guy for a bucket of coal!" the prostitute said.

And the red wine. The laughter. Their voices all lifted together again in Christmas carols.

13

March, Chicago's unavoidable ruffian, came with doubled fists. March cudgeled the city and swaggered through the streets with barrel-chest. The lake wore fantastic white bulwarks and beat the shore with hard, backhand slaps. Buildings huddled to the slush-dirty streets, the sky a gray vulture spreading its tattered wings at their roof tops. Windows were frozen over, or streaked with rain, or tattooed with hail. The scarecrow men on West Madison stumbled along the broken pavement with their necks drawn down into upturned collars and their hands thrust deep into their pockets. March pummeled them. Snow, rain, thaw, sudden storms walked across the city on each other's heels. Then there was a day, gentle as a teenaged girl, that whispered between storms. Even the night made promises.

And it was spring.

Nellie sat in the restaurant with her elbows on the white slab of counter and her chin on her hands. She stared out at the street. Into her vision beyond the large plate glass, like ballet dancers on a stage, or like a burlesquing comedy team stepping from the wings of a theater, came the two drunks in their old and soiled clothes. They came, seesawing across the pavement, and for a moment propped themselves against the restaurant window. Fumbling, fumbling in his back pockets, one of them pulled out a cheap bottle of wine and the other watched the slow, uncertain withdrawal of the bottle. The glazed eyes looked at the bottle, the dirty hands lifted it to the slobbering lips, then passed it to the other spittle-collected lips, holding it there as one would help a child drink. They swayed there in front of the window. Then the man whose pant-knees and hands were muddy where he had fallen, saw a cigarette snipe on the curb. Drunkenly he swerved away from his companion, who, almost falling, banged his shoulder noisily against the restaurant window and hung as if lopsidedly glued there. His partner meanwhile stood at the curb, bending, slowly, waveringly, uncertainly toward the crumpled, muddied cigarette butt, his gnarled and shaking fingers opening, trying to close around the butt, shaking, fumbling, under no control, unable to pick up the bit of smoke on the street curbing. And his friend, glued against the window, opened, with foggy fingers, the fly of his pants and, in broad daylight, started noisily urinating against the front of the restaurant.

"Well, that's it. That's it," Nellie said aloud.

In the evening, when Judge Sullivan came for the English lesson, Nellie said, "I'm not going to bring my kid—my child—up in this neighborhood. I'm not going to raise him here, that's all."

Judge Sullivan said, "One raises cattle, one rears children."

"Well, I'm not going to rear him here. I want to get him out of here. Anything's better'n this."

She went looking for a room somewhere else and found one on Huron Street between North Clark Street and Dearborn. It was really a two-room apartment on the first floor of an old red-brick building. Steps ran up between black iron railings to an uncovered porch. A bay window, framed in gray stone that was set into the flaky red brick, looked out upon a small and lumpy front yard where a few scattered hands of stubborn grass fought up through the scaly ground. Empty beer cans had been thrown here by passing drunks.

Inside the front room there was a bed, a dresser, a gas plate, some dishes in a rack over it and, by the window, a kitchen table covered with oilcloth, three chairs drawn up to it. In a corner was a washstand.

It had once been a private home, and the parlor was separated from what had been the dining room by wide, full-length doors that pushed back into the wall. In this second room there was a bed, a dresser, and windows that looked out half a foot away onto the brick wall of the building next door, which had been erected a few years later on its wedged-in plot of land and had robbed the room of its eyes. In a corner, here, too, was a washstand.

Nellie looked with pleasure and, though the rent was more than she could really afford, told the landlady she would take it: The book said that every child should have its own room, its share of privacy. And she even knew where she was going to hang Nick's picture.

Nellie told Judge Sullivan, "Well, I found a place today. It's near North Clark but it isn't on Clark Street. I don't know what the neighborhood is like beyond Clark Street. It just isn't West Madison Street." She put her hand on Judge Sullivan's. "Come see us, won't you?"

Judge Sullivan said, "Though my business may not be exalted, it also carries me into that neighborhood and I deem it an honor to be invited to see you there."

Nick ran to Judge Sullivan and threw himself into his arms. "We're moving and I don't want to leave you!" He started to bawl.

"I'll come to see you, boy. I'll come to see you."

Max and Phil moved Nellie's few belongings to the new address. Nellie and Nick got off the streetcar on Clark Street. Hand in hand, the small boy and his mother walked toward the Huron Street address.

The blue-black panther followed them, sniffing at their heels.

The front room was Nick's and she put him to bed there, but every night he came through the double doors and snuggled up against her in the room that had no eyes, a musty smell, and cockroaches that darted in all directions when the light was pulled on.

Nick liked the new house, the new neighborhood. He was allowed to walk, just on this side of this street, from Dearborn to the alley just before you came to Clark Street, and he had to come into the house when the street lights went on. He played in the dirt and pulled at the little hands of grass in the tiny front yard where an iron railing was flaking away in rot. A few flowers grew there too, their heads, different colors, just over the rusty-crumbling railing, their green against the sagging board steps, their weak stems, their young, opening leaves reaching for the sun, taking in gasoline fumes and dirt blown from the street that was never cleaned. On Clark Street he could see men like he saw on West Madison. On Dearborn, many, many automobiles went by all day long. Down their street, east, only a few blocks away his mother said, was the lake. He had never seen the lake. Or had he seen the lake when Judge took him to the Field

Museum? He couldn't remember but he could imagine it. And looking that way, toward the lake, there were, a couple of blocks away, lots and lots of trees and the sky opening out blue. Every day his mother took him to school and brought him home, walking him across busy Chicago Avenue. And every day in the house across the street on the second floor, a woman opened the window and set a canary in its cage on the sill. This was beautiful. He liked seeing the little spot of yellow there. On the first floor in the front room with no curtains, he could see the blue-painted outline of a bed.

Judge Sullivan came every day as he had done on West Madison. And those were good times. He took him walking. And at last he saw the lake because Judge took him all the way there and they sat, not talking, just sitting and looking out across all that water . . .

blue, bluer than his blue crayon.

Those were good days because when they weren't walking he sat in the front room or lay across the bed. Mother said this was *his* room. And Judge would be there with Mother, both of them at the table in front of the window with a book between them. Sometimes with glasses there too, the same color as the color in the big half-gallon bottle. At those times, Judge Sullivan's face was very red and he laughed so loud that the room seemed to shake. Well, the cups and the knives and forks did anyway. He liked Judge's face red like that and the sound of his laughter filling the room.

Phil and Norman and Max came to the house, too, and they always had something for him. Or, very often, Norman came early and alone with bundles of food that he would cook, making special salads with oil and wine and garlic in a wooden bowl he bought, and something he called curried chicken and something else, once, called lobsters. They were ugly. But they made funny sounds, breaking them. And they tasted good inside. Then later they would all come. These were like feast days.

Nellie went to see Mike Manos and took him a necktie in a box. She cried a little, telling him she was leaving his restaurant because she had a new job near where she lived and she would be close to Nick.

"It's better for little Nicky," Mike said, patting her shoulder. He followed her to the door.

"Remember, you come back any time. Always there is a job here for you."

Nellie had found a job on North Clark in a cheap barbecue joint with leather-looking chickens on spits in the window where myriad flies banqueted. Here the burlesque girls and their pickups came late at night to nibble at food and drink black coffee before going to one of the hotels east of State Street. Here the pimps and the con-men sucked their manicured fingers over piles of chicken bones. But the tips were good. And she was near her son.

Frank Ramponi came to see her, but always, at her insistence, when Nick was in school. He came often. Then not at all for a long time. This was his pattern. She accepted it.

One of the times when he was leaving, he and Max passed each other on the steps. His cold, unfocused eyes glanced fleetingly at Max, then away, down the street. "What do ya say, Max."

"Hi, Frank."

Max continued up the steps and pushed Nellie's door open without knocking. Nellie had her back to him. She stood by the bed with her head down. She turned when she heard him.

"Hello, Max."

He moved toward her. "Was that guy, Frank, here?"

She nodded without answering.

Max took her wrist between his hard fingers. She went on nodding yes with her eyes closed. He shook her wrist. "He's no good. Do you hear me? He's no good." With her free hand she pushed her blond hair back over her shoulder and went on nodding yes. Her eyes were clenched shut. "I've known him half my life and he's no good," Max said. He was almost shouting it. Nellie winced, but not from the pressure of Max's fingers on her wrist.

14

Nick stood on the bottom step of the porch staring into a flower blossom. The boy was looking at the bee and how it was taking the honey from the flower. Intently he watched, his eyes large and round. And his eyes came up and followed, in a circle, and his head, too, the path of the bee through the sunny air until it again alighted on the flower blossom. It was yellow with black stripes and it made a nice noise. Like the man without any legs on his roller-skate platform. But softer. He wished the bee would land on his hand, and he put his finger out, his small head down close to the flower, his eyes looking.

Along the sidewalk came Frank Ramponi, a rolled newspaper in his hand. He tapped the paper against his leg with each stride he took. And now he stood alongside Nick. He looked at the boy and then the bee. Viciously, with his folded newspaper, he smacked the bee where it now crawled on the black iron railing. The bee fell to the ground and into a puddle there, its wings spread upside down on the water.

The boy looked up at Frank Ramponi and felt hate. He looked down at the bee, there in the water, its nice sounds stopped. He loved the bee. He started crying.

"Go on, get in the house," Ramponi told him.

Nick rubbed his balled fists around in his eyes. When he took them down, his eyes were wet and dirt circled.

He went up the steps, Ramponi following him. "Mother," he said, knocking at the door before opening it.

Ramponi followed him into the room. "Hi." He threw the newspaper on the bed.

Nick went to his mother and hugged her around the knees. Nellie looked down at him and then at Ramponi. She shoved Nick gently away and continued to look at Ramponi. "You go play, honey, I want to talk to Frank."

The boy went obediently.

"I thought I told you not to come when he's here."

"I'm coming when I want, see."

"Oh, no, you're not."

"No?"

"Come tomorrow."

He sat down. He curled a cigarette into a loose paper and handed it to her.

"Smoke this."

He made one for himself.

They smoked silently. She choked a little on the tobacco.

"Mother." Nick knocked timidly on the door.

"Just a little while, honey. Go play for a little while."

She heard him move away from the door. She looked across at Ramponi beseechingly. "You know I—we go to bed together—but —but—" She ran her fingers through her hair. "Don't you see, Frank? Can't you see? Please, Frank."

He sat smiling.

"Frank, can't you be decent?"

He pulled in on the cigarette. It made a loose, noisy sound. "You think more of what that kid might see or think than you do of me, huh?" He had snuffed out the cigarette on the floor and was rolling another one.

"You're goddamn right I do!"

He laughed aloud. He'd hurt her now. He'd tell her and it would hurt her. Who the crap does she think she and her kid is? He laughed again and his handsome face was almost hideous in the sound of the laugh. "Well," he said, "maybe I got kids too. Oh yes . . ." He drew it out, smiling that long, narrow, tight smile of his, his eyes strangely pinpointed. ". . . I never told you before. My sense of humor, I guess." He looked strange. Wild. Especially his eyes. And he laughed again. And Nellie drew back away from the laughter. "I never told you. But I'm married. I was married when we first flopped together. And I have two kids—had them when you dragged me off to bed from the sidewalk." Nastily he mimicked her voice, " 'What do you want? To sleep with me?' " He stretched his long legs out and they made a straight line up to his thin hips. "I'm married." The wild look was still on him. "Yeah, I'm married."

She shrugged. Nothing came as a surprise to her. Nothing disagreeable. No bad news.

Suddenly his long legs snapped up until the soles of his shoes were hard on the floor and he leaned over toward her, took her shoulders between his big hands. "You're a good piece. Do you think I'm going to give you up now?" he asked her roughly. She stared into his pinpoint eyes. He squeezed harder. "Do you?"

"Frank, you're drunk."

"Do you!"

"Frank!— You're hurting me—"

"Do you!"

"Frank—!"

She wrenched away. Her hand lashed out and slapped him across the face.

Instantly his big, hard hand came in a swift, open-palmed blow across her cheek. And as he leaned over in slapping her, a knife fell from his pocket. He picked it up and put it back.

And they sat facing each other. Across his cheek and across hers was the red, fingered mark a slapping hand had left.

And the door came open slowly.

Nick stood just inside. "Mother."

Nellie blinked her eyes, clearing them of the water the slap had brought to them. She forced herself to smile. "Yes, honey. Come on in." She held out her hand to him.

She looked at Frank Ramponi. The wild look was still there but she beat it down with her own eyes.

He stood up.

"See you," he said, a rolled cigarette in the corner of his mouth.

"Maybe," she said.

Judge Sullivan found her there late that afternoon, pale, staring at the floor, looking as if she hadn't moved in hours.

She jumped nervously as he came toward her. "Oh, I'm sorry, Judge."

"What is it, Nellie?" He pulled up a chair and sat next to her. She clutched his hand tightly, and held it as a child might. "Come now, young lady!" Judge said. "Let's talk about it. What's wrong?" And guessed the reason.

"Nothing—it's just—" She disengaged her hand and put the fingers of both hands up into the roots of her hair.

"I've noticed you've been nervous lately," Judge said. "Maybe you need a rest."

She stared at him, one hand slowly massaging her throat. "I'm nervous all right. I never feel good any more." Again she took his hand. "I'm just sort of scared all the time. Frank and—Nicky." Tears stood in her eyes. "I don't want that man coming here any more." Her thin fingers tightened on his old hand. Her fingernails bit in. "No. It's better. For me and for Nick."

"The boy is all that counts," Judge said. He looked back at his son and daughter; and his failure. "All that counts."

Nellie nodded yes and her hand held his for support.

Ramponi came back. She let him come back.

15

Nick's schoolbooks, bound together by a leather strap, were on the edge of the oilcloth-covered table, where some early sunlight fell through the window putting a patch of yellow on the edge of the top book. Near them, the round-faced alarm clock ticked noisily. There was a dish with a little oatmeal and milk in its bottom on the table, an empty glass that was stained a milky-white and a half-piece of bread smeared with red jam and imprinted where his teeth had bitten; but he had not finished it because he didn't want to be late to school.

He stood between his mother's knees and she drew the comb through his hair. Her lips were gently smiling and her eyes tenderly looking down at him as he tightened his belt and squinted his eyes closed against the catching and slightly hurting of the comb.

She kissed the top of his head, gently touching her lips to his hair —my son, my son!—and resumed the combing.

Her eyes were moist with love and happiness: thinking—my son! And bits of those years came back: At five he was an angel. There was no other word for it. Then later he might one moment say, "I love you!" and the next burst out with "I hate you!" She smiled. The children's books had warned her about this and told her that it was natural. She had not been surprised or hurt. She was prepared. And all the curse words he had picked up and enjoyed using, which the book said he would, and which he never used now. His threats to run away. The book said that too. She glanced up at the framed picture of the boy's father as if he had caught her thinking these things, and she smiled. The innocent brown eyes looked back.

"Turn this way, honey," she said to Nick, combing his hair.

"Aw, I can do it myself!"

"I like to do it."

The clock ticked noisily.

"I'm going to be late for school."

"It's only twenty minutes after eight."

She gave his hair a final pat in place. Again she looked up at the picture. The boy followed her glance with his own eyes. "Hello, Father!" he said, childishly, cheerfully.

"Your father was a good man," his mother told him.

"I'm going to be good like my father," Nick said.

"No. You must be better."

Nick had his elbows on his mother's legs, his little pointed chin on the palms of his hands, and was looking up into her face.

"I'll tell you what," Nellie said. "I'll give you a quarter for every good mark you get on your report card."

"Okay!" he said. "Gee, I'm going to be late to school!"

He started to the table for his books. He saw someone coming up the steps. "It's Frank," he announced disapprovingly, grabbed his books, started swiftly for the door, turned back, ran to her quickly, kissed her, and opening the door, brushed past Frank.

"Wait!" Nellie called. "Frank can wait."

She ran after him to walk him to school.

At the school entrance, Nellie kissed her son again and turned back toward Huron Street. She walked slowly, trying to make the distance as long as possible, all the while twisting a handkerchief around and around in her fingers.

On Chicago Avenue, she bought a morning paper. She stood uncertainly on the corner. People were hurrying to work, running to catch streetcars, fumbling for change, blinking sleepy eyes against the day. Already a few drunks had appeared on Clark Street pavement.

Nellie turned down Clark, walking slow, crossed Superior and then turned back. She went into a workingmen's bar and ordered a glass of beer.

Over four glasses of beer she read the entire newspaper but didn't know what she had read. Then she had to go home.

Frank was sitting on the side of the bed.

She stood in the doorway. She wet her lips. She wet them again.

"Frank, I think we're all through."

She paused.

"It's you or my kid."

She paused again.

"I'm settling for my kid."

2 *it could be any man's voice*

16

This is Maxwell and Halsted. The neighborhood awakens. People come out on the street. A parade of hunched shoulders, hard faces, battered felts, baggy pants, ragged coats. Through the hush of half-light they find their way, specters in the city fog of smoke and grit, of lifting dark and spreading dawn. On an empty Maxwell Street streetcar stand a tramp awakens and looks at the dawn with sleep-reddened eyes, stretches the ache of wooden planks from back and shoulders.

Maxwell Street is a small hub around which a little world revolves. This is Jerusalem. The journey to Africa is only one block. It is one block from Africa to Mexico, from Mexico to Italy two blocks, from Italy to Greece three blocks.

And this is Halsted Street. This is the World street, the Mother street. Mother Halsted is wise. Is patient. She knows their tastes, their traditions, their beliefs. She puts the immigrant to sleep in his first New World bed. She holds him in her slum arms. Chicago's most humane street, she adopts them all.

In this neighborhood, from kitchen windows and from bedroom doors, kerosene lamps, in the first pale wash of dawn, beat back the darkness, highlight the poverty. In a basement window a vigil candle, carried from the church, burns in a blessed cup before a plaster saint. A stairway, weather-beaten, debris-littered, stumbles down to a window ledge. The wind looks in. The crumpled papers whisper together.

No grass grows, in smooth green aprons, in this neighborbood. But from every window hang tin pails, crocks and mason jars of green growing things. Surprising growths from milk bottles and tomato cans in front-room windows and on fire escapes. Sweet potato plants. Peppermint. Ferns. Wandering Jew. Memories of the grape lands of Italy, the wide valleys of Mexico, the long fields of the South, the olive-twisted shores of Greece, Gypsy and Jew recollections of the sun-warmed, rain-colored growths of many lands. Evidence of a love of the soil and what it bears.

The sun rises over tenement roofs. Streetcars distribute the slack-eyed night workers from the steel mill and factory back to their cavern shacks—tired blue denim marching off to bed. They meet another file in overall-blue headed for Halsted and crowded cars. Milk trucks circle the dairy on Peoria, one behind the other, ready for morning chores. Bottles clash. Motors throb to the dawn like noisy, bloated frogs.

The synagogue on Union Avenue flings open its wooden arms to the quiet little men, the drab little women, trailing, single-file, down the sidewalk.

Down the steps, through the open doors, beneath the ancient Hebrew script they pass.

St. Francis' calm, slow-stroked bell sounds above the street noises, Halsted's Angelus, calling a sparse flock.

It is six o'clock. Then seven. Workers scatter to their jobs. Children, in shabby clothes, start for school. Women stand in dingy doorways, kissing, waving, admonishing. Some are as dried as corn-stalks in late autumn. Some suckle babies. Some push back straying wisps of hair with heavy, husky hands.

The sun puts a gold-plate on the street.

17

As the neighborhood awakened, Juan walked along Peoria toward Maxwell Street. He was a slim, copper-colored Mexican youth in his twenties. He moved along the sidewalk with easy grace, his hands in the pockets of his unbuttoned suit coat, his shirt open at the neck:

It's too early to open the second-hand shop yet. Nobody's gonna buy anything so early. He used to hang around West Madison Street all the time. Bumming around down there on Skid Row. Shooting pool and screwing around. Sometimes jackrolling. A slow smile eased over the copper face. Now I'm a respectable businessman. No more of that stuff for me. My old man seemed to know about the jack-rolling.

A horse-drawn wagon came down the street toward Juan, a Negro standing with the reins held loosely in his hand, his voice bawling out, "Eeeyes-man!" More smoke and soot was lifting from the sky under the penetrating gaze of the sun.

To keep him out of trouble and off Skid Row his old man had opened the shop. Beat my ass in a couple of times to make me stay working with him. I could of taken him. But who hits his old man?

I gotta meet Max tonight. Again the grin across the copper face. That crazy guy on the phone saying, "Let's put one on! I'll meet you in the neighborhood about ten."

Juan grinned again, and his cheeks and slits of smiling brown eyes met.

That goddamn crazy Max!

Juan moved down the long sewer-like street of two- and three-story frame and red-brick houses, each with an uncovered, high-set porch, steps leading upward between sagging rails, apartments in the basements below. Poorly dressed men and women merchants were setting their goods—old tools, potatoes and tomatoes, carrots—down on newspapers on the curbstones.

Then his old man had died and the second-hand shop was his.

Juan passed the Negro store-front church. The second-hand record shop with music already blasting the neighborhood from scratchy records.

He passed the Gypsy store front: different-colored blankets stretched halfway up the plate glass, and the Gypsy-wrapped heads inside, a small kid running around naked. The Gypsies wore circles and circles of beads hanging to their navels, rounds and rounds of bracelets clanking noisily, many-colored, many-layered petticoats and skirts, hair in long braids, huge circular gold earrings pulling their lobes down out of shape. One of them rapped on the window with her six rings on one hand and made a dirty gesture to Juan. He laughed, nodded yes, and continued down the street. On the sidewalk at the corner, seated on a chair without a back, sat an old black woman. She had a corncob pipe in her mouth, a bony hand holding it in place as she puffed on it contentedly.

Juan crossed Maxwell Street to the other side. He happened to look down at the sidewalk. A large oval of new cement had once patched the old concrete. It, too, was old now and cracked. Into it had been scrawled with a broken piece of stick the names NICK JUAN BUTCH STASH. Scrawled many years ago.

How many? Seven? Eight? More?

Juan looked down.

NICK it said.

Jesus! What a great guy he was! What times we used to have! There was a momentary flash of Nick's face on the screen of his memory. He stood looking down, his straight black hair hanging in two long black scythes at each side of his forehead. A shadow passed quickly across his face. But you don't think about that. Jesus, those were the days! What a swell guy he was! Just about the best friend I ever had.

Beyond that he wouldn't allow himself to think.

He pushed his hair back in place and looked up. Against the tavern front of the Crystal Bar in lazy poses lolled Good-bye George and Seldom Seen. What's Seldom Seen doing around?

"Hi!"

"Hi."

"What you say, man?"

"Nothin', man."

"What's happening, man?"

"Ain't nothin' happening."

Juan continued down the street, past the broken-down restaurant where, glancing in, he saw Big Florabelle sitting on one of the stools. Flora popped a couple of yellow jackets into her mouth and then swallowed hot coffee behind them to get a kick.

"Don't goof with no goof-balls," Juan remembered Seldom Seen telling him once. "You goof with them and pretty soon you're riding the Horse."

Juan moved on down the street. In a doorway, out of sunlight, but looking out, stood Subway. He couldn't read or write but he had his silky black hair slicked down and his shoes were shined and he wore a new tie. He looked out at all the girls who passed by. His hands were in his pants pockets and Juan knew his fingers were protectively fondling the roach of a marijuana cigarette.

On the corner of Roosevelt Road, Juan could see the young priest standing just outside the door of St. Francis' Church. His long black frock belled out a little at his ankles as the wind scurried along. Jesus! I *still* can't believe he's a priest! It don't seem possible. We was raised up together. He lived only about four or five doors from me, and he and I and another kid used to hang around together and we used to go down and break into the boxcars and into a meat-packing place and steal coal off coal cars. And it got so his family couldn't handle him and they threw him in the seminary. A priest! Juan was grinning widely and moving silently toward him. And now he stood next to the priest.

Juan stuck him in the ribs with a forefinger held in his pocket like a gun and was saying hello. The priest looked up into Juan's face with the smile on it like the half-cut of a moon.

"Hello, Juan!"

"Hi, Bill." Juan grinned; then, pretending remorse, "I mean Father Bill." The words Father Bill were always strange in his mouth. Why should he call this guy he grew up with and stole with, Father?

"I don't see you at mass very often."

Again Juan grinned. "Ow, let me up!" he said. Then with his hand companionably on the priest's arm he said, "Do you remember those times when we were little kids and we were playing?"

Father Bill smiled. It was the smile of age rather than youth: sober, kindly, gentle. "Yes, I remember those times. They were wonderful times."

"And the bad times we gave the teachers?"

"Yes." Nodding. Smiling.

They started talking about old times. Sometimes Father Bill's face was a little strained, afraid of what Juan might say next, what other forgotten or wished-to-be-forgotten escapade he might drag out of their boyhood. Now that girl! That girl—little Florence Martin. He shivered in dread and repentance.

"Good morning, Father."

He smiled at the passing parishioners and nodded. "Good morning."

"Good morning, Father."

Again he made himself smile. "Good morning."

And he took Juan's arm warmly. "Come to dinner with me some night!"

"No," Juan said. "You always have the twelve disciples there."

"Don't talk that way," Father Bill admonished, hurt. Then he put his arm around Juan's shoulders. "Why don't you come to dinner? You're a friend of mine."

"Is your housekeeper good-looking?" Juan asked wickedly.

Father Bill chose to ignore this. "Come to dinner," he repeated. "You're a friend of mine."

Juan grinned. He spread out his hands. The grin grew broader. "Well, you're my friend too. But I'll have to call you Bill. I can't call you Father."

"Well, that's all right when we're alone."

"And I don't want to kiss your hand."

"Well, why can't you kiss my hand? That is only symbolic."

Again the mischievous grin on the tan face. "Because your hand is dirty like mine."

The priest was grinning too. "Yes. I guess it is," he said. He put out his hand and mussed Juan's hair as he used to do when they were kids, and suddenly they were scuffling together as they had many times as boys, their arms locked around each other's necks, Bill trying to pull Juan inside the vestibule of the church where no one passing by would see them, Juan trying to pull Bill to the center of the sidewalk. "No!— No, Juan!— Some of my flock may see us!"

They stopped wrestling then, smiling and staring at each other, both a little out of wind.

My flock! Juan said in good-humored belittlement.

"You're the same terrific guy of years and years ago," Bill said.

"Well, I'm not so bad now," Juan said. "Remember the first time you told me to go steal?"

Father Bill disregarded this. The bell had begun to ring for the next mass. People were entering the church, all of them smiling, nodding, saying, "Good morning, Father."

Bill's face became the priest's face again: serene, somewhat detached. "Well," he said to Juan, "if there is anything you want, or need, if I can help you . . ."

"I'm doing okay, Bill."

". . . I'll teach you the right way. I'm a priest in the church. —Good morning, Mrs. Lopez. —When the people need me I am there." He held out his hand to Juan. "I'm still Bill to you"—and complaining a little—"you can't call me Father"—complaining a little more—"you get mad with me because I'm a priest."

"No. I'm not mad at you. It's—" Again Juan gestured. "It's like the ocean between Japan and here—it's just—"

"Well, I'll see you, Juan."

"Yeah—see you—"

Bill and Juan shook hands.

"Well, don't get mad," Father Bill said. "We're still friends. Come to the church whenever you like and I'll be there."

Juan said, grinning, "Well, you come to my shop any time because I'm always there."

"I know you will," the priest said, "and I'll teach you the right way."

Juan, amused and chuckling, moved on down the street.

She was standing before one of the clothing booths.

"Nellie," he said.

"Hello, Juan."

They sometimes accidentally ran into each other.

They looked at one another and seemed to have nothing left to say. It lay between them like an open grave.

"Buying some stuff?" he asked.

"Yes. For my little boy! For Nick!"

The name, in remembrance, cut like a knife.

"He's six and a half years old now!" Nellie said.

It lay between them.

They turned their eyes away.

"Well—" Juan said, "so long."

He turned away.

He walked to his little second-hand shop on Peoria near Fourteenth Street. It walked with him, and as he fitted the key into the lock, it nudged his elbow. He relocked the door. No use opening so soon. He turned and walked back down Peoria.

He lifted his foot up on the curb and stared at the door of the Crystal Bar. His foot, without his knowing it, stepped on the names inscribed there in the sidewalk.

Now you don't need no drink. You know you don't drink during the day. And you gotta meet Max tonight too.

He went in anyway.

It's never too early in this neighborhood for a drink. The place was crowded. The place was jumping. There were several Negro men and women clustered around the bar and the small uncovered wooden tables that were crammed against the wall. Negroes of all shades and varieties of shades. Thick-lipped, heavy-eyed. Thin-lipped. One looking like an Indian and with long straight black-gleaming hair. One with Oriental features. A couple of Mexicans were leaning against the juke box. Several white men, who needed shaves, were sucking from beer bottles and looking at the Negro women covetously. Good-bye George was leaning against the plaster-crumbling wall looking as if he didn't have a friend in the world, his coxcomb of long, kinky hair standing straight up. A high-yellow woman, with a knife scar going along the whole length of her cheek and trying to repeat itself further down on her chin, had her skirt hiked up and was pushing some bills into her stocking top.

Juan walked to the bar and pushed between the people there. "Gimme a beer. Schlitz."

It came. He turned the bottle between the palms of his hands and sipped from it, set it on the bar, began peeling the label off.

Suddenly he felt a closeness to Nellie. He sipped more beer. He remembered Nellie waiting on street corners for Nick. He sipped more beer. To him came a closeness and a responsibility to the kid. He wondered if the kid had been baptized. He'd like to be its *padrino*. How Father Bill would like that! He chuckled. Hey! Stop calling him Father! He chuckled again. He took a big swallow of beer. He wanted Nellie close at that moment, just to squeeze her hand and say, "Hello."

Somebody was sucking on a marijuana butt near the toilet door and somebody else was saying loudly, "Save me the roach, man!" The whole place laughed.

At the table pushed against the window, sat Big Florabelle with a man who was trying, drunkenly, to take her hand, fat as a ham there on the table, into his hand. Florabelle because she was born in the Deep South. Big because she was just that. Big and fat. Almost as wide as she was tall. Black. Good-natured, always laughing, ready to lend a stranger a dollar in exchange for a hard-luck story. She knew you five minutes and she'd give her life for you. Even her face, black and fat and humorous, so black that it shone, swollen with hard, fat wrinkles, made you smile looking at it. And what a smile she had. White teeth shining out of the blackness, several gold teeth set among them like jewelry. A big and honest woman of about twenty-eight. And she was a talker. She could keep you laughing.

The man with her, short, skinny, white-skinned and with the pink eyes and whitish hair of an albino but with exaggerated Negroid features, again tried to take her hand and tell her he loved her.

"Don't you talk that talk," she said. Laughing, she pulled back her big fat hands and threw back her head, laughing loudly, musically, until it filled the place, white teeth showing in the black face. She wiggled her hands, fingers spread wide, and wiggled her shoulders, her watermelon breasts, laughing, singing it: "Don't you talk that talk!"

She got up and started dancing toward the juke box. One of the Mexican youths standing there put his hand down on her broad behind and looked at her through slit and inviting eyes. She smacked his hand away. She half sang, in a humorous southern dialect, " 'You boys is gettin' out of hand. They get twelve years old an' start actin' like a natural man!' "

She put her coin in the juke box. Colored lights gyrated in a rainbow and Ruth Brown began singing:

> You're crazy about love
> And I'm crazy about love mah-self
> Weeellll, you're crazy about love

And I'm crazy about love mah-self
When I'm with you, babe
Can't think about nothin' else . . .

Big Flora grabbed one of the white men she knew. "Come on, boy, loosen up!" and they started dancing.

Everybody was dancing, alone or with partners.

Weeelll, it must be rabbit
'Cause mink don't feel that way
Weeelll, it must be rabbit
'Cause mink don't feel that way
Don't you talk that talk
Don't believe a thing you say . . .

And now Big Flora was dancing alone in the center of the floor, throwing her huge arms above her head, wiggling in front and behind, sawing her stomach back and forth, grinding her huge buttocks in a circle.

They crowded around her, clapping hands rhythmically, keeping time to the music, shouting, "Shake it but don't break it!"

And Ruth Brown:

I got to watch mah-self
You boys is gettin' out of hand
I got to watch mah-self
You boys is gettin' out of hand
They get twelve years old
Start actin' like a natural man . . .

Big Black came in and up to the bar. "You buyin', Juan?"

"What!" Juan said. "You mean to tell me you're drinking, man!"

"I'm drinking because I'm trying to get that feeling off of me," Big Black said.

"The Chinaman's riding you, huh?"

Big Black showed a mournful face. "Ah got that Horse and that Horse won't let me go."

Juan ordered two beers and put the money on the bar.

After a while Little Black wandered in and up.

It was a long story. They had, long ago, challenged each other, or rather, Joe Brown had challenged him: "*Maaaan!* You's even blacker than I is! You's de ace of spades!"

There had been a circle of black and brown faces in a jury. Their hands had been stretched out side by side and the verdict given down. Forever afterward Joe Brown was Big Black, and Charlie Collins, a close second, had to content himself with the title of Little Black and was never again known as Charlie Collins. And Big Black held the title, undisputed, until along came Johnson to the neighborhood. Johnson was blacker than either of them and had been immediately named Extra Black Johnson and crowned the new champ. But he was not among the numbered today. He was in stir. In the county jail doing it cold turkey.

Juan popped for another round of beers and then left, saying, "I got to open up."

Outside the tavern door he looked down at their names in concrete. And there it was again. You don't want to think about it. You let it go.

Behind him Ruth Brown sang:

> I want to go
> NORTH!
> EAST!
> SOUTH!
> WEST!
> Everywhich way
> Long as ahm movin'
> Long as ahm movin'
> Long as ahm movin', ba-be
> Ah don't care . . .

He walked to his shop.

It matched step for step with him . . . out of this friendship long dead, more than six years dead now, dead in the electric chair . . .

"Well—" and Nick was making himself strong now . . .

No . . .

"Hello, Nick . . ."
There was nothing else to say. They looked at him; he looked at them. Then they avoided each other's eyes. Nothing to say. Yet reluctant to go.
Juan looking down: You ain't going to start crying! You ain't going to start blubbering like a kid. You ain't! You ain't!
Juan looking up again at Nick.
And Nick: "How do I look, guys? I'm taking a little rest—in bed every night by seven." The laugh was strained.
And, "Next time you see a cop, give him my love." The laugh was bitter and affectionate.
Juan, Sunshine, Butch, reluctant to go. Then, making themselves

strong, feeling Nick inside the glass and steel making himself strong.

Nick to all of them, "Live fast—yeah—live fast . . ."

Nick, looking at all of them, one face to the other, eye to eye, slowly, a twist of a real and affectionate smile behind the hard mask of a grin.

Nick and all of them making themselves strong, strong to the breaking point. "Well . . . take it easy, guys!"

Nick turning. His head up. His back to them now, walking away from them, from life.

It was the last time he ever saw him.

Juan heard the key turn in the lock and went into his shop and sat down among the second-hand items he sold—repaired alarm clocks, old radios, toasters, chairs, anything—his eyes staring out vacantly at the street. Then, no longer vacant, his eyes were filled with the memory . . .

"Juan Rodriguez!"

The memory came back. He was in the middle of it. He was living it again . . .

On the witness stand his face was pale and his lips trembled. Juan's head was down. His long black hair hung straight at each side of his forehead. He pressed his lips together to try to stop their trembling and the copper color drained out of his face.

Prosecuting Attorney Kerman put his thumbs under the lapels of his coat and moved along the jury rail. "Do you know the defendant, Nicholas Romano?"

Juan's lips trembled. "Yes," he said.

"Tell us if you saw him the night Officer Riley was killed."

Juan glanced up at Judge Drake. "I don't remember," he said.

Kerman's eyes blinked open wide. "You don't remember what?"

"If I saw him."

"Well, were you on the street that night?" Kerman's voice was sharp.

"I don't remember."

Morton looked up at Juan from the shadow of his hand. Kerman half rushed to the witness rail. "What?"

Juan looked straight at him. "I don't remember."

Kerman ground his teeth. "Were you at the poolroom that night at twelve o'clock?"

"I don't remember."

"Were you standing at the end of the alley on Atlantic Avenue and West Madison a little after twelve o'clock the night Officer Riley was killed?" Kerman commanded.

Nick looked over the counsel table at Juan, with grave eyes and lips slightly parted.

"I don't remember."

"You were standing at the entrance of that alley, weren't you?" Kerman yelled.

"I don't remember."

Kerman was staggered by the answer. He seemed about to have an epileptic fit in front of the witness box. His face became red, his arms gesticulated at Juan, his mouth twisted and his nostrils enlarged. "How is it you don't seem to remember anything?" he shouted.

"The cops don't remember when they're on the stand," Juan said loudly, and with an angry ring in his voice.

Nick looked up at Juan and grinned widely. Even Judge Drake smiled a little; but he straightened his lips and pounded his gavel. Kerman looked up at Judge Drake. "I ask your Honor to instruct the witness not to volunteer anything!"

Judge Drake's eyes twinkled a little. "Just answer the counsel's questions," he said kindly.

Kerman, his brows knotted angrily, paced down the length of the jury rail. He stuck his face near Juan's. "What do you remember about this case?"

"I remember that the police picked me up and took me over to the station and beat me up and threatened to kill me if I didn't say I saw Nick coming out of the alley!" Juan's voice grew loud, insolent, angry in the hushed courtroom. It had the sound of fiery truth in it.

Kerman rushed to the foot of Judge Drake's rostrum. "The witness is lying! The witness has perjured himself!— He should be arrested!— I withdraw him as a State witness!"

"Just a minute!" Morton, defense attorney, said, putting his shoulder in front of Kerman. "He won't be withdrawn until I have questioned him on cross-examination." Morton looked up at Judge Drake. "The prosecution called this witness—he is theirs—not ours! They cannot withdraw him until I have had my questions."

"He's a hostile witness! He must be recalled by his Honor as a friend of the Court!" Kerman screamed.

"Not so fast! Not so fast!" Morton told Kerman angrily.

Kerman shouted above him, "I move that anything Mr. Morton has to say—I move that we argue this point out of hearing of the jury." Judge Drake nodded. He ordered the jury to be taken to their room and that Juan be taken to the witness room.

The jury filed back into the courtroom. Juan took the witness stand again.

"Now to whom have you been talking about this case?" Kerman demanded.

"You and the police."

Kerman pointed the red pencil at Juan. "And you told the police and me that you saw Romano—did you not?"

"Yeah—but I lied."

"You're lying now, too, aren't you?"

Morton stood up. "Just a minute—we object."

"You needn't state your objections, Mr. Morton," Judge Drake said. "He is trying to impeach his own witness . . . Objection sustained!"

Kerman narrowed his eyes. "Did you sign a statement that Romano did the killing?"

"Yes."

"Was that the truth?"

"No."

"I have here a photostatic copy of a statement taken by the police . . . I read to you what you said at that time . . . 'Yes, I saw Nick Romano kill Officer Dennis Riley.' . . . Did you ever tell that to the police?"

"Yes, but I was lying."

"Did you testify before the grand jury that you saw the killing?"

"Yes, I lied to the grand jury, too."

Kerman stood up. "You've lied all the time then, haven't you? And you're lying now, aren't you? Aren't you?"

"Object!"

"Sustained!"

Kerman, standing in front of Juan, was jabbing the red pencil in his face. "You're going to be arrested before you leave this building! I'm going to send you up for this!"

Judge Drake shot up to a standing position. He pounded his gavel so loudly that you could hear it clearly, throughout the courtroom. He pointed it at Kerman. "I hold you in contempt! You're not going to threaten any witness in my presence! The witness is under the protection of this Court!"

Morton asked quietly and dryly, "Are you finished, Mr. Kerman?" Kerman didn't answer. With his chair turned toward the witness box and his face in the shadow of his hand, Morton asked the witness, "Did you or did you not see Nick Romano come out of the alley on the night Riley was slain, Juan?"

Juan looked straight into Morton's eyes. "I did not."

"When and where did the police pick you up?"

"A couple days after Riley got killed."

"What did they do?" Morton had his chin in his hands and was leaning forward in the chair looking at Juan.

"They took me to the station and told me that they knew Nick had killed Riley and that I had better tell them he did. I told them I didn't know anything about it."

"That's when they beat you?"

"The first time, yes."

"How many times were you beaten up, Juan?"

"Three times, by four or five policemen."

"Then they got their statement?"

"Yes, sir."

Morton stood up and looked around the courtroom. "Are any of the police officers who beat you in this courtroom?"

"Yes, sir," Juan said.

Morton's eyes swept the chairs that lined the wall under the windows in the business half of the courtroom. "Will you point them out to the jury, Juan?"

Juan stood up in the witness box. "That one there—" He pointed to Murphy.

"Do you mean Officer Murphy?" Morton said.

"Yes, sir."

"Are any of the others here?"

"And the little fat copper slapped me and kicked me in the stomach," Juan said.

"You mean Captain McGillicuddy?" Morton asked in pretended surprise.

"Yes."

"Please stand up, Captain McGillicuddy," Morton said apologetically. "I don't want the witness to make any mistakes."

McGillicuddy, holding his coat on his lap, stood up, flushing and angry-faced.

"That's him," Juan said.

From the benches you could hear the thrill of the crowd. Judge Drake tapped his gavel.

Morton sat down. "Well now," he said calmly, "You say they beat you up . . . tell the jury just what they did."

Juan looked at the jury. "The first two times they beat me with rubber hoses and kicked me." His eyes moved to Morton. "And the last time they threatened to . . . to . . . twist my privates off." And Juan, being the ladies' man he was, flushed and grew angry. "That's when I told them I'd say what they wanted me to."

"After they got their statement what did they do?" Morton asked.

"They let me go—but I had to report three times a week at the station."

"Is there anything else that you remember?"

"Yes—they wanted to give me money after I signed the statement. I told them I didn't want their damn money!"

"You lied to the police, then, Juan, to keep them from beating you a fourth time—is that right?"

"Yes, sir."

"And you told the truth here from the witness stand because you didn't want an innocent person to suffer—is that right?"

"Yes, sir."

"And regardless of anything else, you wanted to see justice done?"

"Yes, sir."

"You didn't think of yourself? You volunteered this information? You realized that telling the truth might put you in bad with the police?"

Juan looked over the witness rail. His head was up. It was held up and tilted back with Mexican pride and loyalty. The dark eyes looked straight out. "I don't care what happens to me. I just ain't a rat and I ain't going to lie so that they can burn Nick!"

"Thank you, Juan," Morton said quietly. "I know you told the truth."

Juan was excused from the witness stand amid a breathless silence throughout the courtroom. He stood up. He smoothed his long black hair over his head with the palm of his hand. He stepped from the box and went proudly across the courtroom. The jurors watched him go. Every eye was on him.

Newspaper headlines said:

OLD PAL TRIES TO SAVE
PRETTY BOY FROM CHAIR

And Nick had done it. Juan was to learn this later, though it would have made no difference in his testimony.

18

Juan locked his shop for the night and went to meet Max. Again he turned down Maxwell Street and moved, in the night, toward the Halsted Street car line.

In the half-dark of the street two women smoked cigarettes. The one in the red blouse, young, an indefinable freshness still folded into her body, was saying, "I was in 7A when I was fourteen and I told my mother, 'Mama, I don't want to go to school any more. I feel I'm grown up now. I think a man can take care of me now.'"

A youth rode along the street on a bicycle. The young prostitute yelled, "Hey! Give me a ride!" Her voice was like a girl's.

The youth made a wide circle at the corner and came back, pedaling slowly. "You give me a ride!" he yelled, grinning.

The women continued to kick their heels against the cross-bar of the streetcar stand. The old, used-up-looking one said, "Tricks are dead bitches tonight."

Juan walked past them toward the corner. In the empty caverns of sidewalk fruitstands bums lolled, curled up on rags and newspapers, their heads pillowed in their arms, eyes closed in sleep or peering out at the people who passed. Those awake, when cars drove up, the occupants climbing out to go to Leavitt's for the restaurant's famed corned-beef sandwiches on pumpernickel, emerged from their caverns and approached with dirty rags and pails, though it was night, hoping for a quick handout: "Want your car washed, mister?"

An old drunk staggered in front of the hot-dog stand on Halsted where well-dressed people from parked cars stood eating hot dogs and drinking pop. He walked with a cane made from a broomstick with a rusted nail sticking from the bottom end to steady him. He staggered first into Juan and then into three Negro youths. The drunk mumbled words at the Negroes, and among them was the word nigger; he continued his stagger down the street.

One of the Negroes stopped and looked back. "Ah ought to go and fix that old bastard," he said. The fellows with him said, "Go 'head, man." And they leaned against a stand, waiting.

"Ah need some backin' up," he said.

One of them waited, the other followed him. He looked over his shoulder at his backing. "Come on, boy."

His backing said, "Oh, go on, man! Ah's here."

The Negro stood in front of the old drunk. "What dat you say?"

The drunk mumbled something and again used the word. The Negro hit him once. In the mouth. The old drunk stretched out on the sidewalk in front of the hot-dog stand on the corner. His cane rolled away from him. His feet, in worn, low-cut tennis shoes, pointed up. Blood on the sidewalk was the color of the fire plug near his head.

The three Negroes vanished quickly into the long black canyon of Maxwell Street. The people eating hot dogs and drinking pop stared unconcerned. The neighborhood people stared unconcerned.

People in this neighborhood mind their own business.

The drunk sat up on the sidewalk, helpless. Finally a loiterer helped him to his feet. Goldie, half a dozen hot dogs on buns lined down her arm, the mustard paddle licking each one in turn, looked over the counter and said, "Get him down a ways from here, will you?"

The drunk staggered down Maxwell to a booth. A stale bun peeped out of his back pocket above the dirty seat of his pants. Blood drooled from his mouth. At the hot-dog stand Goldie said, "He sure asked for it, didn't he?"

A young couple parked an old car alongside the stand in the half-shadow. The youth cut off the motor and put his arm around the frizzy-haired girl. They started necking.

On the corner Juan watched streetcars go by until Max hopped off the back of one.

Grinning, they approached each other.

"Slumming?" Juan asked in routine.

"Yeah. Looking the old neighborhood over," Max answered in routine.

Max poked Juan in the ribs with his elbow and nodded toward the black hole that was Maxwell Street.

Juan knew what he meant.

They walked down and into the Crystal Bar. They bought two armloads of half-gallon bottles of beer. They carried them to an empty stand between Peoria and Maxwell, near the mouth of the alley that runs only north to almost as far as Roosevelt Road, and eased themselves on the hard boards to settle down to some serious drinking.

Max had picked the booth, nodding scowlingly toward it. Juan had said, "Oh?" But this was routine too. They always sat there because they wanted to see Cliff's sister walk by. She was not beautiful, but well proportioned. They uncorked a bottle apiece. Their lips were circles around the circles of the bottles and their Adam's apples worked up and down.

Above them the blue-black panther lay on the roof of a tenement house, its feline chin on the cornice, its yellow-green eyes staring down onto the black night street of Maxwell. Its tail, wagging slowly back and forth, was like a lasso, a noose, sending little shivers of pebbles rolling loosely across the roof.

Again Max and Juan set the bottles to their up-tilted mouths for a long time. Juan came up for air first. "How's Phil?" he asked; and then slyly, ". . . And your friend—Norman?"

"Cut it out!" Max said with a pained grin. "Sure he's my friend. I was going to bring him along to get drunk with us but"— winking—"he had a date." He lifted his bottle in a brawny hand and clicked it against Juan's bottle and said in Spanish, in Mexican salute, "If it doesn't sound, it doesn't taste."

When they met they drank. And looked at women. And talked about women. But mostly they drank.

Again the bottles clicking:

"Health and money."

"And time to spend them."

Cliff's sister came along and their eyes were pleased with her. They drank and waited for her to come back. Something came along that was almost as good, and in that sweater and tight skirt she might as well have been naked.

"¡Ay!" Max said. "I could use some of that!"

"You think I couldn't?"

Again the big bottles tilted up to the eager lips and at last dropped down to the plank boards with a thud. And Juan's face with a crescent moon of a grin: "Hey, Max! I think you got a fly in your beer."

Max squinted his eyes and peered into the amber color of the bottle. Then his tan face crinkled like cellophane and into a wide smile. "Vitamins," he said, and drank.

One bottle apiece gone. Well into the second.

A woman passed showing a very broad backside.

"Ay! Es mucho jamón para dos huevos!"

"Si pero sirve."

Two bottles gone.

"Here's health!"

"And love without a mother-in-law."

Into the third bottle . . . "Hijo de la—! . . . and already arguing as to who was going the half-block for refills.

"Remember that time when we was in grammar school and Bill —Father Bill—" Juan started laughing.

Max, lighting a cigarette, glanced down the street. *"Puta madre! Here comes The Wolf!"* he said in an undertone.

"Frankie," Juan said.

"Here comes The Wolf," Max said again; and, in his own invented slang, "He ain'ta gonna get none!"

"Frankie," Juan said again. Softly. Mockingly.

"The Wolf! The Wolf!" Max said angrily, emphatically.

Max scowled toward the tall approaching figure: But no one calls him The Wolf to his face. No. He's such a bad sonofabitch everybody's scared of him. Always hopped up on marijuana. Nobody hangs around with him much because nobody trusts him. He has no respect for woman, God or anything. He doesn't even respect his own mother. If you have something he likes he wouldn't ask you for it. He'd take it off you. "I'm going to screw you and I'm going to screw you." That's it.

"He ain't going to get any of it," Max said again. "He might stop here and converse and we might have to *offer* him a drink." Max looked at Juan and Juan looked at him. "Ah—we'll hide the bottles."

They hid the bottles, pushing them to the back of the stand and out of sight. Max pulled out a cigarette and began lighting up.

The Wolf moved closer, emerging from the deeper shadows. With him was Subway. Between them walked a colored kid. A kid, because he was young, about eighteen or nineteen. The Wolf was on the inside by the buildings and Subway was on the outside and they had this little colored kid between them and they were talking very chummy-chummy.

"I bet they're blowing tea right now," Max said. "We'll ignore them."

They ignored Max and Juan too.

They walked past them as if they didn't see them and up to the alley. When they got there Subway pushed the colored kid into the alley and struck him as he pushed him, a blow on the back of the neck, and the boy went stumbling, with The Wolf guiding him further into the alley as he was falling.

The Wolf had him then. The Wolf pulled him further into the alley. The Wolf pulled out his knife.

In that moment, in the dark, the kid came to from the blow on the back of the neck. But by this time The Wolf had him; he had a good grip on his collar.

And the kid said, "Frank, whatcha doin', boy, don't!"

The Wolf didn't say a word. He just started stabbing. First he started on his stomach. He stabbed him once or twice and the kid couldn't talk very much. Then The Wolf started hitting him and hitting him with the knife blade.

And the kid went down; he kept going down, down, sinking down to his knees.

And he was on his knees.

The Wolf still had him by the collar.

And the boy: "Frank, whatcha doin', Frank? Frank, I didn't do nothin' to you."

Max and Juan could just barely hear him.

He's talking and pleading with The Wolf . . .

but all the time—

the knife—

sticking—

everywhere—

anywhere that it went.

That's when the kid started kissing his shoes.

"Please, Frank, please, don't, don't kill me, Frank.

And all this time Subway is standing at the mouth of the alley just watching to see that nobody comes by.

And Max and Juan were sitting on the Maxwell Street stand: It's none of our business. We don't want to get involved. Maybe, who knows, what this guy did to them? It's your business. Sorry we got involved in it. You can rest assured we're not going to say a word about it.

And the noise has attracted the attention of the woman who lives in the tenement on the alley. Her window opens. She starts yelling and screaming, "Tu eres Pancho, tu eres cabrón! Déjalo! Déjalo! Leave him alone! Leave him alone! I'll call the police!"

Max said, "Juan, let's take another drink and get out of here."

"No," Juan said quietly, "not yet. It might get pinned on us."

"Yeah. That's right."

The boy in the alley had stopped yelling, stopped talking.

The Wolf walks out of the alley. And here is the woman still yelling her head off. Subway looks around. Nobody's there but Max and Juan. So the Wolf walks out calm, cool, wiping the blade of his knife on a handkerchief. He throws the handkerchief in the alley and they walk away.

As they walked away the sightseeing bus turned off Halsted onto Maxwell. Slowly the rubberneck bus groaned along Maxwell Street, lights out. The windows were open a little at the bottom. They were white with the powdered faces of women.

The rubberneck bus rumbled slowly, its brakes hissed softly, its balloon tires eased the sightseers over the broken Maxwell Street pavement. The spieler had drama in his gestures, in his voice: "Maxwell Street!— The ghetto!— Chicago's gaudy, picturesque outdoor market. Over here you get odor along with your color . . ." The circus barker's voice chuckled. The women stared. The men looked out beyond their pressed and expensive suits.

Max said, "You better give me another slug out of that bottle."

The voices at the windows say, talking to themselves: "How interesting! . . . What an ugly, dirty street! . . . How interesting! . . . There's no excuse for being that poor and that dirty. They make my skin creep!"

The eyes of the slum people come up to the darkened windows of the rubberneck bus, narrow, harden.

A man yells, loudly, "Rubbernecks!" Angrily. Contemptuously.

Charlie, selling hamburgers, says, "Goddamn them! They stare at you like they're looking at pigs. I wonder how they'd like it if we went over where they live and stared at them?"

The corpse lay in the alley.

Several boys had collected rotten tomatoes from the gutter; they began to redden the windows of the rubberneck bus with them. The bus moved protectively away.

A kid got off a stand and ran after the bus. He hooked his heels on the bumper and hung onto the back of the bus. His white oval of sailor cap sat on the back of his head. He shouted in a loud, matter-of-fact voice, imitating the emphasis of the spieler, "This is Maxwell Street. There's a whorehouse right around the corner."

"Now," Juan said. "Let's get out of here."

He and Max took off.

They headed for West Madison Street.

"I gotta have another drink," Max said.

"Yeah. Me too," Juan said. "But quick."

They walked into the Long Bar. Sat far in the back, really trying to get drunk now, working at it, working for over an hour at it, glasses turning on the bar, eyes looking back at it: The guy had stopped yelling by then. I think he was dead by then because of the way he was stabbing him. He was stabbing him all over. Wherever he could get at him. It was dark in there. You can't aim when it's dark. He was sticking him and sticking him. He must have hit him around the neck, around the jaw, around the head. I doubt if he hit him in the head because it would have broken the blade. So he must have been sticking him in the neck.

"Huh? Yeah, I'll have another beer."

And in walked Subway. He walked over to them:

"Hi, fellows! Hi, Max! Hi, Juan! How's everything?"

"Have a drink. Have a drink with us," Max said.

"Sure. Sure! I'll have a drink."

He had a drink. No nervousness showed up. He was as calm as if he had just been swimming.

"How's everything?" Max asked: Nosey me. I gotta find out.

"Fine! Fine!"

Subway popped for another round of beers: We're drinking *his* beer.

Max said, "Hey, Joe, ah . . . how about that monkey you guys just knocked off? Yeah, but tell me, Joe, didn't you feel sort of sorry for the guy? The way he was *kissing* The Wolf's shoes. I mean—the way he was *pleading*. I mean I don't give a damn if he was a nigger"—using a word he never used—"or what the hell he was but you know it could have been any man's voice, you know. Didn't you feel kind of sorry for him?"

Subway said, "Well—yeah. Yeah. He had it coming though."

"Why?"

"You remember the time I was in the hospital for a couple of weeks?"

"Oh, yeah. Yeah. I heard you went out there to the poolroom and you and another guy challenged a whole bunch of colored guys to a knife fight." Max squinted his eyes against the smoke from his cigarette: And they beat the crap out of you and put you in the hospital and you said you'd get even. I guess that's one of the guys. I'll keep digging.

Max kept digging, digging, digging.

Juan said nothing. All the time he sat, with Max between them, just listening, looking forward, looking into the back-bar mirror and following their faces with his eyes.

Max, digging, said, "How about it? Don't you feel sorry for the guy?"

"Kind of—"

:He's breaking, he's going to tell me all about it. Here comes the story.

Subway lit a new cigarette and after a while he said, "I did a little bit but it was too late to feel sorry for him."

"What do you mean?"

"Well, that was the wrong guy."

:The wrong guy!

At that moment Juan picked up his beer bottle. "You *dirty* son-ofabitch!" he said.

Subway was so surprised that he was left with his mouth open. That's when Juan caught him with the full bottle right across the face and the blood began spurting and Subway went over backwards and lay on the floor, out cold.

Juan did it over Max's chest, standing up to do it. Max jumped back out of the way, seeing the blood spill out and not wanting to get any of it on his clothes. "Tee-hee," Max said. "Let me know when you're going to do things like that."

They got out of the bar fast.

As they passed Subway, unconscious on the floor, Juan spat on him. And then he spat on him again. "That's one for your mother too," he said.

19

Even in sleep he was handsome in a hard, masculine way. The sheets took, in long, angular strokes, the long and powerful lines of his body, the square jutting-out of his jaw and the sculpture of his head. His black hair bunched up from under the cover, and moving in his sleep his head edged its way upward on the pillow, revealing, cleanly, in the sunlight, the lines of the jaw, the blueness of beard underneath, the Italian coloring and the strong nose. Then his mouth, like a blubbery sneer. Double-lipped. Puffed out.

He moved again in his sleep, his body tightening together, curled in an egglike shape, his arms between his legs, his legs tightening into them, his head down, now, on his chest, buried there. "Mama! Mama!" his lips mumbled. Urgently. Pleadingly.

"Mama! Mama!"

Some spittle was on his lips.

Trembling in a dream, goose pimples all over his skin: "Mama! Mama!"

The urgency changed to half-wakefulness. His eyes came open slowly. Blinking . . .

"Ma . . . ma . . ."

And Frank Ramponi, The Wolf, came awake.

Against the summer sun of midday he pulled the cover over his head. Then, like a frightened child, slowly pulled it down to his chin. Scared. Rolled his eyes around. Stared. Then knew where he was.

He threw his big arm out from under the sheet. It was long, smooth, well muscled. His fingers went groping around in the drawer of a night table for a cigarette, found it.

The cigarette was a thin tube wrapped in white paper and folded down at the end. It was much thinner than an ordinary cigarette. Greedily he drew the smoke in, making sucking sounds, dragging air down into his lungs along with the smoke. The cigarette made a crackling sound and burned brightly, like a torch. The smoke was acrid.

The Wolf held his breath a long time, as long as he could, before exhaling. A sense of security came to him. Pleasure came. And relaxation. A feeling of increased strength. He inhaled again. Exhilaration struck. Confidence eased itself all along him, all over him, down to the edges of his toes and out along the tips of his fingers. Man! Oh man!

He smoked the cigarette to a fingertip-burning butt and snuffed it out carefully.

The great thing about weed was you always had an appetite. And no hangover.

"Ida!" It was a command. Order.

She came, half frightened, thin, wary-eyed. She was a tired-looking woman with perpetually worried eyes sunk in a thin face framed by straight brown hair and underlined by an expressive slash of red mouth.

"Get me something to eat."

She brought it to him.

"Take these dishes out of here."

She came back into the bedroom and started gathering them up.

"Get in!" he said.

Pulling her dress over her head she crawled in.

He bit her. He roughed her up. She feigned the cries and moans he liked and expected. She hated his guts. Only this. The bed. He had what many women think all weight-lifters, wrestlers and Negroes have. He completely satisfied her. Satisfied her as no other man ever had.

And in this moment: "Mama! Mama!" he shouted sexually at her, his teeth riffling along her shoulder, and over: "Mama! Mama!"

It was, in this moment, the closest he ever got to anybody. And it was only himself.

Afterwards, after she had dressed and taken the dirty dishes to the kitchen, he lay pleasurably sucking on another reefer. Only the hour hand of the clock seemed to move. He could hear every pulsation of the automobiles that moved along the street outside, see a wrinkling of chewing-gum foil on the dresser in its every sparkling detail. Man! Oh man! Again he sucked in the acrid smoke. A feeling of well-being and grandeur came.

Then he sat up, throwing the covers to his navel, revealing his chest, broad and completely covered with heavy black hair, the hair covering his stomach, a thick knot in a heavy curl around his navel.

He stood up, completely naked, and walked across the creaking boards. His compact body stood in front of the dresser. Heavy hair ran down his legs and calves and down onto his toes to their ends. Pimples were on his legs and thighs.

He stood looking in the mirror at himself. Consciously he sucked in his double lip and began combing his hair. He gave no thought to the night before.

Standing close to five-ten, whatever he lacked in height he made up in his shoulders. He slipped into his shorts, pants and shoes, and again stood erect. The shoulders were enormous. He lashed his belt across. He had a terrific, a beautiful slim waistline. He was built like a good middleweight.

The Wolf pulled a white T-shirt over his shoulders. He never dressed up. Nobody had ever seen him in anything but a T-shirt or a black leather jacket.

Pulling the T-shirt over his swelled-out chest he continued to stare into the mirror at himself.

Good looks? He had them too. His face wasn't innocent-looking by a far shot. There was a cruelness, a hardness about it, in the eyes and at the edges of the mouth. A cunning. A shutting out of other people. A face that could turn a coldness and an unforgiveness on a friend. A face some women liked because it suggested sadism.

Again he consciously pulled his lips in tight against his teeth. His mouth still stared double-lipped at him like a half-inflated balloon.

The lift of the marijuana and his mouth sneering at him in the mirror:

They called him The Wolf. But nobody would dare call him The Wolf to his face. Big lips smiling now. They're too damn scared of me. The Wolf. He was proud of the name. And proud because nobody would *dare* call him The Wolf to his face. The Wolf. He worked alone most of the time. Sometimes he'd hook up with Ralph on a heist. The Wolf. Lone Wolf. Why? Why! Grandeur struck him again. Because I work alone and don't split with anybody. Why should I! So the less people with you the less you have to split.

The comb began stroking through his wavy hair again. "The Wolf is in the neighborhood! . . . The Wolf was here!" Everywhere he went the Italian people would make the sign of the cross at him as if he were the devil. This he knew for fact. He took pride in this too . . . He was admired for his stick-ups. He had a reputation all over the city where people knew about weed, holdups, stick-ups.

He had finished combing his hair now. And admired the black gleam of it, the comb still half poised. Then the sneer turned into a scowl. He put the comb on the dresser. He put his hand on his cheek where she had slapped him. Who she think she is? And what she said: "It's you or my kid." He said it aloud, imitating her voice. "Oh, yeah?" Who that broad think she is? On weed or no he never forgot! Nor forgave . . .

She stood in the door. She wet her lips. She wet them again.

"Frank, I think we're all through."

She paused.

"It's you or my kid."

She paused again.

"I'm settling for my kid."

Who she think she is? Who she think she's talkin' to? I been laying this broad for years. Who she think she is? One way I can fix her. Fix her my way for good.

The scowl turned to a double-lipped smirk. The feeling of grandeur came again, like a stoplight turning from red to green. The Wolf! He liked calling himself that. Thing is, Nellie is better in bed than my wife, than anything I ever had. Any broad I ever laid up with. That way I can have it whenever I want. I'll fix her for good. You never let a good lay go till you're tired of it yourself.

He moved to the night table and sat on a chair near it, first pulling down the shade at the long window that looked out on Polk Street and Loomis. He rolled back the rug; a board in the soft-wood floor opened under his fingers, and he lifted it, revealing, in its inner blackness, a foot or less of space between the floor of his bedroom and the ceiling of the apartment below. From it he took out a couple of cigar boxes and a bag. Onto the night table he put them, and began piling marijuana into three little mounds, began manicuring the stuff: began preparing cigarettes of it. The good stuff, in its round cylinders of cigarettes, he stacked in one pile: dynamites. The second-class tea was pushed into a separate stack. And now he mussed his hair, pulling out single strands, snipping them to the length of the marijuana cigarettes he was rolling and inserting a single strand into each cigarette. When it's good stuff it is supposed to crackle when you puff on it. If it isn't it won't. This was the third-grade stuff, each cigarette with a human hair from his head.

Third-grade stuff. Strictly for the suckers. It crackles. They think it's the real McCoy.

The Wolf pulled out another hair, wincing against the slight pain.

"Daddy!" the little boy said, pushing the door open. "Frankie!" The boy came into the bedroom.

"Let me alone."

The boy came anyway, and up to his father's side. "What's that?" His small hand touched one of the piles of dream-stuff.

"Get the hell out of here, you little bastard! Hey—!" to Ida. "Come and get this little sonofabitch out of here!"

He slapped the kid across the face. It was a blow for a man, not a child.

The boy began to scream.

His wife came to the bedroom door. Her eyes tightened but her expression did not change. She gathered the screaming child up into her arms. Tried to smooth away the pain and anguish with an almost uncaring hand. No more kids for him to abuse. She'd see to that. I *hate* your guts. Why couldn't she give this one away to her mother too, like the girl, just to keep it out of harm's way? But no! Frank needed things to abuse.

In the kitchen she tried to pour a teaspoon of sugar into the child's mouth to get it to stop crying. The door opened and Subway entered without knocking. "Where's Frankie?"

She nodded her head toward the bedroom, without speaking. The child was kicking bruises against her legs and stomach.

"Hi, Frankie!"

"Subway."

Frankie didn't turn. He kept at his work, his broad shoulders stooped over it. Subway sat on the side of the bed and waited.

His bedroom was his office, and he went on about what he was doing. He grabbed a capsule and blew hot breath into it. It got damp inside and he took a little stuff, a little adulterated heroin, and put it inside. He capped it and shook it up. The capsule took frosting like a window in the wintertime.

His lips smiled. An ounce makes close to five hundred, I think. He smiled again. Don't forget it's powder and that's a lot of stuff. Take this face powder that women use. An ounce is a big box, you know. When I fill these caps I can make a lot. Selling strictly ounces makes you a lot of take.

The marijuana. The caps. He put the cigar boxes and the bag back into the hole and covered it with the safe-door of the twelve-inch length of softwood board, pulled the rug over it with one foot.

Now he was ready to operate.

"You carry these," he said to Subway: If anything screwed up they weren't going to take little Frankie.

"Okay, Frankie. Sure, Frankie!"

Subway hid them in the lining of his suit coat.

"Okay," Frankie said. He picked up his Bull Durham sack from the dresser. He never smoked tailor-mades. He carried Bull Durham mixed with marijuana. Half marijuana, half tobacco. And he was always charged up. He smoked it the way you smoke cigarettes, not as you smoke marijuana. If he wanted a jolt he'd just step into a side street or an alley and *blow* a good stick.

"Got your short here?" The Wolf asked.

"Yeah."

They went down to his car, which was discreetly parked a block away on a side street.

"Push over," Frankie said, "I'll drive." Not asking him; telling him.

The top was down and they rode in style, Frankie driving slowly, letting the neighborhood get a look at him.

Along Taylor Street they cruised, and past a beauty shop. Two of the operators with nothing to do stared out onto the dull business slum street. Then The Wolf in his T-shirt and at the wheel of the slick, only a few years old, convertible passed along. They rushed to the window and peered out, their faces close to the plate glass, their rumps pushed out behind them in tight-fitting skirts. They watched him every day that he passed on foot or in a car. They watched for him.

One of them pushed her long, sharp, blood-dipped fingernails against the windowpane. "I wouldn't say no to him!" she exclaimed.

The other girl said, sighing sexually, "I hate little bad. That sonofabitch is grand larceny! He's strictly big bad!"

Smiling, head turned on that broad neck, Frankie saw them and, laughing, waved a big hand. He could have almost any girl in the neighborhood just by snapping his fingers. The Wolf! He *liked* that name.

He drove out north to a tea pad where everybody was already hopped up. Everybody but the guy who ran the joint. So The Wolf said, "Look, man, let's go somewhere an' talk."

"Okay with me."

But first The Wolf stepped into the toilet and torched up. Then he and the guy went down the street to a respectable bar.

"Buy you a drink," The Wolf said.

He jiggled his hand in his pocket, feeling the change and the big folded roll next to it. His lips curled. He always had money in his pocket. Big money. And he was always buying one-drink-only. Yeah, one drink only. The rest he got from you.

The Wolf grinned and slapped the guy on the back. They ordered martinis at a far booth away from everybody and talked softly and confidentially.

"Do you go for it?" The Wolf asked.

"If I go for it I'll take a tin."

"You don't have to take it until you sample it, man."

"I'm hip."

The Wolf screwed up his face. "You take that and you still know your name."

The Wolf went back with the guy to pick up Subway. The weed-heads were really blasting the stuff. They were torching up like mad. The muggles were going around like crazy, loose lip to loose lip. The Wolf passed a pack, twenty-five reefers, to a fellow he knew and knew wouldn't double-cross him: "Pass the word around, man."

He picked up Subway. Only a nod of the head did it.

Outside: "It's a nice day. Let's take a ride."

"Sure, Frankie!"

"You drive."

"Okay, Frankie!"

"Turn here."

They turned off onto a dirt road, then another. They turned into nearly impassable roads.

"Torch up!" Frankie said.

They lit the real thing and, free, in the country, blew up a storm, laughing, talking, talking silly, feeling great.

"Stop here!" Frankie said.

The car skidded to a stop.

A lot of people grew their own tea. They had little patches in South Chicago, in Indiana. Wherever there was a highway you just went out there and put your own spread along it. The thing grew so wild, so wild that you could pass in a car and just throw seeds out the window and they'd grow. You remembered where you did it. And you cultivated it the way you cultivate anything else. And you had your own harvests, and you went through all sorts of intricate maneuvers to cure your own stuff and prepare it.

The Wolf sat on the sun-warmed upholstered seat of the convertible, smiling at his field. "Look at all that grass!" he said, torching up again. "Ain't that beautiful grass? And it's all mine!" Like a plantation owner he looked at the tea in its raw state, leaves, stems, sweet

117

young sprouts. Then, almost grudgingly, "Let's get back to town."

They got back. They made the rounds, Subway doing the delivering. Then they bummed around the taverns.

Night came. Night hung in cobwebs over Halsted Street. They ran into Paco. A young Mex. A kid who used to shout, "Hello, Frankie!" and follow him around. Hero worship. Used to chase the pennies he threw.

"Hi, kid!"

He and Subway were blowing weed under the surrealistic lampposts and streetcar wires. Ain't nobody around. What's to fear? They sucked the strong smoke down into their lungs. Great, man!

The Wolf got the kid in between them. About fifteen. Yeah, about fifteen. Good-natured, good-looking kid. Real friendly. Wants to be a man. I'm one of his heroes.

"How you doing, Paco?"

"Fine, Frankie, fine!"

The Wolf pulled his knife. He started chuckling. He put the knife against the young boy's ribs. "Blow, boy, blow!" He pushed the weed over against the boy's lips.

"Blow!" He laughed nastily.

Who she think she's talking to?

The cigarette was against Paco's lips: Please, Frankie, don't pull that on me.

And the kid blew. Or he pretended to blow. He took a big drag and tried to hold it the way he had seen them do, and when Frankie wasn't looking he blew it out fast, out the side of his mouth, and started to go through the usual routine, as if he was trying to keep it down, pretending: Jesus! I got out of it that time!

Who she think she is? Grandeur came and sat like a king on the seat of his thinking. I'll fix her. Fix her good. My way.

20

Juan stood on the street corner. Alice Mae was coming toward him. She was a very light-skinned colored girl and had red hair, long hair, naturally red. Because she was good-looking she made a lot of money hustling. On dope, she was on the street hustling all the time. She had no place to stay and often went to Juan's shop to lie down.

"Juan," she said, and from the way she said it and from the way she walked he knew she had had her needle.

"Hi, Alice Mae."

"Can I sleep in your place?"

"Yeah, go ahead and lay down."

"Wake me up in four or five hours?"

"Okay."

As Alice Mae moved away in narcotic step, Big Black caught up with Juan and put a huge paw on his shoulder.

"Ol' Juan's gettin' tight with that colored gal."

"What do you mean, tight?"

"You's screwing her."

"I'm not tight with her."

"Ol' Juan's getting tight with that colored gal," Big Black repeated. "You better watch out, Juan—niggahs carry razors—that's what the white folks say. Dat gal got a razor. All Mexes carry knives —that's what the white folks say. But niggahs got razors! Razors cut faster, deeper. You watch out, Juan!" His black face grinned in friendliness at Juan. "Niggahs got razors, boy!"

Another Negro voice: "Niggahs and knives. Don't that sound better than niggahs and razors. I've read poetry, man. Read Sandburg." He had. "Read—what's that man's name?—something Eliot. But he don't make sense like Sandburg. Niggahs and knives— They got a name for them words that sound like songs when strung along in a line. If you don't believe me you can find it in your schoolbook."

"But I'm not tight with her," Juan protested. "I never touched the girl or anything."

He hadn't. But the whole neighborhood believed he was tight with her.

Juan moved away down the street, waving a casual good-bye.

Again he accidentally ran into Nellie. With her was a young boy holding tightly to her hand. "Hi, Nellie." Then he grinned down at the kid. "Hey! I know you! You're Nick! Put it here, kid!" He held out his hand.

Nick obediently shook hands.

"Doesn't he look like Nick?" Nellie asked.

He didn't.

"Yes," Juan said.

Nellie smoothed Nick's hair back with her hand.

"What are you doing down here?" Juan asked. "What you got in the boxes?"

"Shoes for—" She smiled and nodded at her son. "They can sure wear them out at his age! I'm buying them while I have the money."

"Hey!" Juan said. "Come on over to my store! I'll fix us some grub. Kids are always hungry."

They went to Juan's second-hand shop and Juan fried some eggs, made coffee, went out for a quart of milk and cookies for the boy.

On a broken-down sofa in the back room Alice Mae slept the sleep of the drugged.

Nick licked cookie crumbs off his fingers, and Juan, stooping down, lifted the boy up in the air and stood him on a table. "Hi, big stuff!" Then suddenly Juan's face became thoughtful. He sat Nick down and handed him a frayed comic book, then, with his head, motioned Nellie to the front of the shop.

"Has the kid been baptized?"

"I don't believe on that stuff," Nellie said, lapsing into slang.

"Neither do I," Juan said; and then, with his face screwed up comically, "But we better not take no chances."

"I don't know—" Nellie said.

"Hey, Nick!" Juan called; and he took Nellie's hand, said to her, "Come on somewhere with me!"

"Where are we going, Juan?"

They went toward the church, Juan grinning all the time: Jesus, is Bill going to get a big surprise!

He hurried them along. Then his face sobered. Jesus, we don't have no *madrina*.

He had to take them a block down a side street. "Wait here!" But his sister-in-law was too drunk to go with them.

Glumly now, he moved toward the church; maybe Bill can find a godmother. Sure he can.

As they passed the dirty window of the broken-down restaurant, Juan happened to look in.

"Wait here!" he said again.

Big Flora, her voluminous breasts under the gingham dress swelled out over the table like turkey set out at Christmastime, popped half a dozen yellow jackets into her mouth and swallowed hot coffee after them.

"Take it easy!" Juan said, standing alongside of her.

"Yes, greasy!"

Her moon face smiled up at him and made him smile in turn. "Man, I'm chewing them like popcorn," she said.

"Why don't you shut it off?"

"Shut what off?"

"Things. Those things."

"It makes me feel like I wanta feel."

"Hey, Flora—you ain't Cath'lic, are you?"

"Man"—she laughed her full-bosomed, musical laugh—"I think

I was the only niggah who was Catholic in the whole state of Georgia."

"Look!" Juan said. "How'd you like to be a godmother?" He pointed to the two figures waiting on the sidewalk outside.

She squinted out the window. "Why not?" she said. "If that white gal will have me." She eased her ample form up off the not too sturdy chair.

Juan made the introductions. "Hello, Nellie, chile," Big Flora said, and Juan took the boy's soft, moist hand and they walked to the church.

Father Bill was all smiles. He shook and held Juan's hand. "I knew you would come. This is your house here."

Juan, grinning, said, "Oh yeah?"

"Any time! Any time! It's so good, Juan—"

"Let's get down to business, Bill. We want the kid baptized."

"I know you are, Juan, in your heart you are—" And he questioned Flora about being a Catholic.

Then to Nellie: "And you are Catholic, of course."

"No, I ain't—"

Judge Sullivan was standing behind her, in memory, correcting her English.

"—I'm not Catholic."

The priest's young eyes in the solemn, almost ashy gray face went from Nellie to Flora and back again. Most unusual.

"And the boy's father—?"

"He don't—doesn't—have a father."

The priest blushed.

"I mean—he's dead. His father was a Catholic—I ain't—his father was an altar boy."

That gave the priest more assurance.

"And the boy will be reared Catholic?"

Again he looked at the three of them and down at the boy and again at them.

Most unusual.

But he was fervent for another soul saved, saved by the Roman Catholic Church.

God works his wonders in many curious ways.

His first non-Catholic conquest!

"Yes," Nellie said, because Juan was nudging her and Big Flora was saying, "You know he will, chile."

"Fine!" Father Bill said, rubbing his hands together. "And may I ask . . . have you a middle name in mind?"

"Well," Nellie said, "if we're going through with this I want him named after the best friends he has and I have—" She held one hand before her and placed the index finger of the other on its index finger. "Judge—"

The priest beamed. "Oh, you mean Jude, the Christian apostle and saint who—"

"No, I mean Judge—" The index finger of her right hand moved to the next finger of her left hand: "—Maximiliano-Philip-Norman —" She had almost run out of fingers and she stopped. "That's what I want his name to be."

Father Bill cleared his throat. "Quite an unusual name, young lady!"

Nick said it to himself: Nick Judge Maximiliano Philip Norman Romano.

Gee, he liked that!

The young priest mumbled. He did some things around Nick's head. "Mother, why is he putting this greasy stuff on me?"

"Shhh!"

The priest mumbled. Nick kept looking up at his mother out of the corners of his eyes, the tip of his tongue sticking out the edge of his mouth and clenched as if it were glued there like a child's tongue to a frozen windowpane.

"Mother, why is he putting water on my head?"

"Shhh!"

Then they all mumbled together, all but Nick—

"I believe in God, the Father-Almighty, creator of heaven and earth, and in Jesus Christ, his son, our Lord, who was conceived of the Holy Ghost and born of the Virgin Mary . . . I believe in the Holy Ghost, the Holy Catholic Church, the communion of saints, the . . ."

Juan couldn't remember all the words and invented some interesting ones of his own. Big Florabelle sang them sonorously in her musical voice, not missing a word. Her smile was happy and motherly. Almost virginal. She looked like a big, fat, black angel.

And then it was over and they were all happy. Father Bill gave Nick a prayer book and a rosary. Father Bill escorted them to the front door of the church and shook hands with all of them. He leaned in his holy robes and kissed Nick on the forehead and Nick squirmed away. Father Bill shook hands again with Juan. "Come when you wish, Juan. Come to dinner. I know you will. And, remember, this is your house."

"I'll come if we can have some of that sacramental wine," Juan said, grinning.

But Father Bill was very happy over the saving of a soul and, grinning boyishly at Juan, said, "Maybe we will!"

And they were all walking along the dirty sidewalk of Roosevelt Road and Juan said, "Hi—godchild!" and punched Nick on the arm. "I'm your godfather!" He hugged Nick over to him.

21

The next day Max, with a secret grin on his face, went to Nellie's house.

Nick was making mud pies with the tops of two shoeshine cans. He was deeply absorbed in his play, and his bottom lip jutted out, his straight brown hair fell over his forehead down toward his small straight nose.

Max stood grinning at him. Max was all in blue and there was a white circle of cloth on his head. And now Nick saw him.

Max knelt down and Nick ran toward him. "Hi'ya, sport!" Max said, and lifted him up into his arms.

They went up the steps, between the black iron railings, Max carrying him; and Max pushed the door open with his foot.

He stood in the door in his navy outfit, grinning at Nellie.

"No, Max!" Nellie said.

"Yes!" Max said, still grinning. He set Nick down. "I haven't got much time. I just came to tell you good-bye."

"Max is going away for a while, honey," Nellie told Nick.

"Yeah, kid. But I'll see you!"

"Tell Max good-bye," Nellie said.

Nick held out his hand to shake. They shook hands. Then Max knelt down on one knee. "Ain't you got a kiss for your Uncle Max?"

"Sure, Uncle Max!"

Max held out his arms and kissed the boy. "For luck," he said, and his burly arms again enfolded the boy.

"For luck," Nick said.

"For luck," Nellie said, the tears running down her cheeks.

Then Max kissed her good-bye. Then Max said, "Take good care of our boy." And they could hear him running down the front steps, taking them two at a time.

She felt lonely—more alone than ever. She remembered Max's

warning about Frank. And she knew he was right. But she had let Frank come back. She was a woman. She was fearful of him, of something inside of him, something she didn't understand—something dark and evil, she was sure. But she let him come back.

22

Juan was at his usual pastime, that of walking the neighborhood to see what was happening.

A girl approached him. He knew her casually. She was a dark-brown-skinned girl about twenty years old, with a good body and regular features accentuated by a thin, straight nose, and if she had been white she would have been considered a very pretty girl.

She walked up to him. "Hello, Juan."

"Hi, Fran."

"Can you do me a favor?"

"Well, if I can help you, I'll do it."

"Well, will you lend me a quarter?"

"Yeah, I'll lend you a quarter."

"Thanks, Juan!"

" 'S all right."

He moved on down the sidewalk toward the Crystal Bar: I wonder about her. I see her hanging around the corner and I know most of these girls who hustle and all that and I have never seen her go away with anybody. She's always just in the tavern anda she's not built bad anda well, you know, I'm going to ask her one of these days, you know, to—if she wants to make some money, you know—

His face crinkled into a bronzed grin. Yeah, I'm going to ask her.

But he was ashamed to ask her because she seemed so different from the other girls.

Juan glanced back down the sidewalk at her: She never approaches no guy. She's always in there just talking to people but never approaches none of these guys. She never tries to catch a trick. I can't place it down.

So, walking along toward the tavern, Juan was wondering about her. Now I know her sister. Now you take Fran's sister, her and her old man, her husband, they did nine months in the City Workhouse for burglary. They turned to burglary to get money to buy dope with. They were using between sixty and a hundred dollars' worth a day between them. I wonder if Fran's on stuff. It's as loose around here as talcum powder.

Juan turned into the Crystal Bar, got a bottle of beer and carried it to a small table against the wall. He began counting. He counted six dope fiends in there. Six, I know of. In this little dump of a place.

The juke box was saying:

Ho-old me
Yes
Aaaand
Thrill me!
NEVAH!
NEVAH!
NEVAH!
Let me go . . .

Juan turned his beer bottle between the palms of his hands and watched: I knew some of these guys for a couple of years and I didn't even know they were on stuff and when I found out I was sure surprised.

He glanced around the bar at the girls hanging out there, looking for tricks, looking for money so they could get some H. Yeah, that's what they call it, H or Horse. Most of these girls around here, they drink—to a certain extent. Not to get drunk. Well, the only time they try to get drunk is when they can't get any money for anything else and they try to get that feeling off of them—that sickness. A real addict, he won't have nothing to do with whiskey. And sex, they ain't interested, really. Take some of these girls that I talked to who are out there hustling. When they get straight—really feeling good from stuff—they don't want to have nothing to do with no man because they get squared. They take off. They get high. And if they have something to do with a man they use all that up and get squared and when they get through then they need more dope. They don't have no more use for a man than regular whores. Less. They're just out there hustling to get money for a fix.

From the brilliantly lighted theater of the juke box Ruth Brown sang, with the orchestra backing her up in blue brass:

I can seeeeee
Eeeeeeevery-body's babe
I don't see mi-ne . . .

Three Negro couples danced, eyes sleepy, bodies clinging close together. The notes from the juke box matched their movements, notes that slithered out of the open lips of saxophones and clarinets, notes that seemed to copulate—and Ruth Brown sang:

Theeeeeeey're lovin' next doah
Theeeeeeey're lovin' up-staaaaairs
People in my house
Theeeeeeey're lovin' eeeeeeeverywhere . . .

Fran entered the bar and dropped her eyes away from Juan's face. She went to talk to a man and woman at a table, and sipped from a bottle of coke offered her.

A man at the bar said, "The Wolf was around today. He was holding a kite."

"A ounce!"

"A ounce!"

"She done dozed off good," Raggedy Bob said, pointing toward Big Florabelle where she sat leaned against the wall.

Juan got himself another bottle of beer: There are a lot of guys who are working every day. They just take enough to go to work and come back and take some at night so they can get up in the morning to go to work. They use enough to keep them going. They go to work like anybody else. You'd never know if you didn't know.

"Listen, gal," a loud, angry woman's voice shouted, "I'm going to turn you every way but loose if you don't stop messing in my business!"

"Aw, niggah!"

"Don't show me your backside, girl! That's all!"

:If you didn't know. You ask them why they ain't eating and they say they're not eating because they don't really want nothing to eat.

Dusty walked into the place. He had killed a couple of men. Everybody knew it. Nobody cared. Even the police knew it.

Juan drank: The places they hide the stuff. The kit. The needle. And then there's the snatch. What a wonderful hiding place!

At the bar a woman, drunk, was showing off. Her companion, a rather gentle man, tall, neatly dressed, said, "I'm going to have to spank her. Tomorrow you wouldn't think she was the same woman. When she gets mad she pulls her dress up. If she does I'm going to slap her."

Instead he leaned over and hugged her.

"I knew it wouldn't be long," she said.

Uncle Sam had his arm around Good-bye George's shoulders and they made their way, unevenly, toward Juan. Good-bye George's mop of kinky hair stood up in a coxcomb above his shiny forehead; it bushed out around the sides of his head and at the back like a lumpy ball of carelessly shaped moss. His thick lips were turned out in a perpetual pout and he had sad, sad eyes. About him there was a humorous sadness; even his drawling voice emphasized it. Around Uncle Sam's neck was a piece of string showing beyond the open collar of his shirt, which he stealthily concealed with his thumb.

They said hello to Juan. Good-bye George said it sadly, and added, "Man, Ah'm gettin' out of this big city, man. Ah'm goin' back to black-eyed peas and ham hock. Ah'm goin' to set me down to some grits and gravy and if Ah happen to be in New Orleans it's red beans and rice. Ah'm gettin' out o' this mean man's town."

Juan and Uncle Sam laughed.

It was said that he was called Good-bye George because he was always going home to Tennessee. Every week he planned it for Friday night. But every Friday night he was drunk.

"What's happening, Uncle Sam?" Juan asked.

"I'm feeling straight, man! I scored. Before I scored I made some bread."

He showed Juan the bread—a roll of bills carried in his trouser pocket.

They called him Uncle Sam not because he was old and had a little white beard but simply because he was white and preferred to hang around with Negroes, went to their pads to get charged up on Horse. He was a young blond boy of nineteen. He was a tough little bastard. Like the rest of them he'd do anything to get his fix. He had this beer-can opener on the string around his neck. He could get into your car with it faster than you could open it with your key. This was a good neighborhood, along Halsted Street, for it. A clothing district. There'd be dresses or pants locked up in cars before they were taken to a retail shop. That little side window of the car, that vent with the rubber guard securing it. The beer-can opener and a flick of the wrist. Then your arm down inside turning the door handle. Over on the North Side and Near North Side the squares sometimes left their suitcases or topcoats and fur coats in their cars. Just to go into a hotel for a minute. That minute was all he needed. Here, in this neighborhood, plenty of places where you could dump that stuff for good money and get your fix. He was a real junkie. A confirmed addict who took a high daily dosage. Only he and Extra Black Johnson could cabaret—have their morning and evening fix and then take some whenever they felt like taking off and really getting charged up.

"I'll buy you a beer—me, I don't want none," Uncle Sam said. "I'm feeling what I want to feel."

"Okay," Juan said: There's some other white guys who come around. Not very much though. They are white guys who come around but they just come to cop. To buy. There probably ain't any in their neighborhood. They can't get none so they come over here and get some and they go back to their neighborhood and take off. Uncle Sam, he's different.

Good-bye George nodded his sad head toward the fat, dozing figure leaning against the wall. "Big Florabelle's on stuff."

"No!" Juan said.

He was shocked.

"Yeah, she's hooked."

Day by day the neighborhood got one or another of them. It starts like anybody else you talk to on the street. They all go from smoking reefers to goof balls and then there's no more excitement so they turn to it. There's nowhere else to go.

At the bar the woman was still showing off. "He's forty-three," she said. "Black folks don't ever show up their age. He can't do no better than a sixty-nine-year-old-man can do."

"Anybody want to test?" he asked good-naturedly.

She said, "He's got that crazy wine up there to drink. Got thirty-five-cent wine. Drinking wine all night long."

In walked Extra Black Johnson. Extra Black Johnson came with yellow shoes, high-yellow shoes, hand-stitched necktie, perfume, a silk shirt, purple, and a diamond ring on his finger. His eyes flashed in that black face like white semaphores. They were big and popped, the lids slow, lazy, like Extra Black Johnson when he slithered across the dance floor in a slow, lazy, dirty shuffle, bony behind poised, mouth puffed out comically.

Big Flora, awakening, shouted in her large, melodious voice, "Look who done flown the coop! Look who done broke out of jail, you-all!"

They crowded around him in childish excitement.

"You look fine, man! You did it cold turkey, man?"

"Cold turkey, hell! Ah got mah supply every day. Got mah fix every day right there in jail!"

"Whooeee!" Big Flora exclaimed.

"Them emeffing guards is bringing it in in fountain pens, selling it like hot dogs at the ball game," Extra Black Johnson announced.

"They musta had you working out in the sun—" the yellow woman said. "You is blacker than ever!"

Extra Black Johnson flashed his eyes and his wide cut of a grin. "Blacker the berry, sweeter the juice," he said. This made him cackle with laughter and he did a little jig to the bar. They followed, crowding around him.

At the bar he took off his white panama with its flashy band and elaborately mopped his bald black head with a red silk handkerchief. More elaborately he took a hundred-dollar bill from his pocket.

"Whooeee!" Big Florabelle exclaimed.

"Buy you-all a drink," Extra Black Johnson said, "that is, all what drinks." Again the big grin. And he let the hundred-dollar bill float down from between his thumb and forefinger to the bar. "Money has no home," he announced philosophically.

Those who drank were ordering good Scotch at Extra Black Johnson's insistence.

"Man," Extra Black Johnson said. "Nutmeg! Now what do you-all use nutmeg for? Cakes. Sweet stuff. Ain't that right? Well, man, in there in that jail they use it for kicks. Man, nutmeg was selling for from seventy-five cents to *three dollars* a can, man! You know how they use it? They cook it in a spoon—just like H—cook it in a spoon with water. Then they eats it. Then"—his eyes rolled comically— "they take a chaser of a dry spoon of nutmeg. Me, man, I has money and I had that old Horse every day. Man, we used to cabaret in there!"

Extra Black Johnson paused in his recital, looking around at his listeners, and then said, like a benevolent pastor who is offering blessing, "Let me buy you-all another drink"—his wicked smile— "all who drinks."

The drinks came.

"One of them guards," Extra Black Johnson said, "was a tier-to-tier peddler. Sure 'nough. That were when I hooked up with him. I'm the contact man on the outside now, man. You think I'm dressed up now?" He pulled at his good clothes. He cackled again and, throwing up one hand, its white palm flashing, did a slow-footed jig. "Man," he said, "I'm sending stuff into that jail, wholesale, by them guards right now!" And, remembering tenderly, his eyelids shut down over his big popped eyes. "Man, we sure used to cabaret in there!"

"Let's go cabaret now," Uncle Sam said.

"Sure thing, white boy," Extra Black Johnson said. "You's all invited up to my pad." Again the wicked smile. "That is, all who don't drink."

Ruth Brown said:

> Ho-old me
> Yes
> Aaaand
> Thrill me!
> NEVAH!
> NEVAH!

NEVAH!
Let me go . . .

Raggedy Bob, Uncle Sam, a couple of the hustlers and several others followed Extra Black Johnson out. And last of all, Big Florabelle.

After still another beer Juan also left.

Behind him:

NEVAH!
NEVAH!
Let me go . . .

The woman and her husband were waiting for him outside his shop. He had known them since he was a kid.

"We got kicked out of our rooming house," the woman said. "We ain't got no place to go."

"Can we stay in your back room for the night? Maybe two nights?" the man asked apologetically.

"Well, okay," Juan said.

"How much will you charge us?" the man asked.

"Well, give me a couple of dollars."

And they didn't have any money.

"Okay," Juan said. "Okay, come on in."

"Maybe we can pay you tomorrow," the man said.

They picked their few things up off the sidewalk and entered the second-hand shop.

"There's no light back there," Juan said. "You'll have to take a lamp in there."

They took the smoking, soot-shaded kerosene lamp and in their old and frayed clothes went into one of the two rear rooms, the man again profusely thanking Juan.

By looking at him he was just average. You meet a man on the street and it could be him.

Yeah. I've known them just about all my life. How old are they? I wouldn't know. They're not young. All I know is that he's been on stuff for about thirty years. I know they used to deal but I don't know if they're dealing now.

Juan sat in front of his shop, feet up against the plate glass, hands working at an old alarm clock he was hoping to repair and sell.

He went into the back room to get some oil.

He had forgotten they were there and they had forgotten to lock the door.

They sat at the table in the dim circle of the lamp. They had bought a piece—a part of an ounce—of heroin with the last money they had.

On the table in front of them was a broken length of mirror and upon it was piled the small amount of heroin. At the man's elbow was scattered a couple of dozen capsules.

You can buy capsules by the thousands in any drug store. Anybody can buy empty capsules.

On the smooth face of the mirror the man had dumped the little pile of dull white heroin. Like baking powder. Like soda. He had a razor blade between his fingers and was chopping it up to get all the lumps out of it. He chopped it up real fine and they figured how many pills they could get out of it and they started cutting, dividing it into little piles. Dull white on the smooth mirror's surface. And they filled the caps. He and his wife each took a cap and breathed into it, put a hot, moist breath of air into it, and then, half filling it, closed the cap and shook it until it looked as if it was filled. If you're a good capper and cap it yourself and sell part of it and use the rest yourself you can double your money. You can keep your habit up.

Anybody can buy empty capsules.

You can buy needles.

You can buy eyedroppers.

Anybody can. You don't have to give reasons. No questions asked.

So they're making a little money, cheating a little to keep their habit up.

Juan walked in. They looked up, startled. Then they relaxed. "Oh, he's all right," the man reassured his wife. "He knows what's happening."

So they just kept right on about their business, capping, cheating a little, keeping their habit up.

The circle of frayed lamplight glowed yellow. The innocent-looking white powder gave no reflection. From lamplight and mirror, shadows fell across the room.

23

"Frank," she said, "I've got a headache." She put the fingers of one hand up into the roots of her long blond hair and, with her elbow on the table, leaned her forehead against the palm of her hand. "One of the worst headaches I ever had."

Frank's double lip tightened in secret smile. He had been waiting for this. Had helped the headache along. It was going to cost him money but he'd get what he wanted whenever he wanted it. Who she think she is?

"I got something that'll fix it," he said.

He put the odorless, dull white powder, as harmless-looking as baking soda, on a dollar bill and held it out under her nose. "Here, sniff this."

She looked from the dollar bill to him, curiously, almost suspiciously.

"It's like powdered aspirin," he said. "It works faster."

She looked up gratefully, her deep eyes pleading. "You do care for me, don't you, Frankie?" Her voice was like that of a child's.

"Sure. Sniff it—"

"I mean besides—besides—just—" Her hand gestured toward the bed.

"Sure."

She lifted her face away from the dollar bill. "You know, in all my life"—and her eyes teared a little—"nobody ever really loved me. I don't think even—" but she would not say Nick's father.

"Sniff it up, baby."

One tear was rolling down her cheek. Her head hurt awfully. "You know, the only thing I love is my little Nicky— I don't mean —" She pushed back her hair from her burning, throbbing forehead. "I don't mean—"

"Sniff it, Nellie."

"—that I don't care for you— I do—but—"

"Yeah, baby. Sniff it and we'll go to bed— I mean when you feel better—"

She began to sniff, her eyes looking up at him gratefully.

"Sniff it," he said.

And she sniffed it.

"All," he said.

And all.

24

And then Fran asked him for a bigger favor. She wanted three dollars.

"No, you can't have three dollars," Juan said; he grinned at her and let out what he had been thinking about, "But if you want to earn them—I'll let you have them."

She turned her dark brown face up to him. She was ashamed. "I don't want to do that with you, Juan." She was actually ashamed. She had a feeling she liked him. Slowly she shook her head in emphasis. "I never want to turn no tricks with you, Juan. I'd"—she lowered her head—"feel funny doing that."

He saw her hanging around the corner a lot after that. And he got on this speaking friendship with her. And he noticed that she always hung around and whenever she had some time she'd be talking to him. So one time he asked her what the score was.

"I go for you, Juan," she said, half turning her head away. "I don't know—I never went for nobody like I go for you."

So Juan said, pleased and proud of her attraction to him though he was, "Well, there's nothing happening, baby. I'm married. I can't give you what you want. But anything else you want, favors, something, if I can help you I'll do it."

Fran said, "Well, I'm not looking for anything. Money or anything. I just like your friendship."

"Well, that's good enough for me," Juan said.

Fran twisted her fingers together and turned to face him on the Maxwell Street stand against which they were leaning. "How about this girl—Alice Mae?—what is she to you?"

"Nothin'. Just a good friend."

"No. It's more than that." Fran stood and, turning away, said, "You're real tight with her."

"No. I'm not tight with her."

"Well, I heard different."

"Well, whatever you heard, there's nothing."

"Okay, Juan." She put her hand against his. "If you don't mind I'd like to know if you got anybody you're tight with."

"No," Juan said. "In my line of business I can't afford to be tight with anybody. Because if I was tight with anybody they'd come around. They'd always want a handout. Or they'd take it for granted that I was making some money and they'd always be asking for some. It's better that I don't have no one—": Anyway, I got a wife I have to support and, man! I don't hardly make enough off of my second-hand store.

"Well, that's good enough for me." She sounded as if she were lonely. As if she didn't have anyone to really talk to nice.

She and Juan saw more and more of each other. They sat on the Maxwell Street stands talking, or at his shop, or at a table in the Crystal Bar playing the juke box.

Everybody knew they were getting tight.

Big Black again humorously warned, "Niggahs got razors, Juan! That gal's going to slice you. That Alice Mae. Colored gals don't let no man get away with that two-timing stuff. And Fran's got herself a old man—a old man, man."

And Salvatore, the barber, with his shop on Newberry, standing in the doorway in his white apron, his handlebar mustachios waxed to points, just smiling knowingly every time Juan went past. He knew everything that was happening. If a fly walked up the side of the Wrigley Building he'd see it. Just his smile and, "Hello, Juan."

Again they sat on a Maxwell Street stand talking and kicking their heels against the bottom support.

The middle-aged man walked past them, glancing at her for a moment. Her eyes cut along the sidewalk in his direction. "I gotta go." She hopped down off the stand. She looked scared.

Fran caught up with the man. He was a short yellow Negro with a big-featured, freckled face, and a portly middle over which a vest was fastened. He wore a hard-brimmed straw hat. Beneath the hat was a hard, shiny roll of fat at the base of his neck.

Looking at them Juan said to himself: Ugly sonofabitch! Juan stared down at the sidewalk: He's dumb but he's in business. You couldn't call a guy in business dumb. He sells ice and coal. So that's the guy.

They were arguing in the middle of the sidewalk and he was gesticulating angrily with his hands; hers were pleading.

Juan watched for a moment longer: Well, it's none of my business. He got up and went down to his shop.

It wasn't an hour before Fran came in.

She glanced at him, and away. "I might as well tell you, Juan. I got an old man. We ain't married but I got a kid by him. The kid's a year old—more—and my mother takes care of him."

"I knew it all the time," Juan said. "Plenty people told me."

She moved close to Juan. She wanted to tell him about it. She did: "I was sixteen at the time . . ."

She was born here in Chicago and had a good upbringing and she was fast.

"By fast, Juan, I mean—what they call fast—I started going out with boys when I was twelve . . ."

She had gone through the third year of high school and had a pretty good education. Beyond that she went to a beautician's college and got a diploma for it.

Her father was a penny-ante politician on the South Side, a precinct captain, and he even owned a restaurant and tavern. That was where she met the old man she had mentioned to him.

"He was a gambler, Juan, and he used to make a lot of money. Lord, he used to come in and give me twenty, twenty-five dollars . . ."

And that kept on. And then her mother said, "Girl, you're crazy if you don't go with him! He's got a *lot* of money. He gives you clothes and all. *Good* clothes. You ain't gonna git nowhere going with these pretty yellow-skinned nigger boys around here!"

"Yeah," Fran said. "What I got to lose?"

So she went with him.

"So the money swayed me, Juan, it turned my head and I was used to this money. That's how it happened, Juan, that's how it all started . . ."

The word "it" seemed important and she tried to swallow it back.

That same night she came back to Juan's shop. He had some stuff to get out and was working late. The black plate glass was like the painting of a realistic artist, with, reflected there, the row of shabby houses across the street, a drunk staggering by, a stray dog curled under a lamppost, a peppering of dimly seen stars in the sky.

Fran was all dressed up.

"Where you been?" Juan asked.

"Oh, I just went to the South Side—went to a night club."

"Well, what are you doing here? Why don't you go home?"

"I don't know. I just came. I wanted to talk to you."

"Okay."

Juan closed his shop and went back and started to talk to her.

When she was ready to leave he made a grab at her as if he were going to kiss her. He could see that she was all for it. But he dropped his arms to his sides: No, this is going too far.

He walked with her toward the door. And he could see, sense, that she had never had anything like real affection shown to her: Maybe this old guy does like her in a way but he never told her anything like that. A feeling of pity took him.

At the door he said, "Look, I'm going home. I'll walk you home."

He didn't know where she was living and had often tried to take her home but she would never let him.

"No," she said.

Juan glanced at her: There's something funny about it. Something I can't figure.

He watched until she got to the corner and turned. Then Juan, detective, locked his store and started following her.

She went down Maxwell and turned off at one of the side streets.

A side street with one-story frame houses and rotten wooden basements. She went down a broken stairway leading into a gash in the ground: a basement.

No, she can't live here. This can't be the goddamn place where she's staying.

He hung around, curious about her, waiting for her to come out.

Well, maybe she just went down there for a while. Just to see somebody.

Juan stood on one foot and then the other. He kept waiting. And then he started laughing at himself—just like a goddamn schoolboy waiting on a corner for a date! Jesus! Am I getting hot for her?

He waited for more than an hour.

She didn't come out.

25

"Have you got some more of that powder?"

"Sure, baby."

"That made me feel real good."

It's costing me money to put her on it. But when I get tired of her I'll dump her.

"That made me feel real good," Nellie repeated.

"Here, baby."

"Real good—"

26

"Who started you on it?" Juan asked bitterly, when he found out Fran was on stuff.

"Who started me on it? Nobody started me on it." She was silent a moment, searching for origins. "I had all this money and nothing to do with it—nothing to do with myself—and I started to smoke reefers—"

Juan lighted a cigarette and handed it to her.

"Well, things went bad for Jake—that's my old man. He fouled up. He lost everything gambling. That's why he's selling ice now. Anyway, I used to smoke reefers and play juke boxes and have people come up and have parties at my sister's flat—anda—pretty soon they all 'joined the ranks.' "

136

Fran paused. She smiled bitterly. "Nobody started me. There was a bunch of people. They were having a party. A lot of guys came from the West Side—around Lake Street." She paused, threw her head back and exhaled smoke. "A lot of guys, and they were on stuff. I was wondering, and I got high on reefers and smoked more reefers and they didn't have no effect and I used to hear those guys saying how nice they felt, so I said, 'Well, let me try it.' "

Again the bitter smile, distorting her face; and she was silent for a long time. Also she could feel the urge for a fix edge its way along her nerves.

She said, "So I told them, 'Let me try it.' They said, 'No! Don't fool with it, gal! Are you crazy?' but I told them, 'Well, I'll try it just one time.' "

She looked back into the present.

She smiled at Juan. Reaching out her hand she clutched at his, her nails biting in. "I tried it one time."

Her fingers tightened into Juan's hand: I need a fix.

Slowly she relaxed her hand and drew it away.

She shrugged. "And here I am."

27

She was shaking. Her nose was running. Her eyes watered. She leaned against the doorway for a moment and then entered.

"Hello, Fran," Juan said.

She couldn't speak. She pointed to the back room.

He nodded.

She went in there and closed the door.

From her body she took her kit: eyedropper, needle, the capsule of H, all wrapped together in cellophane and secreted there inside her body.

After a while she came out.

"I'll feel better in a little while," she said.

He looked up at her from the chair he was mending. There was a great pity in him.

"Look, Juan," she said, "stay away from it. If you ever try anything like that I'll shoot you before you do." She sat down. "It's no good. It's bad enough I'm trying to fight it off."

She sat unevenly in her chair. She began to nod. Her cigarette fell from between her lips and into her lap. Juan retrieved it and snuffed it out.

And later she was more normal.

"You know, Juan," she said, "remember that time that you made like you were going to kiss me?"

"Yeah," Juan said.

"Why didn't you kiss me?" Again the sadness was in her voice.

"I don't know, Fran. Just one of those things, I guess."

Fran said, "I was waiting for you to kiss me. I'd never known anybody that I wanted to kiss. As a matter of fact I've never kissed anybody—not even Jake. He's never kissed me in the way that you would call a kiss. If he wants anything he says, 'Well, I'm ready!' and that's it, see."

The pity, the yearning, that indefinable something stood in a lump in Juan's throat.

"I will now," he said.

He turned out the lights and locked the front door.

They were tight.

28

"I gotta have more. I know there's something in it. Some dope or something. But I gotta have more."

"Sure. First let's go to bed."

"And you will give me more?"

"Yeah. More. Let's go to bed."

"All right, Frankie."

29

"It's better with a needle, baby. You get a quicker lift. But in your ass. Ain't no marks to show. No tiger stripes. And you don't burn the lining out of your nose."

"Yes, Frankie!"

He prepared it. Showed her how to shoot herself.

 *weavers of the night*

30

He liked school. He was nine years old and in the fourth grade. He was shy with the other kids. In school, he liked the drawing class best of all. He got lonesome from the tick-tock of the clock. Mother would see that he was in bed. Mother would say, "I'll be back at twelve o'clock." And he'd wake up. He'd feel for her in the bed. And she wasn't there and he'd hear the clock . . .

tick-tock . . . tick-tock . . .

In school he got such good marks that every time he brought his report card home, his mother said she almost went broke. His mother was sometimes sick now. She would have headaches or say she was dizzy. She didn't eat much. And she didn't keep her jobs very long. Sometimes, when he was in bed, he would see her just sitting in a chair, not really sleeping, but looking like she was sleeping. Her head would go down, down, down, then up again. And she wasn't the clean, sweet-smelling mother she used to be. Her clothes sometimes looked bad. She wasn't the mother she used to be. My mother drinks, he told himself. It made him feel bad.

And once his mother had hurt him real bad and he would never forget it. Frank was in the room with his shirt off and hair all over his chest like an animal. He had his mother by the wrists when Nick walked in. He was dragging his mother toward the other room. His mother was saying, "First, Frank—first—"

"No," Frank said. "Then you won't want to."

"No, Frank . . . no . . . no . . ."

He was dragging his mother and Nick rushed at him, grabbing, too, trying to pull his mother away. Frank let go and his mother had Nick by the shoulders. She twisted him around. She slapped him in the face, once, twice, three times.

He ran out of the house. He sat in the areaway between the two houses all afternoon. He didn't go home until after dark.

His mother didn't even notice that he hadn't been home. And this hurt worse than the slaps.

She sat at the table looking like she was asleep or about to go to sleep.

Phil and Max had been to war and back. Norman had been classified 4F. And now the three of them came together again. With much grinning, and pounding of backs, and a few drinks together in the Loop, they returned to that easy, joking, cursing camaraderie that they had shared.

"How's Judge?" Max asked.

"How's Nellie? How's our boy?" Phil asked.

"Let's go find them!" Max said.

Norm's hand, the fingernails lacquered with clear polish, moved from the side of his cheek to the table. He looked at his hand for a moment. "Judge is older," he said.

"Nellie and the kid?" Max asked.

"Nick's fine." He paused.

"Yeah, and Nellie?"

"Drinking."

They decided to go see Judge Sullivan first. They went to West Madison Street and found him sitting at a table in the Long Bar, his shoebox in front of him, a bottle of beer at his elbow, one shoe eased off under the table, a cane leaning against the back of his chair. He looked up, surprised, pleased, his eyes dancing in his aged face. He did look older and more tired. But his fingers closed like a young man's on theirs and his slaps across their backs were hearty, Max wincing and saying, "Take it easy, Judge! Just because I was in the war—"

And Judge Sullivan, "Well! Well! So the young warriors have come back with their shields! Well! Well! This, young men, calls for a special celebration! Of course"—lifting his arms he let his booming laugh explore the ceiling—"I will have to put it on my tab—*if* I have one here."

"We're loaded," Phil told him. "Navy pay."

They drank in their merriment. And all edged away from the question. They had several rounds. Finally Judge Sullivan said, "Have you seen Nellie?"

"No."

Judge Sullivan turned and called for more drinks and his mustache came away white from the suds.

They couldn't go on forever without asking.

"How are they?" Phil asked.

"Nick is fine," Judge Sullivan said. "I see him every day." He lit a cigarette and, like a young man with young men, said, trying to change the subject, pivot away from it to somewhere else, "Jesus! Look at the legs on that *broad!*" He said "broad" the way they did, mocking himself in the saying, and leaned way out from the table to get a good look.

"Yeah! Yeah!" Max said. "And Nellie?"

Judge Sullivan was suddenly sad-faced and older-looking.

"Fellows, I'm worried about her."

They finished their drinks and, without saying, all knew they were going to see Nellie and Nick. Judge Sullivan put his shoebox under his arm and groped for his cane. The eyes of Max and Phil fastened on the cane, and Judge Sullivan, seeing them, winked extravagantly and said, "Just an affectation, fellows, just an affectation."

They headed for North Clark Street.

She was there. She was in the Shillelagh Club. Her hair hung over her wrists and her head was almost on the table. "Nellie . . . Nellie . . ." Judge said, shaking her gently.

She came out of it partially. She looked up; and after a while, through glazed eyes, recognized him. "Oh . . . hello, Judge." Then she saw the others. "Hello, boys." It was a faraway greeting. "You're back." There were burns on her dress where cigarettes had fallen.

They sat in stunned silence and embarrassment. Max said, "You want a drink, Nellie?" and they all cut their eyes at him; but he didn't know what else to say.

"No . . . no, thanks."

It seemed as if she was falling asleep again.

"How's our boy?" Phil asked.

"Where's Nick?" Max asked.

"Home . . . in . . . bed."

"Nellie, don't you want to go home?" Judge Sullivan said.

"Yes . . . I guess . . . so . . ."

They led her home. She walked as a somnambulist walks.

31

Sergeant Bill Forbes slid into the seat of the car next to his partner. Vice Squad. It sounded exciting and adventurous—but the monotony of it. Jesus! The awful monotony of it. Night after night. Same routine. Same procedure. Same sifting of the dregs of the city. He slumped down in the seat and sighed and he and his partner watched with keen eyes the people who walked the sidewalk under the night sky in the broken-down neighborhood.

Yeah, the most important thing about working on Vice is its monotonous routine. Arresting women for prostitution. He sighed again. You go along and you get hustled by them and taken to the flat and your partner comes in afterwards and you announce that you're police officers and take them to the station and that's that. That's routine.

Fact is, when you and your partner drive down the street in your car, by instinct you get to know a prostitute by her walk, and they're not all bad women. The current thing is: 'I got a baby daughter over in Michigan and she's got to live.' But the idea is that in their walk there's something—and in their attitude—that shows through.

He stopped thinking, abruptly. His eyes had a penetrating look. He and his partner bumped elbows and they were on the trail of another one.

Another. They watched the girl hustle a trick into a basement at LaSalle and North Avenue. They trailed her in their usual way.

When she was letting the man out they flashed their stars and entered, motioning the man inside too.

There was an older woman in the room. She had all the appearances of an addict. When she saw the stars and the policemen she broke down completely, crying hysterically and saying, "That's my daughter. She ain't done nothing wrong. I was here all the time."

Sergeant Forbes looked at the girl. Perhaps twenty-five, she looked forty. Her wrinkled skin and the whites of her eyes were an ugly yellow. In her short-sleeved dress, her pipelike arms were revealed.

The veins had collapsed and there were ugly marks on her arm where the needle had sucked and vomited its venom. On one arm there was a puffed, pus-filled carbuncle, its several openings like the yellow eyes of some weird insect.

"We ain't done nothing! Nothing!" the older woman screamed tearfully.

Quietly, without speaking, Sergeant Forbes and his partner began searching the apartment. They found the needle over a partly opened closet door.

The hysterical crying of the mother brought the landlady down from upstairs, a kimono thrown over her nightgown, her gray hair wildly disarrayed. "I don't tolerate things like this in my house," she said firmly. "I want them out of here. I been trying to get them out of here but they won't leave. Take them with you—"

"Just a minute, lady—" Forbes said.

"—Take them all to jail."

The man who had been hustled leaned against the wall and nervously fidgeted with a cigarette.

"—Just a minute, lady," Sergeant Forbes said again, "these people. They look so thin and run-down—"

"Them people," the landlady said, "have lived on nothing more than tomato juice they get at the Marquis Restaurant."

And the door opened and the father stepped inside.

"They're always out making contacts for dope," the landlady said. "Do you think I want that in my house?" And now she, too, was crying hysterically. "Almost every half-hour," she said, blowing her nose noisily, "they're out prostituting themselves—*mother and daughter*—" She flung herself at the mother and started shaking her. "Bitch! Bitch!" she screamed. Forbes' partner separated them.

Forbes began to question the father. The two older women wailed away noisily. The daughter stood stoically. The hustled trick nervously lighted another cigarette.

"What do you do—what kind of work?" Forbes asked the father.

He was selling spouts for whiskey bottles to tavern keepers so that the bottles wouldn't overflow and would give an exact measurement every time.

"Yeah," the father said, sighing, settling it, "we're all junkies."

Sergeant Forbes washed up to go off night duty. He couldn't get that wretch's face out of his mind. The daughter, diseased and dying.

Whores, poor devils! But this. This.

He rubbed his wet face into the rough towel. He could feel more useful as a responsible citizen tracing it—not the poor devils them-selves, stuck with it like flies on flypaper. But the source—the pushers—the peddlers—the source—

He asked for a transfer to the Narcotics Squad.

32

Max, his curly black hair falling over his brown forehead, held three cigarettes in his mouth. He struck a match and lit them one after the other. Then he handed one to Judge Sullivan, one to Phil, and kept one for himself. He grinned at Phil. Then he said to Judge Sullivan, "Say Judge, how'd you like to go to the whorehouse with us?"

Judge Sullivan's eyes moved back and forth under his shaggy brows; then he said, "Now, if someone of some standing asked me that—but—"

They left Judge and started for their destination. They saw Norm on the stool at a restaurant counter and went in. "They haven't any beer here, ain't it?" Max said; so all three of them went to a tavern. Norm looked around at the young men sitting at the bar. He lit a cork-tipped cigarette and his attention often drifted away from Max and Phil.

"We've gotta go soon," Max said.

"Where are you going?" Norm asked.

"You don't want to go where we're going," Phil said.

"To the whorehouse," Max said emphatically.

Norm flushed a little. He sipped his beer; then again his eyes glanced toward the bar.

"How is it you never went for me?" Phil said.

"Tee-hee," Max said.

"Why, we've always been friends. Just friends," Norm said.

"Yeah," Phil said, "and goddamn it, I like you, you bastard!" He pounded him on the shoulder.

Max swelled out his chest, which was broad and deep, without effort, lifted his arms like the posed models in *Physical Culture* magazine, puffed out his cheeks, scowled, then grunt-growled in a heavy masculine way, "What about me? I'm"—snort! he pulled in air through his nose—"a real he-man."

"You're not my type, Max."

This was not quite true. Once, flushing, Norm had asked.

"I don't go that," Max had said. "If you like what you're doing, stick with it. Get someone who goes it. Get someone on your side."

146

They had become friends.

And sometimes, to tease Norman, Max would call him Sub-Norman or Sub-Normal.

Nevertheless they remained friends, though there were times when Max felt disgust for him deep inside; there were times when Norm left them to pursue his uncharted way. Times when he didn't see them or Nick for weeks, but followed his own wandering from bar to bar, seeking, seeking, paying if necessary. Guilt would come. Guilt would ride him as a horse sometimes rides the rider. Then the fever hit again. And guilt. But need. Max would speak his disgust to Phil, and Phil would say, "They ain't all bad, Max. Live and let live."

They now had a couple more bottles of beer, Max drinking from the bottle as was his custom. Then they got ready to go.

"I'll walk a way with you," Norm said.

Outside, Phil said to Norm, "Where are you going? To the Light-house?"

"Yes."

Norm turned toward Division Street and the bar called the Light-house.

"Good hunting!" Max called after him.

They walked down Huron Street. Nick was sitting on the top step, his elbows on his knees, his chin on his small fists, his head down. The lamppost light threw his shadow in a long splinter down the steps and onto the grimy sidewalk. He saw them and, getting up quickly, quickly came down the steps to them.

"Hi, Nick!" they said.

"Hello." It was a small voice, and sad.

"Where's your mother?"

"I don't know."

"She ain't home?"

"Where are you going?" Nick asked.

"Ah—for a walk."

"Can I come with you?"

"Well—look, kid—"

Max scratched his head until the curly black hair stood up. He and Phil exchanged glances.

"Ah—ah—" Phil said, "look, kid, we gotta go somewhere—"

"Somewhere special," Max said.

"Look—we'll see you, huh?"

"Can't I go?" Small-voiced. Sad-voiced.

"Not this time."

"Aw hell—!" they said, and they both started to give up their project and stay with him.

But the urge was upon them. They said they *had* to go and they'd see him.

When they were almost a block down the street, he followed them.

When they came out, Max with a little mustache of beaded perspiration on his upper lip from effort, Nick sat on the curb waiting for them. "Hello," Nick said. He moved in between them and took their hands.

He walked down the sidewalk between them.

In the bar called the Shack, Nellie sat with Frank, and his cold eyes looked at her vacantly as she spoke. "I guess I'm stuck with you and I don't like it," she whined. "You know you've got me hooked. You've got me hooked good."

Frank pointed to her glass of beer and she picked it up; he lifted his to his lips while his eyes glanced stealthily along the bar and at the neighboring tables. He nodded toward the door in a let's go gesture and, obediently, she stood up. He followed her out. "I just wait around for you," she whined, "until you show up. Sometimes I have to—well, you know—"

She walked unevenly. Her nose was running a little and there was water under her eyes. Not tears, though. But as if she might have a cold.

"I've got a headache, Frank," she said.

He walked a little behind her and on the wrong side of the street. When they got near the alley he said, "Hey!" She halted unevenly. "Gimme your pocketbook." He opened it and dropped something inside. Then he turned and walked away from her.

The four of them were all Nick seemed to have now. He was with them as much as he could be. In restaurants, at the show. They were always good to him. Only once Phil had yelled at him. It was after the show at the Chicago Theater and when they were having sodas at Walgreen's, with Max saying, "Jesus! I'd like to have a beer, ain't it?" Phil had his right hand on the table, spread out palm down. Between the thumb and the first finger in the fleshy part of the hand there was tattooed a little blue cross with two marks over it. Nick put his hand out and felt the tattoo.

"All right, kid!" Phil said angrily. And he put his thumb up over his first finger, hiding the tattoo.

"All right!"

But Phil didn't mean it. Nick knew he didn't.

Norm didn't have a house and Phil didn't either, but Nick's

mother said yes when he asked if he could sleep at Max's house—and so he did one night. Max had nice sisters, and he ate fried beans with cheese and bacon skin in them and flour tortillas and drank a lot of pop. His mother said yes too when he asked to stay one night at the flophouse Judge lived in, and that was exciting, with the chicken wire over the bed and the lights and noises from West Madison Street, but the bed was so small the two of them could hardly fit and Judge snored. His mother said yes to almost everything now. She just seemed to want to be left alone. He wished it was like it used to be between him and his mother.

He wanted terribly to be wanted. He idealized the four of them, Judge, Phil, Norm and Max. He followed them around, waiting outside taverns, poolrooms, whorehouses, bookie joints for them.

And each night that he was with them, they walked him home. Right to the steps and waited until they saw the light come on inside.

He'd go in.

You go to the house and there's no mother there. You don't know where she went.

33

Lee was the kid he liked best at school. Lee had transferred from some other school and they were in seventh grade together. Lee had a shrunken right arm; it was drawn up as if he were leaning on a table with it or had it in a sling. The hand was turned down and a little crooked and it looked something like a claw but you never let yourself think that. When he combed his hair with one hand, you acted like you didn't see. With the book of matches, he bent a match down and struck it by rubbing his thumb along with it, just lifting the thumb in time not to be burned and then lifted the broken match to his cigarette. He was big and husky and it was too bad about his arm.

Lee couldn't play baseball with the fellows in the school playground but he used to sit on the sidelines and watch them. That first day Nick went over, kind of ashamed, and sat next to him. They didn't say anything for a while. Then Lee said, almost as if he was going to cry, "Why don't you go play?"

"I don't like to play."

And it was true. He didn't like sports. He had a crazy idea he wanted to be an artist. Everything in school was crazy or keen. Everything good was keen. He had won first prize in his grammar school for his pictures two years in a row. Last year one was even in a grammar and high school exhibit they had at the Art Institute.

"Why?" Lee asked.

"I don't know."

"I can play checkers good," Lee said.

"I like to draw," Nick said.

"I know that," Lee said. "You're pretty good, ain't you?"

"I don't know."

They became friends. Lee would come over and they would both sit at the oilcloth-covered table with pieces of drawing paper and draw. Maybe the building across the street. Maybe something they made up in their heads. After a while Lee was pretty good. And with his left hand too!

If Nick's mother was there, if she wasn't drunk, Nick would think, she would fix them things like hot chocolate and bring home a cake or some cookies. Sometimes she even made spaghetti for them because she knew he liked it.

Nick and Lee played checkers. They took long walks. They never said much on those long walks, just walked along feeling good to be together. They both were kind of sad, Nick guessed. He knew he was. His mother. But I love her. No, I hate her. How can she do this to me? Sometimes thinking about it, thinking about her drinking, his eyes would kind of water-up.

Nick went over to Lee's house with him. Lee's father was a skinny, intelligent-looking guy not yet old. He had a pasty face with eyes that were always bloodshot and a little sandy-colored mustache. He had long, tobacco-stained fingers. There was always a cigarette clenched tightly, nervously, in between the tobacco stains. His snappy clothes were shabby now.

Lee said, "My old man and my mother are separated."

The house was always upset. The beds never made. The sink and the sink board were filled with dishes piled one into the other, with chop bones, pieces of eggs and greasy uneaten fried potatoes dried into them. Sometimes Lee's old man did the cooking but most of the time Lee had to do it. Every ashtray in the place was filled with twisted butts. On the table were racing forms. And on the table, on the sideboard, on top of the stove, by the side of the bed, were whiskey bottles, half filled and empty. Some lay on their sides.

"My old man gets drunk and blows his check," Lee said.

The air was fetid. It was sickly and thick with the old smell of stale cigarette smoke and strong whiskey fumes. The windows were pulled down; the shades were always drawn.

Lee said, "I think he used to be a gangster."

When Lee's old man got drunk he'd curse and wander around the house stumbling into things. When he went to sleep it was all right. Lee would pull off his shoes and, with Nick's help, roll him onto the bed. Here, with his old man, Lee wasn't like he was at school when he was watching the other boys play ball. He was somebody here.

They'd even undress Lee's old man and pull the covers over him. When they undressed him he mumbled little protesting mumbles. His hair would be damp blond strings on the pillow. His mustache would be frowzy and bristling. His mouth drooled a little. Sweat burst out of him, all over his face and neck. Even the sweat smelled of booze.

Sometimes, when they got him in and the hard electric light was all over his face, his strings of damp hair, his hot flushed cheeks, Lee would push the hair back in place, combing it gently with the fingers of his good hand, and say, affectionately, "My old man!"

Nick watched: I wish I could feel about my mother like that.

"My mother knows he gets drunk all the time," Lee said. "That's why she left him."

A couple of times they went, shamedfaced, through his pockets. He never had anything.

When he had one of his talking and crying jags on, it was awful. He'd stagger around the house like he was blind, bumping into things, knocking over chairs, laughing and crying at the same time. He'd stagger around with his shirt off and his pants open. Sometimes without any clothes on.

All he'd want was a drink, jush another lil' drink.

Lee didn't pay any attention.

But Lee's old man was a swell guy when he was sober. Over there you could smoke. He'd joke with you while his sober hands shook and his sober mouth twitched. And, when he had money, he'd give them cigarettes. Whole packages.

Today he gave them each a pack of Luckies and, with a repentant face that couldn't look at Lee, he went around the house emptying ashtrays, gathering up dirty dishes, spreading blankets over the lumped-up sheets and pillows. He hid the empty whiskey bottles in a bushel basket in the pantry and covered them with newspapers. And he even put the filled bottle away without taking a drink.

151

Lee told Nick, "He knows my mother comes on Thursdays."

And then Lee and Nick sat smoking, waiting for Lee's mother to come. Finally they heard the high heels coming up the stairs. "Hurry!" Lee said, snuffing out his cigarette and making Nick do the same. Lee went quickly to the bathroom and, tossing the fags into the toilet, pulled the chain.

He came right back; and already the high-note knock of a woman's knuckles sounded on the door.

Lee opened the door.

"Hello, Mother."

"Hello, Lee."

The good-looking blond woman in the smartly tailored suit put her powder-smoothed and sweet-scented cheek down and let Lee kiss it.

"How have you been, Lee?"

"Fine, Mother."

Lee's old man was in the front room when they went in there. Lee's mother saw him. She let her eyes touch his face, frigidly, for a moment. "Hello," she said casually. Then she acted as if he wasn't in the room.

Lee's old man said, "Hello, Ruth," and walked out of the room, sheepishly, so that they could talk. It was always like that. Sometimes Lee's old man would say before he left, "How are you getting along?"—"Fine"—a pause—"thank you." She always sounded a little insulted and as if she meant what do you care? What did you *ever* care?

But most of the time Lee's old man would get out of the room right away and go to the toilet or some place.

Today Lee's mother pushed up a window, pushing it up until it banged at the top. "You need fresh air in here, Lee." Then she sat on the edge of a chair.

"Mother, this is Nick."

The pretty blue eyes touched his face a minute. "How do you do, Nick. You're one of Lee's schoolmates?"

"Yes, ma'am."

The pretty blue eyes went away and she forgot Nick was there.

"How are your marks?" and "Do you need any clothes?" and "Have you been well?" Then Lee's mother twisted off one glove, opened her purse and gave Lee four dollars. Every week she gave him four dollars.

She stood up, looking at her small-band wrist watch. She was always in a hurry when she came over to see him. "I've got to go now. I'll see you next week, Lee. Be a good boy." She let him kiss her

soft powdered cheek, bending carefully so as not to muss her hair.
She was gone.

Absently Lee put the money in his pocket. He looked at the door
panels that led downstairs. He looked at them for a long time.

Then in the kitchen Lee was saying, "She's gone."

Lee's old man cleared his throat. Lee's old man said in a husky
voice, "Yes, I know, son."

Because Lee needed money before next Thursday, he took Nick
over to his mother's house with him. Lee's mother lived near 63rd
and Blackstone. It was almost a penthouse. You took a quick-shoot-
ing elevator. And in her house your feet sank into the rugs till it was
almost like walking on snow.

Lee's mother came to answer the soft-speaking, musical bell. She
was dressed like a movie star in her long silky dress that was all shiny
blue. She wasn't glad to see her son. "What are you doing here today, Lee?" she asked; and small displeasure wrinkles gathered over
her pretty eyes when she saw Nick.

"I needed some money so I came."

"Couldn't you wait until Thursday?"

She led them to a side room. From a radio cabinet in the other
room came soft music and from the room, too, came a man's voice
asking, "Who is it, Ruth?"

"It's Lee. Go in and say hello to Mr. Rawlins, Lee."

Lee's mother stepped a little in the way so that only Lee could
squeeze by. Beyond the shiny blue-covered curve of her hip, Nick
could see a man sitting on the low-bottomed sofa. His feet were
stretched out over a loosely thrown rug. He was jiggling a tall glass
with ice in it and a piece of lemon stuck lopsided on it. The ice
tinkled. On his wrist was a watch with a heavy gold band. On one
of his fingers there was an ornate ring. Nick heard Lee say, "How do
you do, sir." Then Lee came right back.

Lee's mother didn't let them stay any longer than she stayed when
she came over to Lee's house. She gave Lee a crisp, clean-looking five-
dollar bill that smelled of perfume, and hustled them out.

On the sidewalk, after the swift leap-down the elevator made, Lee
said, "I guess she isn't too crazy to have me around. She's got a big-
shot boy friend now."

And Nick, on the night street, knew. He sensed and he knew. My
mother was always good to me. She can't help it. When she works
and sometimes when she is out late, she gives me money and tells
me never to give it back to her, even if she asks for it, because it's for
the rent—and sometimes she does ask for it. I'm not nice to her.

"Give me a cigarette, Lee." I'm going to make it up to her. She never had anything. "Thanks, Lee." His voice was very sad.

And when they got back to the neighborhood he told Lee good-bye, that he had to go. Then he went looking for his mother. He looked in the plate glass of the Shebeen Bar but he couldn't see good because there were a lot of men sitting by the front with their backs blocking the view. He crossed the street and went over to the Shack. They were tossing a man out the front door and his hat rolled across the sidewalk ahead of him. Nick stood on tiptoe and looked through the dirty pane. He didn't see her there. Then he went down to the Shillelagh Club. Through the pane, in the crowded, noisy place, he saw her. She was sitting at a table near the back, alone. Her cigarette had fallen from her lips and rolled away from her on the table top. It had burned itself to a long gray ash. Her head hung loosely on her neck as if she was asleep. A half-empty glass of beer was in front of her. Please, Mother, please come out, he prayed to her. And he stood next door to the tavern, waiting, his small shoulders drawn in, his head down in shame. And often he walked to the window and stood on tiptoe. She was still there. In the same position. He waited. He would be late to school tomorrow. He waited, keeping the long vigil. He waited. Twelve years old. And the thousand neon-animal eyes stared at him savagely. He waited. The blue-black panther lashed out its tail, flicking its furry tip against his ankles. He waited.

Two hours and a little more he waited. Then she half staggered out the door, stood uncertainly, blinking with her own eyes at the thousand animal-neon eyes.

He came up close to her. "Mother."

For a moment she stared at him as if she didn't know him.

"Hello—son—"

"Mother, let's go home."

Trancelike, she allowed him to lead her home.

34

The Gypsy woman knocked with her many rings on the plate-glass window and Juan turned his face toward her. She made the customary dirty gesture with her fingers, and, laughing, he nodded yes. He turned back to the sidewalk. Nellie stood in front of him. "I was just coming down to your place," she said. She looked up into his face. "Do you know where I can find Frank—Frank Ramponi? Someone said I could find him down here."

Juan's face hardened. "Stay away from him! Jesus Christ, stay away from him!"

"Yes, Juan."

Juan turned angrily and walked away.

She stood where she was a moment. That was the second time someone had told her to stay away from Frank. She had had the same warning from Max. Too late. Too late.

A little unsteadily she moved back in the direction from which she had come.

At the corner Juan ran into Elijah, Fran's brother-in-law. He and Fran's sister, Opal, were just out of jail after a nine-month burglary sentence.

"Well! You made it, man!" Juan said, enthusiastically pumping his hand up and down and grinning at him: Man, he looks great! He came out big and strong like a bull. Opal, Fran's sister, I saw her already. She has her real nice light complexion back. Man, she's a doll now. She swore to me she wasn't going to get on stuff again.

Elijah said, "I made it, Juan, and, man!—I'm never going to get on stuff again. I never knowed how good it were to be clean. Man, that Chinaman ain't got a chance! Yeah, I seen some of my old friends and they don't have time to talk to you. They say"—talking fast—" 'What you say, man!' " His voice came back to its natural tones. "They're off. They're rippin' an' runnin' to try to get some money to satisfy that Chinaman. That goddamn Chinaman's ridin' them so fast they ain't even got time to talk to you. They say"—again talking fast—" 'What you say, Eli?' and they're gone." He grinned at Juan. "Goddamn it," he said, "I ain't goin' to run like that no more."

Nellie crossed Maxwell Street. Big Flora stood in front of the Crystal Bar and her face broke into that big-hearted, friendly smile when she saw Nellie. She moved toward her, holding out her big fat hand, "Hello, Nellie, chile! How's that godchi—"

Recognition came.

"Lawdy, no!" she said.

Nellie nodded her head yes without speaking. Nodded yes in naked truth.

"I never knowed," Big Flora said.

Nellie closed her eyes. She needed a fix bad. She could feel the cramps coming.

Big Florabelle put one huge arm around Nellie's shoulders. "Now don't you worry none, honey." She looked up and down the street. "Ain't *nothin'* in the neighborhood. The heat is on and all the dopeheads, all the pushers and dealers done took off." She poked Nellie with her huge elbow. "I know where we can make it. It ain't Horse but it will do till that Horse comes along."

Flora steered her to a rusty jitney cab with banged-in fenders and the cabbie asleep with his head down against the steering wheel. "Wake up, niggah!" Flora commanded, shaking him alive.

They got in and Big Flora gave the address.

The cab moved away from the curb and they sat in silence for a while as the cab drove north.

Then Big Flora said, "Yes, girl, you take that short step, that one short step from marijuana or pills, bennies, things to Horse and you're hooked. Ain't no use tryin' to get loose."

She had her head back against the seat and tears ran down her black face.

They drove to LaSalle Street on the Near North Side. "Wait, niggah!" Big Flora told the cabbie.

There was a small shingle that said: DR. THOMPSON, M.D. They went down several concrete steps and into a basement apartment. The front room was a waiting room, the second the doctor's office, and behind them were his living quarters. The row of three chairs in the waiting room had dust-collected seats.

The bell tinkled as they entered and shortly a little round man, sixty or sixty-five years old, came into the waiting room. He had curly gray hair and kindly twinkling blue eyes that were bloodshot; a gold chain stretched across his vest.

"Hello, Miss Wills," he said, smiling and holding out his hand to Big Flora.

He led them over the threadbare rug into his office. His clothes were threadbare, too, at cuff and sleeve, and the collar of his shirt was raveled. He was down on his luck and had been drinking heavily for the last couple of years.

There was a roll-top desk, open, heavy with dust, a straight-backed chair, a stiff wooden examination table. On top of the desk was a straight-standing filing wire with aged and frayed papers stuck into it. On one wall there was a calendar, several months behind time; on another, his doctor's degree and the photograph of a youth with kindly twinkling eyes, dressed in a good suit of clothes.

"Doctor," Big Flora said, "I gotta have one of them perscriptions. I gotta have it bad."

He smiled at her gently, sadly. "I'm afraid I cannot issue you another prescription so soon."

"It's mah friend here, Doctor. She ain't feelin' good. She done said she has pains. A lot of pains."

"Well, that's different."

The doctor gave Nellie a cursory examination, cleared his throat a few times, sat at his roll-top desk and wrote out a prescription.

"Five dollars," he said; and to Flora, "Have it honored—" He nodded, telling her, in the gesture, at the same place.

The cabbie was again asleep and Big Flora again shook him awake.

Dr. Thompson locked his office door and headed for the closest Clark Street bar.

In the cab Big Flora, fondling the prescription, said, "Girl, you can get *ten* high-powered jolts out of this here!"

"Shhh!" Nellie said, nodding toward the cabbie.

Big Flora laughed. "That niggah's charged up right now."

On the staid North Side the cab pulled up in front of a drug store.

The interior was dark, as if the place was so seldom patronized, it napped in the afternoon sun. The window was dirty and flyspecked; its only sign, in dignified gold-leaf letters, read: APOTHECARY. In the center of the window, hanging from bronze chains, were three huge and oddly shaped flasks filled with colored water.

The little bell on a spring attached to the door tinkled musically as they entered; immediately facing them were rows of shelves filled with bottles of loose medicines to be mixed on order. On the counter there was a mortar and pestle and a small scale with a little wooden box containing many tiny bronze weights.

They waited a moment at the counter. Then the druggist entered from the back. He looked as if he had come through a cobwebby door; walking heavily on a cane, he had a clubfoot and wore a shoe with an eight-inch sole. He was humpbacked, almost a midget and had strings of unhealthy blond hair hanging over his eyes.

He took the prescription and put thick spectacles on his long, hooked nose. Big Flora and Nellie began to tremble: What if he wouldn't honor the prescription? And both were having cramps now, their eyes were beginning to tear and their noses to run.

He read, leaning close to the prescription blank, then turned, clearing his throat, and dragged the bottle from a handy shelf.

"Five dollars," he said.

The drug cost three dollars and seventy-five cents.

"Two dollars to honor the prescription," he said. "Seven dollars."

The bottle said:

Warning: May be habit-forming
Usual dose: 2 cc

Federal law prohibits dispensing without prescription
Narcotic blank required
For intramuscular injection only

35

Sergeant Forbes sat at a desk down at the Bureau. This was the morning of every week that the stool pigeon dope fiends came in for their pill. He watched them file in and form a line, and his eyes went along that line. A miserable assortment of pickpockets, prostitutes, petty thieves, shoplifters and jackrollers, most of them were marked with two things in common—their youth and their addiction to drugs. Some others, old and hardened and cunning, were in the line, too, selling information in exchange for their fix.

The government and the city use them and in using them dish out heroin tablets to them. They get a shot according to how useful they are and how dependable they are in their information. Even if they run out in between—if they have a good reason for doing so— they get additional capsules.

They just line up at the Bureau once a week and get them. That's all. But they earn them. No one ever gets it for nothing—for no service.

They serve and get.

They lead us to pushers and peddlers. Not only that, but in other cases where there's information necessary. Cases not related to narcotics. The prosecution of some big man who isn't in right with the administration. Things like that.

Sergeant Forbes' eyes again ran along the faces of the miserable.

For all purposes they are used. It is commonly known that an addict can get off a train in a strange town and instinct—need—his cunning need for the drug will lead him to contacts where he will get it. So that cunning is used to get the information we need in other cases.

Again Sergeant Forbes glanced up at them. Poor devils!

He got up from his desk and went to the water cooler for a drink.

This one young fellow was very nicely dressed and wore a light gray topcoat. He had gotten his capsule in the line-up and was nervously looking for a place to give himself a shot. With a nod of his head, Forbes told him where the washroom was.

The young fellow went in, and when he didn't come out in time Forbes thought he had better go in and see what had happened.

The washroom was a little square place, at most four by four, with just a lavatory and a toilet; the toilet was stopped up and was overflowing on the floor. When Sergeant Forbes opened the door he saw the young fellow lying on the floor in a desperate attempt to give himself the shot. His nerves were in such bad shape that he didn't have the patience to get the process completed, and he was lying on the floor with his new topcoat in the mess of the overflow of the toilet, the needle in nervously shaking fingers.

Sergeant Forbes felt terribly sorry for him. He lifted him up and gave him the shot; having watched so many of them, he knew just how to administer it.

The young man watched with grateful eyes and unmoving lips.

Sergeant Forbes said to him, "Look at your coat. Look at your wonderful clothes."

He didn't seem to care about that at all. That shot was just everything to him.

The following week when they came for their capsules the young man sidled up close to Forbes. "Remember me?"

"Yes. I hope you're feeling better today."

"I been holding out," the young man said. He moved closer. "Dr. Thompson. A druggist named Luchinsky." He gave the addresses and additional information.

The case came to court. Dr. Thompson had been giving an unusually high number of prescriptions for narcotics. Druggist Luchinsky had honored over three hundred of them.

Luchinsky and his lawyer argued that he was in business to honor any prescriptions that were brought in.

Word came down: "The ward committeeman, *The Power*, has fixed it."

Doctor and druggist walked out free.

36

Nellie came more and more often to the neighborhood. And once, during those early visits down there, she was holding. She had her charge but no place to take it. In bad shape she tottered toward Juan's shop, and inside. "Look," she said, "let's face it. I'm a dope fiend."

Juan looked up at her. The Wolf! The sonofabitch! "Go ahead," he said, motioning with his head, "use the back room."

It happened every day. If he had had his way it wouldn't have happened to her. But you can't be sorry for everybody.

"Close the door," he called after her.

Now, what about her kid?

Juan walked out of the shop.

Yeah, what about Nick?

Elijah was leaning against a lamppost. He was torn up. So high he was twisted.

"Hello, Elijah."

Elijah opened his eyes and looked at Juan.

"Yeah, Eli, I see you. That Chinaman's got you ripping and running now, ain't he, Eli?"

Elijah said, "Yeah, Juan, this goddamn Chinaman! He's on me again!" He was almost crying when he said it.

Juan moved away: He and Opal did pretty good at that. They stayed off the stuff for about a month.

And more and more Nellie came to the neighborhood. She knew all the dope fiends now. During the day when Nick was at school Nellie was down there in the neighborhood most of the time.

Big Flora was at the tavern window looking out and singing, " 'Don't you talk that talk, don't believe a thing you say.' " She stopped singing and said, "Here comes mah cousin."

Nellie walked in.

"Hello, Miss Nellie," Big Black said.

"Hello, white girl," the brown girl said.

"Go 'long, Nellie," the black girl said in greeting.

Nellie went along and sat at a table with Big Flora, putting her hand on top of Flora's for a moment. Her morning shot was wearing off and she'd need another soon.

Seldom Seen wandered in for a beer. "Whatcha say?" he said to Flora.

"Man, I just grew up to keep from dying," Big Flora said.

Nellie went to the juke box and put in a coin. Mournful Good-bye George stood there against the wall in dejected pose. Nellie said to him, "I always wanted to ask you why they call you Good-bye George."

The sad face smiled sorrowfully. From his pocket Good-bye George pulled a dollar bill. "You see this here, Miss Nellie? You see who's on this here, missy?—the Father of Our Country. Every time Ah gets one Ah says, 'Hello, George!' Then 'long comes the beer man, 'long comes the rent man, 'long comes the man with the food, or some other man comes 'long, and Ah says, 'Good-bye, George!'"

Back at the table Big Flora, with a recent fix, was nodding away. The brown girl said, "She done dozed off again!"

Big Flora's eyes opened and she said in her large musical voice, "Every shut eye ain't asleep and every good-bye ain't gone." Her belly shook with laughter. Then she started nodding down again.

"Done dozed off," someone said.

Big Flora opened her eyes. "Every shut eye ain't 'sleep," she said.

Out the tavern window they could see the entrance to the alley across the street. Elijah was sitting in the alley on a box. Just sitting there smoking a cigarette. After a while a man walked up to him and they talked. Then the man, motioning that he had to go, held out his hand. Elijah's palm touched his in a handshake. The little capsule changed ownership.

In another group, fifteen feet away, Fran stood, talking, smoking a cigarette. Sometimes her eyes went over to Elijah.

"Jesus Christ!" Juan had said. "I don't want you dealing!"

"I just sell to my friends to keep the curse off of them," Fran had said. "If your friends are sick and you can help them, you do."

Now Elijah gave the sign: No more caps.

Fran crossed the street and came into the bar. "Nellie," she said and put an affectionate hand on her shoulder. Then she went into the toilet. She took out the kit, the needle and eyedropper, and the extra supply of capsules all wrapped together in cellophane. The extra caps for Eli she put in the pocket of her dress. Rewrapping her outfit in the cellophane she tucked it deftly inside her body.

Raggedy Bob wandered into the bar.

"You look put out, man," Subway said.

"I is. I gotta get some bread. The urge is on me."

Hearing him Nellie knew the urge was on her too.

"How much bread you need?"

"'Nuff for my fix."

"Eli's holding. And right across the street, man!"

"I got a cent, man, and I'm squared," Big Black said.

They call everything in small terms. Money is called a cent. One cent is a dollar. Two cents is a dollar or so. A dime is ten dollars. If you're squared, it means you need some stuff. You're not feeling good. A square is a cigarette. And also a quarter. And when you say five-cent pack that means a five-dollar package of Horse. A thing is a dollar-capsule of H.

"When you got that guy on your back you'll go," the brown girl said, "even as sick as you are he'll make you get up and go."

"You going to make it, man?" the black girl asked.

"You emeffing right, I'm going to make it," Raggedy Bob said.

"Everything that looks easy, ain't easy," Subway said.

"Maybe I can borrow a couple cents from Salvatore," Raggedy Bob said, nodding his head toward the barber shop.

"Listen, man, he wouldn't give you the sweat off his balls!" Big Black said.

And Flora, awakening, "Old Raggedy Bob 'spects to find a diamond in a meatball!"

Raggedy Bob went out to make some bread. Big Black walked toward the back of the tavern and put his head close to Nellie's. "Miss Nellie, you got a little bread? Maybe we can make it together."

Again Nellie felt the cramps beginning to come. She dumped her purse upside down on the table top. There were two crumpled dollar bills and a dollar twenty-two cents in change on the table. She looked up into Big Black's eyes that were beginning to weep for need of drug. "Can we make it?"

He shook his head no, slowly and sadly. "I got a little taste here. Got three cents."

"Well, let's try to get somebody else who's got some money."

They waited around, getting sicker. Waited around to see if they could make it with somebody, find somebody who's got some bread.

"How much you got?"

"Well, I ain't got enough."

So they look for another guy that's got it. Maybe a dollar. Enough to make it.

Some is better than none.

They waited around. Waited for somebody, anybody, to come up with a dollar so they could go partners.

Raggedy Bob came back in. He had a dollar. They could get a piece of stuff. A seven-cent pack. A half of a sixteenth.

Big Black made the buy. To Fran he said, "Loan me your key."

They went to Fran's crib.

Fran's crib was in a basement her old man had cleaned out. There was no toilet and no water facilities, and he kept her there.

They went inside. They were three stomachs cramping in pain, three pairs of running eyes, three running noses around a table. The white powder was put on the top of a mirror and a razor blade was brought.

There's a funny thing about dividing. You divide it three solid ways. Even if you have four dollars you still haven't got enough to go by yourself, so you get a guy who has two dollars but between you you still haven't got enough, so you find a guy with a dollar. Some is better than none. Without him your money would be no good. You split it three solid ways.

There's a Queensberry rule about dividing. Whoever divides it, the other fellow or fellows get first choice. I can say I'll divide it or you can say you'll divide it. Say you divide it. Then I get first choice. I say, "Well, I'll take this part." That way you have to be awfully careful how honestly you cut it.

The three small mounds of dull white powder lay between them. Big Black racked one over toward him on top of the mirror with the razor blade, then Nellie, then Raggedy Bob.

They brought out the eyedropper and the needle. One needle was all they had.

They started arguing about who was going first.

"Well, man, you know I'm going first, man, because I'm sick, man," Raggedy Bob said.

And Big Black, "Don't give me no bullshit! Ah'm sick. Ah got to have that first!"

"Aw, you ain't gettin' this first!"

They all say it. Who's going first? They argue about it.

"Please—" Nellie, her hands stretched out to both of them. "Please. I have to have some right away."

"No, Miss Nellie," Big Black said, "you ain't gettin' none of this first! Ah's sick!"

"Who ain't sick, he can wait," Raggedy Bob said. "And man, Ah'm busted up."

"Whoever is sick he ain't going to let nobody else go first. He's going first!" Big Black said. And he grabbed the needle.

And Big Black had his own Horse stashed away for emergencies. Hidden in an alley behind a garbage can.

Big Black grabbed the needle and he made out. Then he gave it to the next one and Nellie made out.

Your family doesn't mean anything. Your kid doesn't mean anything. You like him. You love him. You don't want to hurt him. Yet you're hurting him anyway. But you got to have this stuff.

And they all made out. Their voices thickened. They lit cigarettes. They began to nod, down, down, into the web of night. Their cigarettes fell away, one by one, from their relaxing fingers, onto their clothes or onto the dirt floor to roll away, red in the dark, then dark themselves.

37

Fear is what rules them. They are afraid of the police. The sheriff's force. Of running out of money. Of having to kick it, cold turkey, in jail. Of getting a hot shot. Of being caught with it on them—possession—a one- to five-year sentence. Of an overdose. You fluke out. You die. Say you take too much. Say you got some stuff that was too strong and you didn't know it. You take it and you think you're just taking your right fix and when you shoot it in there you shoot too much. That will stop your heart immediately. And you've got to be careful too that you don't get any air in there—a bubble—because if an air bubble gets in there you're gone too.

They're always afraid something might happen but, still, as scared as they are they still go ahead and use it. And most of all they are afraid of getting sick. A sickness like no sickness man knows.

Fear.

And they were not like criminals but like people living with an incurable disease.

Not like criminals. Like animals caught agonizingly in a trap, whirling insanely on a treadmill.

They're scared of getting sick. Scared of getting those cramps and everything else that goes with it. That's the whole thing. The whole thing behind it—they're—scared of—getting—*sick!*

So they're out there hustling to make that money. They're just trying to make money to keep up their habit.

This girl has been dealing all summer. She walks up and down. She had four or five sixteenths concealed inside her body.

A girl pops a yellow jacket in her mouth: "I don't want this stuff, girl. It just holds me till I can get my fix."

How much does a fix cost you?

It all depends upon what your fix is. Is your fix a sixteenth? It costs you thirty dollars. Is your fix a fourth of a sixteenth?

Your fix is what makes you feel like you want to feel.

And it depends upon who's dealing. The dealers go and buy a piece. And they cap it. The more you buy the bigger piece you get for your money, and the more pills you get out of it and the more profit you make out of it and if you're a real good capper you can fool them. A lot of times some of those crooked dealers, new in the neighborhood, pass off baking soda as stuff or real weak H mixed with baking powder, and you get what's called burned: you're getting a turkey.

Say you need some real bad and somebody gave you a bad lot and you struck yourself with it. You'd know right away. When you hit yourself with it you'd know it wasn't any good.

They can pass it off, yes. But only one time.

Those junkies are an awfully tight group. "Don't buy no stuff off that guy. It's no good."

If they do get turkey, a lot of them go and get their money back.

They're an awfully tight group, the hypos. If some hypo finds out that another hypo is a stool pigeon they give him what is called a hot shot. If you take it you're gone.

They're scared of getting sick. They're out there on the street all day long trying to make some bread to keep that Chinaman off them.

What's your fix? There's no telling. A lot of them get greedy. The more money they have the more stuff they use. Some guys go out and get a nice taste of bread and buy a sixteenth. They shoot it up. Then after about an hour they still have some money in their pockets and they don't know what to do with it so they go buy another. This brings their habit up. And stuff builds up its own tolerance, so you need more. This brings your habit up too.

All day they're out on the street hustling, hustling, to get that money to get that stuff.

Can't get caught with the stuff on you. They hide it in rat holes in the alley, making sure they know where their rat holes are. Wrapped in newspaper they hide it behind garbage cans. They hide it under rocks in empty lots. If it rains they run for it. The rain would spoil their good stuff. The cops know this. The cops wait for it to rain. The cops pick them up.

And a woman has the best hiding place of all.

They're generous with it when they have it. If you're sick and they have it, it's yours too. They know what it is to be sick.

That sickness!

Fear will lead anyone anywhere.

That sickness coming on!

Criminal in behavior but merely self-preservative in intent, when they don't have it, don't have the money for it, they go steal to get the money.

Got to have it!

The living death. Only by having it are they able to go on.

And yet Society sees them criminal.

Society puts them behind bars.

There is no cure in punishment.

Society never sees itself as criminal and so, in punishing and not curing, Society daily weakens itself. Becomes as diseased as those it punishes.

Fear.

"Here comes The Man!"

It went up and down the street.

"Here comes The Man!"

He's The Man. The Man what brings the heat.

Every dope fiend got off the street and hit his hole. There wasn't a fiend to be seen.

Sergeant Bill Forbes walked down the street. Majewski walked with him. They were dressed in sports clothes. Forbes' gray hair was freshly cropped to its habitual crew cut. Majewski was young.

They seemed to know all the dope fiends. They usually stopped them and searched them. And sometimes they just stopped them and took them in on principle. But you have to catch them with something in order to send them to jail. Their eyes roved the street from side to side as they walked along.

Someone hadn't got the word.

"Come on, Pearl," Sergeant Forbes said.

"You jump out of the water pipe at us," she protested.

She was led away.

Fear rules them.

38

They were in Miss Sawyer's room for the last year of grammer school. Miss Sawyer was real old but her hair was dyed brunette. Over her desk, getting bawled out, you could look down at the top of her head and see the gray roots. She had a lined face and the powder caked in the wrinkles; when she stood by her desk, she always had her hand on her hip. She had a little pearl knife. She peeled her apple with the knife. And half the day a toothpick stuck out of the corner of her mouth. She had to have her glass of water on the left side of her desk, always on the left side of her desk. And it was always covered with a little square of paper.

Miss Sawyer was on to everything. She could be writing and you could be whispering and she'd say, "Sneak! You filthy sneak!— What is this world coming to? Nothing but parasites and savages!" The "parasites" were the kids whose folks were on relief and who came to school in charity clothes. She gave little mean-worded speeches at her desk about people who were too lazy to work and had to have the government support them. It was her pet peeve. She'd sit with one hand on her hip, the crystal-glass necklace hanging to her belly and one hand stretched out to the glass from which she took little sips of water between angry sentences. She had grandparents "who came to this country and helped make it; who didn't go crying to the government for help." She had parents who worked their way through college and worked their way up to prominent places in her home town. Most of all, she didn't like Mexicans because they were just too lazy and dirty for words. ". . . It even shows in their school work." She disliked Mexicans more than Negroes because her two grandfathers had "helped free the poor blacks." Her grandparents had helped do that, too, after settling the land. They were straight-backed brave people. *Real* Americans who didn't want anything from the government but to serve their country. If you weren't a Mexican or your folks weren't on relief, you enjoyed these speeches because they sometimes took half an hour, with her grandfolks coming to the Middle West in covered wagons and shooting war-dancing Indian savages. You didn't have to do any work; just sit at the desks and read comic books spread on your knees.

And that wasn't all. She could make you feel like two cents. She'd say, with a nasty snap, if the fellows grabbed at girls, "Why don't you go and pull on your mother like that? I bet she's on the block right now."

It was their last year in grammar school. So it didn't matter about Miss Sawyer. Everybody said eighth grade was easy. It was just a review of the last couple of years.

The good day of graduation came real close, and Judge, Max, Norm and Phil said they were going to buy his graduation suit for him. They had the money in Judge's pocket and they took him to the bargain basement in The Hub, saying it was one of the best men's stores in the city and down there you could get, cheap, a suit you'd pay twice as much for in a lot of other stores. Judge said they should get a sensible blue serge and he could wear it right into high school.

The four of them stood there when the smiling salesman led him out of the little dressing room like a telephone booth, led him out in front of the long, narrow, three-sided mirrors.

He tried on three suits, and Norm, Max, Phil and Judge stood looking at him, feeling the goods, telling him to turn around, turn this way and that way, Nick's eyes following their eyes— Is this suit all right?

It was tied up in a big suit box with the name of the store on the box and they let him carry it.
Then the good day came.

39

This is the day my kid graduates from grammar school. I got to get a fix and get there.

She was happy and proud.

She took his graduation suit from under the protective sheet and brushed it clean of any lint. They had bought his suit for this day. Judge, Max, Phil and Norm. She loved them too. And she was hurting them too.

The first cramp came.

She laid Nick's suit carefully across her bed.

Today of all days she wished she didn't have to have a fix. That she could just go to school with her child as a mother should.

The second cramp came.

She went into Nick's bedroom and stood looking down at him, smiling. Then tears came into her eyes. She put her fingers up into the roots of her hair. She stood there swaying, biting her teeth into her lip, hard, hard. She felt like screaming and screaming. Like never stopping.

A failure as a mother. Shame assaulted her. After trying so hard when he was a little kid. Again shame lashed her.

Limply she dropped her hands from her hair and to her sides; released her lip from her teeth. She walked to the window and looked out. Then, turning slowly, she went back to the bed.

She stooped over her son. She rumpled his hair and ran her hand down over his face, as she used to do when he was a child; over his forehead, eyes, nose, and over his lips.

Nick woke up. He looked up, solemnly, into his mother's eyes. "You will be there, Mother?"

"Yes, dear."

"Do you promise?"

"I promise."

She went into the bathroom and locked the door. When you're real sick and you don't have a fix you use the cotton you have left in the cooker.

She put a little water in it and boiled it in the spoon to get what little Horse was left there. Maybe it will hold me. Maybe I can get to the graduation and then go get my fix.

She struck herself with it.

No kick.

I've got to get there. I've *got* to get to my kid's graduation.

Frantically she started for the neighborhood to get her fix.

It was a hot day, high in the nineties, but she didn't sweat. You sweat when it's cold and don't sweat when it's hot.

Nellie got off the streetcar and started for Maxwell Street. A dilapidated touring car moved down the street. A little packet hit the sidewalk, skidded in front of her and up against a tailor-shop doorway: the policy racket, the illicit numbers game with the packet containing the numbers of winners on the different "books": CAPITAL LIMITED, ATLANTIC, BLUE BOOK. Nellie continued on her unsteady way. Ahead another little packet skidded and slammed against the meat-market door of still another policy agent.

Broken sidewalks and broken asphalt. Lean of lampposts in the hot June sun. Nellie, wandering across them and under them toward a fix. On a doorway stoop sat a big black woman with a razor-cut the length of her cheek. She was singing in a low, mournful voice that carried up and down the street, " 'Nobody loves me, Lord, nobody seems to care . . .' "

On the corner in front of the Crystal Bar was Big Flora.

"What's happening, Flora?" Nellie asked.

"Ain't nothing happening, girl."

Big Flora was drunk.

"I done brought mah habit down, Nellie, chile," she said. "Been drinking three days straight to keep from gettin' back on stuff." She was sweating profusely; great half-moons of moisture dampened the armpits of her dress and repeated themselves below her huge bosom.

They went into the bar and Big Flora ordered a straight shot. "I'm goin' to kick it, honey," she told Nellie.

Fran came in. "I sure hope you can make it," she said sadly to Flora.

Nellie said, "I have to get some": I've got to get there. I've *got* to get there.

Fran said, "Eli and Opal are coming down soon. I think we can make out with them."

They waited around.

Extra Black Johnson came in dressed to kill. He said he had some stuff on him but he was waiting for Uncle Sam.

"Can I make it with you?" Nellie asked. "I don't have any money but I'll get some and pay you back. I have to go somewhere."

"Listen, Miss Nellie," Extra Black Johnson said, "as I always says, them what has should give. Once Ah had a dose—know what Ah mean?—and Ah sure handed it around!" This made him cackle, and he did a slow, dirty shuffle to the bar and back. "Sure you can make out with us, Miss Nellie."

The place began to fill up with dope fiends.

Elijah and Opal showed up. Big Black wandered in. And finally Uncle Sam, young and cocky and bragging about having made some real bread. He had a couple sixteenths on him.

Big Flora just sat. Looking at them. Wanting it. Getting drunker.

"Man," Extra Black Johnson said to everybody, "let's make tracks for mah shootin' gallery."

"No, your crib's too far," Elijah said. "Let's go up to my pad. It's closer."

They all got up to go to Elijah and Opal's apartment.

"Come on, gal!" Big Black said to Flora.

She shook her head no. An unsteady hand brought the shot glass of whiskey up to her lips. Half of it slopped out on the bar.

Extra Black Johnson shuffled over until he stood in front of her. His face was a black balloon before her eyes. "Gal, you knows you's hooked, gal. Come on, gal."

"Leave her alone," Nellie said. "Don't come, Flora."

They all went out under the hot sun. They started for Elijah and Opal's diggings. They were down the street half a block.

Big Flora got up off the bar stool. Maybe she could get that kick back. That first wonderful, out-of-this-world feeling that none of them ever got again.

She followed them.

Heat had dampened the asphalt until it bubbled in small black balloons and ran away in little tricklets.

Down an alley, through an areaway, past a barn with half its roof fallen in, up broken steps, clinging to a sagging banister, and to a door on the third-floor landing they went.

Nellie, leaning on the railing: I've got to get there.

Big Flora, putting her heavy foot on the bottom step, "Wait! I'm comin'!"

They locked the door. They sealed the windows. They pulled the shades down to the sills. They got out the equipment. The heat sweated around them.

Panicky fingers brought out the caps of sixteenths and eighths of heroin. Panicky fingers groped for hypo needles and eyedroppers.

Anybody can buy a needle.

Anybody can buy an eyedropper.

They are sitting around on the bed, on chairs, on a couple of boxes.

Three needles will serve them all. They have a fine wire to keep the needle open before and after they use it. And they blow through the needle two or three times. No, they never boil it. They don't have time.

Fingers taking pieces of paper and tearing off a little piece. Any kind of paper. Nellie's fingers. Fran's fingers. Big Flora's. The rest. Fingers wrapping the small pieces of newspaper, toilet paper, around the end of the eyedropper, tight, to get a tight fit on the needle. And then they stuff the small end of the eyedropper into the head of the needle, snugly, tightly. Shove it in so that no air will get in. The equipment is ready. The needle, sharp, bitter-pointed. The glass tube of the eyedropper. The red rubber top of the dropper like a huge red tear. Ready. Almost ready.

They grab their cookers. The cookers are metal caps off wine bottles, with the cork lining taken out.

They take the cookers. They have a little piece of cotton in each cooker. They dump the dull white power into the cookers. Their fix.

They put the eyedroppers in a glass of water. And they squeeze the rubbers and they draw the water up until it fills the eyedroppers. Then they squeeze all the water into the cooker.

They grab matches and they grab the cookers. And they hold a lighted match under the cooker.

Extra Black Johnson, Uncle Sam and Opal hold the cookers between their thumbs and forefingers. They move the matches back and forth under the cookers.

One match.

Two matches.

Shaking their fingers as the match begins to curl its flame into their flesh and then dies in a black twist.

Three matches.

They cook it.

The stuff begins to boil.

It bubbles. And it gets clear. The color of water.

They cool it off a little, shaking it back and forth in the cookers between thumb and forefinger.

The needles dip into the cookers, drinking like birds.

They stick the needles into the cotton. Not to guard against infection. Only so that the needles will work well. And they draw all the stuff up through the cotton.

They are all mainliners except Nellie and Fran. They go strictly for the veins. Mainlining has a quicker effect. They are in panic for their fix. In shock. Needles shake in quivering fingers. Lips tremble. Eyes begin to weep freely. They start tying their arms up.

Extra Black Johnson frantically pulls his fine silk tie loose and past the collar of his shirt. It makes a hurried whistling sound of cloth against cloth. He bares his arm. Rusty and dirty needles have left a lifetime, tattoo-like, purple-blue strap of flesh on his skin. The main vein is there where the forearm and upper arm come together. He loops his tie around his bicep. He is holding one end of his tie between his teeth now. He is tightening, tightening his tie into a tourniquet. He is tightening the tie tighter and tighter. And while he is squeezing it up tight he clenches his hand into a hard fist, then loosens it. Clenches. Loosens. He is squeezing his hand until the veins pop up. He is moving his fingers, stretching and clenching them, tightening and loosening them.

The veins come out boldly. Like ropes.

They are popping up now.

Opal and Uncle Sam are tying their arms up too. They are using handkerchiefs clenched between their teeth.

Extra Black Johnson's obedient needle turns its sharp-pointed head down to his ropelike, blood-swelled vein. Expertly the sword-point dipped in, going in like a hot poker into butter.

The hypos know when they get a hit. Blood comes up the tube, filling the belly of the eyedropper. When they see that, they loosen up the noose that strangles their arm and they start squeezing the stuff in. They squeeze it all in until the red rubber cap is panting for breath.

Extra Black Johnson, like so many of them, likes to jag-off. Extra Black Johnson is jagging-off. When the red rubber cap is all the way down, pinched between thumb and finger and gasping, pleading for breath, he lets go and the mixed cocktail of blood and heroin rises in the tube, filling it. Again he injects into his arm, jagging-off, getting, getting a second sensation. He fills it up still again and then shoots it back in.

"Oh, Jesus, God!" Extra Black Johnson sighs in ecstasy. "Lord! Lord!"

"Oh, man, give me some of that good stuff!" Big Black says, reaching for the needle.

Uncle Sam just goes—Boom!—the needle tasted blood and it was in.

Uncle Sam jagged-off too.

"Sssssuuuuuuuuuhhhh!" He just sucked in breath. A long, long breath. Like sex. Only better, man, better!

Opal's needle sniffed along her vein. Sniffed there. Smelled the flesh along her arm. She can't find her vein. The injection of impure and adulterated drugs had closed her veins. They were cordlike, almost useless structures. The needle smells the flesh, like a dog, nose down, along a broken path in the woods. She has to wait until she hits. She's biting her lips and digging in, little by little. Biting her lips. Digging. Bit by bit.

And in.

Fran joy-popped. Just hit with the stuff under her skin. Nellie took the needle in her accustomed way. Elijah can't wait. He opens a safety pin with his teeth. He grabs the eyedropper without its biting needle. He grabs the safety pin. In desperation, in greed for a surcease of agony, he jabs the point of the safety pin into his vein, breaking open the skin and the vein wall. Into this bleeding opening he sticks the medicine dropper, directly into the vein, and squeezes the red bulb.

And Big Black is so nervous he can't find that vein. He's in bad shape. He missed the vein. But he thinks he has a hit: He has drawn blood into the medicine dropper and he shoots the stuff in. It just goes under the skin. The skin begins to pop out. It spreads under the skin in swollen protest, like lava slowly flowing, until his whole arm, in irregular pattern, is lumped up under the skin.

Big Flora has been off stuff several days. She grabs the needle. It kneels, like a camel, to the flesh of her arm. She takes a stiff jolt . . .

Peace has come to them. Clean rays of hot summer sunlight fall through the pin-prick holes in the worn green window shades. Dust sifts through the air and on the rays of sunlight—ladders of dream stuff.

At peace . . .

Their voices deepen. Most people would think they were drunk. You can tell drunken people, though. Drunken people act sloppy. A guy on stuff doesn't act like that. He just wants to be left alone. He just wants to nod away.

Their voices deepen . . .

They're taking off now. Opal, when she takes off, gets as if she had a mouthful of spit. She's always like that. She is saying, "Aw, man, ain't nothin' happening. Shit!" Her mouth gets big and full and her eyes start to narrow, getting that sleepy look; and she says, "Man, that stuff is *good*, Jim. I really feel this. It's *nice* stuff."

Different people act differently. Elijah has his fix. The drug is taking him differently. He just starts scratching, scratching his woolly head, scratching his ears and nodding, and picking his nose, and, oh, just scratching all over and just talking to you . . . "Man, that's good stuff" . . . and nodding and just scratching all over.

Nellie says, "How do you feel, Eli?": I've got to get there.

Elijah says, "Man, that's good stuff—that's a nice taste—that."

Extra Black Johnson has stripped down to his shorts. There is no sex in it. Just comfort. There is no sex in any of them.

They are nodding away . . .

Their eyes start drooping. Your eyes start closing as if you're going to sleep. You think they're sleeping and they're not. You can just barely touch them and they know it—you can talk to them. Anything you say to them, they hear you. And they can talk back to you. They're mentally awake. In their fashion.

They are nodding. It is a steady nod. A going down . . .

Nellie has her arms between her legs and is going down, down: Got to—get there. Fran has her hands together and she nods down, down until her hands and her cigarette and even her head are in her lap. Uncle Sam and Big Black go out and come back. They have more stuff and all of them have another fix, cabareting. Uncle Sam and Big Black leave.

They all have their fix. They don't want to have anything to do with anybody. They don't even want to talk. All they want to do is nod. They're in a half-daze.

And Big Flora stirs. Suddenly she sits upright on the side of the bed. Her big bosom heaves. Her breathing came fast and, anxiously, her eyes found Nellie. She half stood. "I feels sick. Sick." Her huge arms lifted out from her sides as if to balance her to her feet. "I needs some fresh air." She rises almost erect. "Sick—" Then falls heavily back to a sitting position. "I's dizzy." Her voice becomes panicky. "Mah eyes can't see good—Nellie, chile—" She gropes out a huge black paw for Nellie's hand. Beads of perspiration had popped out on her forehead.

Nellie takes her hand and tries to lift her erect. "Sick," Big Flora complains. Her eyes looked into Nellie's pleadingly. Between them Nellie and Fran get her to a standing position.

Across the room Opal and Extra Black Johnson are nodding, nodding on their chairs. Elijah is eyes, watching.

Big Flora is now standing unsteadily between Nellie and Fran. She vomits. She begins to gag. Her weight is too heavy for them. She falls back to a sitting position and is that way for a moment, her eyes popped, looking at Nellie. Then she half slides off the bed, her big body toppling over sideways. She has fluked out.

Gone was the big friendly smile, embracing the whole world. Gone the melodious voice, laughing, singing, showing gold teeth among the white. Gone her warmth and friendliness. The shut eye was asleep. The good-bye was gone. Just a ghastly, unwieldy lump of dead flesh there in the bedroom.

"Oh—Lordy, no!" It was a wail and a plea.

They crowded around. And moved away.

"Oh, Lawd, Lawd, Lawd, no!" Extra Black Johnson moaned. He was on the floor, kneeling, his forehead pressed against the splintery softwood boards of the floor, his bald black head sweating now. He was the biggest man there. But he was of no use.

And Elijah was afraid of dead people. Though it was his house and the trouble was there, he took his hat and scurried out the door: Ain't gonna fool with no dead people!

They sat in a stupor, Nellie, Fran, Opal, Extra Black Johnson.

"Can't do nothin' now. Nothin'," Extra Black Johnson said.

"Got to throw suspicion somewhere else," Opal said.

"She didn't buy it here," Fran said. "But she died here."

Nellie was crying into the palms of her hands: Poor, sweet Flora. Poor, poor Flora. Good, sweet Flora. Poor thing.

"Gotta throw suspicion somewhere else—else we all goes to jail," Extra Black Johnson said. "And it's your house it happened in, Opal."

"I can't take it again," Opal said. "I just did a nine-month stretch cold turkey. Another and I flukes out too."

"Gotta wait for night," Extra Black Johnson said.

They waited for night. They were fearful. They were like rats trapped. They were shaking.

Extra Black Johnson took out all the Horse he had and put it on the table. "We all sure needs a fix," he said. "We might as well cabaret."

"No use gettin' scared," Opal said. "No use doin' nothin' till dark."

They cabareted.

Big Flora would have liked it that way.

They nodded, down, down . . .

Dusk drifted a mask of cobwebs over the face of the day.

The corpse lay, a misshapen mess, propped half on the bed, half on the floor.

A cigarette fell in Fran's lap and burned a hole in her dress. Nellie's fingers were clenched in her hair at her temples: Got to get to my son's graduation . . . poor, poor Flora.

Merciful night came.

Extra Black Johnson, the only man there, was of no use. Fran clattered hurriedly down the steps and to the Crystal Bar. Good-bye George was leaning dejectedly outside. "Come up here with me," Fran told him. "We need your help."

Good-bye George stood gaping over what had been Big Flora: Dat gal done died up there. Now Ah know Ah'm going back to Tennessee.

They dragged her, hard to fit, through the back door. No telling moon showed in the sky and they sighed with relief. They stood her half erect, and, straining their backs against her back, moved slowly forward while behind them Extra Black Johnson held a steadying but trembling hand and had to look into the face of the corpse.

Nellie, Fran, Opal, Good-bye George: They moved the corpse off the little wooden platform of porch on the third floor of the apartment building, and it hung, for a moment, over the wooden banister, like a drunk, or an orator giving a speech, or a buffoon entertaining the crowd. Then down a step. Bump! Another. Bump! Another. Another. Another. And the second landing. And Big Flora, as if with a will of her own, wobbled to the rotten wooden railing, clung there a moment as if not wanting to leave, leave life, leave friends—then—with a tearing away of rotten wood and the groaning of rusty nails coming alive in complaint—the corpse of Big Flora flung itself through the banister and down into the rock- and garbage-filled yard below.

They clung to the wall of the building, listening to their hearts pound. They clung there half an hour. Then timidly, fearfully, they went down to the yard and to Big Flora's side, swollen up there in the night.

The pallbearers resumed their duty. They dragged Big Flora past a barn with its roof half fallen in, through an areaway, down an alley.

To throw suspicion off the house, Big Flora was left in an alley, against a garbage can. She was dumped there like a bundle of old papers.

And the frightened ones ran away on their doped legs.

The night wore cobwebs.

40

The good day came and Nick stood grinning and happy on the school stage, the boys lined up on one side and the girls on the other. Grinning and happy, looking out over the seats, over the faces for his mother's face.

And they sang the school song. Good-bye to their school. Good-bye to their friends. Most of the girls had tears in their eyes. And some of the boys. He had tears in his eyes.

In the very back row of the school auditorium sat the four of them. They were an odd-looking foursome. Norman wore a plaid jacket, and he had an ascot scarf around his neck that blossomed in blue silk out the front of his jacket. Phil wore a tight-fitting collar and kept yanking at it with his hand, his coat sleeve slipping up to reveal a tattoo. Judge sat with his cane between his knees and his hands clasped over its handle. Max worked his Mexican face as if he was going to cry.

Then the principal was handing out the diplomas and there were special mentions and awards for some of the students, certificates with gold lettering and blue and yellow ribbons—for the best scholar, the best athlete, the most courteous student, the president of the class. And then his turn came and his was for art. The principal was handing it to him and shaking his hand; and turning to go to his place on the stage with the graduating class, Nick again looked for his mother.

They were standing outside in the sun waiting for him. Judge Sullivan wore no hat and his hair was almost completely white now; his mustache too. He stood leaning forward on his cane and smiling at Nick.

Nick, grinning, hurried over to them, Lee at his side.

"Hello, Uncle Phil, Uncle Norm," and turning, "Uncle Max. Where is Mother?"

"Your mother was too sick to come," Judge Sullivan said.

"You mean she was drunk!" Nick said.

He turned away suddenly.

Then he said, "This is Lee."

Lee had to shake hands with his left hand.

Nick turned away again. He said, "I'll see you later. I want to go with my friend."

He hurried off with Lee.

The sidewalk was empty and just the four of them were there. They were hurt. Especially Judge Sullivan. They themselves wanted to be with him on his graduation day.

"Don't you see," Norman said roughly; and he never spoke roughly, "he wanted his mother to be here."

"Yeah," Phil said.

"That's true," Judge said; and he started to sneak one hand up to his eyes, thought better of it.

"Let's find a tavern," Max said. "I'm going to get drunk." He grinned, his eyes running off into slits. But he didn't feel like grinning. "Some nice cold Pabst," he said.

Nick walked into the house. Twilight lay over the two rooms. He closed the door and locked it. His slow fingers put his diploma and his art award on the bed. He looked across the room at the framed newspaper photograph. He walked over to it. The glass was covered with grit and dirt, smoky. His mother used to keep it washed all the time. Slow shadows crept into the room. He lifted his fingers to the glass and wiped it clean where his father's eyes were. He looked in through the glass at his father. His father looked back at him.

He stood there looking.

"Father," he said.

Tears ran down his cheeks.

4 *night winds call*

41

West Madison Street is a coward. It carries its tail between its legs like any cur. Snarl at the drunk, the panhandler. Kick the bum off the sidewalk. He goes unprotesting, lifting his hat to you, acknowledging his fault in being alive and in your way. Yelping like any common yellow mongrel. Lifting his hat, thanking you for the boot that cleared him from your path.

But this is North Clark Street.

There is, in Chicago, South State Street. There is Maxwell Street. There is West Madison Street. But no street in Chicago like North Clark Street. No cesspool so deep. No night so dark.

North Clark Street is a hustler, hard-eyed, little mustache preened. He's got to have what you have or he won't sleep tonight.

He's got connections. Whore you want? Cheap whore? Fancy, high-class call girl? Drugs you want? Your own sex you want? Anything you want.

He's got connections.

He's the hustler, the con-man, the pimp. The guy you have to look out for.

Under the panama with colored sash for hatband in the summertime, with high-priced, big-brimmed Stetson in winter, his lips are thin and tight and you know there are rotten teeth behind their grimace. His eyes are small, cold, mean, shift back and forth, and you know that out of the corners of them he is watching every sucker comes down to this street.

His hair is plastered stiff in a pompadour with too much grease. The part is like a razor cut. His neck was made for a noose, but no noose will replace the gaudy cravat around that slicker's neck. His buttocks, in creased midnight-blue trousers, for the hot seat. But no hot seat will burn that good suit nor that pimply skin.

He pushes his dirty feet in stiff, holey socks, toes pointed out, toward the Cathedral and the Bible Institute. He breaks wind in front of the Ambassador. He slinks, skinny-shouldered, consumptive, past Newberry Library where the quiet pages of quiet books are turned in research.

Chicago, Chicago, that wonderful town.

This hoodlum, North Clark, roams from the smooth green aprons of Lincoln Park to the restraining ribbon of river, where, across the river, the snow-white steeple of the downtown skyscraper church lifts its delicate spire, halting his prowl like a traffic cop's uplifted hand.

This hustler lives near the good places in Chicago, near the nice people, the good people, the dowagers, society folks, people who like good food and good drinks in nice places. That lady, Michigan Boulevard, with all her airs, is his neighbor. That comic, Bughouse Square, is his neighbor. Northwestern University, Downtown Campus, the Ambassador Hotel, the Water Tower. All are his neighbors.

Many people in high places are in his pay. He is their illegitimate child they dare not claim. But only pay the price for silence.

This is Chicago.

He is Chicago Enemy Number One. He sneers at Chicago. He thumbs his nose at the Gold Coast.

If he were a woman he would be a diseased prostitute sitting there picking her open sores in public.

This is Chicago and this is North Clark Street.

The Cathedral is two blocks away. Moody Bible Institute is a block away. The YMCA, where strange men don't get into strange men's rooms because all must show their room key on the way up in the elevator at night, is a block's distance, with, nearby, a bar for strange men. Michigan Boulevard—THE MAGNIFICENT MILE—

is a few blocks east. And then the clear blue-green lake, yachts tossing on the blue-green water. The Pump Room is a few blocks away. The Loop is within walking distance.

If you knew Chicago you'd talk about it too.

This is the crazy-quilt neighborhood. Two blocks to slums. Two blocks to storied wealth. Rush Street puts down its gaudy carpet of night clubs, grotesquely twisted and twirled new architecture weirdly lit and slapped up over aged brick and frame buildings long condemned. Over the night clubs, on blind second and third floors and behind windows where rooms are presumed to be empty and unused, there are ladies and gambling tables.

If you haven't been in Chicago you haven't been in the United States.

Here, too, in this neighborhood, is the bohemian quarter where painters and writers live. Many along Dearborn, Wabash, State, where the abandoned homes of wealthy Chicagoans lie in slow rot, turned now into apartments and rooming houses. Others where the homeowners hold out against the times, and though they rent out rooms, still live in the houses they have lived in for a quarter of a century or more. The old faces go snooping up stairways for gossip, for sin. The gray heads go snooping out windows or rubbernecking up staircases for scandal concerning the people to whom they have rented.

If you don't know Chicago you don't know yourself.

Here, too, facing Newberry Library and Clark Street, is Bughouse Square, dedicated to free speech, where every night men and women stand on soapboxes and speak their minds.

They are the people from whom the world had slipped away. Their world had died thirty years or more ago. Theirs is a neighborhood, bordering Clark Street on both sides, of gloomy rooming houses. The men shut themselves up in their rooms all day long reading pamphlets, waiting for night, and become so savage and vicious that, when night comes, they have to go down to the square and vent all their pent-up anger. They are impatient for night. For the time when they can climb up on a box and let loose.

They are bitter and broken. They are radicals and religious fanatics. It gives them a certain dignity and a martyrdom to stand alone.

The broken-corpses come into the square to listen. They have nothing else to do. Nowhere else to go. If you brought two trained dogs into the park and started them fighting, you would fill the place.

With the morose and dignified stones of Newberry Library as a backdrop, the spellbinders are going full blast. Here a Moodyite quotes from the Bible. He is made up for the part. He has a shaggy brown beard and uses a flashlight to read from the Holy Scripture. He is like a medieval saint. When they get you leaping like a police dog over those hurdles, you may fall down. He has, now, a convert; and some people can't stand a third degree whether they're in a police station or in a church.

On the boxes in the square, the speakers shout and each one is like a dog gnawing his bone in a corner and growling at the other dogs.

The crowd growls back, arguing, deriding, making filthy remarks.

If the best possible world was made and laid out before them, they'd tear it to pieces.

This speaker gets the crowd with him, and the world's problems are solved and the lions are licking the horses' legs and suddenly—

"Well, I have a little something else to discuss with you—" And he moves through the crowd passing his hat.

That's Chicago for you.

The panther goes roving. This corner they call State and Perversion. It is really State and Division. There's a meeting place for them. There's a bar for them. They are like ballet dancers in their movements back and forth. They are young men and even boys of high school age who go swishing along, swinging their hips like girls while their high voices and shrill laughter trail behind them like colored ribbons blown on the breeze. Some wear a suggestion of make-up. Some have their hair dyed and waved. They go with arms linked. With voices like women. The panther licks its chops with feline, female allure.

You're in Chicago! Is everybody happy!

The panther moves east across the city in his roving. He moves in the city toward the Gold Coast.

Tall towers rise up skyscrapers, testing, with long fingers, the pinkness of sunrise. Are sundials in the afternoon. Mark the coming of the moon at night. A ribbon of highway marks the curvature of the lake. Old mansions and modern skyscraper apartment buildings clothed in glass and housing the rich proudly look out to the lake's blueness.

This is the Gold Coast. This the beautiful woman, Chicago.

The slums are there, behind the backdrop. Smokestacks and water towers stand above broken roofs. Alleys are piled high with garbage and rats skid.

Chicago—The City Beautiful!

The Black Belt is there. Maxwell Street is there. West Madison Street is there. South State is there.

But most of all, North Clark Street is there. Leering. Mocking. Thumbing its nose.

Shadow falls upon shadow. The beast of night wears many eyes. The panther roams his neighborhood. The dead dreams of three million people walk the streets.

Chicago has a painted face and dirty underwear.

42

This the neighborhood of Nick and Nellie. This the worst possible environment for Nick. Nor was the high school any better. To him, the teachers didn't seem to give a damn, most of them. They drew their pay. They had to spend five and six hours with these hoodlums every day to draw it. The kids were tough and didn't want to learn anything. They had to go to school until they got kicked out or until their parents let them quit and go to work; and most of their parents, in that neighborhood, would rather they worked. Their parents didn't even know where they were half the time, or care. Most of the kids refused to get anything out of school. They were just putting in time. Like prisoners in jail. Those kids who did attend classes, even those in the last year, didn't know what they wanted to be. He still had the crazy idea that he wanted to be an artist. He had a job after school now. His voice began to crack and deepen. Hair was beginning to push out from under his armpits and in other places. Sometimes he had funny dreams with girls in them. And the bedsheet would be spotted and he'd be ashamed and make his own bed. He was afraid his mother would say something about it, but she never did. Not even when she changed the sheets. His voice kept breaking up and down.

Lee went to a different school now and he never saw him. This hurt, because Lee had been the only friend he had had in school. He liked school. He wanted to learn. The only friends he had were Judge, Max, Norm and Phil, and he sought them out, was with them whenever he could be, as he had been since he was five years old. There was a loneliness in him, for family, for identity, and there was only his mother. His mother. The words made him feel like crying.

Judge, Phil, Max and Norm were the only family he knew. And

he knew they weren't really his family but he pretended that they were. He didn't know which one he liked the best. Sometimes he thought it was Judge. Other times Phil or Norm. No, Max. Max said to him one day when he had the day off from driving the taxi, "Come on, kid," and he took him to the Art Institute. The taxi driver and the boy walked through the cool art galleries. The kid stood awed in front of the masterpieces. So did the taxi driver. Norm bought him charcoal and pastel chalks and said he wanted to pay for all his art supplies at school. Phil would sneak him off downtown by himself and take him to Goldblatt's and buy socks for him, a couple of shirts, once a pair of shoes. "And listen, kid, don't you tell the rest of them. They'd think I was soft." Phil would put his arm around his shoulders and a tattoo would look out from beyond the shirt cuff at the Chicago skyline. "They'd think I should spend it on drinks for them." And punching him, making it tingle just a little on his arm, "What's better? A pair of socks or a round of drinks for them bums?" Judge he *really* liked. Judge said, once when he was walking with him looking for his mother, "Everybody knows what's good and what's bad. Be yourself and everybody will love you." Judge had put his hand on his shoulder for a little while, pressing his shoulder warmly. "The important thing is to be yourself. Just be Nick." He said it gentle and sad and, in Nick's ear, lastingly. And Judge gave him laughter, and wisdom, and dignity, and—and grown-up companionship. He guessed he liked Judge best. No, he liked them all the same.

His mother.

He lowered his head, looking at his shoes, kicking them along the sidewalk in sadness, hurt.

Your mother can be a true mother for five minutes when she remembers you.

The fifteen-and-a-half-year-old boy, Nick, sat in the Marquis Restaurant on North Clark and Chicago Avenue. His schoolbooks were on the white slab of table that faced the street and he had bought himself a cup of coffee for six cents, the cream already in it, the girl handing him the spoon with her fingers in the end that was used for stirring. He had sat a long time staring out the window, the coffee untouched. Then he had sat, a small notebook in front of him, a soft pencil between his fingers, trying to sketch the head of the old man across from him who sat sleeping, his forefinger still caught in the handle of the heavy white cup. He had put in the oval for the head, the three lines that represented eyes, nose and mouth, the way Mr. Clemson, his art teacher, had shown him. Then again he sat staring. Around him in different postures of dejection and defeat sat the bemused and the lost. The ragged and foully odoriferous overflow from the sidewalk and Bughouse Square. They needed only the price of a cup of coffee to sit here; or, if brash, they came and sat, buying nothing. Sat for hours reading old newspapers and pamphlets, handed them around to one another. Or sat, noisily arguing, until, to be heard above the swell of conversation, men seated at the same table had to shout at each other. Old men in suspenders and caps. Wild-eyed women. Crackpots. Radicals. Religious fanatics. The bohemian outer circle. Sat at the tables with their heads against their hands until spiders wove their webs from their fingers. Or so it seemed to Nick. And, boyishly, he added spider webs to his oval of a head on the notebook page. But the mood of humor broken, he scratched lines through the beginning of his sketch.

His brown eyes again looked out the plate glass and onto Clark Street. A pale, pimply young man, clasping a soft-leather Bible under his arm, went across the window. Horns sounded and the yellow of a taxi made a slow, deliberate, insulting U-turn. A drunk now staggered against the window. For a moment he leaned grotesquely against the pane, as if to keep from crashing into the street. The juke box in the tavern next door was competing winningly against the clanging of streetcar gongs. A Negro starts past the Marquis. The music catches his feet and tangles there. He begins a slow, comic shuffle in time to the music across the stage of the Marquis window. The drunk has now staggered toward the street in a long, looping half-circle. The Marquis window does not crash to the sidewalk. The drunk leans against a parked car and uses the fender for a toilet, vomiting.

Nick's eyes wander across the street. Drug store on the corner, *Beefburger*, then SKIDMORE SHOES (and this is funny to Nick), then BOHEMIAN CLUB, a big, bare tavern and in its window in bragging orange neon: TELEVISION. Then MORRIS KLEIN LOAN SHOP. Followed quickly by a Puerto Rican grocery store, a liquor store:

W
I
N
E
LIQUORS   est.

then   MONEY TO LOAN   1888

and all the things in the windows of loan shops. A man sitting in an open window on the third floor with a huge half-gallon bottle of beer. Looking out. Laughing to himself.

Nick turned the page of his sketchbook and began to rapidly sketch the man.

And Nick again drew scrawls through his sketch and half rose, leaving his coffee untouched.

I'll go home. Maybe my mother is there. The hot air of the street hit him. No, she's not there. He took a hesitating step. No, I'll go to Bughouse Square and sit on the grass.

He crossed the streetcar tracks of Chicago Avenue. He looked into the plate-glass window of Thompson's Restaurant and his lips gladdened in a smile. Inside at a table he saw his friends.

Phil was saying, "I found out one thing about handling broads. You can't treat them nice. You got to slap the shit out of them."

"Shhh! Here comes the kid!" Max warned.

Their voices silenced.

Norman stopped looking at the counter boy.

"Hi, Nick!" they all said when he stood alongside them, grinning.

"Sit down," Max said. "What are you going to have?" and without waiting for an answer, went to the counter and brought him two dips of ice cream and a cut of pie.

Judge came in behind them and playfully tapped Max on the head with his cane. "You sonofa—!" Max started; and put his hand over his mouth, looking at Nick, then turned, saw Judge Sullivan.

"Don't do that, Judge!" he said, laughing. "I swing without looking!"

Judge Sullivan rumpled his hair and eased himself into a chair, placing his shoebox on the table.

"What'll you have?" Max asked.

"Nothing. Nothing. Nothing." His eyes kindled. "Nothing but wine. Or whiskey. Or beer."

"Later," Phil said.

Nick sat, listening to them talk, his eyes rolling from one face to another.

Phil was morose. "Once this street gets a grip on you, it's got you. You're hooked," he said. "I left this street four different times but I always come back."

The conversation went somewhere else. Max had had a few drinks and was expansive.

"There are gods," he said.

"Name one," Phil said.

"Well, Einstein is one."

Norm's laugh was on the upper note of the scale.

Max and Phil frowned at him and Norm lowered the scale of his laughter.

"Max, you're crazy," Phil said.

"And Gandhi was one," Max said.

"Max, you're crazy," Phil said.

"Gods are people who help people," Max said.

They weren't really very happy, and Judge, tired, weary of foot, was unusually quiet and sat resting his fingers against his closed eyes.

"Straight, sober, stone sober," Phil said, "I'll be shaving and looking in the mirror. I'll call myself every name. But I've given up. I'm nothing and have nothing and I'll probably never be nothing. It's a no-good, goddamn life."

It was Norm's turn to frown at Phil.

"We can't lose forever," Max said.

"You gotta live with your fingers crossed," Phil said.

I wonder where my mother is. I better go look for her. I hope she isn't drunk.

Nick stood up, his brown eyes sad. "I have to go."

"Yeah, kid," Max said.

"How about a show tomorrow night?" Norm said.

"All right."

"I'll pop," Phil said.

Nick moved between tables, and for a moment, as he passed, his fingers touched Judge Sullivan's shoulder. "Good-bye."

They sat silent, watching him go, his books under his arm.

At length, Judge Sullivan said, watching him out of his old face, "There he goes, the symbol of the innocence of youth in a horrible, horrible environment."

"Yeah," Max said.

"Ungoof, Judge," Phil said, "and score us in on what you're talking about."

Judge Sullivan's face and eyes came back to levity. "Well, gentlemen," he said, "who's going to pop—pop, is that what you call it? —for the drinks?" And smiling, sharing youthful confidence, "I've been up and down stairs today more than one of those ladies of the night."

"I got holes in my pocket," Phil said.

Norm showed a folded five-dollar bill.

"We're in!" Phil shouted.

"Uuhhh! Tonight I want to really beast it up!" Max said, giving a thoroughly masculine growl. "That is, if I can find a babe who isn't asking too much."

When Nick got home, his mother was there. She was sitting at the table looking out the window.

"Hello, Mother."

"Nicky," she said abstractedly.

Nick set his books on the table.

"There's nothing to eat," Nellie said tonelessly. "We'll have to go out to eat."

"All right."

They went on the street together. They went to a corner hamburger joint. Nellie walked somewhat unsteadily. At the door, Nick said, "Don't go staggering in. That looks bad." His voice was stern. There were tears in his eyes.

Inside, he said he just wanted a hog dog, milk and a cupcake. Nellie wouldn't eat anything. She only took a bite out of Nick's cupcake, taking it from the top where the white icing was.

Again Nick's eyes clouded. On the low stool, he turned toward his mother. "I don't belong to the family," he said.

"What family?" Nellie said uncomprehendingly.

"Your family. I don't feel that I belong. Don't count me." He pulled air through his nose, pulling back wetness and tears. He got up. "I'm going home to do my homework." He walked out.

Finishing his homework, Nick went looking for his mother. Staring through the plate glass of the Shillelagh Club, he saw her sitting at the bar with a man. He walked away, head down. Automatically, as had become his custom, he looked through the windows of the Shanty Inn. He saw Max, Phil and Norm sitting with their elbows on the table, mugs of beer before them, a girl with them. Max was laughing.

He walked back and stood in front of the Shillelagh Club for a while. The man was talking to his mother. His mother was smoking a cigarette. The man put his arm around his mother's waist.

Nick moved away from the window.

He went home. He looked at his drawings for a little while. Then he put out the light and lay across the bed with his face in the crook of his elbow.

It isn't so easy to be so young.

43

When Nick came down to the corner of Chicago Avenue in the morning to get his streetcar for school, Judge Sullivan stepped out of the doorway of the drug store and came slowly toward him on his cane. The brim of his battered felt hat was turned down around his face at different angles and his white mustache hung ragged over his upper lip. "Hello, son," he said in a hoarse whisper, and tapped his chest. "Sick," he said. "And broke." Nick had to listen carefully to hear him; he was so hoarse he could hardly speak. "I need medicine."

Nick reached into his pocket and pulled out his lunch money. "A quarter's all I have. Can you—?"

The old, wrinkled hand came out shakily. "Thank you, son. I'll get some cough medicine." It was a hoarse whisper, almost inaudible. Nodding, pointing, Judge Sullivan indicated that he would wait there until Nick's streetcar came.

"No, you go get the medicine," Nick said.

Judge waited anyway, leaning heavily on his cane.

Nick boarded the car, standing in the back and lifting his hand to Judge.

Judge Sullivan stood watching the streetcar. As soon as it was two blocks down the track, he turned on his cane and walked into a tavern. When he got inside, his voice was no longer hoarse.

The boy Nick hung around with at school was a fellow named Carl, who was first-string fullback on the football team. Their friendship was based only on the fact that Carl, even if he was big and husky and the star of the team, liked English literature too. They often ate lunch together and sat kicking their heels against the stone embankment in front of school and talked about books they were reading and which authors "sent" them. Sometimes they went to shows together. Once to the Art Institute when there was a Van Gogh show and the English teacher promised extra credit for kids who went and wrote an English paper about it. Nick had never seen Carl play football because on Saturdays and Sundays he now worked at a drug-store ice-cream fountain. But he wanted to because he liked Carl. Carl's folks were kind of rich and lived in a big house they owned on State Parkway, but they sent him to public school because, as Carl said, grinning, "They want me to have the common touch—whatever that means."

Finishing his homework, Nick went, as every night, to see what bar his mother was in and then to look for Judge and the rest of them.

He found them at a restaurant where they also served drinks, and when he came in they were all drunk; and when they saw him, they were all trying to pretend to be sober and Norm pulled his eyes away from someone at the next table.

"Have you seen my mother?"

"No, kid," Phil said.

"Sit down, kid," Max said.

"Can I stay in here?"

"Sure, it's a restaurant."

Nick sat down.

Drunk, forgetting he was there, they continued their conversation.

Max was saying, "Yeah, I made the detention home. I wish I knew then what I know now." He took a long swallow of his beer. "I would of said I was eighteen. When you're eighteen you don't go to that crummy joint—and it's really something. I'll take jail any time over it."

"Well, who are you, big shot?" Phil said. "I made the jailhouse. Had a little brush with the law. This other guy. He copped out. He told his guts. It's jail for me."

Norm sat listening, his elbow on the table, his hand and arm like the languid stalk of an Easter lily, a cork-tipped cigarette loosely held between the feminine-poised fingers. Max, momentarily sober, leaned over toward Norm. In a whisper he said, "Hey! Don't hold your cigarette like that!"

Norm's hand came to a stiff, masculine pose. Phil sent Nick to the counter for a bottle of pop and some pie.

"Act more masculine in front of the kid," Phil said.

"Yeah," Max said.

Nick came back with his pie and a bottle of orange soda.

"In the county jail, if you know the right connections, you can pick up on anything," Phil said.

Judge was full of red wine and wisdom. To Nick he said, "If you have respect for yourself, you treat a prostitute like a lady."

A man came along with a small kit, saying wearily, "Razor blades . . . razor blades . . ."

Judge looked up at him and said pleasantly, "I am in that business myself, sir."

The man looked at Judge Sullivan for a silent, unfriendly moment; then, seeing the young men at the table, leaned over toward them and, revealing a small tin box in the palm of his hand, said, "A full dozen for only a quarter."

"Get out of here!" Max said, laughing. "What do you think I am, a rabbit?"

Nick got up. "I have to go look for my mother," he said.

44

The plate-glass window is painted halfway up with muddy green paint. A man can stand on the sidewalk and look inside. It says there in large letters on the dirty, flyspecked plate glass:

THE SHILLELAGH CLUB

The bar seems a block long, and has unpainted, wobbly bar stools placed unevenly in front of it. The cheap bottles of whiskey and wine stand in stiff invitation on the back bar and, incongruously, among them a large vase of wilting flowers. The ancient cash register opens its greedy jaws, then clangs them shut. Tacked to the top paneling of the back bar are gaudily colored placards sold by an itinerant sign painter and boldly proclaiming:

OUR BEER CONTAINS VITAMIN P

THE SULTAN HAD NINE WIVES
EIGHT OF THEM HAD IT PRETTY SOFT

Propped near the cash register is a crudely penciled sign:

BE SURE TO COLLECT FROM ANYONE WHO
IS DRUNK BEFORE YOU SERVE THEM

There is a juke box, a cathedral of a juke box, pushed into a corner near the 26-table. It is turned to its top volume:

He's in the jailhouse now
He's in the jailhouse now . . .

The music shouts to the walls until they seem to shake back and forth. The music shouts to the far door, to the street, to the other side of the street, to people passing in cars. The music assails like an army with cannon.

He's in the jailhouse now
He's in the jailhouse now . . .

With the music, throughout the tavern, heavy, floating on the air, sickening, muggy at the door and out across the sidewalk, is the acrid smell of the brown-stained urinals. Into the clothes of the people, into their pores, it weaves itself like fine hand-knitting.

Across the warped, splintery floor are spit and beer caps and twisted cigarette butts; spilled beer, vomit and urine.

At the dice table the 26-girl sits in boredom. A glass of cheap mixed whiskey stands at her fat elbow. Behind the bar, the two bartenders bend down into beer cases, stand erect, turn, lift cheap whiskey and wine from the back bar, mop, with dirty rags, the suds and spilled drinks, the endless damp circles of glasses within the circles of glasses.

I told him once or twice
He was playin' cards and shootin' dice
He's in the jailhouse now
He's in the jailhouse now
He's in the jailhouse now . . .

Men sit on the stools, and women, big-rumped. They are elbows and glasses down along the length of the bar. A woman's voice cuts across the tavern, laughing and cursing. Another. And another.

There are women, husky and loud-voiced, dressed in sloppy blue jeans. Other women in dirty print dresses or in plain dresses of dark colors that nevertheless show dirt and liquor stains. Some of the younger and tougher-looking women have tattoos on their arms and wrists.

"Hey, Chuck, take over, will you?" one bartender says to another, stripping off his apron. "I'm going to have a sandwich."

Now I don't care if I'm not the first love you've known.
Just so I'll be the last . . .

screams the juke box.

This is the Shillelagh Club. It is on Clark Street just south of Chicago Avenue. It has the worst name on the street. The guy who owns the joint is an ex-con and he knows the score.

At the grimy curbstone in front of the Shillelagh stands the latest-model Cadillac convertible in all its immaculate splendor. It belongs to the owner of the Shillelagh.

Now I don't care if I'm not the first one you've kissed.
Darling, I'll never ask . . .

Nellie half fell into the door. Her long, loose blond hair, slightly tangled, fell to her shoulders. She stumbled at the bar and bummed a cigarette from a man sitting there. He held the match. She winked and, wavering away, said, "I'll see you when your troubles are as big as mine." She wavered back toward tables, toward the deeper darkness of the place. A man leaned over one woman at the bar and said to the woman in blue jeans who sat next to her, "What are you trying to do? Make my wife?" Down a way, a woman with a black eye and a whiskey voice said to her companion, "I'm glad I don't have any children and I'm glad I'm not going to have any. A million dollars' worth I'm glad." She almost slid off her stool.

Nellie found an empty table and wavered down into the chair in front of it. At the bar, a man in overalls who looked like a working man said to a man in a business suit and clean white shirt, a man who didn't look as if he belonged in this place, "All of us are sonsabitches in this life."

Nellie sat at the empty table, her head leaning on her hands, her hair spilled over her wrist and face. In her fingers, above the tangled hair, a cigarette protruded. Its purple-blue smoke rose in long, slow, funereal ribbons. She was a failure as a mother. And she knew why. Don't think about it! I can't stop thinking about it! And I know why. It's my secret. I can't help it. Can't help it. Can't help it.

An elderly woman without teeth, her flesh enveloping the bar stool and spilling over it, said to the equally elderly man in the straw hat without a band, "I used to drive my own big, fine car and it wasn't no Cadillac. I can drive any car you put before me. And you don't walk back. I don't walk back. Nobody don't walk back."

A man walked past her. She grabbed at him, saying, "Hello, sweetheart. Hey, you!—Hello, angel."

Nick stood on tiptoe looking into the Shillelagh Club. Then he went to the door. The bartender saw him standing there and nodded toward the back of the tavern, a swift gesture with his head and neck.

Nick entered and walked toward the back. At a table he passed, a woman was saying to her male pickup, "I was a twisted, mangled mess of a no-good woman. Then I found God. You'd be surprised how that can snap you out of it." She put her hand on his arm. "You gonna buy me another drink?"

A woman of about thirty and weighing at least two hundred and fifty pounds stood by the table talking to Nellie. Her skirt stood out around her hips like a tent. She looked like an elephant standing erect, and she moved about as gracefully. With her, laughing, showing two broken teeth, was a waitress holding a dripping bar rag in one hand. The two women were laughing and his mother was laughing. His mother got up and wandered unevenly to an empty place at the bar. The women went there and stood with her, talking.

Hesitatingly, Nick moved toward his mother. At this stretch of bar he now passed, a man stood with a half-handsome, half-tough-looking boy in his early twenties. There were shot glasses in front of them. The man wore an expensive silk sport shirt with a surrealistic design. His nails had clear polish and there was a heavy and expensive gold chain on his wrist. He leaned over toward the young man and said, "I'd like to have you tonight."

Nick moved to his mother's side. He stood there not speaking. The fat woman and the waitress looked at him. Then his mother, aware that he was there, looked up at him.

"Let's go home, Mother," he said.

"This is my boy!" Nellie said proudly. "This is my son!"

Nick averted his eyes.

"What do you think of my great big boy!" Nellie asked the women.

"Let's go home, Mother."

The women, looking at him, made womanly sounds, chucklings and exclamations.

"How old are you?" his mother asked.

"Sixteen."

"He's sixteen," she told the women.

Nick said, "Let's go home. Your nose is running and you're slobbering. You're drunk."

45

They were drunk as usual and went weaving arm in arm along North Clark pavement taking up all the sidewalk.

Nick came from the opposite direction.

"Hello, Uncle Max. Uncle Norm. Uncle Phil," he said, identifying them.

"Hi, Nick!"

And Max, pretending that he was not drunk, was walking like a giraffe.

"How old are you, big stuff?" Max asked.

"I'm sixteen and a half," Nick said.

Max seemed to digest this. He put his hand on Nick's shoulder for a while and walked along like this—mostly to steady himself.

In front of the Shebeen, they said they were going in, and Nick left them.

Inside, they took a table and ordered drinks. Judge found them there just when, remembering, Max said, "We ain't doing right by our boy." They pulled up a chair for Judge Sullivan and ordered a double wine that rapidly disappeared and stained Judge Sullivan's mustache red.

"What do you say, Judge?" Phil asked, slapping him drunkenly across the shoulder.

Judge Sullivan's eyes, twinkling, followed their faces in a half-circle. "Say? I'm just an observer here from the medical association."

Judge Sullivan got a little drunk too; and a little sleepy. When he wasn't particularly noticing them, Max said, "Pssstt!" softly and, motioning, showed them that he had something to say that he didn't want to say in front of Judge Sullivan: he might be disapproving because he was old.

They walked over to the juke box as if they wanted to select a number. Max, when the three of them were there, leaned his big elbow up on the juke box, up above its shifting rainbow of colors. "The kid's sixteen," Max said.

"Sixteen and a half," Norm corrected.

"Yeah? So what?" Phil said.

Max winced a grin. "W-o-m-a-n." Max spelled it out for them. His lips formed the letters softly, emphatically; drunkenly but carefully.

"Oh! Yeah!" Phil said enthusiastically.

"We'll talk about it later," Max said, jabbing them in the ribs with his elbows, and they moved back toward the table.

Judge Sullivan was headed toward the exit on his cane without saying good-bye. Drunk, but making it. His pants were baggy. He limped a little, but cockily.

They sat with new drinks at their elbows and new cigarettes lit. Max and Phil argued about a girl for Nick, the kind of girl. Norm listened.

"It's got to be a decent girl," Phil said.

"But decent girls don't screw," Max said.

They went over names and ages, color of hair and shape of legs, sizes of bosoms and the possibility of success in their venture toward Nick's manhood.

"Say! What about Gloria?" Phil suggested.

"She's too big. Do you want the kid to go crazy?" Max said, discarding her.

"Maizie?"

"Not a whore. A *nice* girl."

"But, *Max*, nice girls don't screw."

"What about Muriel? She's been putting out for a long time now."

"Naaw! I think she's got a dose." Then Max's eyes went dreamy. He grinned up reminiscence. "Did I ever tell you about that little broad in Tokyo when I—"

"Let's not talk about your romances, huh?" Phil said. "Let's get this thing settled."

"Say! I know a waitress. She ain't cherry. That's for sure. But she's cute and—"

"Look, leave waitresses out of this! They're always lookin' for tips. They're a money-hungry bunch. The kid's broke!"

"That's right."

"You better believe it."

More beer came and there was more talk.

"Yeah," Max said, "but you can't get him a virgin."

"Why not?" Phil said roughly.

Max grinned painfully. "You wouldn't want anybody to do *that* to *your* sister, would you?"

More beer came.

"What about Alice?" Max suggested.

"What! That goddamn P.T. Listen, once I was with her in this guy's car and—"

Max cut in with, "What about Doris?"

She didn't fit the bill either.

"Lorraine?" Phil questioned.

"I call her Lucy," Max said. "Tee-hee."

"And no gang-bang babe for the kid!" Phil warned angrily, as if Max had suggested it.

They finally, after many more drinks and much more discussion, settled on Ann, who they knew had laid a couple of times, but only a couple, and was that close to a virgin and was clean and discreet. She was the one for their boy!

They decided that tomorrow they would tell Nick, and left each other with much handshaking and pleased, wry looks.

They encountered Nick the next day in the back of a hot-dog joint and were pleased that the place was empty. They descended upon him. They slapped him across the back in man-to-man fashion.

"Ah, we want to talk to you, Nick."

"Yes, Uncle Phil." His teeth were white in the hamburger bun, answering.

"Well—ah—look, kid—" Phil began.

"Yes," Max said, encouraging Phil.

"Well, let me put it this way," Phil said. And then sat in silence, having no way to put it.

"Well, look, kid, the sexes are different," Max said.

"Yes, different," Phil said, sweating.

"Well—ah—ah—" Max said, "there comes a time when that little thing stands up—and—ah—" Max halted. He scratched the back of his neck.

"*Look, kid!*" they both said together and then stared at each other.

"Well, you need a woman," Max said roughly.

"Yeah. You need a woman," Phil said roughly.

Nick looked at them in astonishment, from face to face; then his lips began to smile outward. "I had a girl over a year ago," he said.

46

He walked all the way home from school instead of taking the streetcar, thinking, every step of the way, about his mother. He loved her. He hated her. He wished she was different. Like she used to be. For a minute he saw dandelions in yellow circles. The sky bluer than . . . and a Christmas tree . . . a good, good mother. Graduation day. And no mother. Who was my father? She said he was a good man. She loved him. She loved me too. I wish I had him. He could help us now. I don't understand what kind of a drunk she is. Sometimes she snaps out of it. Sometimes she works for a week or two. Sometimes she is almost like she used to be. Sometimes she is like she's in a trance. I love you. I want to help you.

He turned up between the black iron railings, went up the few steps and pushed the door open. His mother sat at the table in front of the window.

She's drunk again.

He laid his books down. Yes, she's drunk. All his love, all his hurt turned to anger, to sarcasm.

"How many drinks did you have today?" he said.

"Well, I had a Tom Collins and I had three martinis, and seven bottles of beer, and three straight shots," his mother said.

Nick sat across from her at the table. "First, I'm going to take you to the doctor to see what is happening to your *wonderful* head," he said.

"I'm going to get a job," she said, her eyes pleading with him for some sort of understanding.

"Aw!"

"Why can't I work?"

"Because you work for two hours and then you go to drink and the next day you forget everything—work—everything—"

Vaguely she remembered her last job. She had fixed herself up. She had tried to get herself straightened out. The job was at one of the girl revue places on the street. She had to sit and drink with the customers, conventioneers, farmers, traveling men. It was a rule in that place, a new wrinkle to get the suckers caught in, that the girls had to order straight rum with a coke chaser. Then the man, the sucker, not believing that they were drinking the real thing, could taste the liquor. The girls took sips from the rum. When they lifted the coke chaser to their mouths they spit the rum into the coke glass. Easy as that. She had had the job three days. And then—and then—

"Yes, I drink," she said to Nick. She laughed. Then there were tears in her eyes and on her cheeks. "You don't know. You don't know," she said.

"Oh, shut up, you."

"What did you say?"

"The same thing you heard."

"You get a pleasure talking to your mother like that?"

"You're not my mother."

"Oh." All of her life went into the one word.

Her nose was running. She began drawing in.

"I'll take my things back to the hotel," Nick said.

He had moved out and lived in a hotel for two days, and then, worrying about his mother, had moved back home.

"And I'll bring them back here," his mother said.

"Okay. We'll see who gets tired first."

"I'm going to the Shillelagh," she said.

"If you go there, I'll smack your face, Mother."

"Well, I'm going there and I don't think you will smack my face."

"Now you're plastered, Mother—and don't talk such ridiculous things."

He looked out the window, looking away, because he had to, from his mother's face. He saw on the window sill on the second floor of the house across the street the little touch of yellow color inside the cage. It had to be another canary. It couldn't be the same one living that long.

He lowered his eyes back into the room. They came beseechingly to his mother's face, asking for yesterday, the things of yesterday. Asking, please love me again and make everything like it used to be. Her eyes looked back out of the frame of her tangled hair. They said none of the love of yesterday. They only looked drunk.

"I'd like for you to be on that goddamn plane that crashed, because I'm ashamed of you," Nick said. His eyes were full of tears.

"Oh, you're ashamed of me. That's good. The voice of experience speaking. Who are kids to judge their parents?"

"You don't want to hear what I'm going to say. Okay. I'm not going to say anything."

"It seems you know everything, and still I'm nineteen years older than you."

"You're in a fog."

"Is that all you know—is to argue with me?"

"You're going to find your way. There are two roads."

"I'm going out." Waveringly she got to her feet.

"No, you're not."

"Oh." Again her nose made a sniffing sound.

He followed her to the door.

She fumbled at the handle.

He grabbed her by the wrist and turned her around. "Take a good look at yourself in the mirror." He forced her to stare into the glass.

It was a horrible face. Only those beautiful blue-gray eyes. But strange. Somewhat wild. And those finely chiseled cheekbones, like his own.

She turned her eyes away. "I'm going out."

She moved to the door. He blocked it. She moved around him.

"Mother, don't go out. Please don't go out." It was desperation and defeat.

She went out.

He followed her.

In that way she had of walking that frightened him, she moved along Clark Street. As if she was asleep. Her feet obeyed. But she was in a fog. Mother! Mother! Please!

Now she leaned with a flabby hand, her arm outstretched, against a drug-store window and, almost feeling her way, moved uncertainly to the clothing-store window, rested there, arm outthrust. Almost bent now with cramps in her stomach, she got to the entrance of the Shillelagh, to its door.

Nick intercepted her, blocking the entrance. He was a half-foot taller than she. She struggled with him, trying to fight her way inside.

Nick stood, frightened, shamed, imagining everybody was looking at them. Her fingernails reached for his face. Everybody was looking at them. He dropped his hands. His mother slipped past him and inside.

Frank was sitting at the bar. His broad shoulders, turned away from her, were huge in the tight T-shirt, his hips slim between bar stool and tight black belt.

She stood alongside him. "Frank," she said pleadingly.

He made no indication that he had heard her.

She slipped onto the stool next to him. "Frank."

"Hi."

He reached over, two places down the bar, and pulled the open pack of cigarettes in front of him. He lifted the pack with one cigarette protruding.

She clutched at the package of cigarettes with both hands.

"Take one! Light one!" he said in a command.

She lit one, her hands trembling. Her eyes held a dazed look staring at him.

His eyes dropped around the tavern for a moment. Then he pushed the pack toward her.

Clutching the package of cigarettes in her hand she got up off the stool.

She moved toward the door without saying good-bye to him.

Nick moved from the window where he had been looking into the tavern. In the doorway he grabbed his mother by the back of her dress, ripping it a little. "Get home!"

Startled, she resisted him. Holding to her dress he pulled at her. Resisting, she sat down on the tavern doorstep. Nick grabbed her fingers, twisting them, bending them backward, forcing her to stand up. Then he led her toward home with his arm around her neck in almost a wrestler's grip. She was wavering so much that he, too, seemed drunk as he tried to hold her erect.

Under dead bars of neon he led her, her neck in the vise of his arm. And he pulled her toward him and kissed her on the forehead, leading her toward home.

At home she locked herself in the toilet. When she finally came out she sat in a chair at the kitchen table by the front window. After a while she started to nod.

As soon as he thought she was asleep, Nick slipped quietly out the door.

Hurt, hurt inside where he knew it would never be cured; he took a long walk, unconscious of his direction or where he was going.

When he looked up he was in front of Lincoln Park.

He went into the park and, away from everybody, lay face down on the grass. Then, after a long, long time, he sat up. He rubbed his face with the palms of his hands. It was almost dark. He went into the bushes to take a leak.

47

Under the shaded green lamp on its long cord Sergeant Bill Forbes sat, his feet propped on a tall stool and crossed at the ankles. Some light from the lamp slanted across the sergeant's face and head, revealing the evenly mixed steel-gray of his crew cut and the squareness of his jaw. Sergeant Forbes was reading.

He sat in a circle of light; elsewhere shadows engulfed the empty room. They reached to the tips of his shoes. Reached toward his shoulders. Reached out as if wishing to caress the blue sleeves of his uniform. In the quiet room the shadows were like condemned men, standing, waiting. Both the innocent and the guilty.

Sergeant Forbes turned a page.

The clock ticked. The shadows stood motionless. Night was a drawn shade at the window. Sergeant Forbes finished what he was reading. He placed the open book, face down, across his knee and leaned back, his hands clasped behind his head.

Long live Thoreau! Long live Jean Jacques Rousseau!

He had just finished reading Thoreau's essay, *Civil Disobedience*. He leaned back now, savoring it, going over, in his mind, some of the phrases. Under the light the upturned book on his knees read: GREAT THINKERS: *Speculative, Social, Political*.

He meditated a long time. Then he looked out into the shadows. The condemned seemed to stand there mute. Chained together. Waiting to be counted. He looked at them and they looked back at him. Other shadows from off the street would soon be standing there inside these shadows. The little petty, piffling crimes. Snatched a purse. Loitering. Disorderly conduct. Drunk. Drunk. Jackrolling. Petty larceny. Over and over. And the charge sheet would fill. The shadows would be dragged away downstairs to the lock-up. Loitering. Drunk. Drunk. Disorderly. Like beads on a string.

He passed a hand over his forehead and his crew cut. Sometimes he felt old and shamed and the criminal himself, there behind the desk recording the minor offenses of the baffled, the weak, the stupid, the sick, the wretchedly poor. Shoplifting. Entering. Disorderly. And, occasionally, the big sin, the big crime that made headlines and fed the morbid appetite of a city. Like being a priest in a confessional under this green-shaded lamp, before this blotter, in front of a shadow that mumbled name, age, address. Petty larceny. Drunk. Drunk. Prostitution.

He didn't like cops, and he was one!

Sergeant Forbes sat up straight and, taking the book off his knees, opened the desk drawer that belonged to him. He shoved the book under arrest sheets at the bottom of the drawer. If the monkeys around here caught him reading this stuff he'd be the butt of endless jokes. He heard a police car drive up into the yard and pushed the drawer closed with his foot. Long live Thoreau! He looked up into the shadows and waited.

They brought the boy in. Between the two policemen he stood in the ring of shadows of the accused. The kid looked scared.

Sergeant Forbes stood up; he was broad and square, with the build of a man twenty years his junior. His head was large, square, the chin and mouth set forcefully into it. The nose was prominent. The eyes, gray and unwavering, held not police inquisition but a deep, sometimes hidden, warmth.

"Indecent exposure," one of the park policemen said. It was said brusquely and as if he were miserly with words.

"You can hold him open," the other cop said, "but this is indecent exposure."

Sergeant Forbes said, "Well, wait a minute, I'll— To what extent is it indecent exposure?"

"Well, we're going to get a witness. We're going to get some people to come in here. Hold him open."

"It's necessary for you to sign a complaint for us to hold him open."

The park police signed the complaint.

Sergeant Forbes took the boy down to a cell. The kid was really scared. On the way down the sergeant looked at the boy, not unkindly. "What's your name?"

"Nick. Nick Romano."

While the park police were out, Sergeant Forbes sat again with his feet on the high stool, his hands behind his head, and thought to himself. Then he let his feet bang down on the floor and went back to the cells.

Nick sat on the edge of the iron bunk with his eyes downcast. He was a thin boy.

"How old are you, Nick?" the sergeant asked.

Nick remembered something Max had said. "Eighteen," he said. He was cracking his knuckles in a habit his father had had.

"Want to talk about it, kid?"

"I just went into the bushes to take a—to urinate."

Later a middle-aged woman and her two children came to the station, sent over by the park police to sign the complaint. They hadn't accompanied her.

The woman said she would sign the complaint "because the children told me that this man walked into the bushes and took his—ah —privates—out." Her young daughters huddled close to her skirt, looking with big eyes out into the new and strange environment of the police station.

"Well, Mrs.—this fellow," Sergeant Forbes said, "I don't know if you know this. This fellow is in his last year of high school, exactly between the ages of eighteen and nineteen. I talked to him and he's never been arrested before, and checked that he has no record, no police record. He was even going to his week-end job tonight. Now —on the strength of the possibility that he may have had to urinate and just went in there not knowing the children were there and never even saw them, he— We can destroy his chance for an education and a living as a member of our society."

The woman put her hands to her head and said, "Oh my God, I never thought of that!"

"Well, think it over," the sergeant said. "We'll hold him, tomorrow being Sunday anyway. Think it over, because this is important."

She said she would.

Sergeant Forbes put the matter aside, but Nick was still in the lockup when he came to work Sunday night.

The sergeant called the park police and told them to send someone over to get a complaint signed legitimately.

The police brought the woman back but she wouldn't sign the complaint.

The park police, disgruntled because their quarry was slipping through their fingers, decided to book him for disorderly.

After they had gone, Sergeant Forbes made himself a pot of coffee and sat looking out at the crouching, invading shadows of the accused while the water boiled on the electric plate. He drank, then refilled the cup and went down to the cells.

The boy still sat dejectedly on the edge of the iron cot.

"Here." The sergeant passed the cup through the bars to the boy. "You're booked for disorderly conduct."

The boy looked up over the edge of the cup fearfully, then set it down, without drinking, on the floor between his feet. "Oh my God, I don't want my mother to know about this! This is awful. I'd rather stay in jail than have her know."

"That's a ten-dollar bond that will get you out," the sergeant said.

"I don't want her to know," Nick said.

"Well, if you want to stay in jail, that's all right with me. You go to court tomorrow morning. But if you want to get out, I can get you a bondsman who will get you out on a ten-dollar bond and your family still don't have to know."

"Get a bondsman for me if you can and I'll go out," Nick said. And he was very grateful to Sergeant Forbes.

Nick made bond and went out. He went to court Monday morning and was discharged.

48

Grant awakened in his Lake Shore apartment. He sat up in bed, pushed his long fingers into his scalp and rubbed vigorously until his hair, which needed cutting, stood up between his fingers. He yawned enjoyably and then stood up tall, threw his bathrobe carelessly over his body. On bare feet he padded to the kitchen, and from the maid got the coffee service.

"I'll take it, Katie."

The maid looked down at his bare feet, always a little shocked at this rich man's behavior.

"Yes, sir."

She was sleeping with one arm thrown back under her head.

With a feather pulled from the pillow casing he tickled her nose.

She wiggled her nose away and he tickled again. Slowly her eyes came open.

"Hi!"

"Hi!"

"Coffee, Mrs. Holloway?"

He stirred in the sugar and cream for her and she sat up in bed.

To him she was as beautiful as she had been almost twenty years ago when they were married.

She smiled and took the cup he held out to her. "You're impossible!" she said.

And when they had finished their coffee and he had set the cups aside, she again said, shaking her head slowly back and forth, "Impossible!— Almost as sweet as—"

"You've got most of the money," Grant said.

"Cut it out," she said.

He started wrestling with her.

"Oh, Grant! You're hurting me!"

He knew he wasn't and he knew she knew he wasn't.

He got a half nelson on her and lay with his face close to hers. "For a man in his fifties you think you're quite the boy, don't you?" she taunted. "Bet I can beat you in golf."

"We're a little too old for this sort of thing," Grant said, lying there pleasurably.

"Golf?" she asked.

"Not today, Wanda."

"What are you doing today? Let's play golf."

"Un-uh, gal. I'm going to start on that assignment. Why don't you play with Bobby?"

"You know Bobby's too good for me—for you too."

Grant grinned. He nodded yes and said, "Ah, the younger generation!" He stood up.

"Oh, Max called you last night," Wanda said.

"Was he drunk or sober?"

"Drunk, of course. He talked to me for half an hour and I don't know what he said."

Grant laughed. "I'll call him today."

Pouring herself another cup of coffee, Wanda watched him dress. He was putting on his oldest clothes. She smiled, knowing him so well. Prowling. For the story. And he'd probably get drunk these first couple of days. Always on the first days of an assignment. Then after that he'd be so absorbed in his work, she'd be almost afraid to talk to him. He'd probably work in his hotel room a week straight and she'd see him only at dinnertime. But she liked him that way. He should do a novel.

He stopped at the door and waved.

"Ta-ta," she said in good-bye.

He went downtown to several agencies and came away with an armload of mimeographed and printed pamphlets and booklets. On impulse he stepped into a telephone booth, called the sheriff's office and gave his name.

After a brief pause the sheriff was talking to him. "Hi, Grant! What's on your mind?"

"Hello, Marty. I'd like to see you. May I come up?— I'm a couple of blocks away."

"Why not come over to dinner tonight or tomorrow, where we can relax?"

"I'd like to see you now for a while."

"Okay. Come on up."

He was shown into Sheriff Cavanaugh's office and they shook hands.

"I never thought a librarian could make it," Grant said and they both laughed.

"This is the first time you've been up here, uh? Well"—and he gestured—"sit down. What's on your mind?"

"I'm doing an eight-part article on narcotics for a national magazine—narcotics, narcotics and crime, narcotics and juvenile delinquency, narcotics and whatever angles I dream up that have broad reader appeal and are also pertinent." He showed his pile of booklets: *The Narcotic Addict in Chicago, Juvenile Narcotic Problem in Chicago, The Facts About Our Teen-Age Drug Addicts*, etc.

Grant smiled at Cavanaugh. "What can you tell me about it— actual cases and—stuff like that?"

"What can I tell you about it? I can tell you plenty." He smiled. "Take out your notebook."

He told Grant plenty about it. He told him about the guards who had smuggled dope into jail in fountain pens and pencils, about nutmeg selling for three dollars a can, about guards who had been tier-to-tier dope peddlers and made contacts with some of the prisoners who were soon to be released and who would then supply them with narcotics. He showed Grant all the paraphernalia—needles, caps of various drugs, samples of marijuana, toy guns used for no reason other than to supply the great need for the drug. He said, "They were sending kites out to contact their pushers—a kite is an illegal letter generally smuggled out by a guard . . . addicts don't want to be with a square. They don't trust him. He doesn't understand their problem. They generally put him on stuff or they won't hang around with him. They are generous with the stuff when they have it . . . there is an impoverished group in jail, a beggar class. The strong-arm men get all their money and they are broke."

He went on talking about drugs for an hour.

Grant kept a room in the Allerton Hotel, where he wrote when he wanted to get away from home; where he also had a wire recorder and where he sometimes interviewed people. Leaving Sheriff Cavanaugh he went there. Scowling, he tossed his armload of informational literature on the bed. Statistics!— How do you make them get up and walk? Go to the people, boy.

Max. He'd call Max. And he'd go to see Juan. Juan had once, in the very infrequent times they ran into each other, casually said that there was a lot of dope in that neighborhood now. I could see Forbes too. No, Juan first. See the people when you want to know about them or write about them.

He called Max's number, and the phone rang a long time while Grant swished the Scotch and water around in his glass. Then Grant smiled. Saturday. Max's off from work. He looked the number up in the book and dialed it, heard the juke box at the Long Bar playing loudly, then Max's voice, "Yeah?"

"Hi, Max! Grant."

"Hi, fellow! I was drunk last night and I wanted to talk to you. I wanted you to get drunk with me."

"Maybe tomorrow," Grant said. "What are you doing tomorrow afternoon? Fine! Will you meet me at Juan's place? Yes, about one o'clock. Fine, Max. Good-bye."

Grant then sprawled out on the bed with his feet on the pillow and the bottle of Scotch near at hand. He read through his pamphlets, making notes and underlining sentences here and there. This took several hours. Then he called Wanda and told her he didn't know when he'd be home. "I'm prowling. I might even get drunk."

"Okay. Be careful." She knew him and smiled in affection, hanging up.

It isn't a far walk from the Allerton to North Clark. On North Clark, Grant went into the Shebeen.

He had a couple bottles of beer and then went across the street to the Shillelagh. As he entered, a woman, her blond hair hanging loosely, her eyes tearing, her gait uneven, stumbled into him. "Oh, excuse me, mister," Nellie said.

Slim, the bartender, was at the end of the bar near the door. "Who is she, Slim?" Grant asked, nodding toward Nellie.

"Aw, she's on stuff—just a junkie."

Grant looked out the plate glass at Nellie feeling her way down the street toward her room and her fix.

Grant sipped his beer. He noticed, at the bar, a young fellow somewhere in his late twenties, but much younger-looking than his age. He was tall and slim and well built, his brown-blond hair worn in a crew cut. He wore a T-shirt and his arms were up on the bar. On each arm were three tattoos. There was a heart with a girl's name in it, an anchor and, high on one arm, on the bicep where it could move with the tightening of his muscle, was a nude girl with her arms clasped behind her head.

The young fellow with the tattoos happened to look around the place and his eyes met Grant's for a moment. Then he looked away.

Grant drank his beer, preparing to leave. He wondered what the young man's story was. He has a story all right. There's something interesting about his face. Something stands in his face. Was it past wildness? Cynical experience? Whatever it is, there's a warmth, a friendliness in his face, too. I wonder what his racket is.

Grant wandered into several other bars along North Clark, sipping beers and making further pencilings in his notebook. Then, when darkness had approached and he was down along Clark Street near Lincoln Park, he went to the house of his friend, the artist, Mark Donnelly, with whom he had shared a room in his youth when they were both going to set the world on fire. "I'm a little drunk," Grant said. "I hope you don't mind."

They sat on the back porch and drank beer from cold cans. Mark's wife brought smoked oysters. O'Leary dropped by. They were old friends, from the days when they had hung around listening to the speakers in Bughouse Square.

"I'm doing this damned series on drugs—" Grant explained to Mark. "Here are the facts—" He began enumerating with his fingers: "It's a slum problem. Negroes are the largest group of dope addicts in big cities like Chicago. Italians are second and the Mexicans are third—though, of course"—and Grant smiled—"the accepted and conventional picture is that *all* Mexicans smoke marijuana." Grant smiled. "Now take marijuana—marijuana isn't habit-forming, though I suppose the big tobacco companies had something to do with its being legally described as a narcotic. But marijuana is the first step for a lot of people—particularly young people—who are looking for 'a bigger kick' . . . The narcotic age group is seventeen to twenty-five, and the youngest addict—according to the pamphlets I've read —was a girl twelve years old." Grant stopped and lit a cigarette.

"Want to hear some more figures?" He laughed and drank instead. Then he said, "But to write about things you have to have more than facts. After the facts are assimilated—people. You're a dead fish if you try to make facts walk around by themselves." He got up. "Excuse me."

When he came back from the toilet he jotted down a note on a loose piece of paper, long hair falling over his forehead. "You know," he said, "when you take a leak you get the best ideas."

"Is that why I see all those writings in public toilets?" O'Leary asked.

They sat among paintings and books and ate steak and salad and talked.

"I'm drunk," Grant said. "I always get drunk when I start out on a new assignment. Statistics always scare me."

Before going home he went back to the Shillelagh for "just one more."

The first person he saw at one of the tables was Max. With him was Edith. "Tee-hee," Max said, "you caught us!"

Edith was a very beautiful dark-blond girl with a soft, cultivated voice that was always that way, even when she was drunk. Grant had known her for several years. Had, in fact, introduced her to Max. And now Max was romancing her. Grant grinned secretly.

Edith was a Ph.D., had an extremely high I.Q., a Phi Beta Kappa key. And she had good jewelry; she had good books; she had good paintings on the walls of her apartment, and lush furniture.

She was now teaching in the public school system. She wanted to feel useful.

She liked this cab driver, the wonderful, crazy, drinking, screwing-around Max, and he liked her. It would be a good experience for both of them. Grant grinned again. He had a deep affection for them. And a smile for their relationship—an impossible one.

Max pulled Grant down into a chair between them and hooked an arm around his neck. The drinks came. "Only one," Grant said. "I have to go home."

They had one . . . two, over Grant's protest . . . three. "Tee-hee," Max said to Grant, "you're a weak character." Four drinks.

Grant said, "You won't forget to meet me tomorrow?"

Max said no.

Edith was talking about school. "When I feel especially bad," she said, "with a hangover, I mean, I'm especially good to them because I know it isn't their fault."

More drinks came.

"Weak character!" Max said, punching Grant on the arm.

"You know, Grant," Edith said, "I wanted to teach them Shakespeare and there were no books available, so I went out and bought a pocket-book edition for each of my pupils. I told them that they could pay me back if they could afford it, and every one of them but one has. And I think, too, that they got something out of Shakespeare."

Max was smiling at her admiringly.

Grant bought a round. Then he began sweating out the statistics again. "I must go," he said, and to Max, "See you tomorrow."

At home he got a chicken leg from the refrigerator, procured a half-glass of Scotch, and sat on a chair in the kitchen chewing on the drumstick. His dog, a boxer, came in and sat looking up at him.

Suddenly Grant had an idea. He went to the phone, walking, he imagined, quietly, so as not to awaken Wanda. He dialed and the phone rang a long time. Finally a sleepy voice answered. "Hello," Grant said, "is this Seminary Avenue? I want to talk to Mr. Potratz. Oh!—Hello, George! Did I get you out of bed? Oh? Sorry. Look, George, you're always talking about Maxwell Street. How'd you like to go down there with me tomorrow? I'd like you to meet a couple Mexican friends of mine. It'll remind you of Mexico. Fine! One o'clock. 'Bye."

The dog followed him back into the kitchen.

"You know you're not supposed to have chicken bones," Grant told the dog. He continued to chew on the bone and take sips from the glass of Scotch. He said aloud, "You have to get with the people to write about it, to write about them. Yes. That's right. So I have all the statistics—say, that's a hard word to say when you're drunk."

The dog, listening intently, put its front paws on Grant's knees and stood there, its head held up regally, its eyes looking into Grant's face. Grant noticed the dog. "Who are you?" he asked. "It's important to be somebody."

Grant took another drink and then spoke to the dog again. "Everybody is somebody but they don't know who they are—and that's bad English."

The kitchen door opened softly and a girl came in. She was young, perhaps seventeen, and was dressed in blue jeans. Her mouth opened a little in surprise. Then she said, "Hi, Grant!"

Grant turned his head sideways, one hand poised with the chicken bone over the dog's mouth. "Hi, Bobby."

She kissed him on the cheek. "I was trying to sneak in," she said.

"So was I," Grant said.

"Mom?"

"She's in bed—I guess—unless she's going to sneak in later."

"I was at a moonlight picnic," the girl explained.

" 'S okay."

"Night, Grant."

"Night, Bobby."

49

Grant finally found a place to park his car several blocks away from Maxwell Street and started out on foot to go over to Juan's shop. A cold beer would be good for his hangover! He hastened his steps through the hot summer day.

George, a tall, thin, elderly man, was waiting in front of Leavitt's as they had arranged, and they started down Maxwell Street, struggling through the mob of Sunday shoppers and sightseers.

Down the middle of the street two shabby, middle-aged Mexican women with babies in their arms pulled wagons loaded with old lumber, laths, house siding. Winter is coming. Wood can be found somewhere. Wood can be carted somehow. They are as thrifty as ants and clean the streets of every twig. They are as far-sighted as squirrels.

Max was already there in front of the shop but Juan hadn't shown up. Max had brought an armload of bottles of beer and he sat on the curb, waiting, with the beer lined up alongside him. He had opened a bottle with his teeth and was enjoyably drinking while he waited.

"Can you do that again?" Grant asked.

Max did it twice again, handed up the beer and was introduced to George.

Juan showed up with the key and they went inside the shop and sat on chairs and stools near the window where they could look out.

They started drinking from the bottles of beer, then George sent out for a fifth of whiskey. Juan found glasses and the whiskey went around. A white fellow and a colored girl came in and had a drink with them. Then they went into the back room and closed the door. George chuckled.

After a short while they came out. They had a drink. The fellow left. And then the girl.

Two other colored girls came in and bottles of beer were passed to them. Max had his arm thrown around the back of the chair in which one of the girls sat and was talking very friendly and confidentially with her. He was smiling and leaning close to her.

Juan grinned at Max. Juan said, "Max, you've got a fat chance of talking any of them girls out of anything. She don't want your friendship."

Max burst out laughing, his black eyes running into slits. Then he sobered. "See how you are?" he complained. "I'm just *talking* to the girl. Ain't I?" he asked Grant.

The girl smiled in agreement, meantime flashing her eyes at Juan. Shortly the two girls left.

"That Polish-looking fellow?" Grant asked in curiosity.

"Most of the white guys are steady for these colored whores," Juan said. "They have steady ones and they come down here about once a week for them. The girls get five dollars." He swallowed out of his bottle of beer. "I charge them a dollar for the room. Everywhere else they have to pay a buck and a half for a room, but I charge only a dollar because I know how hard it is for them." He swallowed beer again.

Outside the window had now come the Sunday sidewalk church meeting: a group of Negroes of various colors, sizes and shapes. Some beat tambourines, others clap their hands together. There is a woman preacher, a big black woman, built like a man and dressed in a purple hat with a white plume, a blue satin dress and pink shoes. *Let the Loooord bleeesss you-all!* A man preacher in flowing gown of yellow and blue satin stripes, a fez of red, its black tassel hanging in one eye. *Come on! Come on, you-all! Lord! Lord! The Lord wants you!* The little group claps hands in rhythm. Their eyes are frantic. Their hands are frantic. Their feet hop like drumsticks against the sidewalk.

"Juan," Grant said, "remember the last time I saw you, you said that there was a lot of dope in this neighborhood."

"Yeah."

"Grant's doing an article on dope for a magazine," Max said.

"Oh," Juan said.

Outside the window the missionaries are saving the neighborhood. A pot-bellied elderly little white man, who looks like all the caricatures of slum missionaries wrapped into one, gets into the act. He has borrowed the Negro preacher's robe and is, himself, preaching now. He is clapping his hands and hopping around on one foot while a spider web of sweat veils his red face. The others are hopping up and down and shaking their hips as their heels hit the sidewalk. They are clapping their hands in rhythm. They are singing something about the Lord coming in a Cadillac. Their hands beat out the rhythm. The slum buildings, the whole neighborhood seems to rock.

George looks out the window and giggles: in appreciation, in understanding of all he has experienced today, the friendship here in this room, the colored girl and the white fellow, the women picking wood up from the streets and alley. He says, "You read it in books and people don't believe it. I couldn't tell anybody in my neighborhood. They'd call me a liar." He chuckled again and again, looked out on the street, enjoying it, finding identity with the city.

"Here you are, fellow," Max said, handing him another bottle of beer.

Juan nodded Grant to the door and down the sidewalk. At the corner he bought a bottle of pop. Then he crossed the street, Grant following him.

It was a row of basement rooms, like a tier of cells in a prison.

Juan pushed the door of one of the windowless rooms open and they entered, light grudgingly following them. On the bed was a young woman wearing a loose dress but with her shoes kicked away. She was doubled in bed, her hands clamped to her stomach.

"Fran."

She turned toward the sound of Juan's voice and her dark face looked up.

"Feeling better?"

She shook her head no.

In her turning, the top of her dress loosened, exposing her breast. Gently Juan folded the dress back over her bosom and fastened it. "Here, I brought you a bottle of pop."

She shook her head no.

"I—I brought someone to meet you. This is Grant, Fran."

She lifted one hand away from her stomach. "Hello, mister." The hand went back to the pain.

"Hello, Fran," Grant said.

"Want me to bring you something to eat?" Juan asked.

"I can't eat," Fran said. Momentarily she grasped his hand, digging in, holding, seeking surcease.

Grant, the writer's eyes, went in scrutiny, everywhere. On the dresser he saw two objects.

Juan nodded to Grant: Let's go.

Back in Juan's shop they drank more beer. A yellow-colored woman came in. "What's Henrietta cooking?" Juan asked.

The yellow woman said, "She ain't cooking. She's doing what you're trying to do—trying to get drunk."

Nevertheless, half an hour later the yellow woman returned with food enough in a pot for all of them—stewed chicken and dumplings.

When she had gone Juan said, "These colored people are really fine when you get to know them. Some people have the wrong idea."

Grant sucked gravy from his fingers. "Would you drop over to my hotel one day next week and talk about—about the neighborhood?" he asked Juan. "I have a wire recorder and we could talk into it. I'll drop down to see you before that."

"Sure. Why not?" Juan said.

"If we can bring beer," Max said.

"I didn't invite you, Max."

"Ouch!" Max said with a pained grin.

"You know you're invited," Grant said.

They opened quart bottles of beer. Grant said, "I'll put the mike here on the bed, and when you see that red light flash every once in a while you'll know we're recording."

He spoke, in illustration: "Chicago, Illinois, July seventh . . . I am, ah, sitting around the Allerton Hotel with my criminal and semi-criminal friends . . ." He laughed and Max said "Tee-hee" into the mike.

GRANT: Oh, Juan, will you tell me first, I have a note here about when you were in jail. Okay, Juan, you do the talking and I'll do the listening.

JUAN: You mean the time I got crabs?

GRANT: No (chuckling), about Fran.

JUAN: Well, before that there's a long story . . .

He began telling of the years of Fran's story . . . and his story . . .

GRANT: You treat her very nicely. I remember when you took me over there Sunday when she was sick and lying there—I noticed, on the dresser, two things, and I want to ask you if you know who they belong to? There was a jumping jack and there was a harmonica. Was that her son's too?

JUAN: Yeah. And her son's a nice kid. He's a real nice guy. He's smart and he knows all the answers, I mean, but he's not getting the right break. I mean, besides seeing all this, I mean, he can't help but notice these things. He's nine years old.

MAX: He's not aware of what dope is, though, is he?

JUAN: Why not! Why, sure he is. Okay—well—one time—numerous times—I've been down there when she'd just tell him, "Turn around."

GRANT: While she's taking the dope?

MAX (lifting the bottle away from his lips): While she shoots herself, huh?

JUAN: Yeah . . . No, Max, you know I don't smoke . . . And I told her time and time again. I said, "What kind of an upbringing is this for your kid?" I said, "Sooner or later he's going to be wondering what it's all about, and before you know it he's going to be turning on that stuff before he even has a chance to grow up."

MAX: Does he go to school?

JUAN: Yeah, he goes to school. He gets pretty good grades. I check them, you know. The kid lives with her now.

GRANT: How does she manage to take care of him if she's on dope most of the time?

JUAN: That I can't figure out.

GRANT: Who pays for the kid?

JUAN: She does. I mean, in a way. After a fashion.

Grant lit a cigarette and squinted against the smoke. Into the microphone he asked, apologetically, as if he were prying, "What are your sincere feelings about her, Juan?"

JUAN: My sincere feelings is pity-like. More or less. I mean, put it in that category.

MAX: But there's nothing you can do to help her kick it?

JUAN: No. She tried it once. I mean she was on a good path—but—she got sick. If she wouldn't of got sick that time she'd a made it. 'Cause she was working every day. She got a job and I guess fate was against her, so—

GRANT: How much does she have to have a day?

JUAN: As much as she can get.

GRANT: Ah—

JUAN: Well—that's that. I was telling you she lived in a basement. Her old man kept her down there. It was a shame the way it was. I found out later from different people that went down there that it was really a shame the way she was living. Like an animal. And occasionally the guy must have stayed down there too. I never found out about the basement until I talked to different people I knew, and I was trying to get at—at the background of all this. And when I found out I—I always tried to bring it up but she would never, she would never admit that she lived down there. She said, "No, I never lived down there. I used to go down there to take off and take my friends down there to take off. I thought that was a nice place to take off."

GRANT: Why doesn't she go to Kentucky to the hospital there for addicts?

MAX: Well, you can't get in there, Grant, it's hard to get in there.

Sometimes it's mighty crowded there. A fellow I know, he's been there three times, and three times they turned him down.

JUAN: Well, you can't just do that. You have to fill out a questionnaire. The thing about going down there is you can get it when you're in there anyway. You can have it sneaked in there like at the jail and the City Workhouse. I know numerous people, actual friends now, who have gone down there and they have kicked it—see—but . . . but—they—come—to—the—same—environment—same—friends—and before they know it, two or three weeks at the most they're back, they're hooked. They got the Chinaman riding them. They got that Horse and that Horse won't let them go. Or that Chinaman's on their back. Take Fran's sister and brother-in-law, Elijah and Opal. They kicked it for a while. About a month. But they're back. They're back. (*Chuckling*) Well, you see the setup between him and his wife is this: Elijah's got a sissy he's staying with and the sissy keeps them both in dope—well, not enough—but some. And he goes home every night to his sissy. And he lets his old lady stand on the streets and make some money. So every morning, his old lady, his wife, has got to have enough for his fix. Or else he beats her up.

MAX: Beats the hell out of her, huh?

GRANT: Does the sissy have a lot of money?

JUAN: No.

The sound of bottles clicking together recorded in the momentary silence.

GRANT: The sissy isn't on dope?

JUAN: I don't know. I've never met him. I've heard a lot about him. He works. I think he works in a restaurant. I'm not sure. At that time he was keeping both Opal and Elijah well dressed. Lately he hasn't. (*Laughing*) Elijah broke the sissy's sister's leg. He took a swing at the sissy with a lamp and he missed him and hit the sister and broke her leg. (*Laughter cackled along the wire*) Last week Elijah told me the sister called him up and said (*Juan's voice took on the worried southern dialect of a Negro woman*), "Eli! Why don't you come home? He's been going crazy about you. Come home before he goes crazy!"

General laughter.

MAX: The sister knows about it, huh?

JUAN: Yes. She said, "He's been worrying me that I go see you and find you and bring you home."

Grant said into the microphone, hesitantly, "I hate to be personal, Juan. But I have heard so many people say that when you are on dope you have no sexual desire. Is that—to be personal—true of Fran?"

JUAN: Well, in some cases it's true and in some cases it's not true. A lot of guys I've talked to, when they get more or less high—what they call "feeling straight"—ah—a lot of guys they want to be with their—ah—woman—with their girl—not just anybody. Because a dope fiend he has no feelings for a woman as such—unless it's a special one— Well . . . if I was on dope and I got high, say, I'd want to be with Fran . . . Hey, Max, hand me a bottle . . . And (*drinking*) . . . then take this thing about dope fiends don't wear no short-sleeve shirts, or girls— That's a lot of bunk, because all them girls wear shorts, they wear sleeveless dresses, and guys, they wear T-shirts. I mean, it all depends where they hit. A lot of people they hit right in here. Right in this vein here.

GRANT: That's between the forefinger and thumb, huh?

JUAN: They hit right here.

The red light flashed as it took their voices.

GRANT: Is that what they call mainlining?

JUAN: Mainlining is when you hit a vein. Joy-popping is when you just hit under the skin. Mainlining has a quicker effect.

GRANT: And greater?

JUAN: Well, no—I'd say just quicker.

GRANT: How quick does it happen?

JUAN: Well, how soon does it take it to get to your nervous system? They hit right here. They hit right in here. Right here is the main one. Or they turn their hand around and they hit in the big vein right here. Or they follow this vein here. Or a lot of them, so it won't be seen, they hit right in here, in this vein here.

"Let's take time out," Grant said, clicking off the machine; and they sat relaxing, drinking.

Grant smiled his crooked smile at Juan. "You know how curious I am," he said, "so I'll plunge in. This is just writer's curiosity and has nothing to do with morals. Well—where does your wife fit in?"

Juan's face became cold for a minute. "Well," he said at last, "she's a good woman."

"Too damn good, uh?" Max said, laughing.

Juan looked at him. Then he said, "Yeah, I guess you're right." He shrugged. "She's a good woman. We live good. Nice, clean house—all that. But, Jesus, she just don't like the things I like. She don't like that neighborhood down there. She was born there—she was born there—but she wants to get as far away from it as she can. Me, I like it. I like the people. She likes"—he grinned—"to play bingo, a couple married people over every Tuesday night—but no drinking —no drinking—dancing at the Mexican Social Club Saturday nights."

"Turn her over to me," Max said, punching Juan on the arm, "and I'll change her for you."

"Max, you want every woman," Juan said. "I only want one." Later they turned back to the mike.

GRANT: Were we on wire when you were telling me about fixing the capsules?

JUAN: No.

GRANT: Well, tell me about that.

JUAN: You can buy caps by the thousands. In any drug store. You can buy hypos. You can buy eyedroppers.

MAX: Anybody can buy empty capsules.

JUAN: Anybody can buy them.

MAX: You don't have to give a reason why you need them.

JUAN: No.

GRANT: Then it seems to me that the laxity begins with the law itself, where you can buy hypo needles wherever and whenever you want, where you can buy capsules.

MAX: Well, how about the diabetics?

JUAN: Yeah, that's true.

MAX: My aunt can buy a needle any time hers breaks. She's diabetic.

GRANT: Well, she should have to go to a doctor to get it or have a card showing that she is diabetic.

JUAN: And then a lot of druggists, instead of charging fifty cents for a needle, they charge a dollar.

GRANT: No question asked?

JUAN: No question asked. So they're making money.

GRANT: How do those girls down there get their money for dope?

JUAN: How do they get their money for it? How do all girls get their money?

GRANT: Now, ah—heroin, cocaine and morphine—which is the most predominant?

JUAN: Heroin. Because it's cheaper. Cocaine is too expensive and the thrill only lasts as long as you hit it with the needle. Once you take the needle out it's gone. There is no more. That's what they call the She.

MAX: The what?

JUAN: The She.

GRANT: S-h-e?

JUAN: The She. Yeah, S-h-e. Because if you take cocaine you have no need for a woman. It makes you—come in your pants. You get that same thrill.

MAX: You mean actually?

JUAN: No, not quite that, but it gives you the same feeling. I mean that's why they call it the She.

MAX: Oh, I see.

JUAN: And as soon as you take the needle out it's gone. It's like taking your thing out of a woman. As soon as you hit it, that sensation is over in about ten seconds.

GRANT: Tell me, where are most of these contacts for sales made? As a rule, is it inside some house, or somewhere, or what?

JUAN: No. On street corners, most of it. But there's some places— Now take this lady that sells, she knows most of them, you have to be an old customer, see, and—

GRANT: Is she young or old?

JUAN: She's an old lady. She's well kept but she uses about an ounce of stuff a day.

MAX: An ounce!

JUAN: An ounce!

GRANT: An ounce!

JUAN: An ounce!

MAX: My God!

JUAN: And the stuff that she uses, these dope fiends couldn't use because they'd get knocked out. That's before it's cut down. She uses it pure. They say that the cotton she uses and leaves in her cooker a dope fiend would get knocked out just putting water in the cotton.

GRANT: Well, I can understand someone who is on it being a sympathetic character because he's trying to make money for his own kick and to help other people in the same boat, but these sonofabitches who aren't on it and sell it and push it—I mean I have no use for them.

MAX: Money, Grant. Money! Money! Why do people kill? Money! Money!

Matches struck. Cigarettes were lighted. They clicked bottles of beer. Then—

JUAN: They never carry stuff on themselves. If they get caught they swallow it. And them girls usually when they got anything they hide it in them.

MAX: Won't it fall out?

JUAN: No. They got it wrapped in thick cellophane paper and then they put it up. And sometimes they even carry their outfits in there. The needle and eyedropper. See, they wrap it up in this plastic and they put a rubber band on the outside and they stick it up.

They opened new bottles and struck them together in friendliness. Then Max said, "Well, tell me, I've read and I've heard—but at

221

what time is it though—that the pupils in your eyes become pin-
points. Is it when you want a fix or is that when you're under the influence?"

Juan said, "That's just something somebody read in a book. It
don't happen. Maybe they got that deal from somebody closing their
eyes and nodding. You know your eyes come down close like this
but they don't get pinpoint."

Max said, "Let me tell you about this bastard. The Wolf, Grant.
The Wolf." Max scowled up at his face. "A worse bastard never
lived. The Wolf."

Max told him about The Wolf. Marijuana. Dope peddling. The
killings he knew about. The one he had seen.

The red bulb flashed painfully. It flashed and stopped a last time,
relieved.

50

Under the flat night sky Grant was walking his beat along North
Clark. He turned into the Shillelagh.

The place was crowded.

Grant sat at the bar on a stool near the front flyspecked window.

Slim came down the bar, wiping mahogany, and up to him. "Hi
there, Grant! What's yours?" he asked in his mile-a-minute jargon.

"Bottle of beer—Schlitz."

Slim is just that, with an eagle-slim face and sharp, fleeting eyes.
He is always dashing from one end of the bar to the other, leaning
over and whispering furtively to various customers he knows.

Once, in a rain-caught day, Slim had told Grant, "The boss
knows about me. He said, 'What you do is your own business. Just
keep it out of the place.' That way"—wiping mahogany frantically—
"I can help both sides. See that the gay guy don't go with no rough
trade and that the studs don't get themselves screwed up with some
goddamn homo-psycho-queer." And back down the length of the
bar. Holding a furtive conversation there. Wiping bar quickly.

Slim brought Grant's beer. Grant sat looking.

Over the warped boards they came, following their warped in-
stincts like so many lost dogs wagging their tails at momentary masters.

They are the twisted cigarette butts that stand at the bar and lean at the tables. They are the discarded beer caps and hawked-up phlegm.

Here: a young man looking for a trick with an arrow like his own.

Here: a blind man pushing his tray of assortments, expertly, into everybody's face, "Buy something just to help me out."

Here: two cops stop in, and Slim, seeing them, without words hands each a pack of cigarettes. Free. Free to law-enforcing, justice-bringing agents.

Here: a woman walking along the bar, half drunk, and speaking to a man, "You goin' to buy me a drink? Somebody's goin' to buy me a drink."

Up and down the bar.

Their mouths are burned with alcohol, brown with tobacco. They are laughing.

Here: a girl playing with the front of a man's pants.

Here: a woman, barefooted, her dress like a shroud, man's coat over it, the cuffs turned back and pinned; matted hair; a scab, drying, like a horse's blinker on the side of her eye, black and dirt-crusted where some fist, male or female, with or without cause, has struck. Looking for a man. Any man.

Here: a man with his pack of cigarettes on the bar.

"Mister, have you got a cigarette?" a bum wandering past asks.

They've got to beat you out of something even if it is only a cigarette.

Here: he was a collar. His dark suit has been pushed away under desire. He is an eye. And two performers found.

"Thirty-five dollars," the mouth whispers, slipping sideways like a knife opening.

Thirty-five dollars, just for that.

But the eye would watch. The arrow would rise. And arch away. To fall to earth, spent.

Is to see, to sin?

Here: one of the soapbox orators from Bughouse Square, counting, in a dirty hand, the money he had collected from the crowd.

Here: from a lush apartment in the tall towers of steel and glass on the Lake Shore, a millionaire. He comes and rests furtively here, like a butterfly in his gaily colored sport shirt, heavy slave bracelet, gold-banded wrist watch, feeling the air with wings and antenna, delicately, for the rosebud of choice. Delicately. Weighing. Measuring. Choosing. Buying. And swift to the blue-jean color of the aster.

223

Outside: the sob and sigh of streetcar and automobile.

They are all broken-down. The young and the old. They are the lost, looking for the lost. Their funeral dirge is the juke box played so loudly that they have to shout to hear each other, tombstone to tombstone.

They come here to drink. They come here to push back the night with another, any other, like themselves.

Elderly homos come here to pick up half-good-looking, half-tough-looking young men. These young men are very masculine—truck-driver-masculine-looking. But willing to go. For sex, some. For money, others. Others in a pretended feminine glance and smile and word, to steal what they can.

Gray-haired women come here. Sleep at tables. Fall off chairs. "Daddy, will you buy me a drink? Daddy . . . Daddy . . ."

The girls are ugly, bold, fat or skinny, pimpled. They dance with each other to the lewd lick of needle on record inside the cathedral of a juke box, to attract men; or dance by themselves for the same purpose, shaking what little or what too much they have of them-selves—like slave masters exhibiting slaves.

Then dance with the men. Some for drinks. Some for bed. All for money.

Girls in blue jeans. Women with tattoos on their arms. Their wrists. Proof of something.

Dancing with old men in caps, high shoes, men old enough to be their fathers. "Daddy . . . Daddy . . ." Dancing with young men in T-shirts, men young enough to be their sons. "Daddy . . . Daddy . . ."

Proof of laughter in the night.

And a voice cuts across the bar—

"Man, I want to make a score!" a young, rough-trade guy says in loud invitation to any man who wants to go. Or any woman.

Grant sits, eyes and ears. Eyes, serious and needle-brown. Ears like wire recorders:

To deny any is to deny yourself.

Every human being is dignified. Or should be. Has something of quality.

God! If you knew the life of any one of them here from cradle to this point. If you knew what brought them here. And they're not completely bad. Sick, yes. Warped, yes. How can anybody judge anyone else? Not, at least, without knowing all of his life and that of his parents and his grandparents. It's easy to judge. It's harder to dig down into the solid rock of cause.

224

Grant twisted his beer bottle between the palms of his hands, thinking, wondering about these people here, feeling a deep sympathy for them.

And spider webs move around him.

And Louie Romano was making his first visit to North Clark Street. Louie Romano and young Paco.

Louie big-shot for the beer, smacking a half-dollar down in front of the woman bartender, a plain big-hipped woman of thirty.

The waitress brought the bottles.

"Hey! Come here!" Louie said, leaning over the bar with his feet propped on the rounds of the stool, the stool tilted on its front legs. "What do you do after work?"

She made a pass at him with the bar rag. "Aw, get out of here, you crazy kid!" She grinned. Her eyes fastened on his. "What do you mean—kid?" Louie protested, hoisting up his trousers and tightening his belt. With a hand on her hip, with the other hip pressed against the bar, she stood laughing at him. Louie drank beer, his eyes even with the glass rim, staring at her. Then, big shot, he turned to Paco. "Want to match?" he asked.

"Nickels?"

Louie tossed his head. He picked up a quarter from the change on the bar. "Game?" he asked, holding the quarter so the waitress could see it.

A broomstick of a man, with a gaunt, tight-skinned face, stood half in shadow, leaning against a piano as broken-down as the guests in the establishment. His owl-shaped eyes looked out. Louie stood with his back to the man. In his tight-fitting pants the outline of his loins and large calves stood out, tracing his heftiness.

Paco sat on a stool at the bar and, turned toward Louie, caught the coin on the back of his hand. Louie tossed, letting his quarter flip to the floor. "Mine!" he shouted, taking Paco's quarter off the back of his hand and stooping to pick his own coin up off the floor. He tossed again, again spinning the quarter in the air and letting it fall to the floor; and as he stooped to pick it up after each toss and rose again, the man propped against the piano, as if propped against life, followed his bending and rising with his eyes.

And Louie noticed.

"Take a good look," Louie said loudly, "you ain't getting none!"

A woman in her forties stood at the bar, her eyes roving up and down the bar at men. Her hair hung in loose, disheveled rags around her head. Her eyes went, calculatingly, along the bar in a half-dazed stare. Her stomach was balled, as if a child asked out. She wore no stockings, and above the heels of her turned-over shoes, rings of crusted dirt, one above the other, were callous-ground into her skin.

The owl-eyed man edged his way from the piano to the bar, near Louie. Ordered a glass of beer and drank it slowly. After a while, letting his finger slide over his book of matches without bringing it out, he asked, touching Louie on the arm, "Have you got a match?"

Louie lit and held the match for him.

"You want a beer?" the man asked.

"Yeah—thanks!"

"Want a sandwich?"

"No. But I'll take another beer as soon as I finish this one."

The man edged closer. "You're a good-looking boy."

"Yeah?"

Swilling beer.

"Would you like to go home with me?"

Louie Romano caved the man's face in with a well-directed punch. A punch waiting all evening for a receiver.

He and Paco got the hell out of there.

They didn't need to hurry. Nobody pays any attention in there to a fight.

Entangling, inescapable spider webs held them. Night. Sand. Dust.

Grant sat in night, sand, dust.

And a cop comes in.

She is sitting on a bar stool. Big, friendly, with a big smile on his red Irish face, he pinches her on the fattest part of her body, her behind, and mischievously looks the other way. She yells, "Ow!" and seeing who it is, says, "What are you trying to do, pick my pocket?"

They both laugh.

They are old buddies. Both on the wrong side of the law.

It was that kind of place.

The young fellow with the tattooed lady on his arm came in. The nude lady, with her hands behind her head, walked past Grant and did a lewd bump, seemed to wink at him. Grant, following her with his eyes, saw the young fellow go to the bar a couple of stools down.

Slim was standing at the bar across from Grant. "Who is that?" Grant asked, indicating the young fellow with the tattoos.

"Hey, Phil!" Slim called.

Phil came over. "I want you to meet Grant—Grant, this is Phil."

Phil shook hands and eyed Grant suspiciously.

It was that kind of place.

Any young fellow talked to by a man thought a proposition was coming.

Grant smiled. And Phil was sizing him up.

Grant wanted to say: Take it easy. Relax. I'm not hot for your body. He looked again at his bicep, smiling.

"Grant's a writer," Slim said. "He wants to talk to you."

"Oh?"

They carried drinks over to a table. They began talking. Grant was amazed at the things Phil told him. It was always amazing to him that people opened up to him, and had since he was a young man. Say you're a writer and everybody has a story to tell. Everybody is a leading character.

Max walked into the place. "Hi, Phil!" Then he saw Grant. "Say"—gesturing—"do you guys know each other?"

"For half an hour," Grant said.

Far in the back of the bar he sits. At a table all alone near the toilet. He sits in night, sand, dust. He had come to pick up a trick.

He is old. He is fat. His long, straight, blondish-washed hair thinning, and his dusk-gray eyes. Holding the desire since youth.

He is old. He is lost. He is unattractive.

Owen sits alone.

He is swollen pink and white and wrinkled flesh around a face that has fallen in like an old woman's.

He is funny-looking. Effeminate-looking. He has taken to putting on a little lipstick and rouge. A little powder. *Mama, look young for the boys.* A scenting of perfume. *The boys like them young, Mama.* Like a woman going through her menopause. A scenting of perfume for paper dolls. A little of these female things. To get the scrapings of the bar. The garbage that came into the place and was left over.

Owen looks down. Owen looks into a goldfish bowl. And around and around.

Slim stands at his side with a young man.

Slim says, "This young fellow wants to know if he can join you."

The boy is in blue jeans. The boy is a man looking for money. The boy says, "Hello, daddy. Want some company?"

Owen shakes his head no.

The powder filters down. The rouge. But the lipstick stays firm.

The boy moves away, blue jeans tight. Slim assaults the mahogany with his bar rag.

Happiness is a temporary thing.

Owen again sees a face.

The only person who ever really cared for me. Was kind to me. Owen looks down. Into a fishbowl Owen looks.

Owen is drunk. Owen is crying. Owen is thinking.

Into a fishbowl he looks.

A solitary fish turns round and round, monotonously, round and round, eternally.

And the spider webs hold them.

They close the place for half an hour to sweep up. But they don't kick you out.

You lift your feet as the broom goes along, sweeping up sin and loss and hope. Most of all, Hope.

Music goes on and drinks keep coming.

They hang onto the bar rail with their curled fingers like bats hanging upside down.

Night winds call to night people.

It was that kind of place.

Night always sat on the rafters. Night, with a laugh between clenched teeth.

Night winds call to night people.

51

Phil sat in front of the wire recorder. "Well—" he said. He looked with astonishment, almost with terror, at the thing that would take down his voice. "Well—" he said, and then grew brave:

"Okay. I'll put it this way. I first joined the Pachuks—short for Pachucos—when I was stationed in California with the navy. Well, we navy boys used to go to San Pedro quite a bit and, of course, after that there used to be a bunch that hung around. Well, I didn't know at that time, but they were Pachucos. It used to be an assorted crew—Americans, Puerto Ricans, Mexicans—just about any nationality you could think of. And we all gathered together in one band and they used to make it a practice mostly to pick up on servicemen. In other words, jackroll them. So after being jackrolled twice, I figured the best thing was to join them rather than to fight them. So a few liberties later I put on a pair of Levis, a sport shirt and a jacket and started hanging around the different sections of town. So I got to know a lot of the kiddies. I got to know a lot of them pretty good after spending quite a bit of dough, buying drinks, going to poolrooms and bars and what not. Finally they accepted me. You better believe it. And so I got in pretty good and I started talking and talking, conversationing it and crazy songs. They found out all about my background and whatnot. So they asked me to join."

Phil took time out to drink his beer halfway down the bottle. "They said they'd have to put me through a test first. This was a melting pot. These people stood together and came out as one. The Gatos. We didn't melt it down to nationality but what we stood for."

GRANT: And, ah, Phil, would you tell me something—something about getting into the group and the tattoo on your thumb.

PHIL (*lighting a cigarette*): I had to be put to the test first to see— as they figured—if I could live up to the code of the Pachucos. I had to go on an armed robbery. I didn't take any actual part in it except to be the wheel man. In other words, the driver of the getaway car. This was taking place in California. It wasn't taking place in Pedro—out near the outskirts of L.A. We didn't operate from our home base except for jackrolling swab jockeys, marines.

MAX (*leaning forward*): You were still in the service?

PHIL: I was still in the service.

MAX: Why did you *want* to get mixed up with these people?

PHIL: I *told* you why. Why fight them if you can join them? So I passed the first test with flying colors. You better believe it. The second test, we had to come off with a rumble—in another town— in other words, a gang war . . . Give me another cigarette, Max . . . Thanks . . . So we all gathered together . . . this night. A lot of 'em were sucking in on marijuana to get up nerve. Me, I never played that stuff. Even when they kept urging me to try it. Lots of things I've done but not that anyway. You better believe it. It just happened I had the weekend off—so all this time I'm wearing civilian clothes. If the service could have known about it— wham!—right then and there I would have been cashiered. So the night the rumble come off we all of us were gathered together, say, about forty or fifty of us. We went over to the other section of town with everything you could think of. Bars, clubs.

MAX: What was the leader's name and age?

GRANT: Wait, Max—

PHIL: We'll call him Mike. Twenty years old. I mean he was rough. Quite a bit. You better believe it. He had knocked around. He knew what all the scoring was. So—anyway—this rumble came off. We moved over to the other section of town. Bottles, knives, zip-guns, tire chains, bricks. Socks loaded with soap. We moved in. It was fast and furious. It lasted exactly, oh, let's see, parts of it at least, about fifteen to twenty minutes. Within that time there were four guys ruined for the rest of their lives. Paralyzed. Cut all to hell.

MAX: Big shot, huh? You were a big shot.

PHIL: No, no, Max. I guess I was just a crazy, goofed-up kid. I'm sorry for it all now. Anyway—

MAX: Big man! Real big!

PHIL: Play it cool, Max. So—some wouldn't be able to walk. Cuts of all kinds. Gun shots of all kinds. A lot of them wouldn't look the same way they looked in the mirror that morning and shaved themselves—if they were old enough to shave. And believe me I was getting a little frightened myself.

GRANT: How did the Pachuco movement come to Chicago? From L.A.?

PHIL: Well, I think the majority of your servicemen brought it back, actually, or else your immigration of Mexicans and Puerto Ricans moving in inland.

GRANT (*rubbing his hand through his hair*): And, Phil, will you tell me a little bit about the tattoo.

PHIL: The tattoo is a cross. It's put in between, generally, on your right hand, between your thumb and your first finger. And for every major engagement you have been in or for any attacks you have made, you get a line above it.

GRANT: Sounds just like our war heroes.

PHIL (*nodding*): In other words, that's to explain to the rest, all your Pachucos, exactly how far you went and what you done.

MAX: Big man, huh?

PHIL: Look, Max, at that time I thought it was something. I don't any more.

GRANT: Isn't that the most important thing to young kids? Belonging to a bunch? You can't be chicken.

PHIL: You can't be chicken. That's right. You have to be part of something. A lot of people don't know this. They figure—they figure—the kids— Well, let's put it this way. They figure if they're left out of something, they're nothing, they're nobody. In other words, they're lames. You're left out. You're a square, in other words. So one kid tries stopping the other. It may lead on just to petty stuff—to taking money from smaller kids or, in other words, like stealing lollipops from them. And the next one will try to outdo him, like taking money out of grocery stores. The next one will lead up to swiping cars. Then that will lead up into—oh, hell —it can go on for years, for Christsake. Jackrolling. Gang fights. And eventually it can lead into your killers. So you figure out— one's got to outdo the other. And they try to do it . . . Max, a cigarette . . . But—all right—the Pachucos are on the West Coast —they were great—they had an organization. One guy got busted and got put in jail. Everybody dug in his pocket for his bond and he never sat there for long. If the rap was too bad the kiddies even told him to cut out. He slid out for another state. Or even into the interior, for a matter of fact, just as long as he wouldn't be around to face that rap. Make it look bad for the rest . . . Look, like I started to say, how it came to Chicago I couldn't really say, except for the immigration. A lot of the servicemen brought it back. They had the cross. A lot of people wondered why. So you hear a lot of tales about what's happening on the West Coast with the kiddies and you say, well, man, if they can do it out there we can do it here. Only you do it in a bigger way.

The opening of beer bottles.

PHIL: All right—so a few of them start hanging together, getting a few more recruits. A lot of new kiddies come to town. They don't know from nothin'. They want to belong. So, okay, man, they hear from different sections. Here's so and so. They know the ropes. You better believe it. They know what to hang onto. So latch on to them if you can. And in Chicago they can be pretty rough. You better believe it. They have, a lot of them, the Pachuco mark. But a lot don't know what the mark means. A tenth of them—in service—knew. Others, who didn't, thought it was a religious cross. And, "I'm a Catholic. I want to be identified." So, wham! Chicago. The cops started picking up, searching, shaking guys down. North Clark Street. South State. Madison. Chicago in general. They started shaking down. Anybody with a cross they grabbed. *And*—here on the North Side there is an organization strictly nothing but Pachuco, the Near North Side.

MAX: I don't get you.

PHIL: Well, I'll tell you. It's bounded by Division and Chicago, Clark and LaSalle. And, man, I'll tell you, them Pachuks can pick up on anything. They peddle marijuana like chewing gum. And over at Sloan's—all the hustlers generally take over the second floor where the pool tables are. That floor is generally taken over by all the hustlers in town. They peddle anything from watches, rings, dope, all the way down to dick. Oh man, it's a great place to pick up on anything. If you want to pick up on pot, on bennies, pick up on any kind of dope. Heroin. There's a lot of kiddies that mainline in the washrooms there. In other words it's a gathering place.

Phil paused. His face reddened a little, then grew taut. He said, "I'll tell you something else, Grant, and it ain't easy to tell. But I ain't holdin' nothing back. You better believe me. Back in the days when I was first in the navy, I didn't know a gay guy from a straight guy. So I started talking to the guy and he said, 'Come on, I'll buy you a drink.' I said, 'I'm sorry, man, I can't make it.' See, I wasn't old enough to go to no bar. 'Well, I've got a few drinks up to my place,' he says.

"So we make it up to his place. Got up there and a few beers.

" 'Make yourself comfortable.'

"Took my neckerchief off.

" 'Make yourself at home.'

" 'All right. I'll slim off.'

"So it's hot and I'm sitting there in my shorts. We're drinking beer.

"So when I leave he said, 'Here, this will help you out on your leave,' and he shook hands and I felt some money in my hand, and when I got outside and looked, it was ten bucks—and I thought, what the hell! That's the easiest ten dollars I ever made in my life. Why am I wasting on a woman what I can get paid for from a man. So I headed back downtown and picked up on some broad and we had a ball.

"So at base I spread the word what had happened. So a lot of the kiddies, they wised me up. They cued me in, you know. They said like it's been happening for years. So I said, oh yeah, then this is for me. So I found out a lot of different spots where them guys hang around. Went to a couple of these spots and wham, just like that. Score after score after score. I'm picking up on bread fine. That's for me."

Phil's voice saddened. "That was a long time ago. Now my feelings are strictly for a woman."

His voice became edged with age and weariness. "The woman I want is the woman I can enjoy being with— I mean not—not just sex. The woman I want is one I can go out with, have a good time with, go to the show with, go out dancing with her." His eyes looked up around the captured room. "I'll put a little time on it. I'll keep looking." The captured room held him captive. "I can still find it if I try hard enough."

52

They walked in deep snow. There were two slow, heavy footsteps and a round hole where Judge Sullivan's cane had pressed. They were followed by three other sets of prints, and they went up the steps between the black iron railings. The window wore a row of icicles.

In the hallway Judge Sullivan tapped softly on the door.

"Just a minute," Nick's voice said.

Then he opened the door and Judge Sullivan said, "Turn around and don't look."

Nick did as he was told. "What is it?" he asked. He wanted to be a man but was a boy.

They came in grinning and on tiptoe.

They set the folding easel up near the window and put the two canvases, the palette and the paint box on the table.

"Okay, now you can look."

"Gee!" Nick said. "Gee!"

Their greatest enjoyment was in doing for the boy. They were a little embarrassed in their goodness. "We'll see you tonight, Nick," they said gruffly, and left.

All but Judge. He said, "I'll sit awhile."

Nick came and sat across from him. Judge smiled and lifted his hand. "No. Don't talk. I just wanted to get my breath back and the cold out of my bones."

"All right, Judge."

Nick moved to the easel and looked at it. His face smiled boyishly, happily.

With a hot, damp cloth Nick wiped the ice from the window, scaling it away in slippery, cold and tissue-paper-thin sheets. He put one of the canvases on the easel.

Judge sat quietly, his cane held between his legs, his hands crossed on its handle, and his eyes went frequently to the boy.

With a paint brush in his hand Nick stood before the empty canvas.

Judge's old mouth smiled and a tear or two stood in his eyes. This is the same boy. The same boy I met on the sidewalk when he was five years old.

The old man's heart quickened with warmth and tenderness, and his eyes took Nick deep within himself. The boy was slim but well built, slight but proportionate. His intent face had a thin handsomeness, an autumn look about it: his eyes and hair were the color of leaves that have left the tree and turned brown. And his nose was thin and perfectly straight. His ears, as when a child, were pointed up, and the ends of his mouth were pointed down. Judge smiled looking at his ears. But the profile was delicate, each feature sharply etched. And his molded cheekbones were delicate too, in their indentation, the deep-set eyes above them. His mouth and his eyes and his voice were sad. Even his smile was sad. There was a quietness about him, a pathos. His walk, the gesture of his hands, the turning of his head. Everyone noticed this quality of sadness about him. And now, looking for the yellow touch of canary, he looked at the building across the street and then moved to the empty canvas. He was seventeen.

Nick's eyes—looking out at his mother, at the four of them, Judge, Phil, Norman and Max, looking out at this, his world of North Clark Street—were always searching for understanding, kindness, warmth.

In his smaller world there was just his mother and the four of them. His feelings hadn't changed for them since he was five; only deepened.

They, too, loved him as they had loved nothing before. He represented to each of them the living over again of his own life and the changing of his own life.

Judge Sullivan put his old hand on Nick's shoulder. He left it there with warmth, trying to impart something from deep inside himself into Nick. "So you see, boy, one must want to do something, to be something. If you want to be an artist—then be one—though" —and he winked—"I do not approve of it from the financial point of view, but, whole-heartedly, aesthetically— Do it with all your ardor, all your heart and being. Wanting is the beginning of getting. Then want it badly and let nothing stand in your way. Neither love nor family nor money. Not even your mother. Nor this old man you see sitting before you, though I want only what you want— But let me take another drink from this bottle of wine, for"—he winked broadly—"as Saint Paul said, 'A little wine for the stomach's sake.'"

Max saw his own life. Quitting high school against his parents' wishes. The gambling, the drinking, the whoring. He saw his friends from the sidewalks and taverns of Halsted Street and Maxwell Street. He saw them jackrolling and knew that some of them went on occasional holdups; and, though he had never gone with them, he had not disapproved. He saw a billfold full of money and Chuck putting the bills in his pocket. In the billfold were the owner's identification cards, driver's license, union card. "Why don't you send the billfold back?"

Chuck had laughed.

"Let me send it back in an envelope. Nobody can trace it to you. I can just drop it in a mailbox." Chuck laughed again, got up and, lifting the lid of the garbage burner, dropped the billfold on the hot coals inside.

Max looked back again. He would have been more like them, gone with them beyond the drinking and gambling and whoring, if it hadn't been for his family: several older sisters, his gentle father, now dead, his impassive mother making the tortillas, tending to the family in its childhood and youth. Wearing. Not showing her wearing. Showing a stoic face and gentle hands.

Max was a little drunk. When he was a little drunk he always talked seriously. "Look, kid," he said to Nick, "my father was a *man*. He's throwing his shadow from the grave. That shadow is falling on me." He pounded his fist roughly into his chest. "You're going to be a *man*, and if you don't I'm going to kick your a—your fanny in." He grabbed Nick to him and hugged him, laughing loudly, warmly. With his other hand he mussed Nick's hair.

Norm had said to Max and Phil, "I'd do anything for that kid."

"Well, not anything," Max said.

"Please, don't get me wrong," Norm had said, flushing. "That will never happen."

Norman now said to Nick, "Always have good manners. Always be a gentleman."

Norman saw his father. He saw himself as a young boy. He had worn glasses as a child because of an eye condition now outgrown. He was thin and weak. But his father was going to make an athlete out of him. When he was only nine, glasses and all, he had to learn how to play catch. If he cried his father jumped on him or made fun of him. All through grammar school and into high school his father forced him to practice athletics. He had no aptitude nor liking for them. But this made no difference. He *had* to practice athletics.

He never knew why. His father was a thin, sickly man with no athletic background, no kindliness about him, no shred of softness or sympathy or real learning. All he had was a lot of money.

It seemed now that his father was always impatient or irritable with him. He grew closer to his mother. Her interests became his. She taught him to appreciate music, the mind, the arts, and insisted that his manners be courtly. Again he saw the ball coming up fast and hard from his father's hand and stinging his small hand inside the heavy, lopsided glove. He smiled with amusement and sadness at the results. And because of the results he had now to live in a half-world, an underworld, to find the pleasures his father's hand had, he was sure, tossed down to him with the hard, white, hurting sphere.

The whole picture, the entire sequence, occurred to him as one sentence linked itself to another and he was saying to Nick, "Always be polite and kind to people and don't force your opinions or desires on them." And glancing at the slim good looks of Nick, "You're a picture. Always make yourself a picture."

Nick looked at Norman with that quiet sadness of his. He saw Norman's delicate, almost effeminate movement of hands and head, the languidness of his neck turning as he moved the cigarette to his lips. With the beginning of knowledge he wanted to say, "I know, Uncle Norm, and it's all right." But he didn't.

Phil looked down at the tattooed mark between his thumb and forefinger. He saw his days with the Pachucos. The switch-blade and water-pipe and homemade-gun gang battles. He saw himself standing in penny arcades on South State Street near Van Buren, having tattoos added along each arm. The smart-aleck holdups, not for money but for the thrill. He saw even more distasteful things— And his eyes turned to Nick. "Yeah, kid, you've got to be better'n us. You got to do all the things us bastards wanted to do. And get an education. An education counts more than anything." He pounded Nick on the shoulder with his fist. "Some day we're going to be proud of you!"

Judge Sullivan took the wine bottle from his lips. "Always be Nick," he said. "Just be Nick and everybody will love you."

Nick idealized them. And he felt sad for them without knowing why. They loved him and were overly protective of him. This was a love, a protectiveness, a friendship built on the realization of the dead-end world of each of them. They could have put their smut on him and they wouldn't.

53

And Bill Forbes sat before the red, tear-stained eye of the recorder:
"But first, Grant, let me tell you this story."

Grant smiled. He knew the story and it hurt, every time he heard it. And Bill would have to tell it.

Bill Forbes said:

"See, this is in the day when the system was far more competitive than it is now and directly after the 1929 crash—roughly two years later. I was working on the wagon. That was before the patrol wagons cruised the city to suppress juvenile crime—but stayed in the station and answered calls.

"As it got near quitting time, ah—a doctor had come in and left word with the desk sergeant that there was ah—ah—removal of a body to go to the morgue.

"Well, back in the barn where we were the phone rang. And we got it. We had to go to this number on Cleveland Avenue. So my partner started to beef right away. We had to go like hell; otherwise we would have to work overtime.

"He was disgusted, you know. People die at such inconvenient times.

"Well, we went over there anda—as we drove up and started taking out the stretcher, ah—the woman next door hollered, 'It's the rear—' Anda—so it was, a frame house that was around Chicago Fire days. Now ah, these people, and many others even to this day, when they buy a lot they build on the back to live in and then work for the day when they can build a good house on the front.

"Well, this was in the back where the family had originally lived and then built a two-flat in front. Anda—ah—we went up the steps and I motioned to my partner to leave the stretcher down until we could get to, ah—ah—see what it was. And this woman again hollered, 'You have to speak loud 'cause she's deaf.'

"Anda we walked into a dark apartment.

"There was no light, but in a room off it was a kerosene lamp burning, and so as I came up to the door I saw a long cot going away from me and a woman with her arm under the pillow and an oldish man laying dead on this couch. And her arm was under the pillow and she was sobbing and sobbing, and I talked in an ordinary tone to her and said, 'We are police.' But no response.

"But she suddenly looked up and she looked startled, because I'm a big guy with the uniform on. And she said, 'Oh, the doctor said that he'd wait a while. There can't be a funeral and he—I was—he was going to let him be with me for a while.'"

Sergeant Bill Forbes looked up with a sad expression on his face, from Grant to Max—and then back down at the man on the cot and the woman at his side. He continued:

"And there was a chart on the table, showing how meticulously she had given him the medicine, and there was a cheap drug-store clock ticking the time off. So raw it sounded. And louder to me all of a sudden.

"And I motioned with my hand back to my partner to hold the stretcher so she wouldn't see it—anda—I tried to talk to her and I—I —I—I—tried to say, well, he can't hear anything or feel anything now —but I couldn't come to that because she couldn't hear me. I just realized that she was completely deaf. So I finally, by motion—ah, tried to tell her that it appeared that she had given him all the flowers she could while he was alive, and I, ah—looked into the big room off which this room was and there was beautiful lamps anda good furniture that showed signs of a better day, you know—of a day when they were prosperous, anda the floor was scrubbed white although the boards were softwood, you know, six-inch boards with the nails up from where the wear was. And we finally talked her into—ah, understanding who we were anda—she let us put the body on the stretcher and we started down the stairs with the body and she kept tucking the blanket, she kept tucking and saying, 'He was such a wonderful man.' And I looked at her and she had the appearance of getting to be an old maid and had passed up her chances of marriage to stick with him, see.

"So it was a chilly night, it was early in November anda—so we had to lay the body and the stretcher down while we opened the wagon door, so she tenderly tucked the blankets over him as if he would catch a cold—anda—we finally pushed the body in and, ah— my partner was in a hurry to slam the door and I held my arm out so she could talk and keep tucking the blankets in, and all she could say, 'He was such a good daddy. Such a good daddy.'

"So finally I slammed the door and—went off—and left—her standing there—that's all there is to it."

Forbes' voice trembled and he stopped talking. Tears stood in his eyes.

"There was no social security or anything in those days, and when we went through that aisle between the two houses you could hear Farley speaking for Roosevelt, promising social security for people who give their all in production so that they won't be abandoned in their old age."

Tears are not for children. Tears are for adults.

And he said, "So help me, God, that's about all there is to it."

Max touched the bottle of beer against Forbes' hand, and he took it, said, somewhat quietly, "But you see how a thing like that can impress you. Fate picks these acts—you know—and you go on doing that work and suddenly things stand up so terribly."

Then:

"So when we got on the seat of the wagon"—laughing, half humorously—"the first thing my partner says, he says, 'For Christsake we're going to have to go like a sonofabitch to get through work on time.'"

Sergeant Forbes began to tell about narcotics. He said, "Grant, can I take my teeth out? I can talk better that way," and slipped them out.

FORBES: Now when a bipartisan is dealing—when the deal is made on a ward level where the opposition both make an underhand agreement—the payoff on narcotics is raised to take care of both sides, so that the amount of heroin in the capsule is reduced and the amount of sugar milk is substituted so that the addict has to buy more often in the exact ratio. So these people are on a treadmill of getting money to get the buy, to make the contact, to get the pill, to go out and prostitute, to get the money, to buy a pill, and so on."

GRANT: You spoke of a political angle to narcotics—

FORBES: Yes. Yes.

GRANT: Would you explain a little more to me as to how the political setup works?

FORBES: Well, in the different wards there's organized—in other words, the privilege of violating is sold to certain people in the form of payoffs which are contributions to the party and so that the payoff on vice, gambling and narcotics, all that stuff, is a part of the system. I'm talking about them days—not now—because now it seems there is a reform but there wasn't then. It was competitive. There was only two kinds of people—takers and take-ins. And it seemed especially cruel where the addict got practically nothing and he was paying the same two dollars for the pill. Of course he came out more often for a buy, and on top of that the immunity that was built up by his system by the added frequency of the pills made it so bad that he'd finally get into a frenzy where he'd do anything.

GRANT: Then in other words, when we get away from the taker of dope—the addict—when we get away from the peddler—it goes to a big, organized crime thing?

FORBES: That's right.

GRANT: The politicians are involved.

FORBES: That's right.

GRANT: It boils down to a few bosses of narcotics.

FORBES: That's right.

GRANT: The privilege of buying.

FORBES: That's right.

The questions and answers came like gunshots.

GRANT: On the other hand, the police are free to pick these little people up.

FORBES: The police can deal with effect at the addict stage—at the addict level, you see—and occasionally peddlers—but can't reach back to the cause. Any more than the police can reach back to the antisocial cause of anything. Or a doctor or a lawyer, for that matter. Because I think every young doctor and every young lawyer has to make a choice between being ethical and poor or a whore. Well, you might say rich or opulent.

GRANT: Then this dope, in a sense, is really a—shall we say—legal transaction among politicians and big gangsters, more or less.

FORBES: Well, yes—in the present sense I don't know if is would apply but was would apply.

Max handed around more bottles of beer.

FORBES: The only thing is—now the political parties, since this national-scale investigation, have lifted their skirts clear of such things, you see, because Lord-God, we're facing a Communist world and you know to have such stains on our clothes wouldn't do. Now there's reform. That is, the reform is genuine as far as the political parties. But as far as the evil itself—where it is rooted in— you couldn't change it that quick. The lifting of skirts wouldn't stop it, see.

GRANT: Have you any way of knowing how these big shipments get to big cities?

FORBES: Oh yes. But they are as many and varied as a person can imagine. Automobile tires and everything. But when they're caught, occasionally, you know, good publicity is given, especially in an extreme case like an automobile tire. Wide publicity is given. See. But they don't have to be that secretive about it be- cause it is a traffic that has become part of the social order, see. But when—you know how the newspapers play up one poor devil who gets nailed for something—but genuine, real desire to stop the dope racket would really stop it—like they could stop political graft if they wanted. Putting the victim in jail doesn't stop it. It's a reform that doesn't think of prosecuting anyone but stopping the sin of it, ah—the evil. I can't quite explain. I guess it's hard to ex- plain—ah—when reform gets genuine nobody will be punished. But it will stop. When reform is sincere. Don't you think so? Be- cause putting a man in prison and continuing the thing under a different name is no—you know—when reform gets genuine and sincere it will not be out to punish the victims of the evil. They'll want to stop the evil. I believe, at least. Don't you? That's about all I can say.

Sergeant Forbes looked across at them. "I wonder—I wonder if narcotics—to people—is not like the effect that truth is stranger than fiction? Fiction is, ah—a—a—poss—a possible turn to dope to escape the horrors of reality in life as we live it—so—ah—that in a way fiction in some ways serves the same purpose mentally as dope does physically to an addict. Do you think?"

He turned to Max, and Max said, "I wasn't following you."

"Well, why does—well, dope eases the horrors of life. As we live it. The effect of life's truth as we live it—not as it was meant to be—but as we live it. Dope gives a person a respite from it. You see, it's an escape. Well, in some ways fiction serves the same purpose. Because truth—that seems to be such an important factor—*truth is stranger than fiction.*

"Truth"—his voice shaking—"oh, man—truth is so much stranger than fiction. It was. Maybe now social reform will modify it but it certainly was. Grant, you know, when you're writing, is it hard for you to believe that fiction is a modification of the horrors of truth on people—?"

Grant said swiftly, "It's easy to."

"It is? Oh, I'm so glad. Then you realize that. Because in a city like this, three or more million, every day there's people dying of whom there's no relatives, nobody knows about the bodies moved away. But the police have to handle it."

"I think that's one of the fundamentals of writing, to know that fiction is the modification of life's true horrors on people. But we face a competitive social order across the line now. The urgency of reform is terrible compared to the amount that has been accomplished. They're, they're still asleep at the switch. They slept for thirty years after World War One, and even if capitalism is a better system of distribution, they better start distributing." Grant laughed. "They're late now."

Grant opened bottles and said, "Bill, now tell me about the time you and your partner picked up this colored woman who was a dope addict."

FORBES: Ohhh, yeah. That was the rawest—ah—the most ironic contrast that I ever knew of. Hit us one night when we were walking and watching, working on Vice. Well, there was a colored girl, a colored woman—she was in her late forties and as wrinkled as a prune and a dope addict to the utmost. There were rumors that she was taking it under her eyelid because of the immunity she built up from constant use, and, of course, she earned the money for the dope from prostitution. Well, we were going along Wabash Avenue, and over where the railroad crosses at about Fifty-eighth Street was— Ah—can I mention names?

GRANT: Sure. It's all right. I can rub it off the wire later.

FORBES: There was one of the Haines Company's little blue coupés. And a salesman in it—we found out later, he was a descendant of one of the wealthy southern families—and he had Alice Woods in the car and— Can I tell that?

GRANT: Sure.

FORBES: And he had been loving her up, and laid her. In that car. And we made the arrest and we started to inquire and here it was post-bellum Civil War days. And she possibly in the social scale at the very bottom. Here he was consorting with her in that car for his own benefit. (*Laughing*) This is a hell of a lot stranger than fiction— I better change the Haines Company name—

GRANT: Well no, I—

FORBES: Well, you rub it out because, ah—I'll some day soon have to live on a pension. (*Laughing a little*)

GRANT: See, because when I finish with this, I erase it—

FORBES: Yeah. Yeah. While I'm talking I don't think of those things.

GRANT: Well, don't worry.

"Let's take time out for a while," Grant said, and switched off the recorder.

They did; but Forbes, still deep in thought, kept on talking.

"About dope— The snatch is what's got us beat. Each peddler has a woman working with him now and she hides the stuff there."

"Won't it fall out?" Max interrupted, asking the same question he'd asked Phil.

"No, sir. It won't fall out. The matron has her undress. She makes her squat and jump up and down but it doesn't come out. We need a law that will give the right to search the human body. Such a law is absolutely necessary."

And switching the subject suddenly: "Let me tell you this. This happened not so long ago. You see, they sometimes switch us back and forth to different details and at the time I was on the desk in a local station. Well—these two park policemen brought in this young fellow and charged him with indecent exposure."

Sergeant Forbes recounted the incident; then went on. "When the captain came to work Monday morning he saw this case on the record. He called the officials of the park board down. See, I was working from four to twelve. He was sure dough was passed and something was wrong—and I was at home and he called me at home and said I should come to the station immediately. I said, 'I'll come to work at my regular time and not before.' I sensed what his evil mind had thought up.

"Well, when I came to work at my regular time there was all the officials of the park board, the newspaper men and everything, and I walked in and I took one look and I said, 'Wait a minute!' I said, 'I'm going to settle this right away.' They had this young fellow there too. I said, 'Did I ask you for a penny?' He said, 'No, sir, you helped me out.' I said, 'I'll take full responsibility for this.' I said, 'Here's a young man who has no record, committed no offense, brought in on complaint signed against him. I booked him according to the officer's word, disorderly conduct, and got him released.' I said, 'I'm to blame? What did I do wrong?' They couldn't say a word. They all dispersed.

"They were going to make a big stinking thing that here was a moron who paid money—and the captain didn't get any—and they were going to squeeze it out of me. So help me, that's all there is to the case. But that young fellow could have been *destroyed*—if that captain had his way, for fear that he was not getting his cut in the dough. And I'll name the sonofabitch!"

Max asked, "What was that sonofabitch's name?"

He and Forbes started chuckling.

Sergeant Forbes said, "Quinn. Captain Quinn. Q-u-i-n-n. And a pious, hypocritical sonofabitch and a more sanctimonious bastard never lived."

Max said, "When he said I'll name the sonofabitch, I thought he was going to say Peterson."

"Aww," Forbes said, "you didn't know that Lorel Peterson had the biggest gambling joint in this goddamn city. Yes! At the time he was trying to push you around, Grant!"

"Jesus!" Grant said.

"Of course," Sergeant Forbes said, "nobody owns a gambling joint. Under the old setup, gambling joints were the administration and in them you could find prostitution and narcotics. Gambling joints were the administration but a guy was the front and took a cut, see, and stood pinches. There isn't a governor that can stop gambling. Nobody. And let me tell you something. Many evils in society begin at the top and work down—and what we have at the bottom is a crude imitation of the top."

54

In the long light of early afternoon Grant walked along North Clark Street, his long legs carrying him forward, his hands stuffed into his pockets, his mind looking down into the pocket that held the rough-penciled outline of his series of articles on narcotics.

And his mind went wandering over the recorded voices. He saw Fran. He saw Phil.

Roughly he put his fingers into his hair and roughly rubbed. The brown eyes grew thoughtful.

You have to take people as you find them. Not as you'd like to have them on a blueprint. This, long his motto; and he now again agreed with himself. Stepping forward, down North Clark. But you want them to change. You want to help change them.

And he heard again what Juan, Phil, Max and Forbes had told him.

So now he had the facts and he had the people.

And these were not completely bad people. Not completely bad. Boys like bats coming out at night, fists clenched, marijuana in their pockets. Boys without identity with good. Dope fiends like abandoned, twisted toothpaste tubes.

Cause. Cause. Search for cause, Forbes says. I second the motion.

As a successful young writer he had had to write a lot of stuff that he did not believe in. Now he wrote only what he believed smacked of the truth. Let them take it or not. He was no longer a pimp.

The square mouth flattened out. The facts and the people. And somehow, somewhere, it was all related. The juvenile delinquency, the narcotic addiction, the living in slums. Yes, the living in slums.

It's a revolt. Against the tried patterns that are as dust in the hands of the parents, are vomit in the hands of the children, dripping through angry, agitating fingers. How criticize the young when we had made such a mess of it ourselves? Handed them the tools of imitation. At the juvenile level it was a crude imitation. So Forbes would say.

It was a revolt, against smugness and self-satisfaction and the shutting out of anything or anyone who was different. So we'll be different. Goddamn the world and goddamn our parents.

Someone known, yet unknown, stood knocking outside the door.

Grant's fingers moved in his pockets and his mind moved over ideas.

Somehow it's all related. And you don't deny any of them. To do so is to deny yourself. Time for a beer, boy!

"Hello, Edith," Grant replied. "Drinking so early in the day?" He sat down.

She was a really beautiful girl. The kind of girl he would be attracted to if he were young and unmarried. Max had good taste. He smiled.

"There's no school today," Edith said. "So?" She gave a small shrug.

The bartender stood at their table. Grant looked at Edith's glass.

"A whiskey sour for the lady and make mine a cold bottle of beer—Schlitz."

No school. But she was full of her students. Over three whiskey sours, while Grant wanted to get away and up to his hotel room to work on his outline, she talked.

"This boy," she said, "gets more out of school than anyone else. He reads in the back of the school English textbook, reads modern short stories, and doesn't even know when the teacher calls on him." She put her small hand on the back of Grant's, in warmth and liking for this boy, in a gesture to hold Grant's attention. Smiling, she said, "He read: 'Come live with me and be my love.' " She lifted her hand from Grant's and inhaled deeply on her cigarette. "He's made for the Syndicate, really. His neighborhood—all that—" She gestured; then put her hand back on top of Grant's. "I said, 'Look, how can you expect anyone to come live with you and be your love if you read it like that?' "

"You really said that?" Grant asked, grinning.

"Why of course. Why not?" Edith said over the rim of her glass. "Much blushing, and then he read it beautifully in this new, deepened voice. And some day he will probably be ashamed that he had this beautiful feeling."

The bartender stood at their table. Edith looked at him and then at Grant.

"The same," Grant said.

The bartender went for them.

"But I'm paying this time," Edith said.

Grant protested vigorously, but Edith took the money from her purse, delicate odors of perfume, rouge, powder and lipstick rising from it, and paid when the waiter brought the drinks.

"The best," Grant said, and they clicked glasses.

Edith said, "This boy, Nick—Nick Romano is his name—is interested in more than comic books and marijuana and gasoline-station holdups."

"What did you say his name is?" Grant asked quietly.

"What is your profession, Mr. Holloway?" Defense Attorney Morton asked.

"I am a writer."

"What do you write about?"

"Economics and the social sciences."

"Are you an authority in this field?" Morton put the question half-humorously.

"I have been called one."

"Do you know the defendant, Nick Romano?"

Grant's brown eyes looked from Morton to Nick. "I know him well."

"How long have you known him, Mr. Holloway?"

"About seven years—since he was fourteen."

"Would you please tell the jury, Mr. Holloway, where and how you met him?"

"When he was a kid in a reform school which I was visiting to investigate conditions." Grant smiled. "We talked about Chicago."

Kerman had jumped up angrily. "I object! Incompetent, irrelevant, immaterial! While this may be very entrancing, it won't prove or tend to prove anything in connection with this dastardly killing with which this heretofore angel-faced-boy—even though in reform school at an early age—is charged!"

"Ohh," Judge Drake said, musing, "I think all this is preliminary to something—though I confess I'm not sure what it is. But I'm equally sure that counsel for the defense knows where he's going. Overruled."

On one of the witness benches Ma Romano wept.

"Mr. Holloway," Morton questioned, "did you see the defendant the night of the killing?"

"Yes, I did."

The tempo of the questions and answers had slowed down.

"At what time, please?"

"At about eleven-thirty."

"How do you fix the time, Mr. Holloway?" Morton's quiet voice asked.

"Because I had just come from the Civic Opera House. I didn't want to go home yet—my wife was away—I didn't feel like working that night. It was raining—I like to ride around in the rain, and started to head for the boulevard. I hadn't seen Nick in some time and wondered what he was doing. Well—I drove down to Halsted Street thinking that perhaps I would find him in the Nickel Plate. When I drove up he was standing in the doorway out of the rain. I swung my car door open and yelled at him. He ran over and jumped in. I said, 'Let's take a ride.' He said no, he had to meet Butch and Sunshine at the Cobra Tap on West Madison. I offered to drive him down there. When we got there Nick said, 'Come on in and have a drink.' I went in. Butch was standing at the bar. We had two rounds of beer and I left."

"What time was this, Mr. Holloway, when you left the Cobra Tap?"

"Exactly twelve midnight."

"How do you fix the time?"

"I had left the radio playing in my car. As I climbed in behind the wheel I heard the radio time signal and heard the announcer say that it was exactly midnight. I looked at my dashboard clock. It was on the minute. I looked at my wrist watch, which was a little fast, and set it."

"Thank you, Mr. Holloway," Morton said, "Cross-examination."

Kerman's face had an angry and tightly drawn look as he began cross-examination.

"How long have you lived in Chicago?"

"All my life."

"And you're a writer. Are you a radical writer?"

"I am interested in facts, not political philosophies."

Kerman ground his teeth. "Your name is in Who's Who among the notables of America, isn't it?"

"I believe so."

"Well my name isn't in it—is it?" Kerman said.

"I've never looked to see, Mr. Kerman. In fact, the only time I have ever seen your name in print was once when the newspapers reported you as saying, 'When I persecute—I persecute!' "

In the jury box the truck driver and the baker grinned.

"The word is prosecute!" Kerman shouted.

Grant shrugged.

Kerman lowered his eyes angrily. "Now then—" he said. "You are privileged to walk among the elite because of your successes, but you spend more time on West Madison, apparently, than you do at your writing— Why?"

Grant said quietly, "I find the people on West Madison interesting."

"Well—" Kerman's eyes narrowed. "Don't you find your North Shore friends more congenial companions than slum dwellers, gangsters, murderers and thieves?"

Grant pulled his tie loose a little—almost with the same gesture with which a man takes off his coat to fight. Grant said, "I don't know any gangsters or murderers—and many of the people I have met on West Madison are more honest and more congenial than many other acquaintances, including some with whom I have come in contact in this courtroom."

Everybody laughed.

"Move to strike as not responsive!" Kerman shouted.

Judge Drake said, smiling, "Sustained—but it is definitely responsive!"

"Now then," Kerman said, getting angrier, "you said that you were at the Civic Opera House on the night of November seventh? How long did it take you to drive from the Civic Opera House where you say you were—"

"Where I was."

"All right! —To the Nickel Plate?"

"A very few minutes."

"And you drove to that rattrap dance hall—tavern—whatever it is? Who's this Butch you say you met there?"

"I don't know his name."

"Are you used to drinking with people whose names you don't know, bums on West Madison Street?"

"I drink with anyone I please," Grant snapped.

"But—ah—" Kerman said, "the radio announcer said it was twelve o'clock when you left there?"

"That's right."

Brooks, Kerman's assistant, leaned over his chair and whispered to Kerman, "You're fastening that Romano was there. Try to tear him down on something else." Kerman pulled his head away and moved his shoulder irritably.

"Mr. Holloway, you're very much interested in the outcome of this case, aren't you? What is there about this defendant"—Kerman's voice took on a high tone—"that fastened your interest upon him and has fastened it upon him all these years!"

"I like him," Grant said.

"Mr. Holloway," Kerman yelled harshly, "why are you—tell the jury honestly—honestly!—why you are interested in this defendant."

Grant pulled his tie loose a little more and said, "I am interested because I have seen a boy, who lived in squalor and misery, sent to reform school for a crime he didn't commit . . . I have seen him during the formative years of his life driven from home by a father who did not understand him, onto the slum streets of the city, where he found companionship and sympathy and understanding . . . I have seen him charged with murder . . . and my belief in the brotherhood of man forces me to do everything in my power to save the life of a boy who is—I believe—the victim of his environment."

For a moment a silence fell in the courtroom. Then Kerman was on his feet, shouting, "Move to strike—all of it."

"You asked for it, Mr. Kerman . . . overruled!" Judge Drake said.

Kerman walked to his chair and banged down in it. "Mr. Holloway," he yelled, "you spoke of the brotherhood of man— Are you a— Communist?"

"No—" Grant said, "I try to be a Christian."

Kerman glared. "You said you'd do anything to have this fellow escape the consequence of his crime—"

"I did not say that. I said I wanted to do all I could to help him escape the bonds which his persecutors are endeavoring to fasten around him."

Brooks leaned over and whispered in Kerman's ear again, "You better let him go!" Kerman pulled away angrily.

"Do you know Andrew Morton, the eminent gentleman on the other side of the table?"

"I do," Grant said.

"How long have you known him?"

"Eight years."

"And you want him to win this case, don't you?"

"I do—because the life of a friend is at stake."

Kerman ground his teeth. "You say you object to persecution?"

"I do."

"Have you ever persecuted anyone?"

"Oh—some of the people I have written about may have felt that I persecuted them," Grant said.

"Oh! You didn't do them justice, eh?"

"I—ah—tried to do them justice but maybe I didn't show them mercy."

"That's all!" Kerman shouted.

Grant walked to the counsel table. A couple of spectators stood up to get a good look at him. Grant stuck his long legs under the table and sat down. Nick, in the chair next to him, looked up at him with his head held down.

"Hello, paisan," Grant said under his breath to Nick.

Newspaper headlines said:

MORTON CALLS SOCIAL AND SLUM
WORLD TO STAND IN ATTEMPT TO
SAVE PRETTY BOY FROM CHAIR

"What did you say his name is?" Grant asked again, quietly.

"Nick Romano," Edith said.

55

The weather had warmed. Trees were pushing out their buds, and the ten o'clock sky showed some stars above North Clark Street. Nick walked along looking for his mother.

Over the cobblestones of North Clark the paddy patrol moved at a crawl, and behind it walked a cop in plain clothes, his rump big, his shoulders like a wrestler's, his hat pulled down over his scowling eyes and hard gray face: *I am the law*. On either side of the street two plain-clothes cops walked: *I am the law*—entering each tavern taking people out, taking people off the sidewalk, leading them to the rear doors of the patrol wagon which stands with its motor idling. The big-rumped cop walking behind prods the wretches inside. Again the paddy wagon moves slowly, slowly down the street. The big-rumped cop walks behind it. He is like a sheepherder taking the flock home.

Alongside the blue-black patrol wagon the blue-black panther walks majestically.

Nick stood in the doorway of the Shillelagh looking inside for his mother. She wasn't there. He turned back toward the sidewalk, started in the direction of the next tavern. Big shoulders, a scowling balloon face and cold gray eyes blocked his way. The detective flashed a badge momentarily in the palm of his big hand. "What are you doing here?"

"Looking for my—"

"Where do you live?" the second detective, a heavy-jowled face over the shoulder of the first cop, said with a mean, accusing mouth. "I—"

The cop's hand was rough on his shoulder. "Let's see your hand." He pulled Nick's hand forward in a strong, big-knuckled paw and turned it over, searching with his eyes the area between his thumb and forefinger. Searching and disappointed.

"What are you doing on North Clark?" the first cop asked.

They prodded him out into the street and toward the open doors of the waiting patrol car.

Gee, you can't even walk down the street.

Gee, you can't even look for your mother.

The door slammed and locked behind him. The patrol moved at its crawl. The sheepherder was taking the flock home for the night.

Along the two long benches, facing each other, sat the scrapings of North Clark. Most of them were drunk. Some had bloody faces and black eyes. There were only two women, Indians, both drunk; one a young girl, half attractive, her hair short and loose over her forehead, her teeth strong and white in her moon-round face; the other a middle-aged woman who looked as if she had slept in her clothes for several nights and who, in her drunkenness, drooled a little.

The patrol bumped slowly over cobblestones. Another man was shoved, stumbling, into it. Another.

Nick sat at the far end of one bench, near the driver, and could see through the small grillwork window. Could see the side of the driver's face and the city as they moved slowly down North Clark picking up more flotsam and jetsam from sidewalk and curbstone and bar.

Across from Nick the two Indian women and a little drunken Irishman in a straw hat, with, unaccountably, a yellow rose stuck in the hatband, were exchanging cigarettes. "Here, Irish," the older woman said, "you better take some of mine. It's a long time till tomorrow and we get out."

"Thanks, lady." Then he turned his face to the grilled window and said to the policeman driver, "Why don't you go out and get thieves? You just take honest people."

Nick looked around at the people locked in with him, then looked out the window. It was strange to sit there and see the familiar crowd standing on street corners, the newsstand, drug stores, people crossing the street.

The two Indian women are now exchanging names with the man with the rose in his hatband.

"What's your name?" the Indian girl asks. "My name is Jacqueline Brown. Just call me Jackie Brown."

The paddy patrol is dense with smoke. A drunk staggers down the line between the two benches silently offering cigarettes to everyone, his shirt tail out of his pants. From her battered purse the older Indian woman pulls out a stack of pornographic photographs the size of a deck of playing cards and about as many. They are bent and curled at the edges. Fingers have soiled them.

"Hey, sister! You better get rid of them!" the man with the rose says.

"Yeah. They'll give you time if they find 'em on you. And they'll keep 'em for themselves," another drunk warns. "Dump 'em behind the seat and leave 'em."

"The hell I will!" She stuffed them back into her purse. "I had too hard a time getting them."

What you do on this street is your own business. Even on the way to the police station. They don't argue with her. They don't even shrug. It's an act performed. A decision made.

A voice at the back of the patrol wagon says, "Christ, we're bums. What the hell, we're bums. We got to stay in jail all night."

Nick looked out at the city passing him. Ahead, pointing a white finger upward as in prayer, was the steeple of the downtown skyscraper church. And Nick could see the driver's face. He was a handsome young blond cop, perhaps twenty-seven years old, with a clean-cut profile and blue eyes.

A man with matted red hair and a matching bruise on his forehead puts his arm around the slatternly Indian woman, in friendliness. They light new cigarettes. On this street your trouble is my trouble when it's the same trouble. We lie, we cheat, we steal for each other when it's the same trouble.

The yellow rose turns with the straw hat, and the owner puts his mouth near the window. "Spending the taxpayers' money to arrest drunks," he says drunkenly, loudly. The cop turns his handsome face and hard mouth back toward the voice. "I can't hear you, sir," he says with polite sarcasm.

The patrol turns off Clark Street, west. Out the rear window Nick could see the downtown skyscrapers.

"You're all stinking bastards. Give a guy a badge and he becomes a bastard," the yellow rose says.

The driver's face turns its mouth toward the caged ones. "You're so smart, why don't you open the door and get out?"

Down the line a drunken voice says, "Don't call them bastards. They're human too."

The patrol wagon now passes Montgomery-Ward's, over the river, across the bridge. The Indian girl and the yellow rose have decided to pose as man and wife and maybe beat the rap. "Don't forget my name," she says to him. "What's yours so I can remember?"

And the patrol pulls up to the station. The doors are unlocked, the street scrapings are herded toward the lockup. The men stand before a desk, to be booked. Behind them are the two large barred cells. In them are the blear-eyed, stupidly drunk faces; the haggard-eyed, scared faces; the sleeping faces with mouths yawned open and flies buzzing around them; the dirty feet in broken shoes, the filthy bodies in filthy clothes, the tattooed arms—the bloodied faces of the animals already trapped in this night.

It has been a good night. The few cots are filled with the shadowy sitting figures of men, their backs bowed, their shoulders slumped. Others sit on the concrete floor. Others stand, for there is no more room to sit.

Behind the desk, booking the new arrivals, is the handsome cop who drove the patrol. He is now questioning the man who was his antagonist on the drive to the station.

"What's your social security number?"

"Twenty-nine, seventy-four, ninety-five." The man gives it quickly and by heart. "It's right here in my pocket," he says. The rose, stuck in the faded hatband, has withered and bobs back and forth on its broken stem.

How can he remember it if he's drunk? Nick wonders, standing in line behind him.

The yellow rose says, "My old lady is here with me."

"Who do you mean? That Indian woman who came in with you?"

"Yeah."

Your trouble is my trouble.

The handsome cop is now frisking him before locking him up.

"You got to satisfy yourself as an officer now, uh, and throw our ass in jail," the yellow rose says.

"Yeah," the cop says. "I get a medal for this, you know."

He moves the yellow rose toward the lockup.

"I'm going to lose my job, you know," the yellow rose says.

"I hope you do." The cop says it casually with his hard, handsome mouth. And he means it.

Nick stepped up to the desk for his turn.

And I don't even have ten dollars with me for bail.

Between the back and front buildings the little square of open lot that was supposed to be a yard was yellow and lumpy. There were ashes in a pile and some old pieces of wood with bent, rusted nails sticking up through them. Some sunlight came, grudgingly, over the sawtooth edge of the building. But most of it fell on the dirty back porches of the front house.

On the first-floor porch of the rear house an elderly woman sat in a rocking chair. Her gray hair was bobbed and artificially waved. She was fat, with large shoulders and swollen-out breasts. There was a big mole, with a long gray hair growing out of it, on her cheek near the corner of her mouth. And the beginning of a black mustache. Spread out on her knees, turned to the horse-racing section, was the morning edition of the afternoon paper. Her eyebrows were pulled together as she studied it, and her lips pouted in concentration. Occasionally she scratched her head with the long yellow pencil she held in one fat hand; occasionally she made a check against the name of a horse or a jockey. At her feet were several copies of *Racing Form*.

A woman came out on the second-floor back porch of the house in front and threw a tomato can over the railing. The can hit the woodpile, rolled onto the lot, its jagged-edged top throwing highlights. The woman went back into the house and the screen door banged after her. The gray-haired woman, sitting on the little sagboard porch two steps off the ground, let the newspaper slide off her fat knees and frowned up at the second-floor banister. "Now wouldn't that freeze you!" she said aloud. Then she leaned back in the old rocker, rocking her big, lumpy form back and forth.

A handsome woman of about thirty-five, a few gray hairs showing in her black hair, came out on the porch.

The elderly woman turned on the rocking chair. "Hi, Ang!" she called in a friendly fat-woman's voice.

"Good morning, Aunt Rosa."

Angela went down into the yard and hung some clothes on the line. Coming back up the steps to the porch she stood in front of Aunt Rosa and nodded toward the kitchen door. "She's worse today."

Aunt Rosa shook her head, her jolly face wrinkling to sadness.

After Ang had gone back into the house Aunt Rosa sat motionless for a long time, staring out across the lumpy back yard. Then, at length, she picked up the newspaper and again bent over the racing sheet, her pencil making checks.

The woman in front came out and threw another can over the banister. Aunt Rosa grunted. "Some people ain't got no decency at all!" she said.

The sun spread out a little more and her pencil made a hesitating mark, thought better of it, flipped upside down in the fat hand and erased. In so doing Aunt Rosa's eyes slipped away from the racing columns for an instant and read the headline of a small news article:

POLICE ROUNDUP
ON NORTH CLARK

Casually she read the article:

> . . . also rounded up last night were seven young suspects between the ages of fifteen and nineteen. Being held are Tony Rocco, 19; Bill Stewart, 16; Beto Lopez, 18; Marco Florette, 15; Nick Romano, 18; Paul Ocampo, 19; and James . . .

Aunt Rosa read the article again. She stared at the name. She went on staring at it. Then she looked at her wrist watch.

The police brought in the defendants from the lockup and lined them up along one wall of the courtroom. From them rose the stench of soured liquor and body odors combined with the lockup smells.

Some of them had faces raw with bruises and puffed with black eyes, eyes wild from liquor the night before and no liquor today. And Nick was among them. In line was the yellow rose. And an honest-faced old man getting over a drunk; and a young fellow just on the verge of becoming a desperado, who had been picked up on the street and charged with vagrancy. Toward the end of the line was a man without a shirt and barefooted. He wore only a pair of pants.

The judge finally arrived, wearing a hat, topcoat and gloves. He removed them carefully and handed them to the clerk. Then he unbuttoned his pin-striped blue suit coat, sat down majestically in his Honor's squeaking swivel chair, and swept the courtroom with his eyes. They narrowed along the line-up against the wall, back and forth, counting them.

"Hear ye!—Hear ye!—" the bailiff began as feet scraped and everyone stood up; and he ended with "Everybody be seated and keep quiet."

The bums and drunks remained standing while the other cases were disposed of. The cases were petty ones, mostly neighborhood quarrels. There were few spectators; some men, who had come as witnesses, stood at the open door outside the courtroom, smoking, listening for the cases to be called for which they would testify.

The man before the bench was a recently arrived Puerto Rican who didn't understand English very well; he had committed a misdemeanor. The judge was a professor giving a lecture. The judge was saying: "There are some nice Puerto Ricans but some of the fellows get out of line. You've got to learn to respect the laws of your country. Case dismissed."

The judge looked up into the courtroom, and was an irate parent when he saw the group of men standing outside the door smoking. He called an attendant. "Will you close that door. I like to conduct my sessions quietly and in order. If those people out there have no respect or interest, they can stay where they are. And we'll keep that door closed. Understand?"

A man, his wife and three small children stood before the bar. The man's father had died and was to be buried today. The night before, the defendant had gone to a bar where his father used to drink, and, drinking heavily, began to believe that the tavern keeper had killed his father by serving him too much liquor. When thoroughly plastered he had gone out into the street and thrown a brick through the window.

The judge was a stern father: "Do you realize that I can send you to jail for this? Do you realize that you will have to pay for this man's property that you have destroyed and I can still send you to jail?" The judge is an advising father: "You can't win in a saloon, you know. I found that out thirty-five years ago, and I quit. Look at those kids of yours, look at those nice-looking kids. They're the ones who suffer with drunken fathers. Do you want to end up like your own father? Do you go to church? When have you been to church last?"

The wife interrupts: "Oh yes, your Honor, the children and I go to church every Sunday morning."

"And your husband? Does he go with you?"

"Well, he—he—"

"Too much time in the tavern Saturday nights, huh?"

The judge is Solomon; he turns to the tavern owner: "What do you want me to do with this man?"

"Give him another chance, Judge."

The wife is crying, and one of the children, too, without knowing why.

The next case is called; this man takes a baby from his wife's arms, the child she has been holding all the time they have been in the courtroom. He cuddles the child in his arms and begins to lavish kisses on it as they move toward the bench.

"He beats me, Judge," the wife says. She wants him to stop beating her. The judge looks down. He is an angry father. He tells the husband to stop acting; makes him hand the baby back to its mother.

And now that the regular cases have been heard, the judge turns to the bums and drunks off the street.

He narrows his eyes upon them again, again counting them. The judge is God. He dismisses two-thirds of them back to North Clark Street, West Madison Street, thirty-cent bottles of rot-gut, taverns, mission meals and doorway beds. Among the dismissals are sentences —few-worded, without sympathy, without interest, without looking up: "Rockpile—rockpile—ten days on the rockpile—rockpile—five days—rockpile"

"Nick Romano!"

Nick walked to the bar. He stood—handsome, sullen, erect.

"D and D. Drunk and disorderly," the bailiff chanted from the sheaf of papers he held in his hand.

"Guilty or not guilty?" the judge said, not looking up.

"Not guilty," Nick said.

"Fifteen days or fifteen dollars," the judge said, still not looking up.

Nick swallowed hard.

"I'll pay the fine," a woman's voice said.

Nick turned around, astonished, and looked in surprise at the gray-haired woman with the beginning of a mustache and the long gray hair growing out of a mole on her cheek. She had her purse open and a big hand was searching around inside it for the money. "Here it is, Judge." She held out the bills.

It wasn't until then that she got a chance to get a good look at Nick.

She had thought he would be bigger.

"Okay!" Aunt Rosa said to Nick. "Let's get out of here!" She said it as if she were half-mad. But the way she looked at him wasn't in anger.

He followed her out into the daylight.

Behind them the judge was God:

"Rockpile—rockpile—ten days on the rockpile—"

Nellie sat at a table in the Shillelagh, an untouched glass of beer in front of her. The juke box said loudly:

> Cross over the bridge!
> Cross over the bridge! . . .

A man stumbled through the front door of the tavern, stumbled quickly, excitedly, urgently. He almost ran to the bar. "Give me a glass of ice water!" It was a quick-spoken plea. His hands and arms were trembling so, jerking so, that he seemed to be clapping them together. The bartender, recognizing urgency, quickly filled the glass with ice cubes and water and set it before the man. The man tried to reach for it, but the back of his hand made the only contact; the glass turned over, the water running along the bar, the ice cubes skidding in it. And the man in a grotesque, leg-twisting dance fell to the floor in a fit.

> Cross over the bridge!
> Cross over the bridge! . . .

the juke box said.

A small, sympathetic crowd of drinkers moved in a circle around the man on the floor. The bartender had hopped over the bar.

"It's a epileptic fit," someone said.

"Get a spoon and put it in his mouth," another said helpfully. "He may bite his tongue."

"Or swallow it," someone added.

> Cross over the bridge!
> Cross over the bridge! . . .

The bartender hopped back across the bar and handed a spoon to a man.

"Move back and give him air," a voice said.

At her table Nellie stared wildly into her beer. She had to get it. She had to get what she needed, quick.

> Cross over the bridge!
> Cross over the bridge! . . .

"Frank!" she called. "Frank! Frank!" almost screaming. She staggered to her feet and out of the tavern.

> Cross over the bridge! . . .

They had assisted the man to a table. He was better now. The violent shaking of his nerves had subdued to an involuntary trembling.

> Cross over the bridge! . . .

On the sidewalk outside the police station, Aunt Rosa said to Nick, looking at him and smiling, then just looking at him, "Come on. I'll pop for something to eat."

"All right."

He followed her. He lowered his head, ashamed of having been in trouble.

"Look, handsome," Aunt Rosa said, "stop feeling bad. Everything's okay now."

"All right."

He glanced up at her. Who is she? Why did she help me—take me out?

She saw a lunchroom and pushed the door open with one of her big arms. "Come on—get a move on!" she said good-naturedly.

They went inside and sat at a table.

Nick looked at her with the sad brownness of his eyes. "Why did you—?"

Her big hand waved his words away. "Let's eat first," she said. The waiter came.

"What do you want, Nicky?" Aunt Rosa asked.

"A hamburger," Nick said, "please."

"Huh!" Aunt Rosa snorted. "You don't look any too well fed!" And to the waiter, "Bring the kid a steak. Make mine the hamburger—with coffee." And, immediately she had stopped talking, her own words came back to her like an echo: You don't look any too well fed.

Her throat tightened and stayed tight. She put her fingers over her eyes and closed them so that the kid wouldn't notice. Oh, my God! Oh, my God!

The headline had said:

MORTON ENGAGED FOR PRETTY BOY!
Chicago's Most Eminent Lawyer
Takes Case of Cop Killer

She had gone to see Nick at the county jail. She said, "Hello, sweetheart! How's my boy friend?"

Nick grinned at her through the heavy glass. "I'm all right, Aunt Rosa."

"Huh! You don't look any too well fed!" She kept her voice even and kidding.

Nick grinned. He lifted his head high until it was tilted back on his neck. He looked down at her and pushed out his chest, pounded it with one fist. Aunt Rosa blinked her eyes hard. Nick lowered his head and his chest. He slowly pushed the curly hair off his forehead.

"Keep your chin up, Nick!" Aunt Rosa said, struggling to keep her voice even.

"I can take it," Nick told her. "Anything they dish out." His eyes were wide and innocent, looking at her through the glass; his lips were soft and said the words huskily. Aunt Rosa felt a lump in her throat. His eyes were brown and guiltless. Aunt Rosa swallowed the lump. He was grinning. Aunt Rosa said, "You got any tips on the horses for me?" Her voice trembled, asking it.

Nick's grin was so wide it made his dimples hard and shiny. Aunt Rosa said, "You keep your chin up, Nick."

Nick grinned. He lifted his chin and, squinting, put his fist against it as if he were punching himself.

Aunt Rosa said, "We're doing everything we can. All of us. That Grant, he's really your friend. You keep your chin up."

And she went home.

With her eyes closed Aunt Rosa pinched the bridge of her nose. And now Louie was her favorite of the family. Was it that you liked the bad ones?

She opened her eyes and looked across the table at Nick. She was surprised that the food was there before them. She attempted to smile at Nick. He smiled back and lowered his eyes.

She watched him eat. And every once in a while he'd glance up at her. Then drop his eyes. Grateful. Ashamed.

Aunt Rosa studied him. This was a sad boy. She studied his face. She looked for something of Nick in his face. She jollied him,

"Okay, handsome, no holding back! Eat it all! You want milk? Coffee?"

Cutting into the meat he looked up at her. "I wasn't drunk," he said. "I don't drink. I wasn't disorderly. I was looking for—I was looking for somebody."

"Where do you live?" Aunt Rosa asked.

He didn't want to tell her. And he didn't want to lie to her. She had been good to him. He told her.

"How old are you?" Aunt Rosa asked.

"I'm only seventeen. Somebody said you should always say you are at least eighteen when you get arrested."

Then Aunt Rosa asked what she had wanted to ask all along. "What is your mother's name?—I mean her first name."

"Nellie," Nick said.

Aunt Rosa saw the girl on the witness stand again. She closed her eyes. She opened them. Almost afraid to ask, afraid to cause the boy to be suspicious, she said, "Say! The pie looks good in here! You want a piece?" And then, "I don't suppose you know what her— her maiden name was?"

"Watkins," Nick said. "Nellie Watkins."

Aunt Rosa closed her eyes: I knew it all the time.

She opened them and looked at the boy. She found little of the father in his face. His mouth? No. His eyes? But good-looking. This is a sad boy. And there *is* something of Nick about him. Something I can't put my finger on. Maybe just his personality.

Nick looked up suddenly. "What is your name?" he asked.

"Just call me Aunt Rosa," she said.

And Nick, quickly, "Why did you ask me about my mother? Why did you help me?"

Aunt Rosa's eyes were full of tears. "Maybe," she said, "I'm related to you."

"Related to me?"

She pushed him with her fat hand. "Go on—eat."

Related to me!

His heart began to beat fast, hopefully. A family!

They had finished eating. Aunt Rosa looked in her purse to find something to write on. All she could find was a race-horse ticket she had lost on. She wrote her name and address on it and handed it to Nick. "I want you to come over sometimes," she said. "Come over and see our boxer pup."

Outside she whistled like a man for a cab. The taxi stopped and she pushed Nick in ahead of her. "I'm going over by Taylor Street. I'll drop you off at Clark and Chicago."

When they got to his corner she said, "Your father was my nephew. I'm your aunt—well, your great-aunt anyway. You come over and see us sometimes or I'll come over and see you." She hugged him over to her and kissed him on the cheek.

When Nick left Aunt Rosa he went home. His eyes were full of tears and he felt that way inside too. Nobody was home. He went to the bathroom and opened the door.

Nellie screamed.

Quickly Nick's brown, sadly moving eyes took it all in. The teaspoon on the washbasin, its underside blackened. His mother with her dress up, revealing the bare flesh to her waist. The hypodermic needle poised like the pointed tongue of a rattlesnake. Like the long, slender, poisonous sting of a scorpion.

Nellie screamed, and the hypodermic fell to the floor, rolling, rattling across the floor, spinning.

Nick turned and walked out of the house, with not enough strength to close the door.

When Nick walked out, even before she knew that he was gone, Nellie fell on her knees, her fingers scrambling across the floor, feeling, searching . . . on her hands and knees, her fingers trembling, searching, searching for it, feeling, like a blind man on his cane, across the linoleum for it. Her arms under the bathtub and her fingers clutching . . . got . . . to . . . get . . . it . . . got to . . . get it . . . have it . . . gottogetithave it . . . got to . . . have to . . . gottogottogotto! got to! got to! get it! get it! find it! have it! . . . where? . . . is it . . . get it . . . have it . . . got to! got to! got to! got to! got to!

nose running. eyes watering. cramps coming. got to!

got to!

got to!

. . . and at last the clutching fingers under the bathtub find the tube with the scorpion's tail.

Nellie is barely able to stand. She pulls her skirt to her hip. Trembling fingers find it almost impossible to hold the rattlesnake's head steady for the stab of bite into flesh. And then, hands trembling, she jabs herself quickly, hungrily, the needle going under the flesh.

She staggered into the front room. She sat on a chair. Her long, thin fingers pulled at her hair, and she leaned against the table, a cigarette between her lips, the smoke curling upward.

She sits at the table by the window. In the building across the street the canary is a touch of yellow in its cage. She nods, nods,

nods. The drug is taking effect. She nods, nods, nods. Is far away. From inside his frame and its grimy glass Nick looks at her. She nods. She is at peace now. Agony gone. Slack. Loosened out. Limp. The cigarette falls from between her lips and into her lap. It burns a hole in her dress before burning itself out.

She is feeling fine . . .

Outside the door the blue-black panther rubs its back like a house cat.

5 A WORLD I NEVER MADE

56

MY MOTHER. With not enough strength to close the door. DOPE. His hand was like an old man's on the black iron rail leading down the steps.

He sat on the bottom step for a while. He got up weakly. He walked down the street. His feet carried him where they willed.

Up one street and down another.

Along this street, with these people, Nick walks.

In the street, in a chorus, the autumn leaves of yesterday's newspapers gossip in the gutter, blown here and there, under streetcar and automobile and passing feet. Go, carried by the wind and grit, in broken, grieving headlines.

An old man, his gray hair plastered flat with sweat, wanders aimlessly into the Shebeen Bar. He has not shaved for two weeks and the gray bristles stick outward like needles. He wears no shirt or underwear top. His pink and sickly white skin hangs in lank layers over his stomach and over his belt. His rounded, freckled shoulders and flabby legs carry him seesawing into the Shebeen.

A woman stumbles up to Nick and asks him where the Shack is.

She is over fifty. She is skinny, her arm bruised and turning black and blue, the side of her face discolored and caked with dry blood, her hair ragged.

Nick points to the Shack.

She stays, standing in front of him and blocking the sidewalk. "Can you let me have a dime for a glass of beer?"

Nick moves around her and continues walking where his feet will take him.

ALL GIRL REVUE the large letters say, cheaply painted but invitingly lurid for visiting conventioneers and farmers: GIRLS! GIRLS! GIRLS!

Up one street and down another, Nick walks.

Ahead is the river.

He found himself in a drug store.

"A pack of cigarettes."

He didn't smoke. He used to but he didn't any more.

"What? Any kind."

Back on the street, trembling fingers lit a cigarette and he choked on it.

Up one street and down another. Not knowing where he was or from what street he had come.

Hours.

He was tired.

He had to sit somewhere.

He went up between the two lions.

He sat in a room. When he was little he could cry and his mother would comfort him. Now there was nowhere to lay his bundle of grief.

He looked around. Colors and shapes, forms in new forms, assailed him.

He wished he could cry. He couldn't. Everything was dried out of him. The boy was a man. Unhappy man.

He looked around. Suddenly knew where he was. He had come here to see the paintings. He must have. His Uncle Max had brought him here years ago. He had come here many times alone, since. Admiring. They had bought him art materials. Encouraged him.

Around him the modern paintings in this, his favorite gallery, seemed like things alive, reshaping, moving to different dimensions, going beyond limits set and established, founding new color, expression, form.

They were like flashes of lightning on the screen of his brain. Then like dew-deep meadows, sun-slashed, sky-streaked. And storms came and failed to break. Then broke.

. . . and the hard stone of reality, his mother and himself.

He sat, his teeth biting into the flesh of his hand, tightening, ever tightening. And the guard, politely tapping him on the shoulder.

"We're closing, sir."

And the street, the night street.

And the streetcar's orange lantern bouncing up the track toward him. It came larger and larger down the track. And a bees' nest humming above it, a sparking as of fireflies.

From behind the streetcar, on the solid surface of the sidewalk, Lee came, with his twisted arm hugged up close to his chin in a claw.

"Nick!"

And dazed, Nick looked into his face.

Lee: They were graduating from grammar school and neither of their mothers showed up.

Lee shook with his left hand, saying, "Jesus, man, it's been a long time!"

Gone was the Lee he had known: sad, ashamed of his hand, timid in front of others.

"Come on up to my place!" Lee said, a wide, careless grin bruising his face. And his eyes were both wild and dreamy and not as Nick had remembered them.

They went into the same broken-down flat. On the same unmade bed lay Lee's father, drunk and passed out, his damp blond strings of hair a veil over his face, empty whiskey bottles and old racing forms scattered across the floor.

But Lee, without looking at his father, gestured Nick to the bathroom and, with the door closed, pulled out from its hiding place a small cylinder of cigarette.

"It's the greatest, man!" he said and lit up.

"What is it?" Nick asked as Lee sucked in like a washbasin relieving itself of water.

"Weed, man—marijuana. The greatest!" He pushed the little poisoned stick toward Nick's lips. "Try it, man!"

"No," Nick said. "I don't want any."

"Just for kicks, Jack," Lee said. "I'll show you what living really is."

"No," Nick said. "I don't want any."

"Jesus, man," Lee said, "it ain't habit-forming."

And his eyes went a little wilder. And he sucked in enjoyably and the weed crackled like the beginning of a brush fire.

Escape.

Escape from the broken-down alcoholic father, the unmade bed and uneaten food drying in the plates. The racing forms that never gave a winner. The empty whiskey bottles that never were empty.

Escape from the good-looking blond woman, his mother, who gave him money and nothing else.

And escape from that clawlike structure, his hand.

Sucking enjoyably.

All's well with the world.

And laughing foolishly, almost insanely, at nothing—the greatest—

Nick got out as soon as he could.

What a lousy, lousy world . . .

Again he walked the street, captured in the city.

He had to sleep somewhere.

He paid for a room in a flophouse on North Clark, not far from where—

Mother!

The loneliness of a room is a terrible thing.

He cracked his knuckles the way his father had.

He went back out on the street.

He didn't know where he slept and it was morning.

He wandered in the morning.

It must be Maxwell Street. Here are the stands. There are the peddlers.

Down the street comes the husky chopped-off man, just shoulders and torso, and arms pushing him along on a roller-skate framework. He whistles loudly as he unpacks his wares. He piles his watches and crystals on an old piece of felt on the sidewalk. The sun catches his watches and crystals and dials. The notes he whistles stride along on long, firm, free-swinging legs and jostle with the passing crowd.

Nick looks back. When I was a kid on West Madison . . .

Someone pushes a pamphlet into Nick's hand:

The Man Upstairs

> To him who doubts there is a God
> And has no faith in prayers . . .

And here Nick stands beside an empty lot on Fourteenth Street. His shirt is wrinkled, his hair mussed. In his hand he carries half a bag of rolls.

In the vacant lot is the hobo jungle camp. The far end of the lot is boarded off, with a few sag-stemmed sunflowers growing against the fence. The jungle population, half a dozen ragged men, sit on rocks and old five-gallon cans, their backs propped against the fence.

They are eating, each from a small pot black with the smoke of many campfires. On the fence rail stands a broken piece of mirror. Squinting into it a man scrapes the beard from his face. He has no razor but holds a razor blade between his fingers and glides it across his bumpy face. In the crushed-down weeds a fat middle-aged Mexican lies sleeping. A dying campfire, long, low flames against the ground, licks at charred pieces of wood. By the fire on bent five-gallon cans sit two men. The wind twists the smoke in spiraling clouds and cuts tears down their grimy cheeks. One man is squat, husky, doglike. He leans over a large tin can set on the fire and stirs the bones and scraps of meat with a clean, flat piece of wood from an orange crate. The man across from him is black and skinny. He, too, looks into the pot with hungry eyes. The mess stews. The coffee is in two discarded cans, coffee grounds swimming serenely on the surface. Half a loaf of bread, wrapped in a ragged piece of newspaper, sits on a rock.

Nick looked with curious sympathy and moved onto the empty lot. The Negro saw him coming and, looking across the little, scratched fire, shouted jovially, "Come on in! You're just in time for breakfast. Here—have a chair." He pulled an oil can up close to the fire and, laughing, said, "But be careful of our furniture. Don't break any of it."

Nick half-hung his head and held out the bag of buns. "Here—I got more than I can eat."

The Negro took them. He divided them into two piles and handed one pile to the other hobo.

The white hobo took them, holding out a hand that was greasy from pawing through the bones. He had a strange face, with big, wide-set eyes that looked their thanks at Nick and then looked swiftly back into the pot. In his fist the broken-board ladle made slow, stirring circles in the stew.

The black man grinned at him. He said, conversationally, "Me an' him's pals. We been hoboing together seventeen years. Been from coast to coast a dozen times. Ain't that right, Billy?"

The big, wide-set eyes looked up at the Negro for a moment.

"We ain't bad guys," the Negro said. "We don't stick up nobody or go jackrollin' nobody. I Simonizes cars." His voice chuckled, his mouth grinned, showing slices of white teeth.

The wide eyes came up to the Negro's face, the greasy hand stirred, the hard mouth grinned.

Nick held out his pack of cigarettes. The black hand and the greasy hand each took one. The Negro said, "You're good people."

"Is it—" Nick asked, "—tough on the road?"

Maybe that's what he'd do.

The Negro laughed good-naturedly. "No. It's a soft life. Me and Billy sometimes go in a store, and while I'm talkin' and spendin' a nickel or a dime Billy steals what we need. I'm the lead man. I lay on the jive and Billy fills his pockets."

This was a good joke, and the Negro laughed loudly.

The greasy hand ladled half the stinking stew into another can and handed it over to the talkative black hobo. Then the silent hobo took his grub and, going out into the weeds, stretched himself out on his belly like an animal and ate.

The Negro pointed to his tongue. "He can't talk," he said. Then, with the big can between his legs, with his back stooped over until his head was close to the can, he ate.

The other hoboes, curious, straggled up to the campfire and sat around in a circle. One of them said, "Hey, kid, how about a smoke?" and all the hands took cigarettes.

"What about a bottle, Slim?" a bum asked the Negro.

"I got a nickel of it," Slim said.

The hoboes took up a collection and Slim went off around the corner. He returned with the rot-gut whiskey. They all stood in a circle and the bottle went from lip to lip. They drank without making faces, as if they needed it. They wiped their mouths with the backs of their hands and silently shoved the bottle around the ring. The bottle went back to Slim. Slim shoved the bottle at Nick. "Here, kid." His voice chuckled. Nick started to shake his head, then saw the faces looking.

Nick gagged on the stuff. All the men laughed at him. Slim laughed loudest. But he said, "That's all right, kid, you're good people."

There was little left. Slim guarded it. He said, standing over the fat Mexican sleeping in the grass, "I got to save him some. He saves plenty stuff for me." He laid the bottle alongside the Mexican's fat-lipped mouth, sticking the cork betwen his lips like a nursing-bottle nipple. Then he prodded the Mexican awake. The Mexican grinned, rose to his wide buttocks, swilled down the rest of the rot-gut and rolled over in the grass again. He went back to sleep immediately.

An old cripple hobbled off the sidewalk and came unevenly across the uneven prairie. At the jungle circle he pulled a bottle from his back pocket. "Look, fellows," he said good-naturedly, generously, "there isn't much here but I want everybody to have a drink." He put his thumb to the label on the back of the bottle and read aloud, "Distilled in Illinois . . . I'm going to take it down to there and then I want everyone to have a smile." He drank, then passed the bottle around the hobo circle. Slim, after swallowing, said to Nick, "Excuse me, I got to take a leak. If you leave before I get back, be sure and close the door when you go out." He grinned and went over and stood with his face to the fence.

Three little boys romped out onto the empty lot, laughing, jumping. They picked some of the sunflowers, tearing them off their drying stalks. Then they skipped away, laughing, carrying the large flowers. An angle of sunlight lay where their feet skipped.

And he wandered all that day.

And night put a thousand eyes watching him. And the city watched too. The cop on the beat, his going, his coming, down many canyons of the city.

And back toward the jungle camp.

Yes, he'd run away. He'd go on the road.

Instead he walked into Juan's shop.

Juan was sitting near the blackened window, the parts of an alarm clock he was repairing strewn around him.

"Juan," Nick said.

"Hello, Nick."

"Juan," Nick said pleadingly.

He sat next to Juan.

And then he could cry.

With his head in his arms and his arms cradled on Juan's shoulder, he began to cry.

"My mother's on dope," he said, through tears, into Juan's shoulder.

"My mother . . . she's a dope fiend . . ." into Juan's shoulder through the blanket of his arms.

"I'm never going back there," through tears.

Juan supported him there on his shoulder. And Juan went on repairing the clock, his eyes concentrating on it, his fingers working with it: Clocks are damn hard to fix. Especially alarm clocks; once the spring gets out of order, it's hard to repair them.

"My mother . . . my mother . . ."

"Wash your face, kid."

"All right."

Nick went toward the toilet. Juan thought about father and son.

Nick came out; Juan's fingers went on working with the workings of the clock.

"I'm going, Godfather."

"All right, Nick."

57

And wandering . . .

Street after street.

Not seeing the people, not noticing the buildings. Like a blind man on a white red-tipped cane, feeling his way to solid surface underneath him.

Block after block.

The city his home and his prison.

Walking.

Another pamphlet was shoved into his hand:

Fifteen Reasons Why Television Is Wrong

Appeals to the flesh—sex, vice, sin . . .
Hell's pipeline into the home.
                    Isaiah V:20
Woe unto them that call evil good, and good evil; that put darkness for light, and light for darkness; that put bitter for sweet and sweet for bitter.

Walking.

He had to do something.

He bought a small drawing pad and a pencil. He found a place in tall grass by the river's edge and within view of the Merchandise Mart. The Haines Company rose from his feet, forty-eight stories high in twin buildings on either side of the river, one reality, the other the dream.

Nick sat there in the tall, bending grass. The river drank from the soil near his feet and dandelions grew, sunflowers tossed on long stems, the Milwaukee Road sent its boxcars slowly along, and many bridges stitched the city together.

Nick put the pad on his knees and drew. He lay on his belly in grass in the heart of the city and drew. His pencil remembered the jungle campfire and the two hoboes. It remembered Judge Sullivan's face. It remembered the legless man on the skate framework. It remembered other faces. And always there was the face of his mother.

His fingers took the sheets and tore them in half. They mingled with the dandelions. And some drifted toward the river.

A young boy in the big city lying on his belly in tall grass, his head buried in his arms.

And night.

He had to eat.

On the sidewalk he looked up and down the street not knowing where to go. THE LIGHTHOUSE the sign winked at him THE LIGHT-HOUSE.

He wandered in, and walked among the tables, looking for a place to sit.

The place was crowded. Someone was talking about the finest Jewish style and someone said something about mushrooms. At a table four young men with bleached and waved hair, worn long and carefully groomed, sat talking in high, excited voices. And one said, "I didn't call you a bitch. I called you a New Orleans bitch!"

This brought squeals of laughter.

And another of the group looked around the restaurant, his hand patting his golden hair into place, said boastfully, "I wonder what happened to the one who wanted me so badly?"

And Nick moves forward looking for a place to sit down. He moves among "truck driver" girls in blue jeans, some of them women baseball players. They are husky and slam around heavily on their feet, swaggering in exaggerated male-like stride, their shoulders thrust back, their hair worn in stiff, masculine pompadours, wishing the hair would thicken on their lips.

A young fellow in a very tight-fitting pair of faded blue jeans walks in. Eyes follow him. "Oh my God! What a basket!" a young man shrills in feminine-like voice.

And Nick walks blindly toward the rear of the place thinking about his mother. And there is no further to go and he stands at a booth against the wall. He looks into the booth.

Carl flushed. Carl, the star fullback on their high school team, sat in the booth with Wally, who ran the hot-dog and soda fountain near school. Wally had his arm around Carl's shoulder and was feeling his muscle. "It's awfully hard, doll," he was saying.

Carl, face red, looked at Nick. But the kid must be with it. Otherwise why would he be in here? They were just finding each other out. "Hello, Nick."

"Carl."

"You haven't been to school for a couple of days."

"No," Nick said.

"Uuuummm!" Wally said, looking Nick up and down. "Come on and sit down—next to me."

He pushed over. Nick obeyed reluctantly and almost sat on top of

Wally's mean little Pekinese, who sat there on the leather of the booth next to its master, perfumed as its master was perfumed. The dog snapped at Nick and crawled into its master's lap.

"No, now!" Wally said in reprimand. "You be nice to this nice boy. You know mama loves *all* her children." And to Nick. "Are you joining the club, doll?"

Bow ties go past the plate glass. Streetcars to 119th and Morgan. Disk jockeys and girls who advertise anything on TV. In orange and blue the neon sign, THE LIGHTHOUSE, blinking on and off, winks lewdly.

Nick ate his hamburger as fast as he could and said he had to go somewhere. He went way to the front of the bar near the window. THE LIGHTHOUSE the sign winked at him THE LIGHTHOUSE.

Maybe he could get drunk. Yes, and forget. He didn't drink but he would now. The only drinks he had ever had were when he was a kid and his mother and Judge would give him a little of their red wine, adding water and sugar.

THE LIGHTHOUSE.

The place was out-and-out gay. The "truck drivers" were here, smacking each other across the back. And the soft-spoken, sweet-voiced young men with the roving eyes.

The men speak in high-pitched voices and laugh in girlish screams, even the old ones. They move their bodies petulantly and sugges-tively. It isn't safe to go into the toilet. The women broad-shoulder their way to the bar in their blue jeans, proud of their tattoos, of their somewhat-muscled arms, their husky voices.

They aren't competition for each other but they don't like each other either. They're here out of necessity. A place to hang out in and look for what they want. A place that won't be raided, because they pay off here and *The Power* has said, "Yeah, let that queer joint over on Division Street operate. It will cost this much—"

Nick stood at the bar . . . I wonder what my mother is doing . . . and got a bottle of beer. He went to a table in a corner. Eyes watched his coming and going.

The beer, to him, was bitter like life.

A dyke in blue jeans, drunk and jealous, throws her bottle. It smacks above the heads of waitress and bartender and into the section of long back-bar mirror, bringing the mirror down in a hail of angrily crying glass.

There are feminine screams from the young men. Howls and guffaws from the young women in blue jeans.

The owner, a big and strong man, comes from behind his cash

register, pot-bellied like himself, comes from his bored speculation on aberrations: But it's a living—and a good one.

"Okay," he says, "you're going to pay for it. You'll have to pay for it"— And is figuring how many bucks more he can get out of the lesbian than the mirror cost him.

Billy, the butch, squares off, putting up her fists. It is an admirable pose, as good as any third-rate pro could pull—left out, right protecting, but ready.

"You want to slug it out?" she asks.

"Yes," the owner says, half kidding. And he doesn't care one way or the other. He could beat the crap out of this butch, and who would care? The police would look the other way. They'd like to do the same thing themselves. It was effrontery to their maleness.

"Okay!" the butch says, shuffling in front of him, fists ready. She's all for it. One year she hit the most home runs in the women's soft-ball league up in—and she had cleaned up on a lot of other butches trying to take her women, a couple of smart men trying the same thing too.

"Okay! Put 'em up!"

The owner nods to the bartender, a little amused at the girl, a little sad. "Go get the police."

The other girl with her, in the same blue-jeans uniform of their adopted masculinity; the other girl, her lover, who is getting jealous of the little feminine waitress, says, "No, no."

But they have no money to pay for the mirror. The owner makes them leave their wrist watches until they can pay, and nods his head toward the door, get!

Going out, Billy says loudly, "I could of wiped the floor with him!" She shoulders some of the little gay boys out of her way, in contempt.

Little jealousies, little arguments are all in the life of any bar. The juke box plays, the boys squeal, the girls guffaw.

And Norman is here in his elegant clothes. "Well," he says to his companion, a friend from out of town, "you wanted to come view the bodies." And smiling, "You look quite butch. Really more like an intimate of the place than a visiting tourist."

It was true, and they sat at the end of the bar near the john.

"Look at the hustlers sparkle!" Norman said, rather proudly.

And the hustlers, the studs, began to converge on them in a line of inspection.

Nick sat alone at a table in a corner of the tavern looking down into his bitter bottle of beer, unaware of what was going on around him. And a queer moved stealthily toward him, a shadow in the shadows of an uncaring wall.

Norman's friend, with many dainty gestures, was telling a homosexual story. The punch line came. Norman began to laugh loudly on the higher scales of laughter. And, still laughing, he looked across the tavern.

The female laughter died in his throat.

He walked to the table where Nick sat. "What are you doing in here!" His voice became almost first-sergeant masculine. "Get up! Get out! Don't ever let me catch you in here again!"

"Yes, Uncle Norman."

Nick went outside.

A boy on the sidewalk was asking a man, who had just left the place, for some money, any small amount, a quarter or a dime, to help get him home to Minnesota.

The man, obviously effeminate, felt in his pocket for some change to help the forlorn kid get back home: Nice-looking kid.

Immediately two men stepped out of the shadows. Their eyes were serpents looking both ways down the street. They flashed phony detective badges.

"You propositioned the boy! Didn't he, kid?"

"Yes, sir," the boy half whined.

THE LIGHTHOUSE THE LIGHTHOUSE laughs the neon sign.

They walk the man down the alley. They want money to let him go. He doesn't have much on him. Thirty-eight dollars. Your watch too. His watch too.

They meet the boy several corners away. Give him five dollars.

58

"The kid knows," Juan said to Max over the phone.

They gathered together in counsel and strategy, Judge, Max, Phil, Juan and Norman. They gathered in a tavern.

"The kid knows and he's disappeared."

Norm said that he had seen him last night. He wouldn't say where. Just in the neighborhood.

Max ordered a round of drinks.

Behind them the juke box said in an old, scratchy voice:

I want to go
NORTH!
EAST!
SOUTH!
WEST!
Everywhich way
Long as ahm movin'
Long as ahm movin'
Long as ahm movin', ba-be
Ah don't care . . .

They sat and they drank. They felt sad.

"Yeah, but he had to find out sometime."

"Yeah, that's right."

"Where do you think he is?"

Shoulders shrugged.

"Now what do we do?"

Shoulders shrugged.

They drank more and more.

Old Judge Sullivan sat, his head bowed, his gnarled cane between his gnarled hands. His mustache hung, weedy, over his bottom lip. "Not I, not anyone," he said, "can travel that road for you. You must travel it for yourself."

"Oh," Max said, "the alcohol is beginning to tickle you, huh?" His curly hair, in his weaving on the stool, brushed Judge Sullivan's forehead. Max said, "But what are we going to do, just sit here?"

"Shut up, Max," Phil said, "you're drunk."

"Awww!" Max said. And he laughed loudly, his head thrown back. But there was no humor in his laugh.

"Maximiliano! Maximiliano!" Judge said sadly. "Don't you understand the significance of those words? And the truth. The beauty."

"I am a child beneath your knees," Max said repentantly.

"There is no beauty without truth," Judge said.

"That sonofabitch!" Juan said.

"Who?"

"The Wolf!"

"We could go beat the sonofabitch up," Max said. He smiled a tight smile of approval and half stood up before his weight flopped him down again.

"That's an idea that has a lot of alcohol in it," Judge said.

"Yeah—more alcohol!" Max said, ordering.

Judge Sullivan didn't object.

"Let me cue you in straight," Phil said. "We got to stick by this kid. You better believe it. We've known him since he was a baby."

"And he ain't like us," Max said.

They nodded.

"He can amount to something," Norm said.

They nodded assent.

"You better believe it."

"The kid's all screwed up and we're the only ones who can help him."

"Who *give* a damn."

"Now let me fill you in," Phil said. "Pick up on this. Nellie, there's nothin' we can do about her—but the kid—"

"Yeah." They nodded assent.

"You better believe it."

"Do you know about his father?" Juan asked.

"No," Phil and Norm and Judge Sullivan said.

"Well, I'll tell you."

He told them.

"May I have something stronger than beer?" Judge asked.

"Sure. Whiskey!" Max yelled at the waiter, and his elbow slipped off the table, his head nearly hit his bottle, ordering.

And the whole bottle of whiskey stood there on the table. Judge Sullivan silently poured himself a second, silently drank it; a third. Then he stood, erect, though weaving. "One of us should be with Nellie," he said. "I'll go there. But keep me informed." He wiped a few tears. Of age. Of liquor. Of love.

The old cane and the old man went slowly toward the tavern door.

And the whiskey bottle went around. It was finished and a second was set on the table.

And they were drunk. But their laughter, their drunkenness, had pain in it.

And Max had a fight, which he won, and they dragged him back to the table. And Juan smoked a cigarette, something he seldom did. A handsome college student, slumming, came to their table and wanted to join them, but Norm sent him away. "Look at that," Max said about a woman with a beautiful body, and Juan said, "I could use some of that." They clicked glasses and their eyes met, without humor, without lust. And Phil looked at all his tattoos as if he were looking at a long time past. And Max wanted to fight with the bartender but they dragged him back to the table.

They were drunk. And they joked. And they were supposed to be having a good time. But they lay down in pain with him. They rose in despair with him.

59

Night is a friend and protector. Night is an enemy. The Judas kiss. The Damon and Pythias handclasp. Night is a good time and a bad time. Night can hurt and it can soothe. So with night.

Nick sank to his bed at the edge of the river. And low in the grass there were dandelions. The dandelions, a bridge across time, linking childhood to young manhood.

Mother!

He lay there. His face buried in his arms.

He lay there.

The wind was his only cover. Night was whispers in his ears.

Your mother is a dope fiend.

River, wandering beneath bridges like a stealthy lover to his meeting place, until it touches lips with the lake. River, shamed, creeping away from slum neighborhood and factory district.

Sleep.

And he dreamed . . .

He was going to the top of the building. Inside the building there were scorpions wearing blue boots and black gloves that were very long. And spiders dressed the same way. They moved about, talking together, whispering together, and all looking at him. He started up the stairway and he met a huge crab on the eleventh landing dressed in the same uniform of blue boots and long black gloves. He got frightened and he started to run down and then he began to fall and fell all the way down, but lightly, as a piece of paper falls, and a scorpion at the bottom of the stairway in the great, wide, round, disklike, moving, slithering entrance hall said he needed an injection and the crab just laughed and they gave him an injection and the crab said, "Now you are one of us."

. . . the dream turned to its millionth reel . . .

No good!

No good!

60

Nick walked into the house. Nellie put her hands up over her face and began to weep.

"Mother," Nick said.

He went to her and put his arms around her. Her weeping shook her frail body. Her eyes went up to him and then lowered. Her weeping continued.

"My mother is on dope," he told them.

Their eyes said they knew it already. Max lit a cigarette, Juan cleared his throat, and Judge Sullivan put his old, wrinkled hand on Nick's shoulder.

"Can't she stop? She said she can't." His eyes looked pleadingly at them.

Juan cleared his throat again. "Look," he said, and he knew it was going to hurt, "for most of them it's almost impossible to stop once they're really hooked. Like everybody else, when they first try it they get a sensation that's out of this world. They really can't describe it, nobody can describe it unless you been on it. I mean, much as I've been around them they still can't tell me how they felt. I mean it's overwhelming. They're carried away. It's a sensation. And everybody I've talked to, they can't describe it. I've talked to hundreds of people over in the neighborhood who are on stuff and they all tell me the first time they take it they get that sensation and from then on all they try to do is get that sensation back. The same sensation they lost. And they never get it. They never get it. But they keep on taking it and trying. Then after a while they keep taking dope to keep from getting sick. That's what everybody around there is right now. They just have to have it to keep from getting sick."

And he stopped.

Nick went on staring at him, and nobody said anything for a moment. Then Max said, "Look, kid, I'm off work tomorrow. Want to go to the Art Institute with me?"

"No," Nick said, "I don't want to."

"What about the show? There's a new picture downtown about that Van Gogh character you like."

"No," Nick said.

"I'll pop—is that right, Max?—for a malted milk," Judge Sullivan said.

"I'm going home," Nick said.

Nick cleaned the house and avoided his father's eyes.

"Look at your clothes," he said to his mother.

He washed her two dresses, ironed them and mended the cigarette holes.

"Why don't you stop?"

"I can't help it. I have to have it."

He fixed the food. "Please eat, Mother."

"I can't."

"Try."

He brought the food on a plate. "Please eat this, Mother." He was now the parent, she the child.

Sitting next to her he lifted the fork of scrambled eggs. "Here, Mother." She only nibbled. "Come on, a little more." She tried to get it down, her eyes looking at him gratefully. "You do love me, don't you?" she said.

Nick lowered his eyes and nodded yes.

They sat a long time, he with the unwanted plate of food on his lap. Then she put her forehead against his shoulder and laughed tragically in sad recollection. "When I was a little girl," she said, "I never got enough to eat—and now—" She lowered her head even further on his shoulder and her blond hair was a shield over sorrow, over eyes remembering. She said, "My Uncle Clarence was a wonderful man. He used to"—her voice chuckled a little—"sneak food to me at night."

Nick stroked his mother's hair. She said, "Let me tell you—" And she told him of her early life and of her mother abandoning her. "And now," she said, "I have done the same thing to you." Wordlessly she slipped to her knees and put her arms around him; and Nick, too, knelt, supporting her, holding her, trying to lift her up. With their arms around each other they tried to hold each other strong from the world outside.

Nick's father looked at them.

And day after day:

"Eat something, Mother."

"Take care of yourself."

"Look at your clothes. Change your dress."

The questions had been there since he knew. They had to come out.

"When did you start?" he asked.

"When you were a little boy."

"Where?"

His fingers twisted together and he cracked his knuckles.

"Here in this room."

"And always I thought you were just drunk," he said sadly. Silence hung like a crepe on a door.

Nick rubbed the toe of his shoe in the sun-pattern on the worn boards of the floor.

"Why can't you stop?"

"Because I can't."

She answered his questions as a child answers an adult.

Nick was trying to rub out the sun-pattern.

"You can't stop."

"No."

Nick buried his head in his arms on the table.

"How much do you have to have?"

"I have to have"—she closed her eyes—"a fix in the morning, the first thing in the morning. Then one or two during the day."

Nick rolled his head sideways out of his arms. His autumn eyes looked into her face. "Who started you on dope?"

She twisted her fingers into her hair, turned her face away.

"I don't know. I can't tell you. I don't want a hot shot."

61

"Who started my mother on dope?"

They turned their eyes away. "We don't know," Max, Judge, Juan and Phil said.

"I think I know," Nick said.

They turned their eyes back.

But he said no more.

When he got home Frank Ramponi was sitting in the front room with his mother.

"Nick, honey," Nellie said, "would you take a walk? I want to talk to Frank."

Nick looked at Frank for a long, angry moment, then turned and walked out.

He walked around. He didn't want to leave his mother there with that guy. He started back soon. Frank was coming down the front steps.

Nick guessed. He said, "You think I don't know where my mother's getting it. There are laws, you know."

Frank smiled at him without trying to conceal his blubbery double lip and continued down the steps.

62

"May I speak to Rosa—Aunt Rosa?" the voice said into the telephone, and after a while the pleasant, fat-woman's voice said, "Hello. This is Aunt Rosa."

"This is an old boy friend of yours!"

"No! And me married!"

"Well, maybe I could take you to lunch anyway."

Aunt Rosa's voice chuckled, grew deliberately coquettish. "Which old boy friend is this?"

"Grant. Grant Holloway. Do you remember me?"

"Remember you! How can I forget the best damn pinochle partner I ever had!" And, just as if it were yesterday, "How's your game?"

"We'll play again sometime," Grant said. "And what about lunch?"

"Huh!" Aunt Rosa said, as if she were mad. "After almost twenty years you have the nerve to call me up and say 'What about lunch' just like that— Yes, I'll go to lunch with you! But I'll have to go to the beauty parlor and pretty-up first."

Grant took her to a very popular and somewhat fancy restaurant-tearoom on Michigan Boulevard. Grant liked the place because here they had a colored waitress working with the white waitresses among the linen tablecloths, candles and vases of flowers. This man didn't have his colored help stuck away in the kitchen or behind a greasy steam table, but out, equally, with the others. The owner had, in breaking precedent, selected carefully and hired an attractive, intelligent and neat colored girl. Grant approved of this, too, and the girl had often waited on him.

He and Aunt Rosa sat now at one of the linen-smoothed tables, but the colored girl wasn't there; another waitress came and waited politely for their order. Aunt Rosa moved her chair noisily under her heavy weight and said, "How about popping for a drink and telling me what's on your mind?"

Grant picked up a spoon and waggled it at her. "Never mind. After lunch."

Then he ordered drinks and they sat, sipping, smiling at each other.

"Well, I wasn't too old to catch a man after all!" Aunt Rosa said.

"I guess bobbing my hair helped. Remember that long braid?" She shook her head. "Jesus, Italian women can be fools when they come here from the old country!"

"Listen," Grant said, "with your pep I'm surprised you haven't been married a couple of times."

"Well, this one," Aunt Rosa said, "sometimes I wonder if I didn't make a mistake. But it's good to have a man around. I met him at a tavern and we went out to the race track together." This seemed to explain everything; she drank and then went on. "Swede, I call him. Don't even remember what his first name is," she pretended; and gesturing with a plump arm, "He's just a big dumb Swede. But a woman gets used to a man."

Grant ordered lunch. While eating they discovered that they both owned boxers.

"Tell you how I got mine," Aunt Rosa said. "This Swede I married, he was crazy about boxers, always talking about boxers. So I bought one, a little puppy."

"Oh—you laid a trap?"

"I don't like you either—" And, laughing a fat woman's healthy laugh, "Yes, I guess I did." She seemed to become angry. "I paid two hundred and fifty dollars for that dog—dog's got papers and all. That damn dog eats better than me. A quart of milk every blessed morning, with an egg in it. A pound of first-choice hamburger for dinner. Bones for presents. Vitamins and things like that."

Grant tapped cigarettes out of his case for each of them. "So the dog came to live with you and shortly after that the Swede came to live with you?"

"That's about right, Grant. But I tell you, if anything happens, the Swede goes and the dog stays!"

And now they were finished with their coffee and were having a liqueur. Aunt Rosa drank hers in one gulp and pushed the glass away. She put her big arms on the table and leaned toward Grant. "Okay, big boy, what's on your mind?"

"There's a kid named Nick Romano."

"Don't you think I know it!" Aunt Rosa said. "I bailed him out of jail not so long ago!"

"What!"

Aunt Rosa told him about it. "And I don't think he was lying when he said he hadn't done anything." She gestured with her plump hand. "Give me a cigarette." Grant offered one and held the match. Over its flare she said, "Yes, he's Nick's son. I checked that."

"I think we better have another drink," Grant said.

"Yes."

They had a couple more. Aunt Rosa said she had to get back to work.

"You're working?"

"With that husband of mine and that dog of his, I better work or we'd starve!" She put her hand over his on top of the table. "The kid gave me his address. We'll go by and see him. Is tomorrow okay with you?"

Grant nodded yes.

"Pick me up at work at five o'clock. The Haines Company. Main entrance."

Aunt Rosa said, "You wait out here in your car and I'll get him," and, as she climbed heavily up the steps, Grant smiled and looked at the rear of his car, where all the bundles of meat and groceries—bread, pie, a half-dozen pairs of socks, a sport shirt and even a quart of ice cream—were stacked. Then he climbed out, lit a cigarette, leaned against the car and wondered what Nick Romano Junior would be like.

Aunt Rosa knocked hard, and the voice on the other side of the door said, "Come in."

She sat there in her cheap dress, a couple of cigarette burns in it, the need for the drug just dimly beginning to make itself known. She sat on the straight-backed chair with her hands clasped in her lap. Aunt Rosa recognized the same, though older, frightened face of the child on the witness stand.

"You must be Nellie," Aunt Rosa said.

Nellie nodded yes.

"My name is Rosa." And she held out her hand.

Nellie took it and looked up at her. Aunt Rosa smiled down into the aged child-face. "Is Nick here?"

"He's in the bathroom. He'll be right out. You—you know Nick? Are you one of his teachers? Hasn't he been doing good in school?"

Aunt Rosa laughed her easygoing fat woman's laugh. "Lord, no, child. I'm his aunt. His great-aunt. I was your—your—husband's aunt."

Nellie stood up, trembling, and put her hand to her throat. "Don't take him away from me," she said. "He's all I've got."

Aunt Rosa put an arm around Nellie's thin shoulders. "Hell, honey, nobody's going to take him away from you. You can bet on that. I just want to take him somewhere for a couple of hours."

Nick walked in at that moment, the two women standing close together, the older woman with an arm around the other.

He flushed. "Hello, Aunt—Rosa."

He looked even sadder to her.

"Hello, sweetheart!" she shouted. "You didn't come to see me so I came to see you."

He lowered his head. "I was waiting until I could save that money to—"

"Awww!" She hugged him over to her and kissed him on the cheek.

Nellie watched fearfully.

"Come on," Aunt Rosa said, "I want to take you somewhere!" And to Nellie, "Can I borrow him for a couple of hours?"

Nellie didn't answer. She was looking at her son.

Nick looked back at his mother. "I'll be back in a little while, Mother."

"Here he is!" Aunt Rosa said. And Grant looked. The boy's son. The boy he had tried so hard to help. In his failure to help the father he felt instinctively close to the son.

"Hello, Nick."

"This is Mr. Grant Holloway," Aunt Rosa said.

"Hello, Mr. Holloway."

"Grant is good enough," Grant said.

"Well, come on!" Aunt Rosa said, moving toward Grant's Cadillac that waited at the curb.

"I was a friend of your father's," Grant said.

"Where are we going?" Nick asked.

"To meet the rest of your family!" Aunt Rosa said.

63

The lamp was low and their faces couldn't be seen distinctly. But it was there. It was on all their faces, in their eyes. It lay on them. And it lay over Aunt Rosa as she entered.

The executed die.

The living go on living.

"Her son died in the electric chair!"

Moving.

"Their brother died in the electric chair!"

Hiding.

286

Until only a few remember; and none in this new neighborhood.

It was a feeling, more than anything else. More than an expression. And Nick lay in their faces. Lay in their thoughts.

The living go on living.

They are the ones who suffer.

Ang and Rosemary sat close together, sewing, talking quietly.

"Hi, everybody!" Aunt Rosa shouted from the door, turning on the overhead light and revealing them all clearly: herself, Ang, Rosemary; Nick and Grant, their arms loaded with shopping bags of food.

The two seated women were both in their late thirties. Rosemary's brown-gold hair with light shimmering in it was worn in a high pile on her head, and her round blue eyes squinted to see who was with Aunt Rosa. Ang's brown eyes also looked up.

Aunt Rosa introduced Grant, and Grant said that he remembered Ang.

Aunt Rosa had the same flair for the dramatic as her nephews, the dead Nick and the living Louie. She said, "And I want you to meet Nick Romano—"

It was like a bombshell.

"—These are your relatives, Nick. This is your Aunt Rosemary—"

Ang was breathing hard.

Rosemary held both of Nick's hands and looked deep into his eyes; and Ang looked, looking for something of her brother Nick, as all of them did when they knew.

"—and your Aunt Angela."

Ang put her arms around him and started crying.

Aunt Rosa shook Ang by the shoulder. "No sniffles. Let's get the food cooked. You, Ang, can peel the potatoes. Rosemary, you make the salad. And I got some Eye-talian olives to go in it. Nobody's going to spoil them steaks—steaks two inches thick! I'm cooking them myself!"

She started taking off her coat and rolling up her sleeves. "All right, fellows, sit down!" She punched Nick playfully on the arm. "You and Grant can do the dishes."

Ang took Nick's hand and led him to a chair, seated him there, her eyes never leaving him. Rosemary looked again, fleetingly, at him, and got Grant a chair.

Aunt Rosa came back into the room, saying, "Jesus God Almighty! I almost forgot!" and lugged out a dusty bottle of wine. "Good dago red!" she announced, and poured glasses. Nick shook his head no. She forced the glass into his hand, telling him it would put hair on his chest.

He took it. He looked across at Grant. Grant was looking at him; he smiled and Nick dropped his eyes.

"Dinner can wait," Aunt Rosa said, and lifted her glass in salute.

One of the bedroom doors opened. Ang and Rosemary exchanged glances.

She came out, an old and skinny woman, her gray hair long and matted. She was barefooted and wore a short bathrobe over a nightgown that showed below it.

"Hi, honey!" Aunt Rosa called.

The old woman came out into the center of the room.

Aunt Rosa said, "Nick, this is your grandmother."

The old woman walked over and stood in front of him. She looked at him. "Nick? Your name is Nick?"

"Yes, ma'am."

"The State took both of my boys," she said, "both of my fine boys."

She turned and walked back into the bedroom.

Ang moved quickly toward the door and, when Grant and Nick weren't looking, slipped the bolt across.

The meal was cooked. The table was set. It was heaped with the food, and glasses of red wine at each plate. Aunt Rosa turned on the television set so Nick could watch while he ate.

They ate.

From behind the bedroom door they could hear Ma Romano humming a lullaby. She hummed it like a dirge.

Aunt Rosa brought out the pie and the ice cream. She made Grant fill his glass with wine again. And another of the bedroom doors came open.

The boy, in his early twenties, came out—wearing nothing but a wrinkled pair of pants and rubbing sleep out of his eyes. Ang frowned at him.

Aunt Rosa yelled, "Hello, handsome! How's *my* boy?"

Nick looked up and Grant looked up.

"My God!" Grant said under his breath.

"It hurts every time I look at him," Aunt Rosa said under her breath to Grant. Then she said loudly, "Nick, I want you to meet your Uncle Louie."

Nick stood up and held out his hand. He was trembling a little.

"Hi, bum!" Louie said casually.

"Aren't you going to shake hands?" Rosemary asked him.

Louie took a hand down from rubbing his eyes and offered it to

Nick. He looked at Nick. His gaze was deep, brown, innocent.

Nick looked at him and looked around the table. This was his true family. And he looked back at Louie. He couldn't take his eyes off Louie. Louie looked just like the picture of his father on the wall at home.

"It's after seven o'clock," Ang told Louie.

"Aw, I was just taking a nap!" Louie said and went off to the bathroom.

Grant and Nick did the dishes, wrapped at their waists in aprons Aunt Rosa had twirled around them. Nick kept looking at Grant. And then his eyes would fall away. He wanted to ask, "What was my father like?"

Grant was nice to him and kept talking, asking him about school, about the kind of books he liked to read, what he was interested in.

"I like to draw and paint."

Grant handed him another of the washed plates for drying. "You sound like a very ambitious boy. Where did you get all these interests?"

Nick lowered his eyes. "My mother started me being ambitious."

The dishes washed, they sat again in the front room. Aunt Rosa asked Nick if he knew how to play pinochle and then said she and Grant would teach him how to play three-handed. She found an old deck of cards. The cards went around. Ang and Rosemary sat watching Nick.

Grant asked Aunt Rosa, in an aside, "Where's the Swede?"

"He and his dog are at the corner tavern," Aunt Rosa said.

A man let himself into the house with a key. A man in a business suit; a studious-looking man with glasses and a briefcase.

"This is your Uncle Abe—Abe Goldstein—your Aunt Angela's husband."

"How do you do, sir?" Nick shook hands politely.

"Do you want something to eat?" Ang asked her husband.

"I ate with some business acquaintances. Shall we go upstairs?"

"I'll be up later," Ang said.

She wanted to sit and look at this boy awhile yet.

Louie was a long time in the bathroom. Then a long time in the bedroom. When he came out he was all dressed up. Not a hair on his head was out of place. No insulting piece of lint was on his suit coat. No part of the surface of his shoes had not been polished to a shine with the bathroom towel.

Nick looked at him with deep and admiring eyes. And Louie went toward the door and at the door turned back, waved to Nick, said, "See you around."

And it came time to go home. In the Cadillac, Grant said, "I go that way. I'll drop you off." In front of the house Grant said, "You'll have to come over to my place sometimes. How about Wednesday? Some young people are coming in." He wrote down the address for Nick.

When Nick went into the house his mother was sitting nodding away, her fix sending her down, down to peace.

Nick led her to her bed. He made her lie down. He put a blanket over her.

Then he sat with his forehead pressed against the window, looking out.

64

"Get the kid on it," The Wolf said.

On the table he laid the dollar bill, and on the bill the dull white powder.

He left, turning at the door to look back at her. Her eyes were staring down at the drug.

The door slammed and she was alone.

A leering street lamp looked in through the window, with one eye atwist on its post where an automobile had hit. Night whispers went running around the darkened room on little rat feet, whispering, laughing, scurrying along, corner to corner, laughing ribaldly, laughing sarcastically. And the old room gave old sighs. And the little heap of dull powder looked up at her.

Nellie looked back.

And Nick, the father, looked.

Her hands were in the roots of her hair and her head was close, now, to the dollar bill, looking.

Her hair hung like a shroud. Her arms hit the table with a loud bang, startling the quieted room and starting little gravelike noises again. A clock ticking. A faucet leaking. A chipped cup rattling in its chipped saucer.

And the moon came bright.

The dull white powder looked into Nellie's face.

Her hair hung like a shroud. Her fingernails bit her hands. And became fists.

They lifted to her forehead. They banged against the table. They beat in a hail of blows against the dollar, the white dust. They beat and beat.

The white dust went as sand goes before wind, as snow before sun, as mist goes, or dew goes. The dollar, under this attack, moved, too, across the table and to the floor, drifting there where the white dust had disappeared in the dirt. The dollar lay there.

And Nellie sat with her head rolled on the table, her fingers twisted into the roots of her hair, pulling, her legs spread listlessly, panting, panting.

And Nick looks from the wall.

And Nellie panting,

Why didn't I take it myself?

panting

panting

65

"Goddamn it!" Grant said, looking into the mirror and, for the third time, knotting the bow tie. Squinting, he moved back from the mirror, his mouth twisted, his hair, graying a little, falling over one eye; and the lopsided tie; and Mrs. J. Reynolds Scott will say, "I simply adored your latest article in the *Atlantic Monthly*" and Wanda would put him next to Dorothy Kirdland at dinner again. I want a beer—preferably on West Madison Street.

Grant yanked the tie loose and started all over again. I'd like to ditch the whole thing. But he really didn't mind. It was Wanda's idea of an occasional good time. He had his bums on West Madison and she had her bums on the Gold Coast.

Grant got the tie almost even and left it that way. He put the comb into his hair. Wanda had said, "It's just a little gathering for dinner. I'm giving a dinner for Lorraine Arlington St. Johns. Her father owned the chain of magazines, you know. Poor man died last summer. I'm very anxious for you to meet Lorraine."

"All right, Wanda." So he'd get another assignment to do another innocuous article for too much money. Thank God for the dope series! Assignment, hell! Job's the word. Like a bricklayer or a

291

truck driver. Only you're having strings pulled for you. By God, I'm going to start on that novel!

Grant got into his coat.

Chauffeur-driven cars pulled up in front of the prize-winning number along the Gold Coast. A private elevator whispered up through steel and stone. Guests began arriving . . .

At dinner Grant looked up with dislike at Ward Committeeman Donald Lockwood and glanced swiftly at Wanda. His eyebrows tightened and his lips tightened on a cigarette. Wanda leaned on an elbow, laughing at him. He ground out the newly lit cigarette. She said, "The kids come in tonight."

"Your art group—the young and very poor intellectuals."

She patted Grant's hand, bringing him around to a good-humored, boyish grin. "Oh, your salon!" he said, chiding her.

"Now don't be mean."

"Well, the menagerie, if you'd rather have it that way."

"You're going to stay for it tonight? Or is it West Madison for a beer to wash your mouth out?" She was smiling good-humoredly at him.

"Yes. I'll entertain your dilettantes with hat tricks."

They sat chuckling together.

"Oh," Grant said, as if he had forgotten, "I've invited someone."

"Who?" Wanda asked.

"Never mind." He wouldn't tell her.

After the dinner guests had left, Grant wandered out on the balcony and wondered where Bobby was and when she would come. She had refused to have dinner with "those people."

And after a while Bobby came. "Hi!" She kissed her mother and father on the cheek and said, "Gee, I ate like a pig at Walgreen's with a couple of friends from school, but I'm still hungry!" She went toward the kitchen, her black hair tied into a pony tail, a red ribbon caught there in a bow.

The young people came. The young intellectuals got out of their coats and immediately began a discussion. Again Wanda sat in one corner of the scroll-end sofa. She liked these kids and was amused by them and amazed by them and hoped that something good would come out of one or two of them.

The little group was on its favorite subject—art. They were discussing, opinionatedly, the trend of modern art. With clear crystal glasses of liquor in their hands they brought out the dead bodies and turned them round and round, turned them inside out, stood them on their heads.

Barbara sat at the other end of the sofa from her mother, her legs drawn under her, her skirt spread out, her fingers laced together in her lap: Gee, I'm bored! They're not sincere. Not like Grant. Not like my mother. Maybe Mario is. I don't know. They're just saying the things they think they should say. Gee whiz!

They praised the ghosts and broke the unhappy shades of famous and long-dead artists. They made the living artists dance to their tune. They said all the bright and not new things.

Grant glanced at his wrist watch. Maybe he can't find the apartment. Indicating to Wanda that he'd be right back, he took the elevator and went downstairs.

Nick stood in the dark shadow of the building. His shoes were shined and his worn suit was pressed. His nut-brown hair was neatly combed. He stood with his shoulders pressed against the stones of the building and his foot scraping along the sidewalk. He stood looking down at his foot, afraid to go inside the lobby.

"Hi, Nick!" Grant said, smiling and knowing. "Come on up!"

Grant had forgotten his key. He rang the buzzer and Nick was surprised to see that when the elevator door opened, it opened right into the apartment.

Then he saw the girl. "Hi," she said, holding out her hand, "I'm Bobby."

"This is my daughter Barbara," Grant said. "Bobby, this is Nick."

Nick sort of half hung his head and took the girl's hand, "Hello," then let his fingers fall away. She had smoke-blue eyes. That was all he noticed. And he dropped his glance.

Grant and Barbara led him to where the young people, sitting on chairs and on the floor, were excitedly talking. "Wanda," Grant said over their heads; and Wanda stood up, smiling and holding out her hand to the new arrival. "Wanda, this is Nick Romano."

Wanda's red-creamed lips parted in shock and surprise; then she smiled and took the boy's hand. "How do you do, Nick? Come, sit here." She made room for him alongside her. "I'll introduce you to the rest later. Or Barbara can."

Nick sat. He drew his legs together and he drew his shoulders together, feeling completely out of place. His armpits dampened a little. He looked at the pattern in the carpet and heard the voices around him. He could smell the sweet smell of Grant's wife.

"Here, Nick."

He looked up. Barbara was handing him a glass. He took it obediently. "Thank you."

For something to do he tasted it; and choked a little and was embarrassed anew.

Grant walked over and offered him a cigarette.

"No, thank you, sir."

Grant sat down next to him and said, "These are a bunch of young people who are all interested in art and literature. I thought you might like to meet them." Grant let his voice chuckle and said, to put the boy at ease, "They talk over their heads a lot but they're nice kids."

Nick glanced at Grant and liked him even more. Then he began self-consciously to look from person to person and tried to understand what they were talking about. They didn't even notice him. They were too busy talking. Occasionally Wanda glanced at him and away.

The young people talked. They bandied the names back and forth. Cézanne. Van Gogh. Blue Period. Picasso. Pink Period. El Greco. Rousseau. Diego Rivera. Gauguin. Picasso.

"Picasso—his immense gift as a creative artist . . ." said Alonzo, who painted.

". . . His protest against the photographic which caused him to create a new form of artistic expression . . ." said Orville, who wrote.

"His refutation of sentimental romanticism . . ." Harriet said. No one knew what Harriet did.

"With pattern! With form! With art!" said Richard.

And Gordon: ". . . the formlessness and too lyrical color of the impressionists . . ."

And Anita: ". . . I find his pink period most interesting."

"Pink period."

"Blue period."

It was a little too much for Grant. He walked out onto the balcony.

African primitives.

American primitives, now so popular.

"Cézanne said everything in nature reduces to the cube, the cone and the cylinder," Orville, the poet, said.

"Yes," said Lawrence, "and it is certain that Picasso got his inspiration from that remark."

"Undoubtedly!" said Anita.

Rousseau. Rivera. Mexican primitives. African primitives. Gauguin. Indian primitives.

Wanda was telling a story about a now famous but then

obscure Chicago artist. ". . . I was getting together a select show and went to see him. He had two very small pieces that I felt I could sell for him—God knows he needed the money. I asked him what his price was. The dear man said that his New York price was eighty-five dollars but that his Chicago price was sixty dollars. I asked him why—" Wanda paused, chuckling. "He said that he liked to keep his children at home, so that if he got lonesome for any of them he would just go and knock at the door of the person who owned them and say he just wanted to come in for a moment and look at them."

Grant wandered back in. Gordon said, "Please tell us, Mr. Holloway!— What is the essential quality of a true artist?"

"Oh, yes, Mr. Holloway!" said several voices.

"A true artist?" Grant smiled, grinned. He combed his hair with his fingers. "Well"—embarrassed—"an artist is a non-conformist. He paints or writes what he pleases, as he pleases. He shouldn't be afraid to paint—or write—anything he wants to. He doesn't give a damn what anybody thinks or says. He has to express himself in his own way—he, he needs humanness and sympathy—" Grant stopped, amazed to find his arms spread out in front of him. He put them down. And he saw Nick looking at him solemnly.

Cézanne. Picasso. Gertrude Stein. D. H. Lawrence. Van Gogh. Proust. James Joyce.

Wanda said, "Let's go into the library. I have some new records you might like." They went down a hallway with paintings crowding its wall. Nick stood, fascinated, then followed the rest.

Wanda put on records of poets reciting their own poetry:

Carl Sandburg spoke about "The People, Yes!"

"Oh! Carl Sandburg!" a voice said.

. . . And Sandburg continued, speaking about "this old anvil."

"Marvelous!— Isn't it?" Then shushing into silence.

Then, from a record, Weldon Johnson gave his version of the creation of the world.

"Oh, I love this!"

Then Gertrude Stein said . . . and her voice went on in neat word after word after word.

"Pure art based on a feeling for words!" a voice enthused.

Wanda sat on a low chair. Others trickled into the room. "Come, Leona, sit here," Wanda said, slipping off the chair, draping her lovely black velvet on the floor, her legs drawn under her, the circle of velvet making a pattern against the floor, one arm draped over the arm of the chair. Leona sat, her elbows on her knees, her hands on either side of her face, her face a study of scowled artistic rapture as she listened . . .

And Gertrude Stein continued in neat, endless word after word after word.

Over Gertrude Stein, Wanda said, "I knew her. She wasn't like that at all. She was a very shrewd woman."

Grant edged toward the door and sneaked out of the room: I guess I shouldn't have asked Nick in for this!

At the end of the evening, as always, they gathered in the kitchen, and Wanda and Barbara prepared hot dogs and grilled sandwiches and made hot coffee. Nick had never seen a kitchen as big as this; it was almost as big as their whole apartment at home, with all sorts of electric gadgets and ovens set high in the wall so that you didn't have to stoop. Uncomfortable and not knowing what to say to these other young people who knew each other so well, he edged into a corner and watched. Grant's wife had changed into a housedress and was slicing onions, which made her eyes run—and it made her look prettier to him, wiping them and slicing more onions. Grant was looking in the refrigerator and brought out a bottle of beer, uncapped it, drank from the bottle.

"Here, Nick."

It was Barbara. She had two hot dogs, mustard oozing, slices of onion and pickle looking out of the rolls.

"Take one," she said.

"Thanks."

She hopped up on the edge of the kitchen table and sat there, patting the place next to her.

He sat next to her. She looked sideways at him, biting down into her hot dog and shaking her head, yes, they're good. Shyly he repeated her gesture. She chewed for a while and when she could talk she said, "What do you do?"

Eyes the color of smoke.

He flushed.

"I'm in the last year of high school. Do—do you go to school?"

"I'm a freshie at the University of Chicago. But I meant—do you paint or write or something?"

"Well"—he glanced away from the smoke-blue eyes—"I do a little drawing." And quickly, "But I'm no good at it."

"Say," Barbara said, "I like you! You're not sophisticated like these other—" She gestured with her hand. Grant had walked over.

"Are you coming over again?" Barbara asked. Nick blushed. Grant said, "Sure, he's coming over again."

"I have to go," Nick said, getting down from the table. "And —and thanks."

He told Grant's wife good-bye. Grant and Barbara walked him to the elevator that was the front door. "Thanks, Mr. Grant."

"Call him Grant, like I do!" Barbara said.

Grant had Barbara by the back of the neck and, laughing, said, "I've already told him that."

"And call me Bobby," Barbara said.

And the elevator was there with the door open.

"See you, huh?" Barbara shouted.

And the elevator door closed.

When they had all gone home and Grant and Wanda sat on the balcony with hot coffee and cigarettes, Grant said, "Do you know who that boy is?"

"Yes, Grant," Wanda said.

66

Every day for many days he thought about Grant and his wife and daughter. He had never thought that people really lived like that or, at least, that he would ever be invited to their house. And he never thought that there were young people his age who could talk like that about art and literature and music. They had invited him to come back, and he wanted to but he was afraid to. And he often thought of the Romanos, especially his Uncle Louie, who looked just like the picture of his father on the wall. He wanted to go back there, too, but he didn't know if he should so soon.

He had been thinking of all of them that evening when he got home.

His mother called out, "Nick! Come here!" Her voice was angry. She stood with a letter in her hand. "This came from school," she said. "It says you haven't been to school for two months."

He looked out the window. "I've been working," he said.

"I want you to go to college," she said. "That's what I want. To see my kid graduate from high school and go to college."

"Maybe one of my children," Nick said.

He walked into his room, and when he came back he carried a

small stack of bills in his hand. "There's a place in Kentucky where they cure you. Please promise me you'll fill out an application. It's free if you haven't got the money, but you have to pay your way to get there. Here's the money for the train fare." He handed the money to his mother. Then he smiled sadly and took the money back, twisting it out of her clasping fingers. "No. I don't trust you. I'll keep it and get the ticket." Again the sad smile.

They all went to the depot with her. She cried and clutched Nick. They all shook hands and spoke in muted voices to her. And she sat at the window looking out at them. She sat as she had when her Uncle Clarence had put her on the train to Detroit, not knowing to what she was going.

The train began to move. Judge Sullivan stood on his cane and, taking off his battered hat, waved it. Nellie leaned her pale face close to the window and Nick ran down the track a way, waving, waving. Then he stood watching, his brown eyes filling up.

"Come on, kid, let's go. The train's gone," Max said.

Nick turned around and grinned broadly at all of them.

His mother was going to be all right.

67

Grant drove up, ran up the steps and knocked. Nick opened the door. He flushed. But he had to say come in, and he was ashamed of the house. And he sneaked the paint brush down to his side, trying to hide it.

Grant walked in. The first thing he saw was the canvas with a composition coming to life in vivid colors: a smoking campfire on a lumpy, tin-can strewn empty lot, tenement houses in the background, ragged figures, hard faces grouped around it, large dandelions, larger than the heads of the gathered hoboes in the foreground, yellow and drooping on their stems and seeming to lean out of the canvas.

"Ummm!" Grant said, standing on his long legs, raking his fingers through his long hair. That was all he said for a long time. Then, turning to Nick, "It's good!"

Nick blushed. He was young enough and sensitive enough to blush often.

"Say," Grant said, "my daughter's mad at you!"

Again Nick's cheeks colored.

He could think of nothing to say but, "Why?"

"Because you haven't been over. She keeps asking about you." And to give the boy confidence, "I think she's got a crush on you."

Nick couldn't say anything. He just stood looking at the floor.

"Why don't you come to dinner? I have the car outside."

"Yes, sir."

In the bathroom Nick, trembling a little, scrubbed paint from his fingers with a bar of laundry soap and got into his worn suit.

Grant stood looking around the two miserable rooms.

At his home Grant said, "Look who's here!"

Barbara said, "Hi! It took you long enough to come to see us again!"

Wanda shook hands rather coolly. "Hello, Nick."

The days that followed were erratic ones for Nick. He was sometimes happier than he had been for years, but these times never lasted long.

He came over many days because Grant said you come over when you feel like it—and Barbara said, "What about us going to the concert in Grant Park tomorrow?" or, "How about the Art Institute on Wednesday?"

And his mother was going to be all right.

Grant even had Aunt Rosa in for dinner one day and she made Nick promise to come to her house the next night to eat.

He did. They were all nice to him. After Aunt Rosa, he liked Aunt Rosemary next. His Aunt Ang was quiet and looked awfully unhappy; sort of always thinking about something else. He didn't see his grandmother or his Uncle Louie. He wanted badly to see his Uncle Louie.

He kept going over to Grant's house.

And he always left suddenly. Feeling—

My mother is a dope fiend.

After his second or third visit Wanda said, "That boy has such a sad expression. Do you think he knows?"

Grant shook his head I don't know, and said, "But we must be kind to him."

"Social worker!" Wanda accused with a smile.

He kept going over there. He and Barbara went to the Art Institute, to free evening lectures called "Adventures in Art." Barbara was taking art classes there because her parents wanted her to, and to these she also took Nick. Afterwards they sat in Walgreen's, with malted milks in front of them, their feet up on the rounds of the stools. They went to a couple of picnics with some of the group that came to Wanda's evenings, but on these occasions Nick was embarrassed and didn't know what to talk about. On the very first day of the football season, with fall crisp and chilly, Barbara and he went to the opening game. They sat high in the stands and Bobby had a bottle of whiskey in her purse. "I stole it from Dad's bar," she confided, and she took a swallow and made him take a swallow "because they all do at football games," and they both choked and coughed and they held chilly hands under the blanket in friendship-like and laughed, and cheered for Illinois because the University of Chicago didn't have a football team.

And, as always at her house, he would get up suddenly and say, "I'm going."

I'm no good, he would think. His eyes would sweep their faces and he'd say thanks for letting me come over.

On the sidewalk outside—

I'm no good.

It was an echo inside an echo. Without knowing it he was speaking his father's words.

All one Sunday they spent the long day drawing. Then, after dinner, they listened to classical records together, lying on the floor, she in slacks, Nick's solemn eyes—his chin perched in his palms, his elbows on the floor—going from the sounds of the music to her face, then to his drawings scattered there on the floor around them like leaves, back to the music, then secretly and sad to her profile.

Grant hadn't been home, and he now came through the room. "Hi, kids."

Grant fixed himself a drink and brought them each a glass of chilled wine. Then he went looking for Wanda.

When he came back into the room Nick and Barbara were sitting at the bar, the wine untouched at their elbows, their elbows on the bar, chins on the palms of their hands and their faces turned toward each other, looking into each other's eyes, playing a game of seeing who could stare at the other the longest without blinking.

Grant chuckled and walked out of the room. One minute you think they're so sophisticated and grown up, that they're adults— they act that way—and the next they're just kids again.

Barbara blinked first. "Heck, you win!"

Nick's half-sorrowful smile came hesitantly, stayed that way; he looked at her hair and her nose, then her eyes.

He got down off the bar stool.

"I've got to go."

Barbara walked him to the elevator that was a door. Because he looked so sad she impulsively lifted her face and kissed him briefly on the cheek; just a brushing of her lips. As a friend. As a sister.

"Good-bye, Nick."

The elevator door started to close.

"Don't forget!" she shouted. "We're going to the forest preserves next Saturday to paint."

That evening when Wanda was tidying up the room she saw Nick's drawings scattered across the floor. She brought them to the bar and, turning on a direct light, studied them a long time with her eyebrows pinching together in concentration.

"Grant," Wanda said.

"Yes?"

She slid Nick's drawings from a large envelope. "The boy has talent. I thought so when I saw these but I wasn't sure." She named a famous Chicago artist. "I took them to him to look at. He said there's no doubt about it. He *does* have talent."

Grant took the drawings and studied them for a long time, each in turn.

Here *was* talent.

He looked up at Wanda. "Maybe we could put him through the Art Institute. Or help with his tuition. We have the money."

"That's what I was thinking," Wanda said.

And Nick came more and more often to their house. Grant hadn't yet approached him about studying art. He knew how sensitive the boy was and that he must put it the right way.

Again Wanda spoke to him. She was plainly worried.

"They're seeing an awful lot of each other," she said.

Grant smiled with his wide, square mouth. His large, serious eyes looked into hers. "Well?" And then, when she made no answer, "We agree, don't we, that there should be no classes? One person is as good as another?"

"His father," Wanda said.

Grant stood at the bar and poured them each a drink.

"She's the only child we have," Wanda said.

Grant handed her her glass and lifted his own. He touched his to hers.

Wanda set her glass down. She put the palm of her hand over his nose. "You big bum." And then, her hand on his shoulder in caress, "Whatever you say."

"The rich. The liberal rich," he said, half accusingly.

She looked at him seriously. She said, "I trust your judgment. I trust Barbara. I know Barbara."

"Bobby's all right," Grant said.

"Is Nick all right?" Wanda asked.

Grant shrugged his lack of knowledge. "I think so," he said.

68

Grant said they were fools to go out into the forest preserves to paint on such a chilly autumn day.

They went anyway, early in the morning, carrying their paint boxes, boards of canvas inside, and their folding easels. It was a long walk from the Gold Coast apartment to the car line, and a very long ride on the streetcar. "Damn!" Barbara said. "Dad won't let me use his car. He says he doesn't want me to be too dependent."

Over deep grass and over red and yellow leaves that crackled like bacon, Barbara said; over the white-crowned heads of dandelions they walked deep into the forest until they came to a little clearing with a view they both agreed they'd like to paint. There they set up their easels and squeezed paint out onto their palettes. Sun was just putting its yellow colors on green colors, and scarlets, tans, all the colors of the autumn forest. Nick said he would use his palette knife. They began to work, and at first, sketching in, Nick looked over at her every once in a while—sweater, blue jeans, her pretty face, and her eyes, her eyes—but more than anything—something about her, something that made him ache. And then . . . in his concentration . . . he forgot all about her. The colors came to his palette knife and went in bold, strong, sure strokes to his paint board.

"Huh?"

Barbara had said something.

"Grant's really wonderful," Barbara said again. "Know what?"

"No, what?" And he was painting.

"He wants me to know about everything. When I was just a kid he gave me a book on all the religions of the world, and then he would ask me questions about the different religions. He even gave me books by atheists. And now he has given me all of Lenin's and Marx's works and those of the great socialist writers. And the philosophers.

He says he wants me to make up my own mind about everything— Oh! I'm sorry! I'm bothering you!"

"No, you're not."

Then silence and the secret, half-heard or unheard sounds of the woods. And their fingers beginning to numb with cold. And Nick gathering wood, making a bonfire in between them.

They painted some more, and now with his picture coming alive Nick sometimes looked over the fire at her and was happy.

And they stopped to eat the sandwiches she had brought. "No! Don't look at my painting until it's finished!" she said, placing herself between him and the canvas.

And more wood on the fire and more painting until late in the afternoon. "Heck!" Barbara said, throwing down her brush. "I can't do any more! It's finished as far as I'm concerned!"

She sat by the fire and watched him. He went on painting for another hour or more, forgetful of her. Then he too was done. Then, very sadly, and for the first time, he painted *Nick Romano* in the corner, thinking of his father.

She stood, wide-legged, looking at his painting. "It's *good*, Nick— but different. I like it though!" She took him by the sleeve. "Now come look at mine."

He dared criticize her. "But that's not right. It should— It's too much like a photograph—I think. It should be more like you feel about it inside."

She laughed. "Who told you that, funny-face?"

She wasn't hurt. She knelt down, rummaging in their stuff for the thermos bottle. "Wonder if there's any more coffee?"

There was. They both knelt by the fire and shared it, and it wasn't very warm any longer.

Barbara sat by the fire, its reflections and the pattern of leaves overhead moving across her face. She undid her ribbon and pushed her hair down into its pony tail with the palms of her hands. Silently Nick handed her his comb. "Thanks." She combed her hair and tied the pony tail with a ribbon the same color as her eyes.

"Sit down, funny-face," she said.

He sat down next to her. He wrapped his arms around his knees and stared into the fire. She scratched on the ground with a piece of broken branch. After a while she said, "You can put your head on my lap if you want to."

His nut-brown eyes, sad, looked at her, and he did so.

She looked again at her painting, still on the easel. She said, "I was lousy on the piano and I'm pretty lousy at painting, too. But I like to do it." She chuckled deep in her throat, and Nick closed his eyes, feeling the chuckle hurt deep down inside of him. She said, "I think I looked out of my cradle at a piano. And voice lessons." Again she chuckled. "Grant would love it if I turned out to be some kind of an artist. I think it's sublimation. Dad would so like to write a novel."

I like her voice.

I like her face. And her eyes.

I like her.

"He's a great guy, Nick!"

"I think so."

They were silent a long time.

Fire warmed them. Sky was the chill of late autumn afternoons.

"What are you thinking?" she asked.

He said, out of nowhere, "You know, sometimes I get lonesome for the tick-tock of a clock, because when I was nine years old my mother would say, 'I'll be back at twelve o'clock,' and I'd wake up and she wasn't there and I'd hear the clock, tick-tock-tick-tock . . ."

"You're a funny guy," Barbara said. She put her forefinger in his hair and started twisting it around. "You've got awfully straight hair. It's just sort of wavy here and there."

He lay with his eyes closed. He wished she would never take her hand out of his hair. He had never been this happy before. He felt good and he felt sad, both at the same time. The empty spots inside of him filled. Like rain filling in around dry stones and small pebbles in a brook at the end of the dry season.

And his feelings came stronger, feelings that slid for a moment to the surface and then submerged, sneaked under rocks as if they had never been there. And he grew afraid and ashamed. He sat up quickly. Kneeling toward her he said, quickly, "I bet I can outstare you!"

She knelt, too, and, with their faces close, they stared into each other's eyes. For only a moment. Then he put his arms around her and kissed her. For only a moment. And he said, "We better go."

He got up immediately and began packing their things.

They were ready now.

Barbara said, "We have to put out the fire."

They stood, not looking at each other, pushing the soles of their shoes against the embers and red-tipped sticks of wood, kicking dirt onto the hot ashes.

Nick, looking down at the red ashes, said, "Please don't laugh." It took him a long time to ask it; then he said, "Do you think I can be an artist?"

304

She nodded a quick yes. She said, "Take my hand."

He took her hand and they walked through the forest and toward the car line.

69

Juan closed his shop and walked down to Maxwell Street. He saw her standing on the corner.

"You're back, Nellie," he said tonelessly.

"Yes, I'm back, Juan. I couldn't take it. It was *too* much."

She wandered off away from him, saying, "I'll see you, Juan," and went looking for Fran and Extra Black Johnson or anyone she could make out for a fix with.

"She's back," Nick told the four of them.

70

Yes, better. Better. By far better.

She must drive him away from her.

She wept over the thought.

But it had to be done. To save him.

She walked as one more dead than alive alongside the table and listlessly, wearily ran her finger across its surface.

The room was full of his paintings and drawings leaning against the walls, the drawings in large portfolios.

She picked up one of the portfolios and, putting it on the table, looked at the drawings, one hand laced into her hair. She sat with his drawings and paintings propped on her lap, looking at each in turn.

She recognized the budding brilliance in him and knew she could not give him the advantages he should have. Inadequacy, despair, her burden of guilt crept like shadows and looked, too, at the drawings: There is so little I can do for him. He must go. What must be done must be done.

There, with the painting lopsided on her lap, she stared out the window as if she were staring into her own grave. The black banister ran downwards. Useless tears ran down her face. Tears that could not take the need of the drug out of her being. Not one tear would alter one day of her life.

Better, much better, what she must do.

She began to hit the skids harder. She began to hit the needle more.

More dope. And more. Partly out of the tolerance for it her body had built up, partly an ineffectual escape from an increasingly sordid reality; and through this desire to see him gone.

She let him see her taking the stuff; and when he didn't see her she made him aware of it.

And nights she would awaken in panic and go to his room, feel for him in the bed to make sure he was there. Then, alone in her own room, cry happily.

She hit the skids a little harder. He didn't go away.

"I'm no good," she told him.

"Mother, don't talk like that!"

"I go out with men. You know what happens."

Moving his eyes away. "You have to have—dope."

"Whoring around, sleeping around." Eyes shrewdly but sadly on him.

"I'm not going to sit here and listen to you talk like that."

She laughed, loudly, vulgarly: the tragic tone was deep-down and hidden. "Your father was no good! We weren't married. You're illegitimate. You're a bastard!"

The awful lightning struck.

He stood up, his eyes flashing at her. "I hate you!"

She put the back of her hand over her mouth. Her eyes were secret with fear and the belief that she had accomplished it. Accomplished what she wanted and what she did not want.

He walked out.

She sat numb. Your mother will never come back, they told her at the detention home. A rat came out from its hole and so silent was the room that it jumped boldly to the table in foray.

The door opened.

Nick hung his head. "I didn't mean it."

And harder the skids. And harder the needle.

But she couldn't drive him away. Try as hard as she would.

"I want to live my own life. I don't want you here any more."

Again he left for that sad walk around several blocks.

"Mother, you didn't mean it."

His loyalty was stronger.

He stayed. He wouldn't leave. He couldn't leave.

Then she must attack him.

She began to berate him regularly. She picked on him while hating herself for doing it. She began to tear down his personality.

"Mother, don't say those things. All we've got is each other."

" 'Mother, don't say those things,' " she mimicked, forcing herself to hold the tears. "Why don't you get out? Why don't you go some place else? I can't even have my friends here. I don't want you around in my way."

He didn't answer.

She put her hands to her mouth: Oh God, let it come, let it come! She took her hands down from her mouth. She said, "Your father was a crook, maybe worse. Your mother is a dope fiend! How can you amount to anything? How can you ever be anything with the mother and father you have?"

. . . and awakening in terror in the black nights, feeling with trembling hands to see if he was in his bed.

71

She sat at the bar in the Shillelagh on the front stool next to the door, broke, needing a fix badly.

A man came in and she said to him, "I am alone and my door is open."

He paid no attention to her.

She took a small sip out of her glass and was terrified to see that it was almost empty.

Another man came in, staggering, this one. She repeated her invitation. He was too drunk to hear and her glass was empty.

The bartender came over and said, "Okay, your bottle's finished. Take off."

"Give me another," she said, scraping the bottom of her purse to pay for it.

You have to have something there in front of you. Else they kick you out.

Another man came in, and Nellie said, "I am alone and my door is open."

He stopped, smiling and looking her over. He was middle-aged and a bum, lost and lonesome, a little money in his pocket.

"Come on, baby," he said, "let's go sit at a table."

They went to a table.

"Who is that?" one of the men who had been given an invitation asked the bartender, referring to Nellie.

"That's the Broom," the bartender said.

"The Broom?"

"Yeah—she sweeps up anything," the bartender said.

They both laughed.

At the table the little sad bum, with some money in his pocket and still a soft heart for a woman and a picture in his mind of one all his own, says, "Do you think I want you because you're pretty?"

"I'm not pretty," Nellie says.

"I want companionship," the bum says.

Nellie got a man.

She got her fix.

And another man.

For money for the rent, Nick's food.

And it is time for her night fix.

Nellie sits on a bar stool between two men. She is leaning against one of them in a childlike friendliness and he has his hand cupped around her breast but she is unaware of this. The other man is making a play for her, too, and behind their friendly and gentlemanly conversation is a cold calculation. And she wants to please. She is patting her hands together like a child in time to the juke box and singing the song it blares. She says to one of the men, "Come on, be a sport and get in tune."

And they are all singing, " 'Have you ever been lonely . . . ?' "

And the night fix and back to the bar. And alone there. And now those eyes, getting sleepier and sleepier, dopier and dopier, sleepier and sleepier in a face chiseled with torture . . .

So nice . . . so nice . . . so pleasant . . .

Nick was alive and he was her husband and they lived together. Her son was a baby. Little Nick was a baby and she was singing to him.

> You are my sunshine
> My only sunshine . . .

. . . so nice . . . so pleasant . . .

She was a kid again. Her mother loved her and didn't leave her in the detention home.

Nick sat next to her, looking at his mother, waiting until she was conscious enough for him to take her home.

72

"Please tell me who started my mother on dope," Nick said.

"Kid, it's almost impossible to get off it," Max said sadly.

"Please tell me."

Max put his full bottle of beer up to his mouth and drank all of it, angrily, head thrown way back. He banged the empty bottle on the table. He was a little drunk. "Do you know who got her on it?" Max said; and angrily, "The Wolf got her on it. The Wolf. Do you know who The Wolf is? Frank! Frank Ramponi!"

Nick sat around gathering temper, temper, temper. And it was not like him to have temper.

"I'm going to kill him!" he said.

Their eyes fell away from his face.

"I'm going to kill him!"

Max was drunk again. He threw back his head and laughed loudly, uproariously. Then he stopped laughing and hugged Nick over to him, rumpling his hair, holding him in a bear hug, his face suddenly gone angry but serious, even angry at Nick. "Now, come on, kid! Come off it!" He was really mad at Nick now for thinking such a thing.

"I'm going to kill him!" Nick said.

A WORLD I NEVER MADE

A WORLD I NEVER MADE

73

Robert Majewski was waiting on the sidewalk outside the house.

"Hi, Pop," he said.

"Hi, Son," Sergeant Forbes said. He threw his arm over his son's shoulders and they walked to the car line together.

Their day off, they went to the Narcotics Division, 1121 South State, and to Room 203 for their pay.

"Think I'll go to the ball game. Want to come?" Bob Majewski asked.

"Naw! To see the Cubs get beat!" Forbes rubbed his big palm across his graying crew cut. "I think I'll get a glow on."

"What will I tell Mom?"

"Well, tell your mother—tell your mother I'm going to get a glow on and not to wait supper for me."

For the place to drink he selected not a secluded or a middle-class bar but one in the slums, in the neighborhood in which he worked, sensing that there was not a hatred between the drug addicts he had to pick up and himself, but an unspoken fraternity, a lonesome camaraderie. He sat in the Crystal Bar. He sat drinking beer at a lop-sided table set on the warped boards of the unclean tavern. And, as men sometimes do, he reviewed his life.

. . . And I was a big, over-six-foot, raw-boned kid who didn't go out for football but read books. Books! Oh, God Almighty, thank man for books!

And, tilting the bottle to his lips: The book, man's greatest invention. Everything man has dreamed, thought, believed, everything man knows is within the covers of a book.

And high school at Carl Schurz High, crew cut half an inch long like newly cut grass and fingers scratching, taking the knowledge inside.

It's 1910-1914.

Debs had been in prison, a socialist martyr. A newspaper strike left the *Chicago Daily Socialist* alone in the field. The Republican party in the city is split wide open. Social science is a hot subject. An aldermanic election was coming up. I join the Young People's Socialist League for a lark.

These men weren't fooling. They came. Upton Sinclair, a master on the effects of law and sociology. They came. William Brose Lloyd, a fifty-per-cent stockholder—inherited—of the *Chicago Tribune*, no less, and a gifted speaker and lawyer. Reverend St. John Tucker, a little giant who reminded me of the "pock-marked thunderer" of the French Revolution; the pastor of the Haymarket Riot anarchists who lived in his district.

Long live Jane Addams!

Long live Governor Altgeld!

And there was Seymour Stealman, corporation lawyer, who flowed out a lucid explanation of utility franchise and finance—how, granted to cliques of lawyers, it established a local ruling class, since under state law the rates allowed a six-per-cent return of each dollar of invested capital. How inventories were rigged to rate equipment and property out of proportion to real value—

Mr. Saltiel, another brilliant expert on tax-exempt bond issues and endowment evasion of taxes—

I *am* getting that glow on!

At a meeting we were told about these political situations, and the party head, knowing we Young People's Socialist League had obtained the Carl Schurz assembly hall as headquarters, consulted us in the selection of a candidate for alderman to try out our civic awareness and as part of our social science subject—the reason we gave so that they'd donate the assembly hall.

We selected Professor John C. Kennedy, who taught at the University of Chicago, and accepted the help of Upton Sinclair and the other leading socialists who took—oh, boy!—full advantage of our permission to use the school assembly hall as headquarters, all inspired by their chance and their instinctive capacity to follow the enlightening facts—

"Pssst! Bring me another beer!"

They soon had all of us students fully class conscious and socially aware. We got the social science training by canvassing the ward as well as the students, their parents and our own parents! Seidel, Mayor of Milwaukee at the time, his record, the city's entire structure was our model. And we won against the great *Chicago Tribune!* Man, oh, man! We elected the only socialist alderman to the city council to this day.

See records.

Long live Debs! Long live the Social Revolution!

Judge Kenesaw Mountain Landis sentenced four youngsters, eighteen to nineteen years old, to twenty years at Leavenworth for having in their possession Young People's Socialist League cards, found in their pockets.

Amen.

And as if talking to Grant: I am guzzling Meister Brau and I do so want to get relaxedly glowed by that wire recorder so I can tell you the rest of it.

He wanted another beer.

And why shouldn't he?

And why shouldn't I?

He ordered another.

These brilliant idealists fired us youngsters with enlightenment that inspired us to influence action and on to victory—and right now, today, I am watching at the Haines Company the Ogden Oswald Bradley case to see the effects of the law courts of a given state deferring to the power of the ruling class. Flies from the stables flew into the Emerson Bradley dining room and infected young Bradley. Rich boy gets in serious trouble. Rich boy gets off. Watch and see.

Man, this beer is good!

The syndicated political organization appoints, indirectly, the judges—a coalition judiciary slate, every four years. The ruling class, in turn, supports and controls the syndicated political organization. The wealthy and connected get justice by appeal to the higher courts beyond the local court's jurisdiction. The masses get local injustice only.

Beer at his elbow. Cigarette smoke twirling upward. Thoughts turning backward and forward:

I joined the Young People's Socialist League.

For a lark.

I was made class-conscious by the speakers who traveled to our Twenty-seventh Ward, volunteered their most inspired speeches and worked so diligently for principle only—

But before I could learn the full truth of their logic from the experience of working for a living, World War I threatened to draft me, so I enlisted.

I go to World War I with this background plus Carlyle and Victor Hugo's French Revolution influence, and to top it off, after the armistice I saw France. Her cathedrals. The Mona Lisa. I touch Joan of Arc's banner. I touch the metal stake at which she was burned in the public square at Rouen. I thumb the edge of Madame Guillotine. I sit in the very tumbrils that brought the aristocrats to the Madame. I touch the pikepoles of the mob and also those used by de Medici for her victims.

Paris. Almost a year in France to make up for schooling lost.

Long live World War I!

I come home woman-hungry and marry a slob who is neurotic and whose sisters are neurotic and whose mother is insane and who is, herself, out to exploit marriage for all it's worth.

A sacred institution.

Dominus vobiscum!

We buy a home: down payment—World War I bonus and mortgage.

One child. Two. Neurotic wife and mother.

What a mess I was in!

What to do? What to do?

I went to Holy Mary Cemetery and sat by my mother's grave. I asked her for the courage to act and give myself a new start.

Mrs. Slob came home at three-thirty A.M. *I acted.* Storm. She reached for my gun on the clothes-closet shelf.

Oh, courage from the grave!

I acted.

I beat hell right out of her.

Packed and left for the YMCA.

And furnished rooms and restaurant meals. And separate maintenance. She gets the custody of the kids. Two years of this.

Back home after the war and to work and first married. Only a single year of industrial work for a living, against the cultural background of my entire life and my long mental fraternity with the masters by way of reading since I was a child, convinced me beyond all other reason that I could only get an even break by climbing on the taxpayer's back or perishing—that is why I joined the police force. Talking to himself or to Grant: Now can you see why I climbed on the taxpayer's back when the going got tough? Before that an eighty-hour week for fifteen dollars per week.

Long live the Social Revolution!

Man, oh, man, how he'd like to get a glow on with Grant in front of that wire recorder!

So, Mrs. Slob out of the picture. The police force. A strictly honest cop is held strictly to the rule book—tie, shoes, shave, and many clever requirements that drive you either nuts or off the job. No word is passed in your presence. The eternal ice, in short.

He was an honest cop.

A cop walks his beat until his feet hurt. There are a few places where, each day, he stops for a cup of coffee, a glass of beer, or a few words of friendship.

The school store was such a place. Lillian is a school store clerk on my beat, twelve dollars a week, three kids—abandoned by a drunkard in a small town in Michigan. She comes to Chicago with the kids and strikes out on her own to fight the social order. Black hair and brown eyes, a ready smile and a nice body.

He signaled for another Meister Brau.

The church has me by the short hairs. My wife won't give me a divorce. Won't let me see my kids. Lillian of the black hair and the brown eyes.

I ask her to common-law with me so that we can have a chance to win. She says no.

I go back to my mother's grave to get courage.

Lillian is afraid and says no again.

I give up and join the navy. Pearl Harbor. Military furlough from the department. Letters to Lillian.

She decides for me when I get back.

And it worked, by God! It worked. It was still working.

Bill Forbes brought the bottle of beer to his lips and drank long and enjoyably.

Back from the war we established a home. Toilet in the hall. Three kids and her. We stand together. Bobby does his hitch, navy, graduates from the University of Wisconsin. Jimmy does his hitch and gets set on a job. Charlie back from Korea and tries Illinois University on the G.I. and flunks. Starts at Wilson Junior College and takes hold because of (well, I guess the old man's influence too) the prosecution of writers before the committee on subversive activities. Interest in their work acquaints him with Debs and the labor movement. I take him, as I had the other boys, to Waldheim, and in the grass there we stand silent before the words written, chiseled in time, on the slab to the martyrs of the Haymarket Riot, the symbol of May Day now celebrated the world over and originating here in Chicago . . .

The day will come when our silence will be more powerful than the voices you are throttling today . . .

And they are *my* boys, the boys of Lillian, my wife. How important that they come from your own body? I am so much in love with my wife. Her story is a story by itself. The economic storm she faced with three youngsters—and my coming on the scene.

And back his mind turned, to his days and years on the police force. All the days of routine. The early days. The days that stood erect in his mind. That burned and seared and left an everlasting scar. The old man dead and his spinster daughter tenderly tucking the blanket around him to keep him warm, *to keep him warm!* Those two old ladies' corpses on the floor over the dispute of a division of a will. And in the welter of his thoughts he saw the boy's face, behind bars, brought in on a false charge of indecent exposure. "They could have ruined that boy's life forever!" he said aloud. And looked up and was in the tavern; ordered another beer. Looked out the window. Saw Fran and Extra Black Johnson go by. Poor devils! I wouldn't make an arrest today if I saw one of them taking a fix outside the window.

Turned to his beer. Getting his son on the police force.

That day when Bobby, out of the University of Wisconsin, out of sociology (my influence), said, "Pop, I want to work on the police force. I want to put sociology to work."

"Well, I'll have to kiss his ass," I said.

He knew father-and-son teams are quite common in the department. It used to be dominated by related groups through church-politico connections.

So I, "I'll get him into the Bureau through a little connection."

I kissed the ward committeeman's ass. I went to Ward Committeeman Don Lockwood, *The Power*, so help me! and told him I wanted the kid on. He knew that I, being on already, would comply with the terms—vote the party, fifty dollars for the doctor, another fifty for the examiner, and whatever *The Power*'s right-hand man asks in dough.

I tell him I want the kid with me. By a phone call it is done. The kid just uses his mother's name—Majewski.

Sergeant Forbes looked out the window.

Well, Fran got her fix.

He saw her standing on the other side of the street leaning against a building, nodding down, down.

He was glad that she had made out.

And he had his glow on.

A WORLD I NEVER MADE

A WORLD I NEVER MADE

74

They told him that he looked just like his brother, who died at the age of twenty-one. His brother had died of some sickness, and he looked enough like him to be his twin. This is what they told Louie Romano.

All he could remember as a small boy was that his brother Nick had been in the hospital often. Once for almost a year.

There was something strange about his family. He could remember whispering. They were always whispering. Women whispering, whispering. Then moving again. Moving to different neighborhoods three or four times.

Whispering. And then their mouths closed, like doors closing, like vaults being sealed, when he came near them. Even their eyes grew hostile. "Now you go play."

Ang, Ma, Rosemary and Aunt Rosa leaning together over a table, in a corner in the kitchen, talking in low tones, hands sometimes up to their mouths, their eyes looking fearfully out the window onto the empty street. Whispering. You move. You hide.

There were too many women around the house. And they spoiled him. They were overprotective to him; then sometimes they seemed not to care, as if they were all thinking about something else. And Ma would hold him close and cry while he tried to wiggle away, and tears got all over his face. Nasty, hot tears.

Whispering again. He never knew what they said, hands held to their mouths: He must never know. Never, never know.

He grew older. He hoped they wouldn't move again. He liked it here. He liked Paco and he liked Giovanni who everybody called Gee.

Women's eyes looking at him and away. Eyes that hid something.

And all those in the family who knew bore the burden. Their faces had never been the same after that night 12:04 A.M. Even smiling their faces showed it. It was a secret that trembled in their eyes, a tragedy that lay there. Reflection of a certain horror and disbelief. What had been done to him had been done to them and must never be done to him, the youngest. They had killed him. Sat him in a chair and killed him. Will we ever get over it? Will we ever forget it? Even when we seem to forget it?

Louie grew older and better-looking. Aunt Rosa said, "You could be his twin brother. You could be him."

Thinking about it now at twenty-two, Louie got up off the bed and, in trousers alone, walked to the mirror. He looked in at the warm coloring of his skin, halfway between red and brown, his broad, square, chiseled face, his wide cheekbones with the red coloring more marked at their peaks, the eyes clear, brown, liquid, innocent, the strong mouth with its well-defined lips that he could make innocent in smile or sad and wistful, as with his eyes, when he wished. He looked innocent now and liked what he saw in the mirror. And now he looked wistful. And now he smiled. Strong white teeth. Even and white. And now he lowered one eye in flirtation. And now, opening his eyes wide, he looked up at his hair. It was brown-black and curled all over his head and around his ears and down over his forehead. He smiled, wide-eyed, at himself again. He was damn good-looking and he knew it.

From a washbasin he threw water on his hair, then rubbed liquid vaseline into it, drew the comb through, saw it begin to lie down, then disobediently rise again in curly waves. He looked at his chest, which was square and flat; at his neck, square and strong; at his arms, which were well muscled and smooth.

He smiled at himself. There was no doubt about it. He was as good-looking as a movie star.

As a kid he hung around with the guys in the neighborhood and they had fun together; and soon, in that neighborhood, when he was only twelve, he found out what it was for and he didn't waste time and he had plenty of girls, 'cause all the girls went for him because he was good-looking and he got any he wanted. He had his pick of girls. Sure he was early spoiled. All those women at home and all those girls outside. He liked it that way.

He had lots of friends in the neighborhood. But best of all he liked Paco and Gee. They used to sit in front of the house when they were fourteen and fifteen waiting for Helen to go by. When she came along the sidewalk they'd nudge each other and yell in unison, "Helen's got the—" then they'd smack the palms of their hands together—clap-clap-clap—

He was the leader of the gang ever since he could remember because—yeah, he knew why—because he was handsome and attracted girls both for himself and for the others—each girl hoping she'd eventually end up with him. First it had been in the alley, behind the school building; later in a vacant flat, over at Gee's house. Now in hotel rooms.

The guys around the neighborhood would yell, "Hey, baby face! Hi, baby face!" at him. But they liked him and they were jealous. He'd wrinkle up his nose at them and grin scornfully. But he liked it. And even if he was handsome he was tough too. He had more fights than any of the other fellows and he always won. He was tough. The guys liked him for this reason too.

Yeah, all the girls went for him. They liked his brown eyes and his curly hair. They liked to touch it. And they all wanted his body. He knew that. They liked looking at him and they liked sleeping with him. Those that got smart, or jealous, those he didn't want, those who put on airs, those who looked at him like they wanted him to take them to bed right there even if he had never seen them before, he'd say right in front of them, "Take a good look, baby. You ain't getting any!"

He enjoyed being a smart aleck.

He turned now and looked at his profile in the mirror, was pleased with it. He turned the other profile and studied it, could find no fault there. Again he looked at himself full-face: He couldn't have been as good-looking as me.

He gave his curly brown-black hair a final caress with the palm of his hand, from forehead to neck. Light caught the little tattooed cross between thumb and forefinger. It had three lines above it.

Smiling again at himself he turned from the mirror and walked to the door.

"Why don't you put a shirt on!" Ang said.

"Aw, why don't you drop dead!" Louie said.

"Hi, sweetheart!" said Aunt Rosa.

Rosemary merely glanced up and looked away.

"What time is it, Aunt Rosa?"

"Eight-thirty," she answered him.

He went into the bathroom, then back to his room. When he came out he was dressed for the street and on his way to the door.

Ma Romano had come from her room. She was smiling and she, too, walked toward the door, in front of which she met Louie. "My boy!" she said. "You're my good son. You're my good boy. They won't take you from me." Smiling, she lifted her face up to him to be kissed. "My good son!" There was a childishness about her mouth and in her eyes, as if a small girl looked out of this old woman's face. No, a rag doll, with that mop of tangled gray hair on top and those thin bones holding the dry flesh half erect. And, smiling, she held her cheek to him.

Louie turned away in disgust. He opened the door and walked out.

"He's a sweet boy!" Ma Romano said, still smiling.

Ang looked at Aunt Rosa and at Rosemary.

They could hear him hurrying down the steps, and they were left facing each other, each with her private thoughts.

And Ang said, looking from Rosemary to Aunt Rosa, "He's going to end up just like Nick."

Old rooms sometimes give strange sounds. The walls, perhaps. The loose boards of the floor. Perhaps the shifting and settling of the foundation. Sounds like sighs. This room gave such a sound.

Nick.

The name had been thought. But it hadn't been spoken aloud in that house for years. And here it stood, feet-high, the owner, the son, the nephew, the brother, standing looking at all of them from the shadow of the name.

Ang had put it into words. She was the one who sat down weakly.

Rosemary walked to the window and looked out, her slim fingers laced behind her back, a tall, still young, pink and white woman with a pile of high-combed blond hair.

Aunt Rosa walked into the toilet and closed the door. It could be true, oh, God! It could be true! ". . . and sentence him to . . . death in the electric chair." The scream was his mother's. She went on screaming.

Ang sat in the chair with the back of her hand across her eyes. Pa died and he wasn't even home for the funeral.

At the window Rosemary looked out at the night, twisted her fingers together and was startled to hear their cracking sound. Strangely, she thought first of her husband, Julian, Nick's brother:

"If you're a pacifist, don't go."

"I am. But I feel a responsibility. Nick—"

And he didn't tell her what he meant by Nick. Just the name and no explanation.

Ang thought:

I ran up the steps after him and said, "Nick—don't tell Ma," and he said:

"It's none of my business what you do."
He pushed my hand away.
"But Abe—it's—he isn't a Catholic."
"The hell with Ma" . . .

He looked down at my stomach. "How are you, Ang?"
"All right."
He held me by the hands.
"Let me look at you, Sis."
We didn't say anything for a while.
"Bring Abe to see me."
"All right."
"You tell him if he doesn't treat you right I'll knock his block off—" And he stopped talking.

There were bars all around us. The last time I saw him.

Rosemary continued to twist her fingers together. And now all that was left of Julian was under her handkerchiefs in the top drawer, the silver star, his letters. The two deaths only a few years apart. First Nick, then Julian. "Why don't you change your name? Why don't you go by your maiden name?" Ang had said. "But I loved your brother." "Yes, but with all the scandal about—about—and all this moving from neighborhood to neighborhood." And all that was left of Julian was the telephone number in his name to perpetuate him as long as she lived.

She twisted her fingers together. She had to do something with her hands. She picked up her knitting, turned on the floor lamp and settled herself under it. Her mind kept up with the needles—and Julian's letter under the handkerchiefs: "I have killed as Nick killed and I feel guilty. I feel unclean. I have killed for country but I do not see how it makes much difference. Mine is legal. His was not. If he killed—and I still cannot believe it. And now I am Nick."

Aunt Rosa came out of the bathroom. Her eyes were red.

Rosemary leaned over the socks she was knitting for her son, a freshman at college. Why did he have to go so far away from home? Columbia. She squinted through the gold-rim glasses she wore for reading and sewing and sometimes in the office when she was alone there, and she tried to concentrate her mind on her son.

Her fingers worked swiftly. Her mind kept pace with them:

They were nice kids. She was a virgin.

Nick's hands had touched her breast. And, after a while, "Unbutton your dress a little."

She moaned and she bled and she cried..

Another time. In a car. And she would have let him. Then suddenly he had pulled her dress down. He got out of the car. "I'm not your kind. I'm no good. Stay away from me!"

Then she had met his brother and they had married. These, the only two men she had loved or had had sex with. Both dead.

Ang said, "I think I better go upstairs. Abe will be home soon."

They had put away the name unspoken for years.

Life goes on. He dies. They live. But they do not live by a clock turned backward and stopped. The face of the clock is not turned to the wall. The minutes tick forward. The everyday things of life.

They were discussing Louie again.

"All those girls coming here, asking for him. Calling on the phone," Ang said.

"He doesn't work," Rosemary said.

"Well, some of the time," Aunt Rosa defended.

"Only half the time," Ang said.

"Do you think he knows?" Rosemary said. "Do you think that somebody from over there could have gotten over here?"

"There isn't a chance in a hundred," Aunt Rosa said. "Anyway, the name Romano is common enough."

"I hope he doesn't know," Ang said. "But why does he act the way he does?"

"Someone should talk to him," Aunt Rosa said.

"I'm going upstairs," Ang said.

Life goes on.

Pestilence comes. Death comes. But when with violence, in war, in electric chair, then it is never forgotten. It need not have been this way.

This shows in their faces.

75

Louie walked out into the night. He swaggered down the street, proud of his broad shoulders and glad to be alive. Alive and Louie Romano. Louie, the good-looking.

At a store-front window he stopped to observe himself; lifted one end of his collar up over the edge of his chin in sloppy but attractive effect. It's early yet. I'll go and have a beer.

He turned into the neighborhood corner tavern. The Swede was there at the bar, his blond and gray hair, both colors mixing evenly, bushing over his forehead. His dog was with him and sat looking up at him. Swede had started out for his night watchman's job an hour before.

Louie walked over to him. "Hi, Swede." Since Aunt Rosa called him Swede, nobody in the family called him anything else.

"Well, look who's here!" Swede said. "Let me buy you a drink."

He was the only one in the family Louie really got along with; they seemed to completely understand each other.

"Never said no," Louie said.

They drank a couple together. The dog kept looking up at Swede, and the Swede, who was already a little drunk, pulled his newspaper-wrapped lunch over in front of him on the bar. "No, you ain't getting none," he told the dog.

Louie was looking down the bar at the dame there. She reminded him of Hazel. He was fifteen then. He tickled the palm of her hand and asked her, "Do you know what that means?"

"No," she said.

"It means I want a kiss." He made his eyes innocent.

"I know what that means," she said.

He got the kiss. That wasn't all he got.

Swede said no to the dog again but unwound the string from around his lunch.

She was my regular lay after that. Regular, hell! Along with five or six others.

Swede fed the dog all the ham from between the sandwiches. Then a bit of cake. Louie ordered a round.

"I'm not going to give you any more," Swede told the dog, and his eyes got misty looking into the uplifted face of the dog, the alert, unblinking eyes watching him steadily. Swede ordered again and, staggering, threw his arm over Louie's shoulder, put a finger up to his lips and said, beyond it, "Don't tell your Aunt Rosa you saw me here."

"Don't worry about that."

The Swede turned to the stranger on the stool next to him. "I guess I might as well give him the rest," he said and carefully spread the remainder of his lunch out on the newspaper and put it on the floor for the dog.

Louie bought again. Dusty came in and Louie pulled him over to the bar for a drink. The Swede walked unevenly to the door and held it open for the dog. "Okay—you go home, Bravo. You're drunk."

When he returned to the bar Louie slapped him across the shoulders. "See you around!"

Again Louie started down the street. Saturday night. He'd go by and pick up Gee and they'd raise some hell.

Walking to Gee's house he started thinking about old times. Them were the days! His life had been one big laugh and good time. He felt more at home at Gee's house than at his own. For one thing, there wasn't any whispering. Giovanni's mother was one of those women who wanted her son to bring his friends there to the house, where "I can see what you do. Here you don't get in trouble." She shoulda known! First it had been checkers when they were young; and later cards. She let them drink beer there in the kitchen. "Just so I have an eye on you. After all, young fellows are going to get drunk and you might as well get drunk right here at home," she would say. There was him and Gee and Paco. Paco—a kid, younger than they were—who was trying to act like a man. Paco with the tan face. The big grin. An open-faced friendliness. The quickly maturing body. Big shoulders. Clothes draped on them as on a man's body. Paco, who went scrambling for pennies across sidewalks.

Louie grinned at the street in front of him and, turning the corner, saw Gee's house.

And Saturday nights, when Gee's old lady dragged the old man to the show, they'd sneak their girl friends in. Only first Gee would always walk his folks to the show to make sure that they went in, Gee pretending that he wanted to get the Sunday paper to see the scores or get "just a couple of beers for us fellows."

Going up the stairs to Gee's house—

Them were the times.

We had our fun and we had our gang. We had our gang wars and they were really great!

Walk silently, hit fast and fade.

The motto still sounded good. Those grownups, yelling, crying about juvenile delinquency, that's a laugh. They don't understand us but we understand ourselves. We ain't any different than they are. We're just imitating them, if they'd take time to think about it.

Louie walked into Gee's house without knocking, as was his custom.

"Hello, Clark Gable!" Gee's mother greeted, dating herself.

Louie went over and hugged her, for he had long ago learned that this always flattered his friends' mothers. They'd ask about you and ask you to stay for dinner and say what a nice polite boy you were.

"Where's Gee?"

"Giovanni—he's at the poolroom."

Louie picked him up there. They headed for West Madison Street. They drank down there for an hour or two and then went to one of the fancier night spots on the street.

They walked in. The show hadn't started yet and the bright lights were still on. They moved toward a front table. He always got a kick out of this, how everybody stared at him. Like he was a celebrity or a movie star. It happened wherever he went. Men would look at him in astonishment. And some men in another way. Girls would stare at him. And women—older women. As if he was the son they'd like to have. Son! Bunk! These older women. They went too. He knew that. Any time one of them old dames would stare at him with her mouth half open and make it too obvious just what she was thinking, he'd say aloud to her, making sure she heard, "Take a good look. You ain't getting any!"

They sat down. They ordered cubas and drank and the floor show started.

They kept drinking and saw the floor show again. There was a broad high-stepping up from the dressing room to the stage, with a red cadet's cap on her head, cocked to one side, a long white plume going up from the stiff bill of the cap and curving over her head, moving up and down as she danced. She came with a red smile, yellow-white frizzed hair dangling around her neck, eyes rolling, legs high-stepping. She had pink net panties that clung to her hips on each side but, in the back, were cut out so that they looked as though they were slipping, the way a kid's pants would slip down. She showed them that, shaking it like jelly; she showed them her breasts, cupped in the palms of her hands.

She gave them the works. The music was a repeated rhythm with a lot of wiggles in it. Her body was intimate with every wiggling note of the music; they undulated together, her body and the music, lewd lovers. Then, in a sudden frenzy, she trotted around the small stage, at its very edge, wiggling, smiling, shaking everything she had, waving her arms. Her behind, with the crescent of panties slipping down, rolled like the drums, shimmied like jelly on a plate, quivered violently, faster—faster— She danced. She shook everything she had.

And the music began again. And she hopped to the bar, danced along the bar, with men sweating and staring up. And she danced among the tables, among the customers.

And as she danced, pausing, shaking, bumping and grinding, Louie grabbed her and kissed the little pink panties. He liked it that way. He liked being a wise guy.

And she turned, squealing in shocked joy, and took his face between her hands.

He leaned back, laughing, stretching his leg out casually, and said, loud, so the people at the next table could hear, "Take a good look, baby. You ain't getting any!"

All the men around him laughed.

When you're young and handsome you can get away with anything.

Louie already knew this.

76

Ma Romano came out of her bedroom. "The boys will be here soon," she said. She smiled in anticipation and said, "Their hands and faces will be dirty, but I will wash them before they come to the table with us."

She smiled at all of them and, as one lost in a sweet dream, went back into her bedroom and closed the door.

They could hear her walking around in there.

Ang lit a cigarette with trembling fingers. She sat down at the table with the rest of them. Her hands were still trembling. "I can't stand it any more," she said; and again, "I can't stand it any more." She looked up at all of them, fearful, frightened, pleading, yet ashamed. She said, "We better send her to—to the proper place."

"Now, now, Angela," Rosemary said.

"Yeah, let's send her to the nuthouse," Louie said.

"Over my dead body," Aunt Rosa said.

They spoke in low voices. Whispers. The same whispers he had heard when he was a child.

"I'm home here with her all day," Ang said. "You don't know. You don't know."

"Over my dead body," Aunt Rosa said again.

Louie got out of the house.

He went to the poolroom. Walking in, he said, "Hi, bums!"

Gee, Paco and Flophouse were there. Flophouse leaned dejectedly against the wall. His hair looked as if it had never been cut, never been combed. The felt hat on the back of his head, with half the brim torn loose, dangled there as dejected as he. There was no collar on his greasy shirt.

"Hi, bums!" Louie looked around. And part of him was still at home: We ain't the finest guys. Nobody would say that.

"Wanta play a game of pool?" Paco asked.

"For money, yes. For nothing, no."

Louie switched on the light over the table and watched Paco pick up a stick, step up to the rail and break the balls viciously.

Funny about me. I go for ugly girls. Tramps. Tomatoes nobody wants much to do with. Funny.

He stepped up for his shot. Underneath the light his face was handsome, boyish, his eyes innocent. Some curly hair fell over his forehead, and he aimed carefully. Two balls went in the pockets. Brilliant! he congratulated himself. He stood erect and, making himself handsome, walked nonchalantly to his next position along the table.

"Jesus, you're a good-looking sonofabitch!" Dusty said derisively, coming into the poolroom from the barber shop across the street.

Gee said, "He ain't good-looking now. You shoulda seen him a couple years ago. He was real pretty then. I used to say, 'Don't ever let me catch you in jail in the same cell as me because we'll shack up for sure!' "

"Hello, eight ball," Louie said to Dusty.

"Hi, ugly!" Dusty said.

They called each other nigger and dago and spick; but that was just among themselves. Let no one else fool with the code!

Dusty was a tan Negro, Louie's age. He was proud of his good hair. It was as straight as hair could be, and brown. He'd say, "You ain't never seen no nigger with hair like this before!" and Louie would say, "You ain't never seen no dago as good-looking as me," and Paco, "Only spicks are good-looking. And good in bed too." Then someone would always say, "How do you know?" and everybody would howl with laughter. Dusty worked at the barber shop, shining shoes and brushing people off for tips.

Dusty had money and bought cokes for all of them. He set Louie's on the rail of the pool table.

"Thanks": One thing we got. One thing most people ain't got.

We hang together. We'd lie, fight, go to jail, or even, I guess, kill for each other.

"What are you doing tonight?" Gee asked everybody.

"Get drunk. What else?" Louie asked.

"Wish I could," Paco said, "but I gotta work."

"You think I was drunk last night?" Louie said. "Wait till you see me tonight!"

"I won't go to work," Paco said. "I'll go with you. Who wants to work anyway?"

They sat in the Long Bar on West Madison. Louie sat with his arm thrown around the back of Dusty's chair. "Come on! I thought you could drink!" he said. "Remember how you and me used to put them on together?" Louie put his head back until he was staring at the ceiling and threw the whiskey down his throat in one swallow. "Now, that's what I call drinking!" he said.

"That's three in a row, man!" Dusty said.

"Aw, Dusty can't drink. He don't know what the stuff's for!" Gee said.

"I'll show you," Dusty said and, like Louie, looked up at the ceiling and drank.

Louie patted his back. "See, fellows, I told you! Hell, Dusty and I used to get *drunk*. They had to kick us out of this joint. They barred us out of here for about a month once because somebody called Dusty a nigger in here and me and him tried to lick the whole goddamn place."

Paco said, "Well, don't talk so much, and drink."

"Solid, Jack!" Louie said.

Dusty scraped some change out of his pocket.

"Put your goddamn money away! I'm treating," Louie said.

The bartender put the bottle of whiskey on the table.

"Can't drink, huh?" Dusty said, and pulled his glass over in front of him. Louie laughed, hugging Dusty, and playfully rubbed his fist against Dusty's cheek. "You sonofabitch!" he said endearingly. Gee winked at Paco and poured his wine into Dusty's glass. Paco went to the bar and then came back, his eyes dreamy. He grinned and hoisted his pants. They knew what was wrong with him before he said it: "I got something on the line." Grinning, he walked away.

They drank more and more. Dusty fell asleep at the table. Gee put a nickel in the juke box that had been silent for all of two minutes.

Louie looked up.

More broads! Jesus!

The two girls walked over to the table, smiled. One walked behind

Gee's chair and put her hands on the back of it. She leaned over until her breast was on his shoulder and her cheek was down near his forehead. "Hello, big boy! How you doing?" Gee turned on his chair and put his arm around her waist. He pulled out a chair with his foot. As she moved to sit down, his head turned so that he could look at her rear. The other tomato stood at the table between Gee and Louie, with hot and ready eyes. Then she saw Dusty. Pride snapped her head up stiffly. "What are you doing with a nigger with you?" she asked disgustedly, looking at handsome and half-drunk Louie.

Louie reached out angrily and grabbed her wrist. "Listen!" he said loudly. "He's with us and we're with him, see, and if you don't like it, get the crap out of here!" His lips twisted nastily and he didn't let go of her arm. "You're muscling in, ain't you? Who the crap asked you to come over here?" She wrestled to get her arm free. Loosening his clamped fingers from around her wrist she nursed the bruise with her other hand. "All right! All right!" she shouted. "You don't have to yell!" She didn't go away. "Sit down, bitch!" Louie said. "Or take a powder." She sat down. Louie grinned. "Now apologize," he said; and, laughing, "Anyway, you ain't getting any."

They sat, getting drunker. The tomatoes lapped it up. Verne sat between Gee and Louie, her arms around the backs of their chairs. Louie sat twisted toward Dot, motioning at her with his glass. "Come on! Drink! What did you come over here for!" Louie was still mad. He didn't care. Why shouldn't Dusty sleep with the little tramps too? What did they have to put on airs about? She smiled at him. A slow smile. Her arm was stretched out on the table, touching against Dusty's tan forehead. She drank. Like a man. Swilling it down one after the other. Making no face. She put her hand out and ran her fingers through Louie's hair. He jerked his head away. "Cut it out, bitch!" And, laughing, "You ain't getting any!"

At the Romano home Ma Romano looked out the window. "I can't understand where they are. They should have been home hours ago."

"Yeah, Ma," Ang said dully.

77

Funny about me. I don't get it. I go for these cheap broads. Maybe because they're so easy to have. Maybe I got what they call an inferiority complex. Maybe I'm ashamed because I'm so good-looking. Or maybe I'm giving them a break. Yeah, that's it. They see guys like me in the movies and they can never have them. And the good ones, the decent ones, the nice-looking ones, especially if they try playing up to me, try making me— Take a good look, you ain't getting any!

Louie waited half an hour until it was time for her to knock off. When she came out in her wrinkled coat with the sleeve armpit torn, he said, "Aw, it's too early for you to go home. It's Saturday night. Tell your mother anything."

Betty was only about sixteen. Her face was pimpled. Her skin was slightly blotched. Paco said that if you stuck two toothpicks in an olive for her legs, that would give you an idea of her body. When she talked she always sounded as if she had a mouthful of mush.

"Come on!" Louie urged.

"I don't know," she said, like chewing mashed potatoes.

He had her by the arm, forcing her. "It's only nine o'clock."

They went between buildings and he was feeling her. They were both in the mood.

But she said, "Wait, I want to tell you something."

"Oh, never mind!" Louie said angrily. "You can tell me later."

"No. I want to tell you now."

"Oh, all right."

Then she told him. "I'm sick."

He moved back, looked at her pallid face. She got ready, as if she expected him to hit her. "Ain't you going to hit me?" she asked. "The others did when I told them."

He put his arm around her. "No. You're all right," he said.

Jesus, he was being nice to this little whore and he felt funny about it.

They walked to the corner in silence. Then he said, "But I would have hit you if you hadn't told me."

She turned away. "Hey! Wait!" he said. And then he did a crazy fool thing. He pulled some bills out of his pocket. "Go see some doctor and get fixed up."

He turned and walked away. He was mad at himself for letting some money go. But he felt kind of good about it too.

78

So went the days and nights for Louie.

And one day Aunt Rosa said, "This is your nephew. This is Nick."

He didn't look like much to Louie.

79

And now he was going with this broad, Maria, from South Chicago. I'm getting out of the bargain basement anyway. She's good-looking for a change and not a tramp. At least I don't think so. Well stacked too. Nice behind. I like to see her walk. There's something funny about it though. When I go out there to South Chicago she rushes me off at certain times with some crazy excuse. But he knew broads. Probably shacking up with some other guy too. Maybe married. So what? As long as she pleased him he'd string along.

They came out of the hotel, and he said, "I'm going to play some pool. You can sit and wait and I'll ride out there with you on the streetcar."

"All right, Louie."

In front of the poolroom he took her arm and steered her in.

Paco was there, and Louie nodded his head toward the tables. Paco picked up a cue stick. "Buy us a coke," Louie told Maria.

She bought it. They played. She sat on the bench along the wall, bored and waiting, chewing a stick of gum.

He was quite a big guy, tall, a dishwater blond, but Italian. Blondie or Whitey you'd call him if you didn't know his name. He stood hunched over, looking in the poolroom window, his hand up to his eyes, shielding them from the sun. Louie had finished his game, racked up his cue stick and was standing, one foot up on the bench, his hand on top of Maria's head in a rough caress.

The blond guy walked in. "Maria!" he said. His voice was rough and angry and his eyes cut over at Louie. Louie looked up. Slowly, elaborately, he put his hands behind his head, stretched, his chest swelling out, and leaned against a post that held the ceiling up; scratched his back in a slow back-and-forth diagonal as if it itched. Then he made a complete circle around the post, his back sliding along it, and came face to face with the fellow. "Who's the guy?" he asked Maria, looking at the fellow.

"Hey, that's my broad!" the guy said.

"Yeah?" Louie said.

"Yeah."

Against the wall was the rack of pool cues, the sticks fastened to it in a long, upright row. Louie leaned away from the post and ran his long, square-tipped fingers across them as one would strum across the strings of a harp, but strongly and with authority. "Want to play a game of pool?" he asked.

"Yeah."

Louie lifted a cue stick from the rack.

They played. The girl sat, scared.

Louie won. He won again. He said, "Well, I won. I'll buy you a drink."

"Okay." The fellow's eyes were hard and narrow.

"Come on!" Louie said to Maria.

She walked behind them.

They went into the bar. They sat on stools. The guy motioned to the girl. "Sit down!" he said.

"I wasn't doin' nothing," she said. "I was just talking to him." She sat on a stool a seat away.

"Go to the can," Louie told her. "Go ahead! You heard me!"

She went to the toilet.

"What'll it be?" Louie asked the guy.

"A shot."

"Two shots," Louie told the bartender.

The bartender brought the cheap whiskey. They sat, looking over the shots, looking each other over.

"Here's luck," Louie said, lifting his.

"Luck." They drank.

The guy set his glass down.

"Tony's my name," he said.

"Yeah?"

"What's yours?"

"I don't know it's any of your business, but it's Louie—Louie Romano."

"Bring us two more," Tony told the bartender.

"I'll pay," Louie said.

"If you want."

The girl, having come out of the toilet, sat at the end of the bar.

"What do you do?" Tony asked; his eyes were hard on Louie.

"Nothing. And you?"

"I work at the steel mills."

"Oh."

"It's my day off."

"Oh."

They gulped their glasses.

Louie put his empty glass on the mahogany, and laughed. "So she's been two-timing you," he said. "Me too."

"Got her signals mixed up," Tony said bitterly.

"What are you going to do about it?" Louie asked.

"Nothing," Tony said. "Why fight over this broad? I'll just take the bitch home."

He took her home.

That began it.

80

Let the bitch go. But she was a good lay. Well, she'll have to come back to me. And she will. He was good-looking.

It wasn't a week before she was back. "You know I love you, honey! I don't care nothin' about that other guy."

He laughed at her. He was sprawled on the hotel bed in nothing but his shorts. "Come here!" he said. She came over. He grabbed her by the wrist and pulled her down beside him.

After that Louie would go over there to see her when Tony was working; she took care of that, saying, "Me and Tony's all washed up," but saw to it that their paths didn't cross; and she came to Chicago to see him. It was like that. They were carrying on this affair.

But in South Chicago there is a whole bunch of people, a whole gang. They weren't people, because none of them were over twenty years old. But mean, tough little guys. A gang.

They saw Louie's comings and his goings. And, though Louie didn't know it, they reported back. Not knowing this but seeing in their eyes their hatred of him, the outsider, he decided to stay away. He figured he didn't want to get his good-looking face messed up. Not for no broad.

They met on the sneak and he didn't like that, and he didn't believe her when she said she never saw Tony any more.

So he brought her to Chicago. He kept her in Chicago for almost three weeks.

That last morning he got out of the hotel bed, naked, and went toward the bathroom.

"Gee, you got a nice body, honey!" Maria said.

"I know it," he said.

And when he came back: "And you're so good-looking, honey. Like a regular movie star."

He got into his clothes.

"Where's my honey going?"

"To eat," he told her.

When he got back she was sitting at the window.

"I saw you coming, honey."

Louie stretched. "You bore me," he said.

"Honey doesn't mean that."

Louie took out a cigarette. He didn't offer her one. He tossed his in the air and caught it in his mouth. "Tell that bum you ain't much," he said.

"What do you mean?"

"That's all for you," he said. "You had all you're going to get!"

He sent her home.

81

Tony's pride had been hurt. His honor was at stake.

"Let's go downtown!" he said.

In South Chicago when they say downtown they mean they're going to Chicago.

They went to Chicago and to Louie's neighborhood for revenge. Tony brought five or six fellows with him, and they didn't care who they caught. They just knew that they were guys from the other side of the tracks. "South Chicago!" they yelled, beating the guys up, "Remember South Chicago!"

That started it in earnest.

They came a second and a third time in their night forays, to where Louie and his friends hung around. There they caught a couple kids alone and beat them up—bad.

And as wild as Louie and his gang of fellows in the neighborhood were, it was a challenge.

Louie threw a pool ball with all his might through the open door of the poolroom and out onto the street, and the proprietor hadn't better say anything; he didn't, he sent the house man after the ball.

Gee and Flophouse and Paco looked up. Dusty said, "Man, that dago's got a temper!"

Louie walked over to them. He showed his thumb with its cross and three bars. Flophouse and Dusty showed theirs. Gee showed his with two bars. Paco was ashamed that he didn't have any to show.

"The Lobos! The Old Lobos!" Gee said reverently.

"Walk silently, hit fast and fade," Louie said.

They began to organize again. All the Italian guys in the neighborhood—and Paco and Dusty.

It began to build up. Little raids out there. Little raids "downtown."

Going out there, and anybody you caught on the street, giving it to them. And then shooting back here.

And "downtown" had its stool pigeon. He was a guy who used to live in Chicago but lived out there now and was afraid of them. A kid called Seven Leagues because he was less than five feet tall. He was cute and good-looking, a miniature man, and he had a car and he would come and tell them all the action that was going on out there. Or he would phone from South Chicago: "Three cars just left from here. Watch it."

So they'd be waiting for it.

Little raids back and forth.

They caught Gee alone. They were laying low, down on the floor of the car, and the guy driving pulled up to the curb: "Hey, buddy, can you tell me where—?"

"What?"

Gee went over.

The door came open and they dragged him inside. They drove along railroad tracks and into a coal yard and beat him something awful. They left him unconscious in front of the poolhall and some guy painted a big S.C. on the sidewalk.

Retaliation.

Louie, Flophouse and Dusty went over there in a stolen car. Just the three of them, with baseball bats.

They knew the poolroom was the place to catch them. They waited in the car. After a while three of the South Chicago fellows came out. One of them got on a bicycle and the other two walked along beside him. They were kidding and laughing about something.

"I'll take care of the kiddie on the bicycle," Louie said.

Flophouse nodded okay.

The fellow bumped off the curbstone on his bicycle and onto the street and the bicycle started to gain speed. Louie stood in the street, waiting: If I swing at his head I might miss. I'll play dirty and take care of the bicycle first.

When the fellow saw him and, pedaling faster, tried to turn away toward the opposite curb, Louie stuck the bat in the spokes of the front wheel and the bicycle tipped over onto the street. He stopped the bicycle dead. That took care of that. The fellow, dazed, got to his feet and started to run. And that's when Louie caught him, right below the knees. It could have been a home run. Louie knew he wouldn't walk for a long, long time.

Meanwhile Dusty and Flophouse caught the other two fellows. Dusty hit the guy in the back, in the arms, in the back again, over the neck, like hitting a pig. Flophouse hit his guy over the head, over the head again, and again. Flophouse didn't even lose his hat.

They left the three of them lying in the middle of the street and ran for the stolen car.

The motor was running and they took off. But not far. They went fast around the block, swerved to keep from running over the guys lying in the street, and threw a brick through the poolroom window.

Then they took off.

That really started it. But good. That kept it going.

82

Finally it began to get in the newspapers:

The Italian boys are killing each other off.

The adults got together:

Nobody's dead yet, but eventually these guys are going to get killed.

The adults formed committees. The parents from South Chicago and the parents from "downtown."

The young fellows were all sitting around in the poolroom. Paco sat there too. His new shoes hurt at the back and he kept lifting his heels out of them. On his lap he held a round piece of wood, about eleven inches long, that a fellow had given him: This will make a good rolling pin for my sister. What the thing used to be, I don't know. Maybe the inside of a printing machine, a roller from a press. I'll get all the varnish off, sandpaper it, take it to the wood shop and make a rolling pin.

"Hey, Louie, loan me your knife."

Louie lay on one of the benches, half asleep, his feet propped up against the wall and his hat pulled over his face. He felt under his belt, and pulling out the knife, tossed it underhand to Paco. It had a big reindeer foot, and closed it was about ten inches long. Open, it was like a bayonet.

Paco started scraping varnish. It was very, very hard wood.

Gee, Slim, Flophouse and The Muscle were playing a loud, razzing game of pool. Dusty and Cue Ball were hand-wrestling, and the rest of the fellows were just loafing around.

They were all sitting around, fooling around, when this man entered. He wore a freshly pressed suit, white shirt and tie, nice hat and a worried, yet paternal look. He approached them and said, "Fellows, I'm here to represent the parents of the South Chicago people out there—anda—we, ah, we think that you people should stop all this nonsense because, ah, actually, gang wars—well, because somebody's going to get hurt."

He passed his pack of Luckies around and they all took one. If this guy's going to give out cigarettes, we might as well help ourselves. "Why don't you fellows come over tonight? We're having a party."

Seven Leagues came in. "I brought Mr. Leonski over in my car," he said; and the fellows looked and knew it must be all right if Seven Leagues was with the guy.

Mr. Leonski said, "We're having a party over there at Turner Hall, out near Ninety-first and Commercial. We're inviting all you fellows, but please come peaceful-like because we aim to put an end to all this foolishness. All you kids hurting each other."

Paco looked at Louie. "What do you think?"

"Okay," Louie said.

And the man said, "There's just one thing I want you people to know. Believe me, when you fellows get there, there'll be only one person armed and that's the cop at the door. He's the only one who will have a weapon. So please—I beg you fellows, not to bring anything with you."

"Who's got anything?"

"We don't need anything."

"Nobody's got nothin',"

voices said.

Flophouse said, turning to the owner of the poolroom, "Tell him you'll take the responsibility for the weapons."

So the owner spoke up. "Yes," he said, "I can trust my boys here. In fact, I'm going to show you how nice they are." He rolled the cigar to the other end of his mouth. "Now I want all you guys to drop your tools here, here on the pool table. Anything you got."

They all dropped their knives, blackjacks, everything.

Paco felt the rolling pin under his sweater: Un-un. Why should I drop this? I'm going to take this home. I want this as a rolling pin.

He left it right there.

Guys were dropping everything.

"Louie, drop your knife," Paco said to him in an undertone.

"It's my knife!" Louie said, nasty-like.

Paco looked at him.

Louie dropped something. It wasn't the deer foot. It was the pocket knife.

:I know he's still got it in his belt.

Paco leaned over and whispered, "What are you going to do?"

"Nothin'." Soft and mean.

But everybody else—Slim, Gee, Dusty, Flophouse, Cue Ball, Doubtful Dick, everybody—they all dropped everything.

We're going out there to make peace.

They goofed around at the poolhall all afternoon and evening. They may have been a little happy, had a few drinks, a little high, but not drunk. They chipped in for gas and for booze. About five carloads started out there.

They got there a little after twelve o'clock, when there wouldn't be any charge to get in.

So they didn't have to pay, and they walked into the dance hall. The guys standing out in front didn't say hello, but inside, the elderly people: "Hello! Hello! Make yourself at home! Go dance with this one and that one."

But little hoodlums that they were, they lined up all around the dance hall.

But they didn't have weapons.

They stood around, half an hour, longer.

Gee said to Paco, "Let's go to the crapper."

Dracula said, "I'll go with youse guys."

They went upstairs to the toilet. They weren't there long when Paco said, "Listen!"

—paah! paaaah!—

Downstairs.

All of a sudden.

"Hey, Gee," Paco said, "them ain't firecrackers!"

—paaah!

"Yeah, that's right. They don't sound like firecrackers."

"Let's get out of here."

By the time they got downstairs the whole hall was empty, and it was a very large hall too. There had been people lined up against the wall, watching, waiting to dance. The dance floor had been crowded. There had been women. There were no women now. By the time they got down from the second floor, there were just men. It seemed as if all the men from South Chicago were against the wall near the open doors and on the sidewalk immediately outside. And all of Paco's friends from downtown, unarmed, were on the street.

Paco hit the bottom step from the balcony and stood, looking around. The first thing that crossed his eye was Louie. Louie was wavering. But Paco knew he wasn't drunk. Then Paco looked at his hand and saw the deer foot. And Paco saw the red spot at his shoulder that was trickling sickeningly down, forming a gummy pool at his uncertain feet. He had been shot. Through the shoulder and through the wrist. And he was going down . . . down. With his slow-moving eyes Paco measured the distance—one—two—about twelve feet away stood Tony. And he was standing there with a thirty-two. He was holding it in both hands. Fear. Or gaining nerve. Or aiming for the kill. "Don't come near me, Louie! Don't come near me, because I'll kill you!" And in back of Louie, Dusty—Dusty and Flophouse and The Muscle. "Louie! Don't move! Don't move! When the police come we'll take the knife and you can claim self-defense."

But Louie was stubborn and mean.

He says, "No!" He takes a wavering step toward Tony. "You sonofabitch, look what you did to me. You shot me. I'm going to kill you, I'm going to kill you, I'm going to kill you." Quietly. And all the time walking up, real slow, as fast as his body would permit him without losing balance.

He keeps walking toward him.

And Paco and Gee, at the bottom of the balcony, see what is going to happen. They have come down the stairs on the side of the hall where all the South Chicago people are. They begin to circle, to move to a position behind Tony. Quickly, yet slowly, so that Tony and the men of South Chicago won't notice. And now they are behind Tony. Paco is almost shoulder to shoulder with him. And Gee stands almost directly in front of him but to the side and still a part of the watching crowd. And Louie, walking, saying, "I'm going to kill you, I'm going to kill you."

Saying that.

He is doubled up in pain. I'm shot. I'm going to kill this rat.

345

He is walking, and walking, and walking.

And Tony is scared. Scared to shoot. Scared of this thing that won't fall down.

And at the same time Flophouse and Dusty and all these other guys from "downtown" are telling him:

"Don't! Don't, Louie! Stay there! Stay there! The police will be here!"

And all of a sudden Gee runs in from the crowd and swings at Tony. In his excitement he doesn't hit him good. He just taps him, but enough to make him lose his balance and go back. And when he went back, Paco automatically pulled out the rolling pin he had under his sweater and slugged him good.

Boom!

He dropped down.

And Louie kept walking toward him until, about five or six feet from him, he dropped. Louie dropped. To his knees.

Tony made an effort to get up. Paco slugged him again. This time he caught him across the face, splitting it wide from forehead to nose.

Then everything went to pieces. The tight, intense, fearful yet fascinated crowd, close pressed and panting as if they themselves were the struggle, became a mob. Guns came out. And knives, blackjacks, zip-guns, broken bottles, bricks, clubs. All the guys from South Chicago. And the others unarmed. Armed only in the struggle for a gun, a bottle, a club. Chicago jumped the guys from South Chicago, who had guns because they were all scared. And the fellows from South Chicago didn't want to use the guns to begin with. And the fellows from South Chicago *did* know how to use guns.

And in the struggle both sides were half armed.

Bricks, clubs, bullets were showering everywhere. A lot of people got hurt. People even got hurt in their own homes.

The parents were on the sidelines, shouting, "Don't, don't, don't! Stop!"

Stop . . . shit, man, this has gone too far already!

And in the center of it Louie crawls up to Tony. Louie half passes out. "Paco! Help me. Push him this way—'cause I can't make it—"

Louie is crawling on one arm only. The other feels paralyzed.

"No! No! Get up! Let's get out of here! There's too much shooting going on!"

And all of a sudden a man who lived next door to the hall opened his window and started shooting at everybody—anything he saw moving. They were disturbing his slumber.

"Louie, come on! Let's get out of here!"

346

"No, let me, move over there, push the guy closer, I want to take care of him."

"There's a lot of guys out there, Louie! They all have guns!"

Louie laughs. "Tony's got one."

And Louie crawls. Louie is on top of Tony. He holds the knife like a dagger. He sticks him in the back. He sticks him in the shoulder blade, and he couldn't, he couldn't get it in.

Paco stands helpless.

"Help me, Paco."

:Un-un. I ain't going to help you there. You're going to kill the guy. "Come on, Louie! Let's get out of here!"

And the hall is deserted. The fight is on the street. Maybe two hundred people. The fight is being pushed from one block to the other, back and forth, all this shooting, people ducking.

In the long, wide, empty, silent hall Louie and Tony. Paco.

And an empty bandstand. Some curtains blowing at open windows.

Paco hears, from half a block away, a bunch of fellows coming running, yelling, yelling Louie's name, Tony's name.

"Come on, Louie! They're coming for us!"

"Yeah, yeah, all right . . . but one more shot at him with this."

Louie raises the knife in a slow hand.

"No, no, leave him alone."

Louie manages to push his hand over Tony's neck and tries to pull the knife across the skin, but the strength of his hand is completely gone now. He can't use the right hand because he'd been shot through it. He can't use his left hand because he's leaning on it.

He was lying down too. They were lying close together. Almost on top of each other.

Paco picked him up.

"Can you run?"

"Yeah, I can walk."

They ran down the street and they ran down another street.

It was quiet.

:I'll take him in an alley and sit down and see how bad he's hurt, and then from there I can decide what the next move is going to be.

Paco, the boy, was suddenly man.

They were still running down the street. Then not running because Louie could no longer even walk very well.

Paco is holding him with one arm and trying to run with the rest of his body.

A car comes toward them. There are three couples in the car, top down, radio playing, car cruising along slowly.

Some of the South Chicago gang have turned the corner in pursuit of Paco and Louie and are shooting at them.

Paco had heard the shots when he was in the toilet; they sounded like cap guns but he knew they were bullets. Now! And Louie hardly able to keep moving.

They weren't going any faster than the carload of cruising lovers. And as they neared the car Paco saw a bullet go through the windshield: Boy, these guns mean business! Almost crying he tried to get Louie to move faster. And as soon as the bullet went through the windshield all the doors opened on that car—whissss—people flew out of there and ducked. They left the car right in the middle of the street.

Paco kept pulling Louie along.

"Ahhhh—" It was like the long exhaust of air from an inner tube. "I can't run any more," Louie said. "I can't—I can't— Go ahead, Paco. Go ahead, go ahead, take off, leave me alone."

"No. Naw. I can't.": What the hell, what are you going to do? Leave the guy there? They're going to shoot his tomato off. I know that.

"Come on. Try! Try!"

Louie said, "Don't be a fool! Take off!" There was command in his voice.

They got to the corner and there was a lamppost there. No buildings. No nothing. Just a big old lamppost sticking out in the middle of nowhere.

"Leave me here and you go on," Louie said. "Go ahead."

"Can you hold on?"

"Yeah."

:Sorry, but this is it.

So Paco took off and left him there.

He was holding onto the lamppost with his left arm and he still had the open knife in his right hand.

And that is where they caught him.

Paco could see him. Could see them coming to get him. Paco had gone only to the mouth of the alley. He had on a brand-new pair of shoes and they had hurt him in the back all day every time he had taken a step. They hurt like hell. He pulled them off.

That's when he saw that they had caught him.

But they didn't go near Louie.

They stood away from him. They stood in the middle of the street.

This big guy, Dago Red, said, "Why, you sonofabitch!"

"Hello, Dago Red," Louie said.

"Why, you sonofabitch, I caughtcha!"

"Yeah, Dago," Louie said, "come on, come on up here. I want to talk to you." With the knife, "Come on up, I want to talk to you."

"No. I'm going to shoot you down like a dog."

Louie laughed through his pain. "You're not man enough to shoot anybody."

He wasn't. He flipped his gun in the direction Paco had gone. "Get the other guy," he said.

Paco took off down the alley. And Paco is running again and these little bullets—zee—zee—all over his head. Running: I'm with my shoes in my hands. Running.

And he is just runningrunningrunning.

He made a sharp turn down a side alley and ducked in an area-way. They shot by. They went by like a little bullet. They wanted to lose him. And Paco knew this: These guys didn't have nerve enough to kill Louie. You're just chasing me to make it look good. He got his nerve back.

So, fifteen minutes later, when he walked out of the mouth of the alley, he was looking around: I haven't got a dime on me 'cause I chipped it all in on gas to get out here and for bottles of booze. He sat down and pulled his shoes on: Here's a new territory, I mean like a strange town. But I'll get back, eventually I'll get back. But I want to get back right now 'cause it's kind of hot here.

A car stopped across the street by a lamp. Paco recognized it as The Muscle's car.

"Hey, Bob! Bob, it's me!"

And in the back they had Dusty, Cue Ball and Flophouse. And they had Louie spread across their knees. He was in sad shape.

They dropped Louie off at a hospital out there and left one guy with him. Some guy with a clean record: "I found this man lying in the street. I'm bringing him in."

Next day they heard that Louie and Tony were in the same hospital. In the same room.

And when the fellows went to see Louie, they were still fighting it out. Louie with his leg stretched out and his arm way up in the air in a sling and needles stuck all over him, and Tony dying a couple beds away, or so he was for a while.

And people used to go see Tony, but not many to see Louie. They didn't want to get implicated. Tony worked and this was the first trouble he'd been in. Well, Louie, he didn't work and he had a reputation.

People brought Tony flowers and candy and cigarettes.

"He's a cute character, this Louie," Gee said proudly. "He conned one of the nurses into stealing for him. She goes and steals cigarettes from Tony for Louie."

And one day Louie had two visitors. Cops!

:I can smell them two miles away with the wind blowing away from me. You can tell them by the looks on their faces even if they wear formals.

His visitors said, "We got a little trip all lined up for you when you're able and ready to travel."

And out in South Chicago the guys gave Maria, the cause of it all, a baldhead haircut and she had to move.

83

Louie came out of jail. Ang wouldn't talk to him. Ma wasn't aware that he had been away. Rosemary said, "You better eat something." Aunt Rosa came home from work. "Hello, Louie." She sat down heavily in a chair. She twisted off her shoes, one foot against the other. Her feet were swollen. They hurt. It wasn't her feet that hurt. It was her head. Her heart. It was Louie that hurt.

She looked across the room at him: This has gone far enough. Again she looked at Louie, then at the others sitting around the table before food they didn't feel like eating.

"Okay," she said to Louie, "I want to talk to you."

She nodded to the bathroom.

Moving toward the door she wondered: Could their family be diseased? Could crime be inherited just as they said insanity was? Would Louie end up like Nick?

She closed the bathroom door and, with her hand, waved him down on the edge of the bathtub.

"I want to talk to you."

And in that moment she was back in the jail, that last time.

. . . "Hello, Aunt Rosa." Then, softly, "Sit down."
They sat side by side on the bench against the bars.
She reached out slowly and put her hand on his knee. Tightened

it. "I don't want you to break down, Nick," she said gruffly. "You're a Romano and—what's more—a Pelitani. They can't hurt you, Nick. Nothing they do to you. And you ain't bad. Whatever you done. Whatever you done—God—Christ, Nick! I don't want to talk like this." Her hand fastened down tight and shook his knee. "Come on, grin at your old aunt. Ain't nothing can keep us from grinning. Now or ever. We're like that, Nick—you and me—"

He took her shoulders between his hands and gently shook her. Then, very gently, one hand moved itself from the cloth of her coat. The fingers gently wiped away the tears that had gathered in her lashes. Then his embarrassed hand came away, lay on his knee. Neither spoke for a long time.

"You been working hard, Aunt Rosa?"

"Not too hard."

"You been taking care of us a long time, ain't you, Aunt Rosa? Ma—she did all right. She meant all right. I couldn't tell her, Aunt Rosa, but I can tell you. She taught us right and tried to—to make me do right. You even managed Ma and—kept us together." Color came to his cheekbones and he was silent. Then he said, laughing a little, "How are the horses going, Aunt Rosa?"

"Oh, so-so."

"You win lately?"

"Didn't play since—for a long time."

"How's Julian?"

"He's all right."

"How's—Rosemary?"

"She's just fine and that kid of hers—he's a cute one." Aunt Rosa took a long time between each answer.

"How's Junior?"

"Getting awfully big, Nick—and bad."

"Aunt Rosa—will you do me a favor?" Staring at the toes of his shoes. "Don't let him get too bad—don't let him end up like— You beat hell out of him, Aunt Rosa! You see that he does right!"

Nodding her head hard and fast without answering.

Then he told her about Ang and Abe. "You keep an eye on Ang too, will you? Ang is all right. You help them, Aunt Rosa."

"I will, Nick." She took his hands between hers.

"What's wrong with this lousy world, Aunt Rosa?" And he turned his head away, rubbing his ear against the bars.

"There's nothing wrong with the world, Nick. There's nothing wrong with people, Nick. There's something good in everybody. I— I don't know how to talk about it—but I know people are all right. People don't do no wrong. Not when they're left alone." She was *holding his hand on the palm of one of hers, moving each finger a little to the side and looking at it, gently moving them all together and looking at them as she talked. "Sometimes I think there's no good or bad in the world. It's just people looking for something— trying to find something, somebody to love—somebody or something to feel good about— Some find it, some don't, but there's nothing wrong with people, Nick."*

They sat in a long silence, side by side, their backs against the bars, their hands touching on the bench between them. And at last they must part. Aunt Rosa stood looking at him. Then she smiled slowly. Her old, fat hand patted his cheek. "Kiss your old aunt good-bye." And she held him in her arms with the firm protectiveness of one holding a child from harm.

Now she no longer knew if she believed what she had told Nick. She had grown older, and suffered more, and given more, and, in turn, had made others suffer. Sometimes not meaning to, other times with what she thought was reason enough. Knowing all, maybe you can't condemn or even judge, but Jesus-God-Almighty!—there is right and wrong and that's why I have to talk to Louie, tell him— make him see that everybody is responsible for his actions—tell him—

Now, to Louie, she said, "I have something to tell you."

And then she didn't have anything to say for a long while.

Finally, "Light me a cigarette."

He lit one for both of them. She sat there on the toilet seat, an old woman, smoking in despair, smoking the cigarette to a butt and crushing it out before speaking again. "Your brother," she said, "died in the electric chair."

The whispers were words.

"We used to tell you he was sick in the hospital when he was in jail."

The tears were running down her cheeks, unchecked.

"He used to say, 'Live fast, die young and have a good-looking corpse!'—Is that what you want to do?"

Louie felt the sickness of the question rising in his throat. He turned his head away from the tears, and asked, "Did he—did he do it?"

With her eyes clenched tight and her lips pressed together, holding back the moan, she nodded her head yes.

She rocked a little on the seat, forced her eyes open and again looked at Louie.

"Your brother—your brother told me to see that you were good and wouldn't end up like him. And—and I promised him—I promised Nick you would be good."

She stopped talking awhile and blew her nose noisily. Then she told him about Ang and Abe. And more about Nick.

"I promised him—"

She raised her right hand, as though repeating an oath.

"—the last time I saw him—I promised him— Oh, Louie!"

Now she gestured with her fat hand, dismissing him. She couldn't say another word.

"Thanks, Aunt Rosa," Louie said.

He walked out of the room and out of the house.

 *too late for tears*

84

"The kid got slugged," Juan said. "He's in the hospital."

Max's face tightened. "Who did it?"

"Nobody seems to know."

They went to see Nick at the hospital several days in a row. Max, Phil and Norman were there the day he regained consciousness.

"Who hit me?" he asked, still half-conscious.

"We'll find out," Max said quietly.

"How did it happen?" Norm asked on the streets below.

"Somebody hit him from behind. They hit him with a brick, a blackjack or a piece of pipe. Over by Maxwell Street. But we'll find out."

They went over to Maxwell and, with Juan, they went around asking people if anybody had seen what or who hit the kid.

Nobody would talk.

Nobody would tell them anything.

Later Max and Juan sat at the Crystal Bar. Max said, "Salvatore, the barber." He lit a cigarette. "That guy, that guy can see anything. I don't care what time of the night or day it happened. That guy knows everything. If you want the latest you just go to him. If a cockroach walked past his door at midnight he'd know it. If it happened in the neighborhood he'd know about it."

Juan was already paying for the drinks.

They went across the street.

"What do you say, Sally!"

"Hello there, boys."

And Max, coming to the point, "The kid got hit here." He pointed to the back of his head. "Who did it? What happened?"

"I don't know a damn thing."

He wouldn't talk. He wouldn't tell them anything. He was scared.

He knew who had done it and they knew too. Or at least they had their suspicions.

"Nobody except this character Frank would do a thing like that to the kid," Max said.

But they wanted definite proof.

We'll find out. And when we find out—

Finally, about two weeks later, they got that proof. This guy, Corky, was going back to Texas and he knew he wasn't coming back. He was in a hurry to get there.

One night he tapped on the window of Juan's shop and came secretly in. They were all there, Juan, Max, Phil, Norm and old Judge Sullivan, because they had just brought the kid home from the hospital that evening and were having a quiet drink or two in the darkness there.

"Hello, Corky—" Juan waved his hand at the bottle. "Have one?"

"No." He looked around nervously, then said, "If it's worth anything to you guys I'll tell you—because I saw—I know—"

"Okay," Max said into the tightness of the room, "spill it."

"The Wolf," Corky said.

They looked from one to the other. Max laughed shortly. "Just as I thought. That sweet character."

Corky said, "I better have that drink now."

Juan pulled out a twenty-dollar bill. "Here," he said, "this will help with your passport, and thanks!"

Corky drank and left. Max turned to Judge Sullivan. "You stay out of this. It's going to be dirty and it's going to be right."

"Yeah," Phil said, "you better believe it."

Max turned to Norman and said, so that Judge couldn't hear him, "And you too, doll."

And Max, pulling the bottle to him and pouring, looking over it, "We're five guys—we're together. We don't bother nobody, so we don't want nobody to bother us. But he hit the kid. The kid. The same thing would have happened if he had hit any of us, we'd feel the same way about it. But the kid. So we're going to even the score."

They drank in the dark room.

"Okay, okay," they said, very softly, "he asked for it. Now we'll give it to him. But good!"

They said it softly, in the dark, but with decisiveness.

The next night Juan, Max and Phil went to see a good friend of Juan's. They went into a housing project and into a nice apartment with a piano, a television set and a bicycle in the kitchen. Juan's friend, a man close to forty, poured them drinks, chased his wife and his kids and closed the door.

Juan's friend had been a professional stick-up man, a guy who had never worked a day in his life until after the war. Then his kids were getting bigger and he didn't want them to know the score. That he was a bum, that he didn't work. Now he was working for a cheap outfit making fifty dollars a week and nothing in comparison to 1936 and 1937, the good old days when he was making good dough. Even the whiskey he poured them was cheap.

"Well, boys?" he said, smiling and showing several gold teeth.

"Just a social visit," Juan said, grinning.

"Oh yeah?"

Juan came to the point. "Loan us your gun."

He knew. He knew. He kept tabs on the neighborhood. And he had no love for The Wolf. His eyes stayed steadily on each of them in turn. Juan was his personal friend of long years. Juan had even bailed him out once. He knew that anything Juan and Max did or said was sincere, that they wouldn't mess around, go showing off with a gun. He trusted them. He caught Juan's glance and held it, saying at the same time, "Any time that you want to, if you want me, I'll take care of the bum myself."

"No. This is a personal affair. We'll take care of it by ourselves. Just lend us the gun and nobody will know about it."

He unlocked the desk drawer and handed them a forty-five automatic.

They celebrated the gun. They locked it up in Juan's shop and then went down to the Crystal Bar and drank.

They drank for three nights, because then they were going on the wagon until they had taken care of The Wolf. On the third night in the Crystal Bar, Seldom Seen was sitting alone at a table against the wall, his hand up to his face. He was smoking one cigarette after another and not drinking. Seldom Seen was long and tall. Women called him Daddy-Long-Legs and liked to go to bed with him. He had gray eyes, sleepy-looking, but nevertheless watchful, almost evil-looking. There was only the hint of tan over his skin, and a sprinkling of freckles on his face. He was lean, almost tubercular thin. Max and Juan had played basketball with him in high school and, as kids, they had done a lot of petty stealing together.

"Hey, Seldom!" Juan called. "Come on over and join us!"

Seldom practically crept over and sat down, his hand again against his face.

"What you so sad about?"

"Nothin', man."

They made him drink with them. They drank for two hours. Still Seldom Seen didn't come out of it.

They bought another bottle. At last Seldom Seen looked up at them. His eyes were filled with tears. He nodded his head toward the alley half a block down the street. "A little colored kid got killed in that alley some years ago," he said. He stared at his long fingers and tightened them into fists. "The Mexican lady upstairs told me who done it. She just told me today." From gray eyes tears fell on the table top. "That was my sister's only child. The only relative we had. No maw. No paw. Just she and me and that kid."

"I saw it!" Max said roughly.

"Me too!" Juan said.

"I'm going to kill that white sonofabitch!" Seldom Seen said.

"Un-un!" Max said with emphasis. "We are!"

"I'm going to get him, man! I'm going to get him!" Seldom Seen said.

They met the next night in Juan's shop: Juan, Phil, Max and Seldom Seen. They argued about who was going to pack the gun, do it. "Me, man!" Seldom Seen said. "I want the pleasure."

They finally agreed that each would take a day carrying the gun. They drew lots for this. Max, with a malicious smile, secreted the gun on his body, having won for the first day's vigil.

Nick said, "It was Frank, wasn't it?"

"We know who it was, kid," Phil said, "and we're going to handle it. You better believe it. And we don't want you involved."

"It was Frank, wasn't it?"

"Get home!" Max said roughly. "We'll handle this."

"Well, I'll get him alone," Nick said.

They used to booze like hell. Now they decided they weren't going to drink any more. They'd stay on the wagon until they caught up with The Wolf.

Seldom Seen was always seen. Seen with Max and Phil and Juan. He had a quietness about him. A dedication.

They followed The Wolf's activities. They knew he was making stick-ups with Ralph Pizarro. But they never came to the neighborhood.

"He'll come, he'll come," Max said. "One day he'll come."

They followed his activities.

They stayed sober.

85

Nick stood, as always a little frightened and embarrassed, as the elevator stopped at the apartment door.

Would they treat him the same?

Would Barbara be as nice to him?

What if they knew about his mother—?

And the elevator door opened.

"Nick!" Barbara said. She moved toward him as he stepped into the room. "Where have you been?" she asked.

"I—"

"I'm mad at you!" she whispered.

"I've been sick."

"Oh. I'm sorry. I thought you didn't like us any more." She took his hand and led him to where Grant and Wanda were. "Look what I found in the elevator!"

"Hello, Nick!" Grant said. He held out his hand.

"No you don't!" Barbara said to her father, not releasing Nick's hand and leading him to the bar. "Look!" she said.

Nick looked where she pointed. There, in a frame over one end of the bar, was one of the drawings he had done, lying here on the

361

floor in their apartment one Sunday afternoon. He flushed. He looked at Barbara and away. His brown glance went to Grant. "Do you like it, sir?" and he half lowered his head in embarrassment.

Grant laughed. "No. I put it there because there's a hole in the plaster. Come, sit down, Nick."

Wanda said, "Hello, Nick. So good to see you again."

He glanced shyly at her. "Thank you."

"Yes, the drawing is good," Grant said. "Your drawings are good— Cigarette?"

"No, thank you. I don't smoke."

"Well, I do," Barbara said, and took one from her father. Smiling up at her Grant took it back, lit it, then handed it to her. She sat, hugging her knees, smoking, looking at Nick.

Wanda said, "I'll make us some coffee. We can have it out on the balcony. It's such a lovely night."

Barbara said, "Nick, tell me what you've been doing. You know, we haven't seen you in such a long time."

Wanda called from the kitchen, "Barbara, come give me a hand."

"You were sick!" Barbara said to Nick. "I bet you just didn't want to come over this far."

"Bobby!" Grant said.

"Oh, heck!" Barbara said and got up, and went to the kitchen to help her mother.

Grant mixed himself a drink at the bar. He brought it, and a glass of wine for Nick. "Here. It will make the coffee taste better."

"Thank you."

Grant tilted his glass, looking at the color of the liquor, letting the ice tingle, finding pleasure in the sound. "Nice night.": Come to the point.

Grant eased his long legs out in front of him. "Yes. We all looked at your drawings. Here is talent. You've got it." He looked at Nick. Nick glanced down at his feet. "You've got it," Grant said. "But it's hard work." He smiled. "And painting doesn't pay unless you're the lucky exception."

The boy sat silent, his head down.

Grant said, "My wife showed your drawings to an artist. A pretty famous artist."

Nick looked up, surprise and fear in his face.

Grant smiled. "Drink your wine," he said. "The artist said that you have the makings." Grant tried a joke. "The makings—you know, like tobacco and paper for a cigarette."

Nick looked up. He couldn't look at Grant; he stared at the far wall. "I'd like to be a painter," he said.

Wanda and Barbara came in with the coffee service. "The balcony, children!" Wanda said cheerfully.

They sat out there, a breeze ruffling hair and shirt collar, Barbara's ribbon tied to her pony tail, spoons tinkling on saucers, lump sugar dropped gently into thin porcelain cups.

And Barbara patted the low seat next to her. "Sit over here, Nick."

Nick looked at Grant and Wanda as if to ask permission, then went and sat next to Barbara.

They sat talking in half-whispers, giggling; and Nick looked sometimes at Grant and Wanda: Is it all right?

To her parents Barbara announced, "We're going painting in the woods again!"

"Oh?" Grant said.

"Look, Nick—" Wanda said. She pointed to the Chicago skyline. "Isn't it beautiful?"

His autumn eyes held hers, then held the Chicago skyline.

Barbara nudged him and said something low and softly laughed.

Wanda sipped her coffee. The lip of the cup was very thin, pleasant to the touch of her lip, and she remembered where she had bought it and how frightfully expensive the set had been, really. And a part of her observed Nick and Barbara nervously. She had nothing against the boy—and the boy had talent—but—but—

Nick thought of his mother. Was she alone?

"I have to go," he said.

"Hey, Mom!" Barbara said. "I'm going to walk Nick to the streetcar. I need the air. All right, Grant?"

"Sure, honey."

Grant and Wanda stood on the balcony. Wanda pretended she was looking at the skyline. Grant looked down. He watched them go. They were small down there on the sidewalk, going under a tree, and Bobby had taken Nick's arm. What did he know, really, about this boy?

Wanda was watching them too.

Grant put his arm around his wife.

86

Louie went into the main branch of the public library on Randolph Street. He asked for the back issues of the papers. He began leafing through them. Half an hour later he stopped and gasped. He was looking down at his own photograph! Just as if he had been looking in a mirror, he was seeing his own face. Nick looked back at him. His gaze was deep, brown, innocent. The headline said:

PRETTY BOY ROMANO DIES TONIGHT!

Louie closed the heavy cover of the book of bound newspapers and put his forehead down on it. Brother! Brother!

For half an hour he sat like this. Then he got up and walked out of the library.

The next day he went back and again turned the pages of the old newspapers:

GRAND JURY INDICTS
PRETTY BOY ROMANO

Laughs. Says, "I can take it!"

KILLER IDENTIFIED!

Goddamn it! Forget it!

He went over near the neighborhood, stopping at tavern after tavern.

A girl was standing on the corner in a pair of shorts and a thin blouse and she was well stacked. He looked her up and down, stopping, standing there in front of her. "Jesus! That's really nice!" he said in Italian.

"Why don't you say it in English?" she said.

He looked her up and down again. "Jesus, that's nice!" he said in English.

She smiled at him.

He had his own cigarettes but he said, "Give me a cigarette."

"Here. But buy your own next time."

"Okay, babe." And he wandered on.

Another tavern.

There at the bar he ran into Cue Ball and they drank until night talking about old times, bragging about the gang wars and the big fight in South Chicago, laughing about the broads they had shacked up with together, and Louie said, "Let's go down to West Madison."

They went down to West Madison, and their money was getting short. As they used to do in the old days they followed a well-dressed drunk. He turned into an alley and they turned in after him. He stood up against a post in the dark and they went into action. Louie grabbed him around the neck from behind, cutting off his voice, and Cue Ball went through his pockets. They dumped him.

But not before Louie had punched him in the mouth a couple of times.

"Come on, man, let's get out of here!" Cue Ball yelled. "Do you want to kill him!"

They got out, divided the sixty-one dollars and threw the billfold away.

"Let's get a couple more guys," Louie said.

"We got enough to drink on, man!" Cue Ball said.

Louie said, "Aw, screw you!" and walked away.

Following him, Cue Ball said, "Well, okay, I'll go with you. But just a couple. No use stretching our luck."

Louie said, "Aw, beat it!"

"Okay! Screw you then!" And Cue Ball turned into a bar.

Louie jackrolled three other drunks. Then he bought himself a quart of whiskey, went over to the neighborhood and rented himself a room, locked himself inside with the bottle.

The next day the girl was on the corner again. "Got your own cigarettes today, huh?"

"Yeah, want one?"

He gave her one. Then he said, "Come on up to my room. I want to talk to you."

"I don't trust Eye-talians," she said.

But she went.

They stayed up there three days, drinking, getting drunk, going to bed, drinking some more, going back to bed.

Then he woke up with a hangover.

Your brother died in the electric chair was the first thing he remembered.

She was puckered and unattractive in drunken sleep. He put all the stolen money, except for a couple of dollars, on the dresser where she would see it. He didn't know why he did that.

Your brother died in the electric chair.

Brother! Brother!

And back to the library.

POLICE-KILLER AT LARGE

COMB CITY FOR KILLER

STATE ASKS DEATH
IN ROMANO CASE

TOUGH GUY ROMANO BETS PACK
OF CIGARETTES HE'LL GET CHAIR

He left the library. The guilt was on him, too, now. And the shame. Oh, my God! Oh, my God!

A world I never made.

He stayed out all night. Until dawn. Thinking. Drinking a little beer. Not getting drunk. Just thinking about things.

And a little all-night restaurant, one neon sign down a black street until dawn erased the blackness and the neon closed its red eye. Cup after cup of coffee, each saucer twisted with brown-stained cigarette butts. Headache. Eyes tired. Go home. Not sleepy. "Gimme a order of hot cakes." Two bites. Can't get them down. No. Pushing them away. "Hey—another java!"

Down this street is home. In an areaway, a few doors from home and three steps down, he saw the old man sprawled there in drunken sleep, legs spread, arms spread, head at an angle, gray hair spilling over his forehead and the big dog lying across him protectively, its paws across his stomach, its huge head resting on its paws.

Louie went down the steps to the man. The dog opened its eyes and growled; then it recognized Louie. But it didn't leave its vigil position. "Swede!" Louie said, shaking him. "Swede!"

It took five minutes before his eyes came open. "Oh, hullo, Louie." He propped himself up on his elbows. "Just couldn't make it home last night."

Louie struggled him to his feet. "Come on, Swede, upsee-daisy!" He adjusted one of Swede's arms around his shoulders, held it there and half carried him home. The dog followed gratefully.

At the steps leading to the house Louie had to put Swede over his back and carry him up.

Louie kicked the door open with his foot. Aunt Rosa was up, half dressed for work, and having a cup of coffee. "Laundry!" Louie yelled at her and deposited the Swede on a chair, where he hung over its edge perilously.

"Huh! Garbage!" Aunt Rosa said. But she wasn't mad. She was glad her husband was home safe.

"Say!" Louie said, walking to the stove. "That smells good!"

"Want a cup, handsome?"

"Yes, Aunt Rosa."

"Here—let me get it for you."

She brought it to the table. "Where was Good-Looking prowling all night?"

"Well, you could kiss me good morning." He didn't know what made him say that; he hadn't kissed her since he was a kid.

She looked at him for a moment, surprised, then took his face between her hands and kissed him.

Louie said, "I bet you ain't had a good-looking guy kiss—" And then he stopped.

Ang came down. "Hi, Sis," Louie said. She looked at him for a moment. "Hello, Louie." It was the first time she had spoken to him since he had come out of jail.

Louie stayed home all day. In the late afternoon he went down to the poolroom, but turned and walked out right away. Then he went and lay on the grass in the park. It was almost dark when he felt like going home. He stopped at one of the landscaped flower beds and, looking all around to see that none of the park officials were behind any of the neighboring trees, cut long stalks of gladiolas. He used the deer-foot knife.

He walked to the lagoon to wash his hands, and laid the flowers down alongside him. It was a good idea, so he pulled off his shoes and socks and let his feet dangle in the water. As he sat there he tossed the knife up in the air so that it came down blade-point in the grass. Then he put it on the back of his hand and slapped his hand and made the knife again stick in the ground. Then, as deftly as he had done that, he took the knife, broke the blade over his knee and threw both parts in the lagoon.

He put on his shoes and went home.

He hid them behind his back, then brought them out with a grin and, gesturing awkwardly with them, said, "I brought you broads some flowers."

"How nice of you, Louie," Rosemary said.

"Do you want to eat now, Louie?" Ang asked.

"Humph!" Aunt Rosa said. "Ain't we a little too old for you to be bringing us flowers?"

They had eaten, and Ang and Rosemary were gathering up the dishes, when Ma Romano came out of her room. Just in her night-gown. "The boys are sleeping," she announced.

"Look, Ma. Come here," Louie said, very gently. "Sit down." He drew up a chair for her, next to him, with one of his long legs.

She sat down, smoothing the skirt of her nightgown primly and smiling up at him. Louie put his arm around the back of her chair. "Look, Ma—" He took his arm away and turned from her, hugging his knees and putting his forehead down on his arms. He turned back to her. "Look, Ma." Clumsily he tried to brush her hair back off her forehead with his clumsy palm. "Ma . . ." He gestured helplessly with his hand, making several circles in the air. "They're dead." He turned on the seat of the chair, toward her. "D-e-a-d, Ma. Don't you understand?"

For a moment her eyes held terror.

"My boys dead?"

Then she smiled at him. "Louie! You're such a joker!" She slapped at him playfully, childishly. "Why, I just put them to bed. Don't be foolish."

As Louie's arms came up in a gesture of helplessness his mother's hand rumpled his hair and she said, "I'm going right now to see about them."

She went into the bedroom and, after a brief moment, stuck her head past the door. "They're both sleeping," she said. She closed the bedroom door.

"Yeah, sleeping, all right," Louie said. "Say Aunt Rosa, what about a two-handed game of pinochle?"

"You're on, boy!" Aunt Rosa said. "Want to make any bets?"

They started playing. From inside the bedroom door Ma Romano's voice carried, singing a lullaby as if it were a dirge.

Ang walked to the window and looked out. "Oh, I wish she would stop that . . . stop . . . stop . . . stop . . ."

"Get yourself a cold bottle of beer out of the icebox," Aunt Rosa said, putting down a card. "I brought some home."

They played, and Aunt Rosa beat him three games straight before he won one. They played some more. Then, the cards still spread on the table, Louie suddenly got up. "Hey, Aunt Rosa—"

He didn't say anything for a while. He took one of the gladiolas out of the water pitcher where Aunt Rosa had put them and held it like a sword. He squinted down the blade. He made several swipes at a fly. Then, "Do me a favor, will you? Bring that kid over—you know"—and turning his face from the rest of the family, gesturing a touché with the gladiola—"Nick's son."

Ang walked to the window and wept, her back turned to them.

Saturday afternoon Aunt Rosa stopped by for Nick. He was sketching. Nellie looked again at her with frightened eyes. Aunt Rosa said, "Here, honey, I brought you something," and handed her a box of candy. To Nick she said, "Your Uncle Louie told me he wanted to see you."

Nick flushed with pleasure. "Can we go now?"

"Sure. Why not?"

"I'll be back before dark, Mother."

They all fussed over Nick. Louie said, "Let's take a walk. There's too many dames around here."

They walked under cottonwood trees and past slum houses, past corner taverns and grocery stores, down a hot summer sidewalk. Nick glanced often at his uncle, in admiration. Just like my father in the picture on the wall.

"Where do you live, Nick?"

Nick told him.

"What do you want to be?"

"An artist."

"Well! Ain't that something!" Louie said. He threw a friendly arm over Nick's shoulders. "A Romano an artist! That's great, kid! Say, I'll be rooting for you, and some day I'll probably be asking for your autograph. How'd you like that?"

Nick grinned and couldn't find anything to say. Louie slapped him on the back. "You got a girl?"

"Well—sort of. I wish she was!"

"I'd like to meet her."

"We're painting in the woods next Sunday. Do you want to go with us?"

"Are you sure you want me along?"

"Sure!"

"Hey, I'll race you to the corner and buy you a soda."

They ran down to the corner and went into the drug store and had a soda. Then Louie said, "I want to show you something."

He led Nick into a playground and to the long, high children's slide. "Watch this!" he said, mounting, and slid down, letting out a blood-curdling howl. "Now you!" And Nick slid down too.

Louie was at the bottom to topple him over, and they lay on the ground for a while. Then Louie took him to the bars so that they could chin themselves. But Nick wasn't any good at it, so Louie pulled off his shirt and stood on his hands, walked on them, his body arched muscularly in the air, his curly brown-black hair hanging down. "Now you!"

"I can't!" Nick said.

"It's easy! I'll show you how."

Louie held Nick's legs aloft and together, and Nick tried, taking two or three steps on his hands before collapsing. They tried again, and Louie, holding Nick's legs high, asked, "How did you like your father?"

Nick tried to look up into Louie's face, but he couldn't with his legs above his head like that. All he knew was that his mother had told him he was good and then that he was bad.

"I didn't know him," Nick said; blood was running to his head fast from being upside-down so long. "My mother said he was a good man," he shouted.

"Sure he was!" Louie said.

And Sunday he went with them to the woods where they were going to paint. "This is my Uncle Louie!" Nick told Barbara proudly when she met them at the drug store near her house.

"Hello, Louie."

They shook hands and all had a soda.

"We'll have to take the streetcar," Nick told Louie apologetically.

"I'll steal a car," Louie said jokingly.

They set their canvases up near a river, having decided what they wanted to paint. Louie watched for an hour, then said, "Say! This is kind of monotonous," and went over in the grass and fell asleep.

Hours later Nick prodded him awake. "Uncle Louie!" And then, "Gee, I've got so many uncles! I want you to meet all of them."

Louie stretched and turned on his stomach and stretched again. "Yeah. But don't call me uncle. Just call me Louie. Now let's go look at the art."

Louie said, forthright, "I like yours, Barbara, but I don't understand Nick's. That don't look like a river to me."

Barbara said, "Well, Nick's a better painter. Maybe that's why it's hard to understand right away. I just do it for fun."

"I was trying an abstraction," Nick said apologetically.

And they ate. They talked, lying on their stomachs, faces in a circle. "You and Nick ought to paint me," Louie said, "I'm good-looking." Then he was ashamed. Now he was sorry about his looks.

"Yes, you're good-looking," Barbara said. "Do you think it matters?"

And it was time to go home, and Louie said, "I'll take the stuff," and carried both their paint boxes, staggering, pretending they were very heavy. And on the streetcar he made them sit together on the seat in front of him. He sat with his feet propped up and his hat on the back of his head, and he sang loudly, his voice carrying the length of the car.

People turned around to look, frowning as they turned; and then they saw him.

They smiled. He was young. He was good-looking.

Nick felt glad to have Barbara's shoulder touching his and to be with his uncle who looked like his father. He said to Barbara, "Gee, I like my uncle. He's just like my father."

87

And back to the library. A fascination and a horror seemed to draw him back.

PRETTY BOY ROMANO

GETS ELECTRIC CHAIR

A photograph of Nick. And a caption underneath:

> Pretty Boy Romano collecting bet
> of a package of cigarettes from bail-
> iff in court today. "I win. You owe
> me a pack of cigarettes," Romano
> said, in a cocky, almost amused
> tone.

Louie sat looking down at himself on the yellowing front page of the newspaper.

> Walking into court in a new brown
> suit with his curly black hair neatly
> combed, Nick (Pretty Boy) Ro-
> mano smiled broadly and looked
> around the courtroom . . .

PRETTY BOY GETS STAY

SUPREME COURT SAYS
PRETTY BOY MUST DIE

NO REPRIEVE: ROMANO DIES FRIDAY

RUTHLESS KILLER GOES TO CHAIR UNSHAKEN

Louie went down the steps of the library. He stood in the glare of the noonday sun, not knowing where he wanted to go, letting his legs decide for him. Nick, his brother, had become a strange, a tragic, even majestic figure to him. And he saw his family as it was. Not to be held in contempt by him, but a group, chilled to the bone by the pain of the things that had been, warmed around the table lamp because they had suffered and they had stood together. And Ang. Aunt Rosa had told him her tragedy too. Ma. Poor Ma! She had been all right. And then both Nick and Julian being killed, and so close together.

His eyes were filled with tears. He saw a door and he entered.

He sat down at a table. Then he looked around. He saw a white linen cloth, roses in a narrow-necked vase, and candles burning on the table. What am I doing in this fancy joint?

A waitress approached him.

"Yes, sir?"

"What about a drink, baby?" he said.

"Are you planning to have lunch, sir?"

"No, just a bottle of beer."

"I'm very sorry but we do not serve drinks without meals."

"I ain't hungry."

Her lips quivered in the smallest of smiles. "Sorry, sir."

"Okay! You win!" he said. "Give me a club sandwich."

"Potato salad, cole slaw or potato chips?"

"You make up my mind for me." He waved her away.

Gee, I need a drink. Lousy dump! And as she moved away to fill his order he looked at her curiously and casually and from a short distance.

She brought the beer, well iced, wrapped in a paper napkin, a vaselike glass to drink it from, also iced.

He finished the beer and wanted another, and the girl hadn't even showed up with his sandwich. Lousy service in these fancy dumps!

He looked up angrily. First he noticed her hips and how she walked, moving toward him with the sandwich. Then he looked up at her face. He stared at her with unbroken attention. For the first time he saw her. He kept staring at her.

She set the sandwich before him, and a damask napkin.

"Thank you."

He watched her moving back to the little group of idle waitresses near the service counter, all of them prim and pretty in white starched uniforms with lace collars and cuffs.

Something was happening inside of him. Some new something.

Still staring at her he took a bite out of the sandwich.

He gestured and she came over. "Another beer—please."

When she brought it he said, "Working here long?"

"For a while."

"Do you live near here?"

She flushed and didn't answer.

"What is your name?"

"Sorry, sir, we are not allowed to converse with the customers."

"Ho!"

She moved back to the group of other waitresses. He half finished the sandwich and gulped his beer. Then he raised his hand in a signal.

She came reluctantly. "Something wrong, sir?"

"Yeah. It's wrong that you don't talk to me."

She walked away without replying.

He finished and left a big tip for her.

As he walked out the other girls were looking at him.

But she wasn't.

88

He kept going back to the tearoom. The first time he sat at the same table and she waited on him. He was polite and didn't try to talk to her; just looked at her and tried to catch her eye. No luck. The other times that he went in she was waiting on other tables; and when, in turn, he moved to them, she was working at the far end of the quiet, leaded-windowed room. "Where's the other waitress?" he asked the girl who waited on him. "Her service station has been changed." She looked at him coolly.

The waitresses were all sore at him:

"Hump!"

"Here he comes again!"

"You'd think—" She didn't say what you'd think.

"After all—!"

Even the colored woman who washed dishes came to stare when he entered, and was mad at him too. "After all—!"

And Louie sat with another and another club sandwich, changing from potato salad to cole slaw to potato chips, and a bottle of beer, day after day, looking across the room at her. He wanted to talk to her—more than to anybody he had ever known or seen. He didn't know why. He just wanted to.

If she was aware that he entered every day and sat looking at her, she gave no indication of it.

He waited outside. He waited a long time. At last the only lights burning were the night light and those in the kitchen. The waitresses left in little friendly groups of two and three. And then she came.

Alone.

He accosted her under a lamppost. "Hello."

"Oh!" She put her hand up to her throat.

"Please talk to me a minute."

Her hand was still at her throat. "You," she said.

"Will you talk to me?"

She moved around him and continued down Michigan Boulevard. He followed alongside her.

"Please!" he said.

"Leave me alone," she said.

They came to the second lamppost. There was a small stone on the sidewalk and he kicked it with his foot. He followed her. When he caught up to the pebble he kicked it again.

"Please," he said.

"If you don't stop bothering me I'm going to call a policeman," she said.

"Talk to me for just a minute."

"Go away!"

"I won't bother you. I won't hurt you."

They were under the next lamppost.

"I—I'm colored," she said.

"Do you think I can't tell that?" he asked roughly.

He looked at her cinnamon skin and her bee-stung lips.

She stopped walking. They stood under this lamppost. Standing on her high heels, one hand suddenly on her hip, she looked up at him and said somewhat bitterly, "What are you trying to do—change your luck?"

He flushed. "What do you mean?"

He knew. He knew . . . in the neighborhood they'd say, Go to bed with a nigger and change your luck. The gang used to go sometimes to the colored whorehouse. The pimps would eye them narrowly, with evilness lurking behind the look. The girls: What the hell. A man's a man, in our book, none of them amounts to a shake of a stick. Whatever color. Except one. The money's the thing that counts. For the one. Mechanical action and metallic money. Next!

He remembered all the nasty sayings of his friends: Dark meat. Change your luck.

"Go away," she said again.

Instead he followed her. They were at the next lamppost. He put his broad, square hands on it, jumped down from the curb, jumped up the other side and faced her.

"Come on!" he pleaded, his dark brown eyes looking at her.

"Please don't bother me!"

She tried to brush past him. He would have only a minute to talk to her and she would be gone.

"My brother died in the electric chair," he said. "Now will you talk to me?"

"What?— What did you say?"

"I said now will you talk to me?"

"What do you want to talk to me about?"

"I don't know. I just wanted to talk to you."

They were walking alongside each other. His shoe found another rock and he kept kicking it along in front of them.

"All right"—she gestured with her hand—"I'll listen."

"My name's Louie," he said.

"Glad to meet you, Louie," she said, and he couldn't tell if it was irony or not.

"You're not working now," he said. "What's your name?"

"Judy."

He held out his arm like a traffic cop and she had to stop walking. Then he held out his hand.

"Hi, Judy."

"Hi."

They shook hands.

They started to walk again, but he circled back, got his pebble with the toe of his shoe and began kicking it along in front of them.

Judy shook her head in the dark. "You're strange. You're awfully strange," she said.

"Interesting?"

"I didn't say that."

"You smoke?"

She nodded yes.

He gave her one, took one himself, lit a match and held it and looked at her hair. It was an Italian cut, sculptured to her head, with little tufts turning up about her face and as black as hair could be. It shaped and molded her face. It was like a little cap. A snug cap.

He shook his fingers where the match had burned.

She smiled slightly. He liked her smile. It was sort of sad and yet compassionate.

"You better be careful, boy," she said.

They started down the sidewalk again. "Wait!" he said. He went back to retrieve his pebble.

They walked in silence around the block, and again around the block. "We been walking around this same block for half an hour," Louie said. "Let's go have a Coke." He picked up the stone and put it in his pocket.

At the Coke bar, in a booth at the back where she wanted to sit, she looked even prettier to him.

"The service is better here," he said.

He looked at her bee-stung lips. He liked to look at her lips.

On the street outside he put his little stone on the sidewalk and again began nudging it along in front of him.

At the corner she said, "I have to catch my car. You better go." She turned from him.

He stooped down and put the rock in his pocket. "Thanks for letting me talk to you."

"You better go."

"Okay." Then he touched her lightly on the shoulders. "Stand there! Let me look at you." He looked at her and grinned. "You can bet and win that I'll see you again!" he said.

He turned and sprinted down the sidewalk.

89

On the wagon for weeks, they waited. All the time they stayed sober, just looking around for The Wolf.

The Fourth of July came. There was going to be a big dance at the Marconi Auditorium. Max said, "I know everybody's going to be there. People like, for instance, wife deserters and wife beaters or guys who beat alimony and all that. Their wives will be there with a cop and a warrant."

Phil laughed.

"No. I mean it serious," Max said. "I know damn well that that's the place all the dagos will congregate. That day, and on their special holidays, all the Italians from Indiana, Wisconsin, Michigan, they all come to that particular place."

"Yeah," Juan said. "I know goddamn well he's not going to stay away. He's *got* to come there for some reason or another."

They went to the dance. Max sat in the balcony. Juan was by the door and Seldom Seen and Phil were by the orchestra, one on each side, to watch, to make sure if The Wolf showed up. And Seldom Seen, who didn't weigh more than a hundred pounds soaking wet, was in charge of the artillery; it was his turn.

They stayed there until ten to one, watching, waiting.

They held a conference.

"He's not around."

"He musta left town."

"Let's go."

From there they went to Max's sister's house, where there was a party.

"I'd sure like a beer," Max said.

They had one beer apiece, one with the food. Then they took off.

The next day they met at the Crystal Bar and they heard the news.

The Wolf *had* been there. He'd been there with his wife and his two brothers. Ralph Pizarro was there too.

They got this from a guy who had been there:

The Wolf walked in—way after one o'clock so he wouldn't have to pay. The Wolf goes and has a drink, then he makes his way to the men's toilet and he stands by the door and he threw everybody out of the toilet—everybody. And he stepped outside.

If some guy wants to go to the crapper:

"Where you going?" Short. Sharp.

"I'm going to take a leak. I want to get by."

"Drop it!"

"What do you mean, drop it?"

"You got to pay."

"What do you mean, *pay?*"

"You *heard* me! If you want to go in there it'll cost you a quarter."

Max said, incredulous, "He was *charging* people to go in there and take a leak!"

"He was charging," the guy said.

The Wolf was charging. First he had had his drags on his weed in that same toilet, then he'd ordered them all out. If a giant had walked up to the door, The Wolf would have said, "You better drop it, buddy!"

They all paid. There was a cop at the door to see that there was peace, just in case anybody got smart.

"The cop didn't say nothing," the fellow who was telling the story said. "Because, I guess, the cop was getting a piece of it. So he didn't say a damn thing, until the committee, or whoever was in charge of the whole shebang, all the people together said, 'Hey, this isn't right!' so the cop told him to knock it off. Do you think they'd take him to jail? Naaaw!"

"I'm telling you," Max interrupted, "they're so damned scared of that lousy bastard! Everybody trembles when he walks in. He's got three killings behind him. Two that I actually saw. And they told me that before he left grammar school he knocked off a little kid. Supposedly accidental. But once you met The Wolf you knew nothing he did was accidental."

"Let me tell you the rest," the fellow said impatiently. "So he stopped, and that was when he met with Pizarro."

. . . Ramponi and Pizarro had been on many jobs together. Recently they had made a round of holdups where the both of them walked in and one guy took care of the register. And The Wolf was the man, the money man, the cashier, or the bank. Pizarro just covered the entry and the retreat. "We'll meet some other place. Count it. Split it."

After the last few stick-ups The Wolf had taken off completely—with the bank.

This was their first meeting since then.

"Ho, big man!" Pizarro said. "So you did the disappearing act, uh?"

"Something like that he said," the fellow continued. "And The Wolf's there with his whole damn family—about twelve of them, man! Anyways, Ralphie's just there with his brother. Ralphie Pizarro's got this older brother who is a ex-pug. A stick-up man now. A beautiful—I mean, that is, if you admire stick-up men, ah—like you admire bullfighters or baseball players, you'd say Tex was the coolest man you ever saw when it comes to making a stick-up. Never smiled at nobody. Nobody ever saw him smile. I don't think his mother even saw him smile. Well, he was there, anyway, by the time this happened. So the only friends there with Ralphie was his brother Tex and some character named Rudy. Sooo, one word leads to another and they say, 'There are too many people in here. Let's go outside.' So they go outside. They slugged it out."

The guy kept on telling the story. "And they beat the hell out of Pizarro. The Wolf, and his cousins. And I think The Wolf's wife got a few slaps in there with her purse or her heel or something. You see —at first they began to fight with fists, but Pizarro got the best of The Wolf; but later, with that crowd, every time The Wolf hit Ralph and he would go down, one of The Wolf's relatives would sneak a foot in there through the crowd and kick him, you know. At one time Ralph turned a complete flip until he was on his hands and knees, and then he was turned over in the air by a kick from one of The Wolf's cousins. Man, it was something! In other words, he wasn't fighting just The Wolf. He was fighting the whole damn family. And

Rudy tried to get in to help Ralph but they told Rudy you—you get out of here. So Rudy ain't much of a fighter. You know Rudy. He's very handsome and he don't want to get his features lifted—so he took off."

The guy stopped to light a cigarette, continued, "Then The Wolf peeled his knife. He got to cutting Ralph when he was down, see— he jumped on him and started cutting him. He hit him across the cheek with the knife and he split his face all the way to the cheek-bone. Meanwhile, all the time the cousins is holding Pizarro's brother back; the ex-pug's got his arms pinned back. Then The Wolf starts stabbing Ralph. The Wolf, he wasn't drunk because he don't drink too much. He was high on stuff. He was high. He was so high, man, he was twisted. His eyes just dots. And you know his mouth. It got that way. Double-lipped and sneering."

"Dirty sonofabitch!" Max said.

And the guy telling the story: "You know Subway? Well, Subway is a friend of both sides. He's a friend of Ralphie and of The Wolf, and he goes up there and he tries to humor The Wolf. 'Aw, come on, Frankie boy—' because nobody would call him The Wolf to his face —they call him Frank— 'Frank, come on, I *know you* since 1935—' and tried to give him a line of bull, you know. He said, 'Subway, leave me alone! Leave me alone! Because I'll cut you too!' And he had the knife by Subway's ear. But he didn't have the whole knife, just the tip of it. He said, 'Subway, I like you. You're a nice kid. But leave me alone. 'Cause if you hold me I'm going to cut you.' Well" —and he stopped to light another cigarette—"Subway tried to grab him and said, 'Aw, come on, you're kidding.' "

The guy nodded his head. "He cut him. He give him a big scar over here—" pointing.

"Then Subway's little brother—just a kid, said, 'Look what you done to my brother! Leave him alone! That's enough!' The Wolf said, 'Jim, get out of the way. You're one of the family too,' and— boom!—he sliced him. On the arm, like this, like a half-moon. From near the elbow it was, down to the wrist. And I know it went to the bone.

"So that took care of that."

90

The Wolf took off. But he didn't leave town. The next day when Pizarro was in the hospital he sent his wife over to see him. The

Wolf's wife sat in a chair close to the bed, a thin woman with large sunken eyes and an expressive slash of red mouth, her fingers twisted together in her lap, looking more like a missionary than a stick-up man's wife.

She said, "Ah—Ralph—I want you to know that Frank says he is sorry for the—ah, little fight and misunderstanding you guys had last night. He"—she twisted her fingers again—"he wants to apologize but he's ashamed to come over here, and besides, you know— how he gets when he blows tea—too much tea—you know—ahhh— enough is all right, he can handle enough, but last night he was a little bit too far gone—anda—he, he wants to know if you'll accept this as—a sort of a, ah—get well—ahhh—token, or let's be friends."

She handed him his cut of the stick-ups plus The Wolf's cut. He had turned every bit of the winnings over to Pizarro: Let's forget about it and shake hands.

Pizarro grabbed the money. He slapped it against the palm of his hand. "Here! Here's the dough! Give it back to Frank and tell him— stick it— Tell him the next time I see him I'm going to kill him!"

She was his wife. She began to cry, sitting there by the bed. "Please, please, Ralph. Please don't talk like that."

"Putting on the tears. Trying to cop a plea, uh?" he said, laughing; and lay back in the bed panting hard.

He was all messed up. He got stabbed. He got cut in the stomach. He got cut all over the face. That was the worst part of it. He put one hand up to the bandages over his face.

She went out.

91

He stuck his head from behind a Michigan Boulevard tree.

"Did you think you had lost me?"

"You!"

"Yeah, me. You didn't think I'd let you get away, did you?"

She smiled a little.

"Coke? Same place?" he asked.

"Well—" She was a little amused, a little lonesome, a little sorry for this boy—and she didn't know why. And a little daring too.

"Well means yes," he said.

"Okay. Yes," she said.

They started down the sidewalk together.

"No stones tonight?"

"No. I got corns."

Over Cokes he said, "See, you could've won that bet."

She was suddenly very quiet and very serious, and she looked at him several times before she spoke; then she said, "Was that true what you said?"

"What?"

"Nothing."

"Sure it's true! Do you want dates? Do you want to look it up in the papers?"

She touched his wrist fleetingly. He looked where she had touched; and up at her. "Go with me, Judy."

She lowered her eyes and her white teeth went over her full bottom lip for a moment. "Look," she said, "you're nice-looking and all that, but it just won't work."

"I could say I'm lonesome. I'm lost." The clear brown eyes looked at her. Then he grinned. "That would be corny."

"Awfully corny," Judy said, looking at her fingernails.

"It's true."

"A good-looking—I almost said white boy, that would be impolite —boy like you."

"It's true, Judy."

"Look here, boy," she said.

He liked that; the slight southern drawl, Negro dialect, whatever you want to call it.

He looked at her. And kept looking.

"I think it's true," Judy said.

Louie said, "I made my confession. Now tell me about you."

"Nothing much to tell. I went three years to college—in New York—": That was vain. Sure it was vain. I wanted it to be that way. Does he think he can pick me up just like that, like some cheap girl— colored, in this instance—to go to bed with?

"I need you, Judy," Louie said.

She smiled a little. When she smiled her eyes closed down a little. Gee, her eyes were black! And he noticed that her lashes pointed down over them instead of turning up. They threw long shadows over her cheekbones.

She said, jokingly, "Do you tell that to all the girls?"

"Only to you so far."

"You mean you don't want to sleep with me?"

"It doesn't have to be that way. I like to be with you. I like to look at you."

"Oh!" And then, poisonously, "All male Negroes want to sleep with white females, it says right here in 'Negro-White relations—

U.S.A.' Isn't it true when you turn it around the other way, or when you divide and then multiply you don't get the same answer?" She stopped. She put her hand on top of his. "I'm sorry, Louie, that was nasty."

He looked and kept looking at the quick, fluttering beat of the pulse in her throat.

"Go with me, Judy."

"It wouldn't work."

"You mean Society wouldn't approve?"

"It just wouldn't work."

"There have to be some rebels."

Somebody had put a coin in the juke box and a song was playing. At first they weren't aware of it. Then, first subconsciously and a little later consciously, they were aware of the words:

> We could make believe I love you
> Only make believe that you love me
> Others find peace of mind in pre-tend-ing
> Couldn't you, couldn't I, couldn't we?
> Make believe . . .

"That's an oldie," Louie said.

Then they didn't say anything for a while. Instead Louie went to the counter. She watched him go. She looked at him as he stood at the counter, curly hair, handsome square face, warm Italian coloring.

He came back with hamburgers and malted milks. He winked at her and slid the tray onto the table.

"Oh, look!" he said, feeling in his pocket. "I brought you something."

He laid a small silver pencil on the table in front of her. "That's so you won't keep breaking the point on your pencil like when you were waiting on me." And, grinning, "I don't ever want another club sandwich! That's all I could afford with the prices you charge! Why are they so high—to pay for them flowers and candles?"

Her eyes had misted when she looked down at the pencil, but now she looked up, surprised at his words, and laughed.

He leaned over and deliberately, afraid, though, that she would repulse him, tapped his thumb against one of her fingernails. "If you'd give me your address," he said, "I'd hang around in front of your house."

"You wouldn't like it," Judy said. "My grandmother smokes a pipe. My mother sings spirituals."

"Say, my mother's nuts!" Louie said. "You don't believe that, huh?"

Judy looked at her watch. "I've got to go home."

"Let me take you home."

"I can't."

"Why?"

"I can't. I just can't," she said half angrily.

"Boy friend, uh? I'll compete. Let me compete. Let me take you home."

"Louie—" she said, "do you think—"

"I like your hair," he said, "I like the way you've got it cut."

"Louie—Louie—Louie—"

"You like that name, huh?"

She had to smile. "Yes, I like that name. Once upon a time I had a boy friend by that name and he had green hair, but where I lived all the people had blue hair and—and that's why you can't take me home."

"I'll get a sun tan."

"Don't be nasty."

"I'm sorry."

"I want to pay my half of the bill, Louie."

"Don't be silly."

"No, really. I want to. I don't think it's right for a girl to—"

"If you let me take you home."

That made the tears rise in her eyes. She leaned forward. "Look, Louie," she said, "please listen carefully." She looked away and ran a fingernail slowly along the edge of the table, her eyes carefully following it as she spoke. "Do you think I can take you into that neighborhood? Do you know what everybody would say? Do you think I could get married?"

"Do you want to get married?"

"Of course. Every girl does sometime. You're not listening."

"Yes, I am. And I still like your hair. I like your eyes too. But most of all I like your lips. No, most of all I like you."

"Listen to me." Her voice was shaking. But she looked at him and her eyes forced him to look back. She said, "No decent fellow would ever want to marry me. They'd all think—well, you know what they'd think— And they'd all be making nothing but nasty, dirty passes at me every time I walked down the street."

He took her to the car line. "Same tree tomorrow night?" he asked.

"All right."

He helped her onto the streetcar and then hung onto the back platform, hanging there as the car started and gradually gained momentum. "I'll hang by my tail!" he shouted at her, let go of the streetcar railing and dropped down to the cobblestones.

92

They continued to see each other. For the first time he was afraid of a girl. He was always shy with her, half afraid even to put his arm around her. Afraid of being repulsed. With other girls he would just have grabbed them and kissed them—and he had always gotten away with it.

Somehow this was different. And he hadn't had the desire to be with another girl since he had met Judy.

"You're too good for me," he said.

"Who's too good for whom?" she said.

They sat on a park bench. "Just let me hold you close."

"People are looking."

"I don't care."

He moved over closer to her, put his arm around her. She didn't say don't. "Thanks, Judy," he said.

And they sat and it was night.

"I've got to kiss you, Judy."

"Well, what's stopping you?"

And she couldn't realize or believe that he liked her and wanted nothing.

"Where shall we go?"

Where could they go?

"They may not serve us."

"People will look at us."

"I don't care."

They could eat or drink on Michigan Boulevard. They could be college students or lovers. People wouldn't care. Or if some of them did, it wouldn't matter much. Most people wouldn't even pay any attention. But to go to Clark Street cafeterias, or shabby cocktail lounges there on the side streets leading from Michigan to Clark, was another story. There'd be dirty looks, or sneers; maybe open insults.

"Let's go out to the South Side."

"No, Louie. We better not."

"To a colored place."

"No."

And yet they continued to see each other. It was a challenge to both of them, this relationship of theirs. Like everything that is "sinful" or "wrong."

She smiled at him. The innocent brown stare of his eyes met hers. He squeezed her arm.

There are different answers for different people. This was his answer.

A month. And every night they saw each other. A walk. A Coke. Long talks.

And they were on this joking basis.

"Listen, colored girl—"

"Listen, white boy—"

Two months. And two kisses in all that time.

"Here, hold my hat."

She took it.

"Look!" he said. He sprinted down the street to the next lamp-post, grabbed it with his hands and hung there, waiting for her, feet propped against the post, his body a stiff angle.

She caught up with him and pulled him down. "Oh, you fool! You fool!" she said, laughing.

She still held his hat. He put his arm around her shoulders and leaned on her. "I'm drunk," he said, walking unsteadily down the street a few steps. "Drunk with you."

She stopped and handed him his hat. Then she put her hands over her face and started to cry. "I love you," she said through her fingers.

He pulled her hands down. "Does that make you cry?" he asked roughly. They kissed.

"Let's have fun!" he said. "Let's go to a colored night club."

"All right."

They walked in. Negro eyes picked them up. First casually. Then in various types of concentration. The music was loud and sensual and definitely Negro-style. People danced, rubbing their bodies together. Glasses and bottles of liquor and setups stood on red-checkered tablecloths, the tables pushed close together.

Louie took Judy's arm and steered her toward one of the front tables at the foot of the tiny bandstand. Two dark girls saw Louie and brightened up, their teeth white flashes in their dark faces, red lips pulled away in smiles. "That chick done caught herself something mighty fine!" one of them said.

"She sure has, white meat!"

The other girl shrugged. "You never can tell." Then she brightened again. "Good-looking, ain't he!"

"Not like some of them ofays come here with race girls. All broken down and beaten up and looking like something the cat dragged in," the other girl said. "No wonder their own kind don't want them."

"You right, girl," and, like all women, leaning out, looking Judy over from head to foot, legs last, in a slow, appraising stare. "That little hooker's built."

Judy and Louie drank, danced, sat holding hands over the table; Louie relieved to be alone with her somewhere where there were four walls and he could dance, hold her close, feel the tickling, slightly itching touch of her hair against his cheek, look at her.

It was a place where the dance floor was so small that you could hardly find room for your feet; where the tables were shoved so close together, they could have been one large table. People were spilling over onto each other. Shoulders touched or knees touched. A woman's shoulder-strap purse was in the small of your back. You heard each other's conversations.

At the next table the two couples had already noticed them. They leaned together, whispering, often glancing in their direction. And once when Louie and Judy happened to glance over, the big black woman in the evening gown smiled quickly at them; but the little yellow man with the mustache and glasses, who looked like a doctor, turned his eyes away, and the other couple just went on staring, unfriendly.

At the table behind them a young Negro sat alone. Drunk, or only angry, he said, loud enough for them to hear, ". . . white." And a little later, ". . . white bastard," just loud enough for them to hear.

He was on his home field, in his own ball park. He had been pushed around in theirs.

Louie flushed a little and looked at Judy. He could tell that she, too, had heard. "Shall we dance, honey?"

They got up to dance. When they came back the Negro had his foot stuck out just far enough. Louie stumbled over it.

"Sorry, man," Louie said, "it's awfully dark in here." He put his hand on the Negro's shoulder in apology.

The Negro looked at him and didn't say anything. But he brushed off the shoulder of his suit where Louie's hand had touched.

Louie and Judy sat down again. They pretended nothing had happened. Louie smiled and held his glass to touch it against hers.

The Negro said, more loudly now, ". . . white trash"; and, ". . . picking up our girls."

Judy had her back to him. She turned, facing him, and said, "He's colored just like us."

The Negro was genuinely sorry. He leaned over to their table.

" 'Scuse me, man," he said, "I thought you was one of them ofays."

Louie laughed; and his eyes held Judy's. Some of her hurt went into him. He understood a little better now. Still looking deep into her eyes, he said to the Negro, "It's all right. Why don't you have a drink with us?"

"Well—if you and your girl don't mind, man, because I want to apologize good. After all, I insulted you."

Louie pulled out a chair and the Negro came over to their table. "Us niggahs are getting to look more and more like them white folks every day. You take Walter White," the Negro said. "You passing for white when you ain't with your people?"

"Yeah," Louie said.

Judy looked at him, her eyes misty.

"That's the only way to get a good job," the Negro said. "Fight fire with fire."

"Yeah," Louie said.

"Go be white," the Negro said, "if you can. In the white man's world."

A week later Judy told him that she had a friend, a Japanese man who was married to a colored girl. A man she had known at college. "They give parties up at their place. They live in the colored district and they have people in. Mixed couples. They have open house every Sunday. Would you like to go? I think we might—might have a good time."

Even in the taxi they were a little embarrassed—as if they were doing something wrong—and sat not too close together. Not like sweethearts. Who knows taxi drivers? Do they think like most of the rest of them who say we shouldn't be sitting here together? That there's something immoral? That even if we paid our way in this public vehicle we must act as strangers?

They rode through the night, moving past other cars in the cabbie's greedy pursuit; lights turned red-green-green-red; and they spoke softly to each other. Louie tried to take her hand and she slowly withdrew it. Their eyes met in the rear-view mirror, both looking to see if the driver had seen.

It was a luxuriously furnished apartment. The Japanese husband was a technical engineer, his wife a public accountant. The group was composed of mixed couples only—their special and apart club—most of them married. A Puerto Rican and his blond wife. A Jewish girl secretly married to a Gentile and still living home with her parents. Cuban, Negro; Jew, Gentile.

They had to be careful outside. Only now, entering the house, taking off their coats, smiling and greeting each other; holding cocktail glasses, listening to records, dancing, talking together about little trifling things, and things like books, classical music, concerts, politics; buffet snack later—in this little oasis of bookcase and chairs, phonograph, cocktail table and wall photographs, refilling glasses, talking together, each marked the same, each marked by one thing— only now could they smile and be themselves.

They talked intellectually. They had fun, or tried to. They really couldn't—or, rather, could only for that short while. They were freed people, chained together in an isolation.

The city waited outside.

"Have a good time?" Judy asked him.

"They talked over my head!" Louie complained; and, "Say, you like barbecued ribs!— Look, there's a sign down there on the corner!"

"All colored folks like barbecued ribs," Judy told him.

"Listen, colored girl—" he said.

"Listen, white boy—" she said. And she put her chin down against his arm.

Chewing on ribs, his white teeth biting, face showing hard dimples, he moved his eyes to her. "I'm going to see you tomorrow?"

"No."

"Yes, I am."

"I can't, Louie. I promised my brother I'd come to see him play baseball for his high school."

"I'm going with you."

"No."

"I'll pretend I don't know you."

The next day he stumbled over people's feet in the stands for half an hour. Then at last he saw her. He squeezed in next to her, getting a dirty look from the girl he had forced to make room for him.

Judy looked up at him.

"Which is your brother?" he asked.

"The real black one," she said, pointing.

"I'm colored just like you are," he said.

She put her head down against his shoulder.

93

They were still laying for The Wolf. It was already late fall. Then one day someone said, "The Wolf was here last night!"

Max turned grim. "Oh yeah," he said, softly, quietly.

Then, thinking: Like a little fairy story. The Wolf came, you know. The sheep all hidden, and all that bullshit. He tried to remember the end of Little Red Riding Hood and found himself laughing.

When they went around to see the proof, all they had to do was walk up to the corner and there they could see that all the windows in the tavern were out. The Wolf had been around—and evidently he had had an argument with somebody in the tavern and they had either asked him to leave or he had left of his own accord.

So they knew he had been around.

Two days later, in the early afternoon, Max and Juan and Seldom Seen came down Pacific Avenue after playing handball. Now that they weren't drinking, they played handball or catch in the afternoons when they weren't working. Max had a girl who lived on the second floor of a tenement in the neighborhood, and he was going up there to take a shower.

"Come on up," he said.

"No. I'll wait here," Juan said.

"Well, I'll be right out. It won't take me more than fifteen minutes."

He and Seldom Seen went up.

Juan stood waiting and smoking a cigarette. Then, all of a sudden, as if something had directed his eyes, he looked across the street and there was *The Wolf!*

The Wolf was standing one door north of the barber shop, on a little stairway. He was wearing a white T-shirt. He was handsome, with his belt pulled tight, his thin waist, his enormous shoulders.

There he was, standing out there throwing pennies at a bunch of little neighborhood kids and making them fight over them. "Don't anybody pick up a penny unless you beat the hell out of somebody or hit somebody, at least. First hit somebody and then go for the pennies."

The kids were kicking hell out of each other and picking up

pennies. And The Wolf standing there; "Ho! Ho! Ho!" in this big, loud horse laugh.

Juan turned and ran up the steps.

"He's in the bathroom," Max's girl said. "He'll be right out."

"Tell him to hurry up! Max! Max!"

She went to knock on the door but Juan beat her there. "Hey, Max! The Wolf! Right across the street! The Wolf! Big as hell!"

Seldom Seen stood up. The bathroom door was flung open. "Where! Where!" Max wanted to run out.

"Get some clothes on, Max. Take it easy!"

Max went back to hurriedly pull on shirt and pants, put on his shoes without lacing them.

Seldom Seen stood looking out the window. "Hurry, Max!"

Juan went and stood alongside Seldom Seen. The Wolf was still there, throwing pennies.

Their eyes hardened on him.

It is the middle of the day.

Autumn.

The sun is still out brightly, warming things.

Juan and Seldom Seen saw a car pull up. The car pulled up and stopped and someone got out of it. They recognized him right away as Ralph Pizarro.

The first time they have met since The Wolf knifed him.

The Wolf made no effort to run away.

He's still throwing pennies.

Pizarro is standing not too close to him. The Wolf is about three steps up the stairway, pennies in his hand, shaking them, casually, as if they were a pair of dice. Pizarro is between him and the car. The car is parked right at the curb, right in front of the house, right in front of the stairway where The Wolf stands. Pizarro is right in the middle of the sidewalk, not too close to the car, just between the car and The Wolf.

The window is closed and Juan and Seldom Seen cannot hear what they are saying, but they are pointing their fingers at each other and a lot of talking is going on.

Finally Pizarro walks away, turns, points his finger again. The finger seems to say, "I'll be right back, you sonofabitch! You wait right there."

And into the car.

"I'll be right back!"

So okay.

The Wolf throws pennies.

Max comes bursting out of the bathroom. He is dressed. Now he has his shirt on, unbuttoned, his pants and his shoes, a towel wrapped around his hand. Within the towel he has the gun.

"No. Drop the towel," Juan said, and Max put the gun into his pants. "Let's go!"

"Wait! Wait!" Juan says. "Pizarro was just here talking to him. Wait a while. Let's wait and see what happens."

"Noooo!"

Juan is blocking the stairway. Blocking Max and Seldom Seen, trying to wrestle with Max and—

Just then Pizarro's car pulled up.

And this time Pizarro isn't driving. His brother, the ex-pug, is driving.

And The Wolf has been there all the time.

He don't care for nothing.

He's just there, still throwing pennies.

He doesn't have a gun. Only when he goes on stick-ups. But he always carries a knife.

The car pulls up.

Juan is saying, "Wait, wait, Max! Let's see what they do. If they don't take care of him, then we will walk across the street and take care of the guy."

The car pulls up. Pizarro gets out. He holds a forty-five in his hand. He lifts it in The Wolf's direction. The gun turns and looks, like a sleepy dog.

Pizarro walks to the middle of the sidewalk and starts pumping lead into The Wolf.

No talking.

No nothing.

The talk has been done already.

Just business.

Just blasting.

And he emptied the gun into him.

At the time there was a strike going on down the street at the shirt factory, and people were used to seeing men go back and forth, pulling up in cars with rifles and guns on their sides, hoods protecting the scabs, and so when they heard shooting they were only mildly surprised. But there was a family that had just moved into the neighborhood above the barber shop a couple of days before, and one of the girls stuck her head out of the window and started to scream.

Pizarro said, "Get back in there," and pointed the gun at her. Then the gun looked at The Wolf again.

The girl didn't faint but she did a fast disappearance. The next day they moved away from there.

The gun looked at The Wolf—

Juan is holding Max back. "Take it easy. The guy got it already. Let's see what happens."

:Un-un.

He's fighting to get out of there.

When the gun first looked, when The Wolf saw Pizarro with the gun, he immediately peeled his knife, his blubbery lip sneering, and, blade open, started toward Pizarro.

But it was too late.

He was shot at two times by the time he raised his arm. But he made it. He made one step down and then he lost co-ordination. Then all Pizarro had to do was to empty the gun into him. The Wolf falls flat on his face.

. . . this is it. He saw a little park. A woman with her child. And dandelions. Gray-headed dying dandelions. Regret is a long-time thing. His white teeth were biting at the sidewalk, looking for succor. "Ma . . . ma."

And so passed The Wolf.

And Pizarro nonchalantly walked to his car, got in, said, "Okay. Don't even speed away."

They strolled away.

And Max breaks away from Juan. He and Seldom Seen clatter down the steps, Juan following them.

Max ran across the street. Max looked down at The Wolf. He was bouncing up and down, lying on his face, his midsection bouncing. Max looked down: Like a snake bouncing. As if he was laying somebody.

And Max put the gun to his head.

Juan saw; and knew you can't miss a man from here up to there and he's dead already.

Just as Juan kicked Max's arm, the gun went off and a big cement chip of the sidewalk flew off and scattered away. "Man, don't be crazy!" Juan shouted. "That sonofabitch is going to die anyway. Why should we get the rap for it? You know Ralph killed him. He'll die. He'll die. I'm sure he'll die."

So they took off through the alleys, Seldom Seen kicking The Wolf as he ran by.

They circled the block and came back; watching from Max's girl's window, they could see where The Wolf was lying—nobody had come out to look at him. Nobody would come out, they thought.

But they were wrong. Finally . . . little by little . . . a lot of people came out. A lot of them.

There was an old, gray-haired Irish woman. She seemed to have known him since he was six years old and she said, "Oh, Frank, they finally got you! May God have pity on your soul." Then she spat on him. "You sonofabitch! You had it coming!"

People came from the surrounding neighborhoods, as word spread that The Wolf was dead. They all came down, and they all looked at him, and then they were sure he was dead.

He was dead all right.

The little boys who had been chasing the pennies were the first ones back after he was shot. Why should they be afraid? They were his friends. He wasn't going to hurt them.

"Those little characters ain't afraid of nothing," Max grunted from his girl's window.

And the little boys were saying: "Oh, look at the hole, look at the blood coming out."

And Max from the window: "You have to watch those little bastards. Little animals. That's all they are."

The police came. Photographs were taken. The Wolf's family was notified. His wife came over. "Frankie! Frankie! Frankie!"

And Max at the window: Big joke. She's putting on a good act. After all, it's her husband and all that, her husband by the church, but I bet inside herself she's saying, "You sonofabitch, I'm glad you're gone!"

Max turned into the room and said to the rest of them, "When he died he cried like a sonofabitch, cried for his mama!"

The city came for the body.

It was just as if you found a dead dog in an alley and you cleaned up—that was all.

94

Everybody saw who killed him. It was broad daylight.

Ralph Pizarro went to his night job at the usual time. They picked him up at work. A suspect. They questioned him and they let him go. Then they picked him up again.

So what did he have?

"I have a car. Here, sell it and it's yours. And I got eight hundred dollars in the bank. And you can have that too. Forget about it."

Factory strike, you know. Yes, factory strike.

They didn't make a fuss about it.

Nobody made a fuss about it.

That took care of that.

There are a lot of unsolved murders in a big city like Chicago.

95

They had the wake. A lot of hoodlums and weedheads showed up. Hoodlums who admired stick-up men. Reefer smokers he had partied with or sold to. They talked in quiet corners, about his smooth jobs and about how much weed he could blow in a single day. They took bottles out of their pockets and took big slugs and there was a peculiar smell in the room.

Max, Phil, Seldom Seen and Juan went out of pleasure. They wanted to see the guy in his casket. "Oh, yeah, yeah. That's right. Too bad." Inside they were still mad, and as soon as they got out of there they'd go pick up Judge Sullivan and Norm and get drunk.

The father came into the room, a beaten man. They had caught him broke. He said, "Since my son passed away"—he didn't use the words got killed—"I haven't taken my shoes off. I've been running here and there making arrangements, and I haven't got money enough for the funeral. I'm trying to make up a collection and—"

He took it very bad. He said, "Somehow I feel I've failed my son."

In another part of the room one of The Wolf's aunts was crying, and people said, "Don't cry. He's better off." They said this guardedly and quietly.

The aunt said, "I'm not crying because he's dead. I'm glad! I'm happy!"

And the father said, "I'm trying to make up a collection—and I haven't got anything to mark the grave with. I thought I'd ask you people if you think this is worthy of his grave. Please excuse me a minute. I'll go in here and get it."

He came back into the room with a beautiful cross he had made out of wood and tin, beautifully engraved.

"Do you think this is worthy of his grave?" he asked the assemblage piteously.

Max looked down at it: Well, Christ, if a dog had peed on a stick, that would have been worthy of his grave as far as I'm concerned.

They didn't have any pallbearers—and went around the room asking if he would serve, or he would serve.

They got three. Fellows who used to idolize him for the stick-ups and holdups he used to pull.

They asked Max. It was just what he was waiting for. "Sure, I'll volunteer."

Outside, Juan and Phil said, "Why, you crazy sonofabitch!"

Max laughed. He said, "I want to make sure that this sonofabitch *leaves!* That he won't come back any more."

They headed for a bar to get drunk, to celebrate.

Max went to the funeral. He helped carry the heavy box, thinking: So it all caught up with you, Wolf, huh?

He didn't see The Wolf's mother. If she was there, she stayed in one of the cars.

At the Crystal Bar that night he told the rest of the fellows, "Well, I saw them throw dirt in his face. He won't be back any more."

They all drank up; and Max added, as an afterthought, "And **we** don't have to stay sober any more."

96

She had just had another fight with Rosemary and Aunt Rosa about Ma.

Ang stood in the kitchen, quietly crying, watching the tears fall down into the dishwater, fall on her arms and run away in long rivulets over her arms . . .

Ma was walking the floor in the dining room, again with the pillow in her arm, calling it Nick.

"Isn't he a pretty baby?"

Ma tickled the pillow with her finger where a baby's belly button would be. She put her face down into the pillow. "My little-bitty baby!"

"Please, Ma! Please!" Ang said. She had taken the pillow away from her mother.

Ma sat on the edge of the bed and wept like a child, her face in her hands. "Let me have my baby. Please let me have my baby back."

Rosemary came over and took the pillow away from Ang and handed it back to Ma.

Aunt Rosa said, "Damn it, Ang! You just ain't co-operative."

"Oh, please! We've got to do something!" Ang pleaded.

More tears dropped into the dishwater. She'd probably beat Ma to the insane asylum if this sort of thing didn't stop.

Why did Aunt Rosa have to treat everything so tolerantly? Like everything was a part of life and you had to accept it. Why did Rosemary have to be so superior? Because she had a good education and I didn't? Because her mother was one of the officials at Hull House? Rosemary can be that way. She has a son. This is irrational thinking, Ang. But she does have a son. Some things hurt . . . The years leafed backward . . . She and her brother . . .

"Nick—I had to see you. I've got to talk to you."

She sat on the sofa, her head down. Her fingers pulled at the handkerchief. Nick asked, gently, "What's the matter?"

"Nick, I—I—"

Her fingers twisted the handkerchief. She was quiet a long time. Nick rubbed the toe of his shoe against the rug, looking at it; she remembered that. "Come on—you can tell me."

"Nick, I—I—" She stopped. Her hand wrapped the handkerchief around her two fingers, hard, like a bandage. "I know I can tell you, Nick. You're the only one I can tell. I couldn't even tell Aunt Rosa—" She stopped again, her lip caught between her teeth; and then said, "I'm going to have a baby."

Silence hit the room.

Ang's fingers twisted. "It's Abe's."

Again the room was silent. At last Ang said, "I've got to get rid of it." She went on swiftly then. "I—I don't know who to go to— what doctor—or what you do or anything." Her voice was trembling again. "You were the only one I could ask." She spoke so low he could hardly hear her. "Please tell me where I can go, Nick."

"Why do you want to throw the kid down the drain? Why don't you have him?" Nick said, his voice hardening.

"I—I can't, Nick. Oh, I can't. You know Ma—that would kill her. Me not married and—and—Abe being Jewish. She wouldn't let me marry him. You know that."

"You have to live your own life," Nick said, hard-boiled. "She lived her life, didn't she? The hell with her!"

"No, Nick, I've got to think about her." Ang was turned toward him, her hand on top of his. "She's had so much trouble.

*You know all the trouble she's had. Pa dying—and—and—she's had
a lot of trouble."*

"Me!— Go ahead and say it!" Nick told her.

*Ang shook her head no. She twisted the handkerchief around and
around, looking at her slim, helpless fingers.*

*Nick looked at his sister. "I'll find out tomorrow about a doctor
who'll do it."*

*She cried. He kept his arm around her. Leaning against him she
cried herself out.*

"It—it isn't murder, is it, Nick?" she asked wretchedly.

He shook his head no.

"Will God forgive me, Nick?"

"Sure, he will!"

"I love Abe. I don't care."

Nick gave her the address. She went over to Milwaukee Avenue
and to "Sophia with the long sword." The saving sword of respectability had cut the child away. And this lay like a scar on her, on her
and Aunt Rosa, as lay the death of Nick on all of them.

*She went to see him. "Nick," she said, when he was standing be-
hind the glass in front of her.*

"Hello, Ang."

*He looked down at her stomach. "How are you, Ang? Is—are
you all right?"*

She nodded her head yes.

*They stood with the section of thick glass between them, their
heads down, not looking at each other.*

"Bring Abe to see me, huh?"

"All right."

Her child lost. And she could never have another. And all her
life seemed desolate around her and she was getting old.

Ang wiped her eyes against her upper arms. She dried the dishes.
Then she heard Louie come into the house.

"What's to eat?" he was saying, and she heard the scrape of the
chair as he pulled up to the table.

As soon as Ang entered the room, he announced to all of them,
"I'm bringing my girl over Sunday."

"A new one?" Aunt Rosa asked.

"Yeah."

"My boy has too many girls," Aunt Rosa said. "It's time you got
serious about just one."

"This pizza ain't very good," Louie said. "Where'd you get it—at that dump on the corner?"

"I'll make scallopini for Sunday dinner," Aunt Rosa said.

"Can we get some candles for the table?" Louie asked. "I'll buy some flowers."

They met in Lincoln Park near the zoo. Almost immediately Louie said, "I'm taking you to my house for dinner Sunday."

"Louie!" She stopped on the sidewalk. "I can't go. I won't go."

"What's all this about?" He took her arm roughly.

"I won't go!"

"Yes, you will!"

"They won't like me."

"Yes, they will!"

"No, no, Louie."

"And if they don't? Do we care?"

"Louie, please call it off." She stood rubbing the calf of one leg with the instep of her other foot. "I'm scared."

"So what? You're with me. I'm with you."

She had to smile then. Leaning against him she quoted, " 'Till death do us part.' "

"Sort of right," he said.

And, still leaning against him, "No. I don't want to go, Louie."

"It's all arranged." He mussed her hair. She leaned against him, still scratching the calf of her leg with her instep. "Please call it off."

"No." He rubbed his nose against hers. He put his hands up into her hair.

"Why does it—? Why is it—?" she asked; but she didn't finish. Instead, "Hold me tight!"

"You're the one who's holding me tight," Louie said. "Without you— Hey! Let's go look at the monkeys!"

"Lend me your comb, Louie."

He handed it to her. "Hey! We gotta buy some peanuts first!"

"I'm scared," Judy said. Her breath was coming fast. "They aren't going to like me," she said.

Louie swung the door open.

Louie walked in, holding Judy by the arm. There was something of his brother Nick in him, his slight swagger and the small grin curving only the edges of his mouth, knowing he was bringing shock with him. "This is my girl," he said. He was like Aunt Rosa. He enjoyed it, these shocks to the family.

"Judy"—he smiled at her, his face dimpling, his brown eyes on her earnestly—"this is Aunt Rosa—Ang—Rosemary—" And he wrinkled his forehead and brought his eyes, his mouth down in a grimace. "Nothing but women around here. Uncle Abe—he's Jewish—you'll like him—he's golfing with some of his law partners. The Swede is probably drunk somewhere. Right, Aunt Rosa!"

"Right," Aunt Rosa said absently.

Rosemary smiled with her blue eyes and held out her hand. "Hello, Judy."

Ang said, "How do you do?" A pulse was beating in her throat.

Aunt Rosa said, "Hi, Judy! Sit down. Make yourself at home."

They all looked at her. It was another bombshell exploded in the parlor.

Then the three women of the family looked flutteringly at each other, their surprise and shock communicating itself.

"How do you like the flowers?" Louie asked, pointing. "And candles. Just like that joint you work at! Come on—sit down!" He pulled her over to a chair.

Ang said, "Excuse me," and went into the kitchen.

Rosemary said, "I'll go see how dinner is getting on."

Aunt Rosa sat with them. Not knowing what to say she said, "Sunday. *Come é bello el dolce far niente.*"

In the kitchen Ang said, "*Oh, my God! Oh, my God!*"

In the parlor Judy smiled and said, "It's so nice to do nothing." It didn't sound like her voice to her. Her smile was so forced it hurt her face.

"You know what that means!" Aunt Rosa said. "Were you raised in a Eye-talian neighborhood?"

"I learned a little Italian in—in college."

"Hey, Ang!" Aunt Rosa yelled. "Bring in that dago red! This girl speaks some Eye-talian!"

Ang brought the bottle and glasses. Her hands shook as she set them down on the cocktail table. She immediately went back into the kitchen.

Rosemary was standing looking out the window.

"Oh, my God!" Ang said.

Rosemary turned slowly away from the window.

"Oh, my God!" Ang said again. "The disgrace!"

"Ang, how can you possibly—?"

"Oh, my God!"

Rosemary came and stood beside her. She said, so that their voices wouldn't be heard in the front room, "Ang!" As if to awaken her. As if to bring her out of shock. Then, "I'm a little shocked too." And, smiling slowly, "I think Louie planned it that way."

"I haven't got anything against colored people," Ang said. "It's only—it's only—"

They could hear Louie laugh. Aunt Rosa was laughing too. It wasn't quite like Aunt Rosa's laugh.

"Maybe he's just going to sleep with her," Ang said hopefully.

Rosemary went to the kitchen door and quietly closed it so that they couldn't be overheard in the other room.

"Yes, maybe he's only going to sleep with her," she said to Ang when she returned. There was no inflection in her voice whatsoever.

"It's just that I can't get used to the idea—" Ang said.

Rosemary went to the pantry. She reached past a bottle of wine and took, instead, the bottle of whiskey. She poured a shot for herself and one for Ang.

They drank. Ang's eyes were piteous on her. Rosemary smiled a little, partly in scorn, partly in pity; and smiled at the same time, in the same manner, at something in herself.

"Maybe he's only going to sleep with her. I hope he's only going to sleep with her," Ang said, and bitterly, "Did you ever see him so attentive to a girl before? Candles! Flowers!" And, pleading, "Do you think he's only going to sleep with her?" With shaky hands she poured herself another drink. "If it happens I won't like it, but I'll take it. I'll have to take it."

Rosemary was mad at herself. She heard Ang say, again, "I'll take it."— "Like brother Nick?" she asked scornfully; and immediately put her hand on Ang's shoulder. "Oh, I'm sorry." She turned away then, and said quietly to Ang, "I'll tell you something I've never told anybody. I slept with Nick."

With her back turned she explained.

Ang seemed not to hear her. "Maybe he's only going to sleep with her," she said again. "Her! And there are so many nice white girls."

Rosemary turned to her. Enough was enough: After all, I was an anthropology and sociology major. And I've lived at Hull House.

Rosemary was mad at herself and mad at this woman, her sister-in-law. She suddenly realized what the girl in the front room was going through.

"Yes—I guess he just wants to go to bed with her," Ang said.

"Like you and Abe?" Rosemary said.

"All right, throw it up to me," Ang said. "My Jewish husband."

"I'm not throwing it up. I've got nothing against Jews. I love Abe."

"Well, throw it up to me that I slept with him for several years before we were married—because—until—until Ma was too crazy to know even if Abe was as black as that girl in there in our parlor!"

"Ang!"

"And you slept with Nick! You just told me you did. Nobody's ever touched me but Abe."

Then Ang was crying, was leaning against Rosemary for support, her fingernails digging into Rosemary's arms. "Oh, I'm sorry, Rosemary! I'm sorry! I'm sorry!"

Rosemary put her arms around her sister-in-law. Ang said, "And I threw it away. The only child we ever could have had. Abe has never forgiven me. I'm—I'm—I guess, like Ma, with her two sons gone. I guess—I mean—I hope Louie will be happy—if it has to happen— No, I don't mean that—I just hope he only sleeps with her. It would be so hard—so hard on all of us. Like Aunt Rosa said, I should have had that child."

Rosemary tried to comfort her. Ang went on crying softly. Ang said, "You've got a son in college. I'd have a kid about his age— maybe in college too. Abe says so. Sometimes—sometimes I hate my mother. Yes, I guess I hate Ma. Sometimes I understand Nick. If this thing happens I won't like it but I'll take it."

Rosemary said quietly, "You have a husband. I lost my husband."

Rosemary needed another drink, and poured it. One for Ang too. Ang was at the sink patting cold water against her red eyes.

"Here!" Rosemary said.

Ang took it, and lit a cigarette.

Rosemary said, "Let's face it. Louie's been a bum. You and I know it. Maybe this will help him. Maybe she's only a tramp." And still mad at herself Rosemary said, "A nigger tramp. Do you like that word? But let's give them a chance."

In the parlor Aunt Rosa said, "I'm going to see what the hell is holding dinner up!"

When she got to the kitchen Ang was setting out salad plates and Rosemary was dishing up the scallopini.

Aunt Rosa looked at them and knew—knew how they felt, what they had been talking about.

"Everything smells good!" she said gruffly; then, "Well, so what!" This was said belligerently, and she waited for an answer.

No answer came; only the look in Ang's eyes.

"Them salads look good," Aunt Rosa said.

"It's just that I can't get used to the idea," Ang said.

"We moved before. We ran before," Aunt Rosa said. "We can move again."

She took another bottle of wine into the parlor. She returned. Her mind had been working. "After all," she said, "we got a Jew and a Swede in the family—and what the hell are you, Rosemary? —so we might as well make it a United Nations. So what—the whole damn world's a family of people, ain't it? We'll have to hide and lie and cheat and maybe move." With this she moved toward the door. "You know, they got good music in that neighborhood," she said.

She had still another thought. At the door she turned and said, "And don't forget what a bum Louie used to be."

She hoped Louie hadn't heard her. And she said, loudly, "Look, kids! Let's make a hole in that bottle of wine! Dinner's coming up soon!"

Dinner was served. Rosemary smiled graciously and passed the dishes. Ang had put powder on her face, under her eyes. She was polite and quiet. Aunt Rosa said, "This girl speaks pretty good Eye-talian! We been talking in Eye-talian."

Judy looked up. "Mrs.—"

"Just call me Aunt Rosa. Everybody else does."

"Come on, honey, eat!" Louie said to Judy. He put his hand on top of her head. "What do you think of this haircut?" he asked.

Aunt Rosa said, "I'm going out with you two some night. I like that music."

The veal scallopini was very good. Nobody enjoyed it but Louie. Cramming some into his mouth he leaned close to Judy and whispered, "Hello, colored girl!"

And after dinner Ma Romano came out of the bedroom, its lock having been forgotten when Judy showed up. Ma was carrying her pillow in her arms. "Yeah, Ma," Louie said; "Ma, this is my girl." And he got her back to her room before she could say anything.

At the door Aunt Rosa said, "I'm going to see you again!" Ang said, "So glad you came to dinner." Rosemary smiled and held out her hand.

And they were on the street.

Ang unlocked the bedroom door so that Ma Romano could eat. Ma came out into the room. "You say that was Louie's girl?" she asked. "Oh . . . by the way . . . she was colored . . . wasn't she? . . . Well, I'm going to see if the boys are on their way home." She went to the window and looked out.

In the dark below, Louie and Judy walked to the car line together.

"Have a good time?" Louie asked.

"Yes," Judy lied.

"I'm glad." He squeezed her arm.

They waited for the streetcar.

Judy put the palm of her hand against his nose for a moment. "I love you less than tomorrow but more than yesterday," she said. "That's a French saying."

And the streetcar came.

97

Nick was at the house again. He and Barbara stood under the tree near the apartment building for a long time.

"Barbara," Grant said when she came back upstairs, "I want to talk to you." He sounded very severe, even to himself; and he seldom called her Barbara.

"Yes, Grant?"

"Sit down."

He hardly knew how to start the conversation. "Ah—"

He got up, mixed himself a drink and brought it back with him; sat across from her, their knees almost touching.

"Cigarette?" He gave her one, lighted it and lit one for himself.

For a while in the darkened room there were just the two red-glowing cigarettes.

Finally Grant said, "Ah," again; and then, "I don't know how to explain this to you. His father wasn't a—a good man."

"What has that to do with him?"

"His father was my friend," Grant said.

He got up and poured himself another drink. A stiff one. Daughters were difficult problems.

He half emptied his glass before he spoke. Barbara was fidgeting.

"You're eighteen now?"

"Yes."

"What I have to tell you will perhaps be shocking to you—"

"Not that you're not my father." Her lips smiled over the kidding words.

"Now, now."

"Say it, Grant."

"Well—" Long pause. "Look—I suppose this isn't good advice for a father to give a daughter. But I'm going to give it to you, thinking it's right. Look—there are two types of girls. I don't know which type you are. Look—there's nothing wrong with sex. It's an important function of the body." He was embarrassed at his own words, but went on. "There are, as I said, two types of girls. Some girls want to wait until they're married. If you're the kind who cannot or does not want to wait, and if you care enough about a boy—really, sincerely care—take Nick, for instance—and think that you are in love with him, well, I think—and this is only my opinion—then you should sleep with him and find out how much you really care for him. That way, don't you see, Bobby—?" He swallowed his drink. "—Well, you won't mess up your life and marry someone you can't—you can't make it with."

He got up to pour himself another drink. Silence from Barbara's chair. Utter silence and utter quiet.

He came back and sat down, reluctantly, yet knowing that he had to finish what he had started. He said, "There are ways to protect yourself—but you'd better ask your mother about that. No—on second thought, you'd better not tell her anything about our conversation." He gestured helplessly. "I don't know what type you are, Barbara. It's—well—it's up to you. I just don't want you to mess your life up. I want you to know."

He stood up and drained his glass. "Well, I'm going to bed."

As he moved off toward the door, her voice spoke behind him. "Daddy," she said, "I think I love him. Maybe I will, Daddy."

98

Nellies was to suffer from The Wolf's death. He had kept her in a little dope. He had shown her a little affection. Now and then, not very often, he had brought her a dress. Most of all he had brought dope to her.

She was broke. She was sick. Her body functions were slowing down. She hustled, hanging out at the Shillelagh bar. "Here comes the Broom." They all laughed. Her door was open. Wide open.

She came unevenly along the Clark Street sidewalk as the sun opened a red, bloodshot eye to the day.

She stopped the man in overalls. "Mister, are you holding a dime?"

"Yes. And I'm holding onto it. I worked hard to get it."

She wandered into a restaurant, open for the early morning trade. A workingman sat at the counter. She took the stool next to him. Sleepy and tired, on his way to work, he nevertheless became immediately aware of her.

"Mister, you got a dime?"

"Sure. Who ain't got a dime?"

She edged over. "Can you let me have a dime?"

"Well, now, a dime isn't much."

He let his knee hit hers and held it there. He let his hand fall down to her leg. "Sure, I *could* let you have a dime." He played with her leg and suddenly, even with eyes tearing and nose running, she realized he was kidding her. She cursed him and turned away. Another workingman had come in. She turned to him. "What time is it, mister?"

"Seven o'clock."

"The taverns are open!" Nellie said.

She left and went to the Shillelagh.

She sits at the bar. She goes out of the bar. Always she went out with men. She always came back alone. She sits there and has a drink and has another drink. But then there's nobody to have a drink with any more.

And all she wants is a fix. And a little money for the house.

Nick watched her as one watches a loved person who is dying.

He tried to take care of her. He tried to make her take care of herself. If he had ever been sad he was sad now.

Resentment is a long-lived sore. And love is a longer-lived thing.

Nick watched his mother. His eyes, in their sadness, seemed to say that they had seen too much.

He watched it all. He was like one without emotions.

"Okay. You're killing yourself. It's your own business."

One part said, Remember and paint.

But this was the false part.

He loved her.

A world I never made.

I love you.

He was controlled—he had to be controlled.

"You're making a fool of yourself, Mother."

He was so cold emotionally that it seemed he couldn't be hurt.

"Let's go home, Mother."

99

Grant sat in the low-down West Madison Street bar. You can always find friends when you walk into a bar and put a dollar down. You sit somewhere and listen. Maybe it's a poolroom, a tavern or a street corner. Grant sat back and listened.

They like to talk. They all tell on themselves. Grant sat with his arm stretched out in front of him, his hand turning the glass around and around: So you listen, you keep your face straight. Keep your lips curled back in the civilized sneer, even when your stomach is retching. What they say doesn't make sense. Doesn't fit into the neat little grooves of civilization. Maybe it's just a part of life. The dirty end of the stick . . . That's what Society handed them, Grant, the dirty end of the stick. And they're not completely bad. Jesus Christ, no! There's something decent in every one of them. Grant twisted the beer glass: You figure it out. He looked, slowly, from one hard, one cunning, one dissolute face to the other: One's a pimp. One's a jackroller. One's a queer. One doesn't know how to read or write. One's obviously on the needle. Maybe you're not like them—but don't brag. You're a coward. You conform to the pack you travel with just as they conform to their crowd. You compromise with life. Everybody does. You make compromises with life on your own level. Everybody does. So the boy's father died in the electric chair. So what does that have to do with him? Sleep with my daughter but don't come inside the house! You're a coward, Grant. A goddamn coward. Everybody's a coward . . . That's not right, either. Well, yes, it is. Now we've learned how to destroy all of humanity with a couple of bombs, and we're rather proud of the fact. Nobody says no. We follow the pack. So you don't try to figure it out—you listen.

One of the fellows, Mexican, was saying, "If I make a good score I'm going to live with a girl, don't forget that!" He grinned, a white crescent in a copper-colored face. He said, dreamily, "I wonder who's the next woman I'm going to lay in bed with until I get tired." He moved his arms away from his body, expressively, and, still grinning, said, "Then I'll get another one—and another one—and another one —until I get too old. Then go and drink whiskey."

Grant got up and went home.

Barbara came in. Her face was shining.

"Grant!" she called.

"Here, Bobby."

She came over. "Shall I tell you what happened?"

"I don't think you'd better."

"He was scared, Daddy—actually scared— I said—I said, 'You can have me if you want—' "

"Barbara!"

"And he said, he said he loved me and that he didn't want to do that. That he loved me and that was why—why— Daddy! Are you listening!"

Grant drew a long breath. "Yes, Bobby."

"Did you hear what I said?— And I said—"

Grant put his arm around her, loving her, loving Nick. All he could think to say was, "Ho! So that's the type of girl my daughter is!"

She began to cry. "I'm so happy!" she said.

She cried some more on his shoulder. Then the appalling thought struck her. "Maybe I'm ugly, Grant!" This made her cry too; but in a moment she said, "I'm so happy!"

Grant said, "Go to bed. Women make me sick."

She kissed him quickly and again said that she was so happy.

When she had gone to bed Grant stepped out onto the balcony. He held his glass in salute to the sky, to Chicago. He thought of Nick the father and Nick the son. "We have played and won, Wanda!" he said.

100

"He's dead," they had told him.

Nick knew who they meant.

"I'm sorry."

"What do you mean, you're sorry!"

"I mean I'm sorry for him."

He looked for his mother. He couldn't find her.

And later he looked again.

She was at the Shillelagh.

The bartender was yelling, "Jesus, Chuck! Can't you wait a minute! I'm waiting on a cash customer. You're just a credit customer here. When you have money I don't see you. You walk on the other side of the street. This side ain't good enough for you. Christsake, shut up! See how you are when you start eating it—I can always tell when you're eating it."

As Nick walked toward his mother, he heard a sag-faced woman with lots of rouge ask another woman with a face as heavily smeared with make-up, "Hey, girl, how did you do last night?"

And the other, "I caught a fish."

"Tell me about it! What's his name?"

"I don't bother about names. All I bother about is billfolds."

His mother was with a man. She had taken the man's hat and put it on her head. "How about another drink?" Nellie asked. He swayed toward the bar, upsetting a glass. "Two more!" he demanded, loose-mouthed, his elbows holding the upper part of his body up off the bar.

Nick walked toward her.

My mother.

My father.

Where else is there to go from here?

"Mother," he said.

The man touched her hand and her leg, saying, "You don't need any money."

"All right," Nellie said, "but don't feel me. You're paying for the drinks. Not the feels."

"Mother."

"You don't mind if I hold your hand?"

"No. Hold anything."

"Your husband isn't around, is he?"

"Huh?"

"Your husband isn't around?"

For a while Nellie's eyes cleared. Then they grew bleary again.

"No. He's under the ground."

"I don't know how to begin," the man said out of his haze.

"Well, I'll start," Nellie said, "and we'll have a photo finish."

"You're not drunk yet?"

"Naw."

"Mother."

The man pushed her glass toward her. They drank. Over the rim of her glass she said, "You're not playing me for a sucker, are you?"

"Say," the man said, "you've got a nice figure there. You ought to do all right."

"Well, I'm not putting millions in the bank."

"You've got nice-looking legs."

"Huh?"

"You've got nice-looking legs."

She looked down at them. "Well, they ought to be nice. I stand on them."

The man was feeling her.

Nick turned and walked out.

Again he met Lee on the street. Lee threw his good arm around Nick's shoulders. Lee's other arm was a claw under his chin, shriveled thinner than Nick had remembered it, like the leg cut off a chicken and thrown away.

"I'm going to a party," Lee said. "Come on with me."

My mother.

"All right."

Nick didn't even notice the people or the house.

My mother.

Lee came over. He had a smoking cigarette in his hand. "Here, Nick—take a puff—like this." He showed him how. "It ain't habit-forming. I can take you to the library and prove it."

He pushed the cigarette into Nick's fingers.

Nick held the cigarette listlessly. The smoke curled up his wrist and arm like a snake. The blue-black panther licked his hand.

 *the long, lonely, lonesome road*

101

Why not? He brought the cigarette up to his lips. The acrid smoke burned in.

It took only a few seconds.

It started from his feet, up his legs, up his back, along his neck, creeping pleasurably, up into his face and his head, the roots of his hair, the very ends of his hair. Uuuuuhhhhhh! . . . .
. . . Uuuuuhhhhhhh!

Aaahhhhhh . . .

He was relaxed and kind of sleepy. He had forgotten about his mother. About everything. He was feeling better than he ever knew you could feel on this earth. It made him feel good. Good! He had no problems in the world. Everything was okay. He felt more normal than he had ever felt in his life. Relaxed and kind of sleepy. You're talking to somebody and then you close your eyes and coast—like when you're not drunk and not sober. You close your eyes and coast —and you feel fine, real nice and fine.

Oh . . . so good!

102

The rain was throwing little silver daggers at the sidewalk in the night and she was walking toward him. His heart contracted a little because she was walking toward him.

"White boy," she said. She tickled his ear with a piece of grass she had pulled.

He pulled his head away. "Don't, colored girl."

He put his arm around her.

"Don't," she said.

"Why not?"

"I can't hold out any longer," she said.

"Do you think I'm a superman or one of those—those—you know, they have soprano voices."

"Where can we go?"

"I don't know."

A half-moon hung over the river. Rain sprayed its gentle silver strings across it. They walked. They walked over bridges through the city. It was a long time before it would be late at night—and these things are done at dark, late in the darkness.

They sat in the drug store where they had first talked, at the same table.

She looked at him and lowered her eyes. He glanced away, out of the booth. There was now a shyness about them.

"Louie—"

He squeezed her hand and made no response.

Outside, black asphalt was gleaming under street light and rain. The dampness of their clothes touched their skin. The wet smell of their clothes was intimate.

By mutual consent they arose and left the drug store.

Walking closer together now, they moved down the sidewalk in the soft-whispering rain, past lamppost after lamppost.

She put her head down against his shoulder.

"I'm not a virgin," she said, "but it hasn't happened many times."

"I'm not asking what I can't give," he said.

They came to a place. HOTEL. In a stiff bar of red neon. No more. Sign like a sphinx. Sign like a priest sworn to the secrecy of the confessional. Sign like a lewd leer set against the night. Sign and invitation to: Who? What? Sign like a pimp—in this door.

They went in that door.

Judy stood with her back turned and her face half turned away toward the street. Rain pelted the dirty window.

Artificial two-foot palm. Tile floor strewn with cigarette butts, gum wrappers and phlegm. Doors set, one after the other, two sides of a long hall. Like secrets or sins set side by side.

OFFICE: A cubicle the size of a telephone booth.

Louie laid a ten-dollar bill down on the desk. "No change," he said.

The evil face smiled evilly. The bony hand took the ten-dollar bill, and a key attached to a square of masonite was placed where it had been.

One of the doors of secrets and sins opened. It closed. The key turned in the lock.

Bed. Chair. Washbasin and towel. A naked bulb on a dangling cord.

Louie put his arms around Judy and she responded as warmly. They held each other. And were both afraid or ashamed to look at each other. Double was their sin. Double their secret. The city moved in night around them.

"Judy! . . . Judy!"

They held each other.

Then they sat alongside each other on the bed. But not too close together. The bare bulb watched them.

"Well, here we are," Louie said.

"Here we are," Judy answered.

"Can you do this?" Louie asked, and pulled his forefinger way back, showing her he was double-jointed.

"No," she said. "When I was a kid I used to turn my eyelids back."

"There ain't a radio in this room," Louie said.

"No, there isn't."

"You're good-looking," Louie said.

Her eyes filled. "You're kind of good-looking yourself, white boy."

"I love you, Judy."

He took her hands. He was kissing them. And she was pulling his hands over to her lips, kissing them.

Footsteps went along the long, secret hallway and they stared at each other fearfully.

The steps went away. They sat side by side. Louie put his arm around her. He sat staring at the floor.

She looked at his ankles and his feet and, secretly, at his profile. His nose was straight. He had dimples. His dark hair was curling across his forehead.

He looked up at her. "Our clothes are wet."

"Yes, they are."

His white body and her brown body showed themselves to each other.

It had never been to either of them before.

And they dressed. But they did not leave. They lay side by side on the bed along the corridor of secret and sin, their arms around each other, their faces turned looking at each other. They slept and they awakened and they moved closer together, holding each other, and they slept.

The troubled night moved over them, moved through the city. Sometimes like a bully, when thunder came and rain increased. Like a thief or pickpocket, when clouds obscured the sky. Then more peacefully, sleepily.

And night moved.

And the half-moon lowered itself.

The window showed the raw neighborhood in daylight, like a scab on the city's leg.

They awakened and looked at each other and held each other. She put her face against his chest, hiding it there. "My husband," she said. She cried there. "My wife," he said. And took her head in his hands, put his fingers into her hair, placed his lips against hers, gently, kept them there, gently.

They held each other. There was this. Loving someone. In tenderness. In giving. In warmth. Your forehead. The touch of your hand. To look at you. The way your hair is. To see you walk. The— the look of you.

And sun rises high. The city waits. No life stands still. They must move from this room to the ordinary ordering of each day.

Judy shakes out his damp and wrinkled coat. "If I had an iron I'd press it for you."

Louie took the coat from her and put it on. "If I had a thousand dollars right now I'd take you downtown and buy you a whole new outfit—from inside to outside—fancy high-heeled shoes and a fur coat."

The secret, sinful room was a home to them and they sat, side by side, on the bed.

"I wanted to give you that," Judy said, "and I wanted to have that. I wanted both of us to remember it—" She lifted his hand to her cheek and pressed it there. "We have loved each other more than most people. We've been lucky."

" 'Have'— You sound like it's over."

He took her shoulders between his hands and turned her toward him until they were facing each other.

"I wanted you to have that, Louie—so that, when you disappear—"

"I'll never disappear. I'll never leave you."

"When you leave—"

"Hush! Judy." He put his hand over her mouth.

She moved her face away. "Wherever I am in the future, wherever you are, I'll always love you and I know you'll love me—remember me—"

Tears were running but no sound came. "—remember me—and—and—"

He tried to interrupt.

This time she put her fingers over his lips. "Listen to me—please listen—"

And head against his shoulder. "We've loved each other more than most people because—because it has been harder."

103

The group Lee ran around with and introduced Nick to was a wild bunch of kids. They were just learning to smoke and drink and find out that a woman is a woman. A couple of the older fellows had already introduced them to marijuana; a couple of them were even on heroin and encouraging others not to be chicken, to just try it for kicks, for the big bang. The group had graduated from its gang warfare days. They had had that too. But now they didn't need the thrill of gang wars. They had outgrown that. They had a bigger kick now.

There were three or four girls in the group. One was called Cowboy Sally. She got the name when she was fifteen and they were still engaging in gang fights. During one of the neighborhood battles—boys slugging it out with knives, bricks, zip-guns, baseball bats, whatever—she rode a boy piggy-back, stabbing him all the time. Now, when they ran out of money for muggles or H, she prostituted herself for the fellows and got the money to get the kicks.

Carl, Nick's high school friend, was one of the gang. He and a couple of the other fellows had their own hot rods and tore around the neighborhood in them. When Carl's folks were out of town or on vacation he took the crowd up to his parents' place and they had parties there.

They hung around candy stores and jive joints and poolrooms, places where teen-agers hang out. There was a drug store. Anybody could go in there and say "my Uncle Bennie sent me," throw down a five-dollar bill on the counter and get all the benzedrine tablets he wanted. They took the bennies for kicks. Or red jackets and yellow jackets: goof balls. Or reds or yellows with bennies to give an additional kick.

They had their contact near the high school. He sold ice cream bars from a bicycle with a cart attached to it and a bell that summoned them. From him they could also buy marijuana and, if he really knew you, the stronger stuff.

After his first experience Nick went back to see Lee. With Lee were a couple of other fellows.

Lee poked Nick and said, "Let's go take off."

They went up to Lee's house and into the bathroom.

They lit up.

Nick wanted to leave and didn't want to leave. He remembered the first time.

Lee passed the roach to him. "Here, Nick. Get hot!"

Nick sucked in.

It picked him up immediately.

Everything was coming from the bottom of his soles up through his head.

They went out onto the street. People were around but he didn't know it. He was walking on air. And feeling a little sleepy.

"Man, he's the gonest!" one of the fellows said.

"It sure picks you up, don't it, Nick!" Lee said.

"Like—you know—man—" the other fellow said.

"Cool, man, cool—"

"I'm hip, man—"

Nick didn't say anything. He didn't feel like talking. He felt drowsy and happy and contented and everything—everything!—was all right!

He went into a store for a bottle of pop.

Nick fell in with the crowd. Out of loneliness, confusion, an ever-changing feeling of love, hate and pity for his mother. A knowledge that he was illegitimate. A feeling that he wasn't good enough to be with Barbara, that he was no good, could never do anything, never be anything. After all, look who he was.

104

Nellie sat, clenching and unclenching her fingers. She needed her fix. Needed it badly. But before she went off the deep end and had to go out into the street and get it somehow, somewhere, she had to figure this out. Had to. Where was Nick? He was almost never home. He didn't seem to care any more about anything. Even his drawing. My fault! My fault! I've lost him.

She sat in the lowering twilight, her hands held there on her lap as if in a prison. Four walls, and you wish somebody would come even if it's the cops.

And somebody came. The door swung open. He stood there in the picture frame the door made.

Nellie stood up, trembling. She clutched the back of the chair and started breathing hard, one hand held tightly against her throat.

For a moment she thought that she had lost her mind. Had the dope done that? Or had she had her fix and was this a hallucination? No. I've lost my mind.

The apparition spoke.

"I'm Nick Romano's brother."

No, I haven't lost my mind.

"Yes, I know it," she said.

"My name is Louie."

She held out a trembling hand and then crumpled into a chair, her fingers laced, her head down. She looked up at him and at the picture on the wall, and back at him. A ghost had crept through the crack of the door and sat in warmth and light across the table from her. She began to cry. "What do you want? What do you want?" she asked.

"I came to tell you something," he said. He looked at his brother and then at her. "I get all the dago news," he said in explanation.

He got up and looked out the window, turned back into the room, walked to her. "Your son, Nick—" he said. "Your son is on dope."

"You lie!" She stood up. "You're a goddamn liar!"

Louie shrugged. "Take it easy," he said. He looked at the picture again, then back to Nellie. "I *know*. And the kid's on stuff. I been rotten. But that's one thing I never did. Dope."

She tried to hit him, tears running down her cheeks, and he backed away. Again she called him a goddamn liar. He moved away until his back touched the door. "Jesus Christ! I'm just telling you!" he said. "He's your son. Take care of the kid."

He walked out.

105

He walked in again the next day.

"Where's your mother?" he asked.

419

"I don't know," Nick said.

Louie came further into the room, broad-shouldering his way in. "So?" he said.

"Yes, Uncle Louie."

"Yes, Uncle Louie," he mimicked.

He looked around. He saw the paintings on the wall. "Ummm!" Louie walked over and started looking at them. "They're better than that thing you did in the woods."

Nick stood looking at his shoes.

Louie moved to the other wall. He stood there, looking in past the frame, looking at the picture of his brother hanging there. Looking at himself. He whirled around and faced Nick. "I could tell you something, you little sonofabitch!"

But he didn't tell him.

He walked up to Nick. "You're on dope, ain't you?" He slapped Nick.

Nick didn't feel the pain. He felt the words.

"Ain't you!" Louie repeated.

"No, I'm not."

"Take them off!" Louie said. "Take off your clothes. I'm going to find out."

Nick tried to move away from him. Louie grabbed him. The shirt made tearing sounds and was in shreds around his waist. They were both panting. "Take them off! The pants!" Louie commanded.

Fear in his eyes, and hurt and panic, Nick unbuckled his pants and slipped out of them.

"The shorts too!"

Louie examined him. He could find no needle marks, no tell-tale tattoo of blue penciling running along the veins.

And Louie, looking at Nick: But I know, I know you are . . .

And they were standing there in the middle of the room, the uncle and the nephew, both crying, the arms of the uncle around the nephew, shielding.

106

Nick walked into Juan's shop. He looked up pleadingly at Juan. "Can I use your back room?"

Juan walked over to him and looked at him. "Let me look at you, Nick."

Nick glanced fleetingly and lowered his eyes.

And Juan knew.

Juan's fist lashed out and hit Nick in the mouth.

"Leave him alone! Don't you hit that boy!" Fran said.

Juan looked at her. For the first time he hated her.

Nick stood, stopping the blood with his hand, looking at his damp fingers.

Fran went to him and put her arm around him. "Are you hooked?" she asked.

Nick nodded yes.

"Are you sure, honey? Sure, real sure?"

Nick nodded yes. He wiped his bloody fingers on his pants and stared down at his feet.

"It's a living death," Fran said. "A emeffing death."

"You ain't going to use my place. No, sir!" Juan said.

Fran touched Nick's hand. "Come with me."

He moved with her toward the door.

Juan sat down heavily in a chair.

At the door Nick turned back. "Please don't tell Uncle Max and the others."

Juan didn't answer. He was staring at the floor. And when they had gone he got up, locked up the shop and went down to the drug store. Into the telephone he said to Max, "I gotta see you tonight."

When Nick got home his mother was sitting at the table in her accustomed pose, balanced between relief and the pain and panic to come before relief again.

Nick came in slowly. He walked and stood before her. "I'm one of you," he said.

107

Max was drunk. When those brown eyes got drunk in that brown face, they were really drunk. His hair was wild and standing up curly.

"Well, what was so urgent?" he asked, good-naturedly.

"We better wait until the rest get here," Juan said.

"In that case we better have a drink," Max said.

"Yes, I need one."

They came, one by one, into the broken-down West Madison Street bar. Judge Sullivan, his shoes no longer shined, tie carelessly tied by aged fingers, but tied; his hair almost completely white now, and the tobacco-stained mustache drooping over his mouth; his cane moving him forward slowly to where they waited. Phil, saying, "Well, I got here. You better believe it," and, sitting down, "What the hell's up?" Norman, immaculately dressed, his long blond hair waved but straight at the edges. Norman casting an eye at the young men along the bar as he entered.

When they were all seated and after they had had another drink, Juan looked at all of them and said, "Let's go to the crapper."

They all filed into the toilet.

Juan closed the door and stood with his foot against it so nobody else could enter. "The kid's on dope."

"No!"

They stood there, wordless, helpless and hurt.

Judge Sullivan was unashamedly crying.

108

They met again the next night.

"What are we going to do about it?"

"We could send him to that place in Kentucky."

"Narco," Juan said.

"That costs money."

"No, it's free."

"We can get the money. We can save it."

"We got to send him there."

"It costs seven dollars a day and they're supposed to stay four and a half months, at least," Juan said. "If they can't pay they get in free."

"We'll pay for him. He won't be any charity case."

"We'll get the money."

"It's hard to get in there," Juan said.

Judge Sullivan, wiping his eyes, saw a small Christmas tree for a small boy and an electric train they had all chipped in to buy, saving the money for a month ahead of time. "We can start saving money now," he said.

"Yes," they said.

In another part of the city, at the same time, Louie and Judy sat over a Coke.

Louie looked up into her eyes. "And now," he said, "my nephew, that goddamn kid I love, is on dope."

She took his hands. She was massaging his fingers.

"His mother wanted to practically kill me for making such accusations. 'My son! My wonderful son!' She even tried to hit me. I walked away. I said, 'The hell with you if that's the way you feel about it!' And she wouldn't believe me, and *he is! I know he is!* So—what are you going to do?"

Judy kept massaging his fingers, her eyes looking at his hands, her eyes filling with tears.

He pulled his hands away roughly. "Let's go get a drink somewhere."

She started gathering up her things.

Louie said, "Maybe I can get him to go to that government hospital for dope fiends."

"That's in Kentucky," Judy said. "That's in the South."

"Yeah," and, feeling her sensitivity, "they're not prejudiced there. They have both colored and white there."

109

Nick supported his habit. He and Lee, also on heroin now, went to the house of Lee's mother that cold blond woman who, on a certain day each week, gave Lee an "allowance," so that he would stay away and not bother her. Lee was older now and he could ask for more money. Once he slipped a silver table cigarette lighter into his pocket, another time he pocketed one of her wrist watches and a ring from her bedroom. They pawned them and turned the money into H. When Carl was around they could always party; his folks were loaded and gave him a lot of money. They seemed to have only this way of showing their love for him.

They had started out on the grand kick, the big bang. Now they brought their habit up.

Now they needed more every day. They could afford to buy only the very cheapest, sometimes stuff that was about eighty or ninety per cent adulterated. It's weak. But you start taking a little more and a little more and you bring your habit up.

When they were under the influence they were at their peak. They knew what they were doing but they didn't care. That wonderful drowsy, relaxed phase. They could get away from it all. Yeah, you're at your peak. You're avoiding the emotional strains of life. You're not unhappy. You gain happiness. You're not restless any more. Or sad. Everybody who isn't a user seems like a phony. You think you know everything. You have no illusions about anything. You know everything. The more you use, the more withdrawn you become.

When you really get strung out you don't care about anything but your next fix. You're always hustling to get your fix. You think two or three days ahead how to get your fix. If you know you must get it or stay sick two or three days, you go get it, it doesn't matter where or how.

When you don't have it, your nerves and bones ache, you puke, you get cramps, your nose and eyes water. If you're a hypo you go get it.

It all starts when you don't know what the hell you're doing. You can become an addict in from three days to a week if you hit it hard. And then—

And then—

Your mornings are hell until you get it. Your pillow is wet with sweat. You have to have at least two more fixes during the day—and as many more as you can get.

Who started you? It looks innocent enough. You're anxious to be a regular fellow. You don't want to be chicken. Somebody, maybe a close girl or boy friend, says, "Try it just once—" a marijuana. You want to be one of the gang. I can handle it. Just this once, I ain't chicken. You want their respect. You want to be one of the gang. You become! You become!

And from there it's just one tiny step to a bigger kick. You become one of the lured ones. Some mule pulls you in. Maybe a best friend. You can count on it that one kid on H is going to lure about five others in.

And you're hooked.

Nick was one of the lured ones.

When he didn't have his fix he had to get it somewhere. He sold fake magazine subscriptions, saying he was going to college and working his way through. He felt like crying when he thought about it. Then the needle went in and he felt good. He panhandled money, begging it on street corners, "I'm trying to get back home to Iowa." He was a kid trying to get a fin or a sawbuck a day to keep his habit up. With Lee he helped steal cash and trinkets from Lee's mother's house.

I want to quit. I don't like it. I better try to stop. I can't stop. I have to have it.

When he had funds for the next shot he was satisfied. When he didn't—

But it takes nerve to go out and steal from strangers. And he feared arrest. Arrested, he wouldn't be able to get his fix.

Twice, with other hypos, he helped steal batteries out of parked cars. And was scared to death. But he had to have his fix.

:I better go to that place where my mother was. Maybe I can stop.

And his addiction grew and became worse and worse.

He stood in front of the Lighthouse. There in the shadow of the door where the two men had told him to stand. He could see the men looking in the drug-store window, down the sidewalk a way, as if they were interested in something to buy, their snap-brim hats turned down over their eyes.

Inside the Lighthouse, at the far end of the bar near the toilet, sat a young man. The collar of his pink-colored sport shirt was worn open and lay outside his suit collar in two long hand-stitched pointed V's. His hand was up to his cheek, fingers spread. He leaned on a delicate arm. He smoked a long cork-tipped cigarette, and as he exhaled long, lazy streamers of smoke he tossed his head back gently.

Two middle-aged men sat at the bar near the window, looking like caricatures. They were fat, dumpy, double-chinned. One had his arm thrown around the other companionably. He said, "That's nature." And the other, "Oh, nature is *terrible*." The other started talking to the bartender, and said, "People live the life they want to." The bartender said, "Yeah, a fellow knows what he's doing." And the caricature, "I live the life I like."

A man walked past them. He was short, ugly, red-faced, about forty. With a face like that he could have been an ex-pug. But he walked with a twist. "There goes the movie queen!" said one of the caricatures in a voice like a woman's; and then, loudly, "Oh, Queen!" The man looked around. "Hello, girl!" he called, batting his eyes and twisting over to the bar. "How are you, dear?" He held out his hand, with the back of it arched gracefully. A woman, coming from the toilet and having wandered into this place with her escort by mistake, looked at him queerly. He stared her down. Then he said to his friend at the bar, "Have respect for the opposite sex. Have respect for all the gay bitches!" They laughed. He said, "I'm a lady but still a bitch!" He stuck his tongue between his lips and rolled it from one end of his mouth to the other lewdly.

Outside Nick waited.

One of the effeminate men came out of the Lighthouse. Nick approached him and, looking up into his face pleadingly with his innocent brown-eyed look, said, "Mister, could you help me? I'm hungry and I'm from out of town."

The effeminate face looked at the boy sympathetically, and the man pulled some change from his pocket for the kid.

The two snake-eyed men appeared, burly and closing in on the boy and the man in a hard circle.

"He was propositioning you, wasn't he, kid?"

"He asked you to do something dirty, didn't he, kid?"

Nick looked at the man. Then at the two men.

"No—no. He was going to help me."

Nick turned and ran down the street.

The next day he and Lee found over thirty dollars in Lee's mother's jewel case, at the bottom of it, under rings and bracelets. They left quickly.

After his fix Nick went home. "I've got some good stuff!" he told his mother. "Some *real fine* stuff!"

They cooked it. They shot it.

Nick went for the mainline.

110

Ward Committeeman Don Lockwood, born Chet Kosinski—Don Lockwood, *The Power*—was talking with his wife.

"Your sister was here today," Irene said.

She knew this infuriated him, *goddamn* her!

"We had a nice lunch. Your family asked about you." She smiled thinly.

He moved a little closer to her, his metal and leather leg dragging. His red-flushed, blue-veined face looked at her and he tried to smile. "I'm going away today on a short trip. Just a few days."

Her chocolate-brown eyes looked at him. "Yes?" There was unconcern in her eyes.

Goddamn her! he thought.

He took one of her hands. She allowed him this but there was no response in her fingertips.

Your mother. He wondered why she hadn't thrown that up to him too.

The more disdainful she got, the more desirable. The more she frustrated him, the more he wanted her.

In the city he was known as *The Power*. It was a gangster name, but he was a politician. Powerful. Giving favors. Taking them away. At home, with her, he was a nothing. Disdain in her eyes. A mocking smile. And, always, he had to make a peace with her at any cost. He wanted her love at any cost.

But he had made his pact with life, his bargain, and paid the price: I want power. As long as I have this I have my entrance anywhere, patting his pocket. I like a buck just like anybody else. As long as you have money you can buy just about anything you want. She had been another possession, like his car and his diamond ring. He was the Polish boy from the slum who had made good. That was something he didn't feel good about now. And the child. *His son.* He knew it was Christopher's child. It looked exactly like Christopher. Same curly black hair and slim chiseled features. This was another anger, another frustration.

"Irene, it's—your seeing Christopher all the time that I don't approve of. He's married and has several children. You and he at night clubs together when I'm working. Why, it's positively indecent!"

Her chocolate-brown eyes unwavering. "Was it indecent when your mother died and you didn't even go to the funeral, Mr. Power? Was it indecent—?" And she marked off his faults on her fingers. There were many.

Did she think he hadn't wanted to go to his mother's funeral? Did she think he could afford to go? If there had been any hint of a connection—

But he couldn't make an answer.

He tried to make up to the child, but Irene would have none of it. It was *her son.* She continued to treat Don with cold disdain, and Christopher was a friend of the family. He, *The Power*, needed Irene and she knew this.

And now he stood holding her hand, her listless fingers resting on his.

He had loved her. And he had used her. Now that she, who had loved him for a short while, loved him no longer, he found her desirable, he wanted her, wanted her, wanted her to love him again, wanted to crush her, and then love her again as before, as it had been when they had truly loved, and this was lost, lost, lost, as a dream is lost on awakening, lost as the foam from a wave, lost and so far gone that it was as though it had never been.

And he respected her, even with Christopher, her lover. She only despised him.

"Would you like me to bring you something, Irene?"

"No, thank you."

He passed his hand over his hair. He would need a toupee soon.

She allowed him to kiss her good-bye.

With time yet to spare, he went to a plush cocktail lounge in his district. Most of the men went there for but one purpose. There was no spirit of friendliness. The girls run to mold. They have a brassy beauty, but a hard look, and are always stunningly dressed. They are like lazy, preening, fur-licking cats on their tall upholstered stools and in the brightly painted leather arms of booths. They touch their hair. They purse their lips in damp cups. They pull their blouses tight or stretch languorously in their satin until their breasts are hard against the cloth in a signal. They oil their lips with the red heads of lipsticks that peel out of hard metal sticks, daintily holding them to their half-opened lips. The men buy them drinks and speak to them in low intimate voices. The men sit and drink and drink until they decide that now is the time to go up to a room.

Don Lockwood sat over cocktails until it was time to catch his plane.

Ace sat in his office before the huge mahogany desk, his hand stretched out toward the silver decanter, a cork-tipped cigarette dangling from his thin lips, and his baggy eyes squinting against the smoke.

He had a couple more drinks, consulted his wrist watch, then pressed the buzzer and had a boy carry his bags down to his car. Then he walked through his place, past the lavish bar and to the roulette wheel where well-dressed men and women, some in evening clothes, stood playing.

He stood, smiling, shaking hands with some of his patrons, then went under the sign that said $\begin{smallmatrix} \text{DINE} \\ \text{DANCE} \end{smallmatrix}$, the words jerking into each other in red and blue neon, and got into his car.

They took separate planes to Mexico. They took separate planes to Puerto Vallarta in Mexico. Hell, whoever heard of Puerto Vallarta?

It was the slack season, the burning hot summer season. There were few Americans there.

They both liked sun. They met on the beach.

They met without blinking their eyes.

"American too?" Ace asked Don Lockwood.

"Yes. From Toledo."

"Not far from Chicago. I'm from Chicago."

They discovered that they both liked fishing, and Don Lockwood said he was looking for someone to share a boat with him. The Ace said he'd be glad to share expenses, and the hotel manager brought a young man around.

"This is Rudy Lepe," the manager said, "He has boats. He speaks English."

Don Lockwood and the Ace looked distrustfully at Rudy's white skin and blue-green eyes. They said, "We'll take your boat. But we want a fisherman who doesn't speak English. We don't want to be bothered. Or talked to."

Early in the morning they set out in the little boat, fishing poles in hand.

They sat an hour in silence.

"Sure they don't understand English?" *The Power* asked.

The Ace shrugged his shoulders.

They sent the boatman and the fisherman, by hand signs, up to the other end of the boat.

They had a stiff slug of Scotch out of their respective silver hip flasks.

"Here's a big piece of change if you want to handle it in your set-up," Ace told Don Lockwood.

He explained it. "I got contacts. I got connections. In several big cities."

The Power frowned at his cigar. "We politicians can't buy immunity, you know. It's a federal rap now."

"Look—" Ace said.

They both looked. It looked this way: The fix was to let it be known to certain cops in the night club and surrounding slum area not to "molest" certain known or suspected pushers—our boys in the setup.

"And this other thing—the big thing—the distribution—" Ace said.

. . . It is a dark, sinister thing, moving across the world as night moves, hushed and secret. From smuggler to distributor to wholesalers and jobbers, pushers, peddlers, recruits, to the kid on the sidewalk in front of his high school. It's big business. For two hundred dollars in Turkey two pounds can be bought. By the time it is cut and capped and sold to the user, it brings a hundred thousand dollars. It's a big business. If the legal market is surfeited, you sell it anywhere you can. You're a businessman. You're selling. You're looking for your profit. You're out to sell the stuff. Period. For three thousand dollars in some countries you can buy two pounds of pure heroin. When the last cut is made with milk sugar, the stuff is lucky to be five per cent pure heroin by the time it reaches the user and all the businessmen have made their profit. Profit. Over three hundred thousand dollars. Planes shuttle back and forth between New York and other cities in the United States engaged in the traffic.

The businessmen work at it just as hard and as steadily as the businessmen do at any other business . . ."

"It's *big* money," the Ace said. "*Big* money."

"Yeah," *The Power* said.

"We can set it up soundproof, foolproof," the Ace said.

"I'm keeping myself clean. I'm keeping my skirts clean," *The Power* said.

"I'm keeping myself clean too," the Ace said.

"Hell, after all, somebody's going to be using it anyway. Let it run," *The Power* said, giving the okay.

111

"I sent for the application," Max said. He laid it out in front of them: APPLICATION FOR VOLUNTARY ADMISSION TO U.S. PUBLIC HEALTH SERVICE HOSPITAL.

They started filling it out.

"His mother has to sign it," Max said.

"She will," Judge Sullivan said. "After all, she loves that boy."

"Yeah, and she tried the cure down there herself," Juan said.

"It will take close to a thousand dollars," Norman said.

"We'll get it," Phil said.

"I've got some now," Max said, and put ten dollars on the table.

"Well, boys," Judge Sullivan said, "here it is."

It was in small coins, mostly nickels and dimes.

It amounted to four dollars and thirty-five cents. Judge Sullivan said, "Tomorrow I've got enough for my eye opener of wine and—well, I'll make it tomorrow, and next week I hope to have more for the fund. Much more, with luck." He put his nose down into the stein of beer Phil had bought him.

"Will you be treasurer?" Max asked him.

The old man lifted his head and smiled. "Again," he said, "I deem it an honor—but this time I must decline. You know"—he smiled gently—"in my old age I find myself—ah—with the years advancing, Bacchus calls much more frequently—and I do not cherish the responsibility for—how, Max?—holding onto the dough."

They went about getting the money to send Nick for the cure.

Juan had three hundred dollars in the bank and pledged half of it.

Phil got a very close shave, had his crew cut trimmed, put on a tight-fitting pair of Levis and a T-shirt. He went downtown to the bus depot. He went up to the mezzanine and stood outside the drug store.

In a little while a man walked up. "Buddy, have you got a match?" the man asked.

"Sure. Here."

The man started a conversation: "I'm here early. I have two hours to wait for my bus. How about having a drink with me?"

"Okay. Fine, man."

Phil went over to Bughouse Square. He sat on a bench to see if he could still work it. Three or four men were hanging around. They all looked at him. Then one sat down at the other end of the bench and quickly glanced over at him. Phil put his elbows on his knees and his chin in the palms of his hands and looked across at the man. The man sidled down the bench closer to him, and Phil smelled a faint whiff of perfume coming from his clothes. They sat silent. In a little while Phil again glanced at the man with that practiced look of dejection and innocence. The man moved an inch or two closer. "What's the matter, kid? You look as if you just lost your best friend." Underneath the friendly tones there was a searching sound.

"Aw, I'm broke and I ain't got a room for the night," Phil said.

The man offered him a cigarette. Phil's eyes, in the match-flare, said thanks, and what's the score, and what do you want, then—go ahead.

Phil leaned back against the bench, shoving down on his spine and spreading his legs a little. Almost immediately the man said, "You can come over and stay at my place if you want."

"No—that would be imposing—and I just met you."

"No, it wouldn't. It wouldn't at all! Don't you want to go over there?"

"These benches are hard. Let's go sit on the lawn for a while and talk about it."

The man said all right immediately.

Max drove his taxi around the Loop and the night-club district on the night shift. So the kid needs money. So I'll go along with this little gag. He didn't like doing it even if there was good money in it. The out-of-town men, the small-town men, the conventioneers, an occasional city guy out on the town, all looking for a good time. Fat, evil, sex-ridden, neurosis-ridden, lewd-faced, good suits strapped around their big bellies, thick, wise-cracking lips, dirty with dirty ideas. If it was some clean-looking kid, half-scared, needing this—well, that was different. But this scum!—Well, the kid needs the money.

Cab door coming open.

Another of the species climbing in, just like the one before, fat, middle-aged, looking like he's suffering from ulcers or something. Maybe just too much to eat and drink.

"Where to?"

Lewd-smiling face in the frame of the rear-view mirror.

"Know where I can go for a good time—know what I mean? I'm new in town."

Max stares back at the ugly face: Yeah, every cabbie's a pimp, mister, here to serve you.

"Well, it will cost you something, buddy."

The face smiles. "I'll give you a good tip. Somewhere where the women are—" The face shuts one eye down in a wink.

"How about ten bucks? It's generally five but I got a wife and sick kid at home—": Get out if you want, you sonofabitch.

Max stares back through the rear-view mirror: And I used to say, "Get yourself another taxi, buddy . . ." Well, the kid needs the money.

"Ten. Okay. But they'd better be nice!"

"What you're looking for, mister."

The cab leaped forward. Max delivered the livestock. He drove around the block and came back. The doorman gave him five bucks, as were his orders for every cabbie who brought a sucker to the place.

And Max, on his day off, got drunk. He found Phil alone in a bar doing the same thing.

"You sonofabitch! I don't like the way you're raising the money," Max said, meaning it.

Phil took another long drink before answering. "Do you think I'm enjoying it?" he asked.

"No. I don't like it," Max said.

"Okay, Max."

"And I don't like the way Norm will get his either."

"Okay, Max."

"Sure, the money's for a good cause but—"

"Yeah, Max."

"His old man didn't make a queer out of him," Max said. "Or if he did, he didn't mean to—and why don't the sonofabitch work like the rest of us?" Max drank. Then he said, "Sometimes I can't stand the guy."

"You mean—" Phil said, "—like always expecting us to pay for his drinks?"

Max nodded grim-faced, emphatic agreement.

"Yeah. I always notice that," Phil said. "And I don't like it either.

You better believe it. He's broke. Or he's waiting for a check from his father. Or he just lets you pay."

"I don't care what he does. But he could at least *work*," Max said. "He wants to be treated like a *woman*." And Max burst out into one of his wild, wrathful laughs.

And Norman wrote the letter. He polished up the phrases but brought in the innuendo that would bring fear and panic to his father: I need four hundred dollars to hush this thing up.

He smiled over the rereading and delicately folded the letter, inserted it into the envelope, sealed it. He knew how to handle his father—and his life was a sort of revenge on his father.

The fund for Nick was being raised.

112

Louie walked in without knocking. "Hi, Maw!" he said to Gee's old lady.

Gee's mother wore only a loose and dirty slip as she pattered around the kitchen barefooted, making coffee, dragging things back into place. The night before had been a big night. Cigarette butts and a couple of chips were scattered over the floor, and on the bed reserved for the purpose, where he had been dragged and thrown across it fully dressed, was one of the old man's gambling and drinking partners. Through the open door of Gee's old man's room you could see the edge of the bed and the old man wrapped and twisted in a sheet.

When Gee's old lady saw who it was, she made a big fuss over Louie. She patted his back and turned him around and around to look at him. "Where you been, Louie? Why don't you come to see us? Your old friends, they no good now?"

She patted his cheek with her big-boned foreign hand. "Gee he sometimes talk about you. He wonder too. Gee he work in steel mills now. Make plenty money. Gee he asleep. You go wake. Then I feed my boys."

Gee was sound asleep, with his mouth open and his hair licked down over his forehead by sweat. Louie shook his shoulder and pushed him around in the bed. Only grunts came out of him. Louie lifted the foot of the bed and dropped it back on its legs noisily. Several times he did this. "Goddamn—cut out—cut out—" Gee mumbled. Once he opened his eyes, looked straight at Louie, and closed them again. Then immediately they blinked open. "Hey!—For Christsake!" And Gee leaped out of bed, naked, shouting, wrestling, his arm wrapped around Louie's neck, until they both sat down hard in the middle of the floor while Gee's old lady stood in the doorway in her slip with her hands on her hips laughing at them.

Gee wiggled into his clothes, pushed his fingers through his hair, then came out into the kitchen barefooted. Paco happened to drop by too. They sat around all afternoon and part of the evening, shooting the bull, laughing and talking.

"Remember—remember the night out in South Chicago?" Gee said. "When you and that guy Tony had it out?"

"Remember?—Sure!" Louie said.

"I took off down the street," Gee said. "I took off to my aunt's house. She only lived about two blocks away. She said, 'What are you doing here?' I said, 'I'm going to *stay* here,' and I crawled into bed and I went to sleep and I got up early in the morning. I got up and I got on the streetcar—" Turning to Paco, "You lost one of your shoes, didn't you?"

"I took them off." And, grinning, "Oh, I got my feet all cut from glass and nails and every damn thing. But I got away though."

Gee grinned in remembrance. "I took off to my aunt's house. Man, I was sweating. I was crying."

Restless, and with something on his mind, Louie said, "I'm going." Nothing would hold him there.

"No, I gotta go somewhere," he said.

They met in the drug store where they had first talked, in the same booth.

He kept looking at her.

"What are you looking at, white boy?"

"Nothing." And he didn't pay her a compliment as he usually did.

Then he leaned over and said, "I want to marry you."

He was looking in her eyes and didn't see the pulse start pumping in her throat.

"I want to marry you," he said again, and here was the most beautiful person she had ever seen in her life.

"You see, it was more than just sleeping with you," he said. His eyes were sad and brown and deep and were looking at her. "Will you marry me?"

"Oh, baby—baby—" She took his head between her hands, her fingers curling into his ears, the nails biting in a bit as if, perhaps, to hold him, to keep him.

434

"I want to marry you, Judy."

"Do you know what you're saying?" Tears filling her eyes.

"I want to marry you."

"Your nephew?" she asked. "Has he gone to the hospital?" As if to get things back into focus. To balance things.

"I talked to him again. He said he'd go to take the cure." And, looking at her, "Did you hear what I said?" He took her shoulders roughly. "About an hour ago."

"I heard you."

"And?"

"Louie—Louie—"

He grabbed her wrists. "My brother died in the electric chair. Will you marry me?"

"Oh, Louie . . ."

She put her head down on his arms.

She was crying.

He let her cry for a while, then lifted her face. "Will you?"

She put her fingers against his lips. He opened his mouth and clamped his teeth down on a couple of them. Without letting loose he said, "Will you?"

Judy looked at him. Tears were running again. "They wouldn't let us live. It would be hell. Neither of them would let us live."

"The hell with them. We've got each other," Louie said.

"We've got two strikes against us," Judy said.

113

Carl's parents were out of town. He said, "Let's go up to my pad," and they went to his house on State Parkway to throw a party. About twenty of them.

They put only one record on the phonograph, and it played over and over:

> Down around the corner
> In a little school
> Children learn their lessons
> And the Golden Rule . . .

They danced, girls and boys in blue jeans, boys with their shirts out of their pants sloppily, girls chewing gum, dragging on marijuana cigarettes.

Every single morning
It's the same old thing
All the kids are waiting
For the bell to ring . . .

They shot themselves, those who were that advanced. All of them, the weedheads and the hypos, lay around in all sorts of positions on the floor and on couches, talking, taking off, feeling fine, dozing down.

Well, readin', writin', a-rith-me-tic
Taught to the tune of a licorice stick . . .

"Give me the roach, man."
"Here you are, man. Get hot!"
"Pick up on it, man."
"Like—everything's great, man—"
They just lay there. Lee on the couch, legs stretched out wide. All of them talking silly. Talking about fishes and flying, and cats and dogs—any kind of nonsense. Just rambling on and on.

No education is ever complete
Without a boogie-woogie-woo-gie beat
Well, all reet . . .

Any time any of the weedheads said something, it seemed so funny to them that they all giggled like a bunch of school kids.
"Just getting kicks, man!"
"Just for kicks!"

All the kids are waiting
For the bell to ring
When they hear it ringing
They all jump in line
Walk into the classroom
Feeling mighty fine . . .

Carl said, "It's a funny thing, but when you're on stuff there's no desire for sex."

To learn their A,B,C's
With rhythm and ease . . .

"Only the unnatural forms," Carl said.

Cause they got a teacher
Up on Basin Street . . .

They were now all nodding, slouching, nodding down in sleep.

And she does her teaching
With a boogie beat . . .

They torched up again. They blasted again. The hypos hit themselves again.

"He really comes on, man!"

Teacher is so happy
'Cause she's done her bit
To educate the kids
And really make them fit . . .

"I got something special, man! Let's try it, man!"

Nick, Lee and the other fellow who had just come to the party bared their arms and started tying them up.

To educate the kids
And really make them fit
To say their A,B,C's
With rhythm and ease . . .

Lee was in such a hurry . . . *Well, readin', writin', a-rith-me-tic* . . . that he opened his vein wide for the tip of the eyedropper to enter easily . . . *Is ever complete without a boogie-woogie beat . . . well, all reet . . .*

"What's happening, man?" someone asked Carl.

"Aw, you get tired of girls when you've had as many as I've had." And, pulling on his marijuana, sneering, "Poor little rich boy."

Woo-gie beat
Well, all reet . . .

Needles passing. Cigarette butts passing. "Get with it, man!"—"Cool, man!"—"Like—cool—" Some of them disrobing. Carl and another boy, nude, walking with their arms around each other into a room and closing the door.

And she does her teaching
With a boogie beat
Teaching the A,B,C's
With rhythm and ease . . .

"I know two fellows on stuff for twenty years, man, and the veins in their arms and legs and back of their necks are burned out."

"Yeah, they picked him up. He was going to canary and the pusher went around to jail and told him, 'Don't talk. We'll be around when you get out.' "

Well, all reet . . .

And the police, on the neighbors' complaints, made a raid in this fashionable neighborhood, to this respectable house. The raid was led by Sergeant Forbes.

Woo-gie beat . . .

The kids were all lined up on the thick rug under the crystal chandelier in the bookcase-lined front room.

Well, readin', writin', a-rith-me-tic
Taught to the tune of . . .

While the policemen held them there, listening to their lies, their pathetic protestations of innocence, their lies, their frightened pleas for mercy, their lies, Sergeant Forbes and another officer went through the rest of the house, searching it.

Sergeant Forbes opened the bathroom door.

The boy stood with his foot on the toilet seat and his shoe unlaced. He was taking some cotton from the tongue of the shoe for his hypo needle. The boy was shaking and running at the nose.

As the door opened the boy looked up.

Sergeant Forbes had never seen such distress, such an abandoned look in a pair of eyes before.

"Okay. Finish," Forbes said.

Nick injected himself.

"Give me the kit."

Nick handed it to him.

He looked again at the boy. Then he was staring at him. "I know you," Forbes said. "I remember you—I remember you from somewhere." Then recognition came. Slowly recognition came. Forbes looked straight into him, saying, "I know you dope fiends. You lie and lie and lie. Okay. Was it?"

"Was it what?" Nick asked, hanging his head.

"Indecent exposure."

Nick looked up at him.

"No, sir."

Forbes held his glance until he believed him.

"Okay," Forbes said. "I'm going to let you go. But get this straight —get it straight, buddy—if I ever see you under the influence again I'm going to see that you get cold turkey. I'm going to stick your ass in jail as far as I can and throw the key away!" And Forbes stood outside himself: Listen to you talk, you big slob! Acting tough. You big slob you! You know how soft you are.

He gave Nick a push toward the window. He opened the window and shoved Nick. "All right! Beat it!"

Nick climbed out the window and ran.

The phonograph said—

A *boogie-woogie-woo-gie beat*
Well, all reet . . .

114

The rain had been gently pock-marking the sidewalks for a long time. Old hats, shielding rough, bearded faces, wept with rain. Hard faces came out of the shadows into the shine of street lamps and passed back into the shadows.

A group of men were standing in front of a flophouse, their backs turned to the sidewalk, facing the doorway. They were looking up beyond the sign EXCELSIOR ROOMS 35¢. The voices said, "Some guy croaked in there. Some old guy." The curious crowd waited. The men's eyes shifted back and forth. Always their eyes went back toward the door. Through the glass they could see a long and dirty lobby with a clerk's cage and stairs disappearing up to the several layers of thirty-five-cents-a-night rooms; rooms large enough for only a bed and a chair, partitioned halfway up, then chicken wire going the rest of the way to the ceiling.

The men stood quietly on the sidewalk. Their eyes watched. Their voices were low and respectful. They said, "Yeah, he's been there all day."—"Did he starve to death?"—"I don't know."—"It's a wonder he didn't rot before they found him."—"He didn't have no papers on him saying who he was."—"Left it a blank, huh?"—"Yeah; it's better to leave it a blank."—"Sure is. Nobody's goin' to miss none of us anyhow."—"Christ, no!"—"Passed away in his sleep." "Old guy."—"Used to sell razor blades and shoe laces."—"He went out peacefully. That's the way I want to go. In my sleep."—"Jesus, I don't want to croak in no flophouse cage!"—"Why not! Better than on the street. Or maybe you want to be in the county hospital dying by inches for a couple of years."—"If he had stayed in there overnight the rats would of ate him."—"You're sure right, fellow!"—"I knew him. The old guy didn't have no flesh on his bones. I didn't know what his name was but I used to see him hobbling around an' I used to buy my shaving stuff off him."—"What room is he in? I wouldn't want that room."—"You don't think they're going to let nobody know what room! They'd never be able to rent it again."

They said it gruffly. Hard-boiled. In casual, kidding, iron-stomached terms. But their voices were low. Their voices were respect-ful. Their eyes were half scared. Their minds thought ahead: "I want to clear off this street. I don't want to peg out on Skid Row."—"Who does, buddy? Me, I'd like to live on a farm somewhere like when I was young."—"What difference does it make where you die?"—"What are they going to do with his body? They give them to the University for them to cut up, don't they?"—"Christ! I don't want no bastard cuttin' on me!"—"I heard they give fifty dollars for bodies."—"Crap! They're going to dump him in potter's field."—"I'd sell my carcass to the University for fifty bucks if I could. Think of all the whiskey you could buy with that!"—"Not me!"—"What the hell! Why not? When your number's up it don't matter where you croak or what they do with you. You ain't goin' to feel it none."—"Just the same, I don't want them cuttin' on me!"—"Won't they take him over to the morgue and pickle him?"—"Naw, they take you out to potter's field."—"Yeah, and they don't even put you in no box."—"Shovel you in, huh?"—"That's right, buddy. Just dig a hole like for a dog and cover you over."—"You pay your insurance this week yet, Smitty?"—"Hell! I drank that up when I left my old lady."—"They use quicklime, don't they?"—"Yeah, they throw some in on top of you so that it will eat you up quick."—"Christ! It ain't that you're going to know it. It's just—"

"Here he comes!"

There was quick silence. The eyes of the men looked up. Looked through the door, past the large letters: ROOMS 35¢. Their eyes saw the blue legs of a policeman appearing on the steps. Then hands holding the end of a stretcher. The stretcher coming down the steps at a steep angle. The stretcher wrapped in a black canvas and tied at both ends with a rope. The outline of the frail and bony body under the canvas.

The men angled their eyes toward the stretcher. The police car-ried the stretcher across the lobby, out beyond the doors of the flop-house and onto the sidewalk. "Poor guy."—"The poor old devil."—"Poor guy."—"Well, we all gotta go."

Their respectful bodies moved back, forming a little aisle. Their curious eyes looked down. From under the black canvas the dead man's feet stuck out. They were bloodless. They were stiff. They were turned in toward each other as if protecting pride or self and the rope of the canvas was knotted tightly around their ankles. They were like wax.

The police carried the dead man to the curb where the patrol was backed. They shoved the stretcher up into the wagon. It banged against the floor.

The men wavered in front of the flophouse for a while. Then they began to trickle away, aimlessly down the sidewalk. A couple of them went into the first tavern.

At a street corner a legless man let himself down off the curb on his roller-skate framework. He wore a red wool sweater. In his hands were his pads. The skates bumped over the car tracks and whirred softly against the cobblestones, leaving damp streaks behind them.

Their eyes were filled with tears.

Nick said, "You told me to meet you here."

"Yes, sit down."

They said, "We been saving money for you to take the cure in Kentucky."

They said, "Your mother signed the paper and you're going."

"I want to go," Nick said.

He couldn't look at them.

"We think we got just about enough money," they said.

They began counting it, piling it up on the table there in Juan's shop.

"Here," Norman said. "I put the touch on my folks." He didn't say any more but put four crisp hundred-dollar bills on the table.

Phil put a wad of small bills on the table on top of Norm's. "Never mind how I got it," he said. "I got it."

"Oh, you're still a good-looking guy, huh?" Max said.

"Some people think so."

"I got news for you," Max said. Then he remembered and shut up.

Nick said, "Where is Judge?"

Again their eyes filled with tears.

They told him.

"We knocked."

"The door was open."

"We went in."

His few possessions were there. A picture of his kids when they were young. One of his wife, yellow and fading. An envelope.

They handed him the envelope.

It said in an old man's handwriting: "For my boy, Nick."

"We ain't going to let him be buried just anywhere," Max said.

"We'll have to get a grave for him, and a box," Phil said.

"We'll have to get some more money."

Norman began composing the next letter to his father.

Nick kept twisting the thick envelope between his fingers without opening it. One tear came. And then another. They fell on the envelope.

Juan took the envelope out of his hands.

"What a great guy he was," Max said.

They counted what was in the envelope.

They placed thirty-four dollars and eleven cents with the rest of the money.

Nick put his head on the table and began to cry.

115

A prostitute in a doorway calls, "SSSssszzzz! Want to have some fun? Want to have a good time, honey?" Brave girl, dress so thin, so short, only a sweater pulled over the upper part of her. Brave, hell! Hungry! Rent due too. Gotta show the boys what you got if you're going to scratch a living. Gotta advertise. Damn tough going in this neighborhood. Plenty of competition. All whores. Almost any gal in this neighborhood, out alone after midnight, will turn a trick. Gotta live, honey.

Judy hurried along these night streets, walking all the way. Slanting snow followed her as shadow follows. Her feet were wet and cold. Her ears cold. The end of her nose. She hurried, shivering. She had to get there.

She stood, shivering, in a doorway near the house. She stood there an hour.

At last a figure came out of the house. Judy tensed. Then forlornly she relaxed. Felt another little shiver of cold go through her.

Her eyes saw the fat, bundled figure stooping against the wind and the snow.

"Aunt Rosa!" she called.

The fat woman stopped, looked, then came and stood close to her. "Judy, child! What are you doing here?"

"Is Louie there?"

Aunt Rosa put her arm around her. "You'll freeze here. Come on in the house."

Judy drew back in fear. "No." She tightened her cold, damp toes against the soles of her shoes. "I have to see Louie."

"Come on in."

"No. I don't want to. I'll wait here," Judy said.

"I'll go get him," Aunt Rosa said.

Louie came out at a trot, a suit coat thrown on, its collar turned up around his neck.

"Honey!" he said; and took her hands, rubbing them between his, trying to warm them.

"Louie, I had to see you."

"Come on in."

"No. I don't want to. Ang—the way she looks at me."

He kissed her.

"Where can we go?" she asked pitifully.

He thought helplessly and could think of nowhere. He put his arm around her to warm her and they commenced walking.

They walked four blocks. The wind helped blow them, the snow was icy against their necks, numbed their ears. A cold, faceless moon, a moon without expression, rode the night.

Somewhere in some house they passed they heard a Negro woman singing in lament: " 'You ain't the one. You ain't the one for me.' " Singing full-throated, lamenting every word of the way.

They walked another block or two, not talking. Then Louie remembered. He turned her around on the sidewalk and they went in the other direction.

They walked for a long time, until they were in a better neighborhood of well-kept two- and three-story apartment buildings.

"Wait here."

He left her on the corner. He went down the street a distance and in between buildings, then down several concrete steps. It was warm there against the door, and he knocked. The door came open, and for a moment, in the sudden light, he couldn't see anything—then the red glow of the furnace door.

"Hullo, Louie!" Swede said. "Come on in."

Louie pushed into the apartment building boiler room where Swede was the janitor and took care of the furnace.

"Just stoked her up for the night," the Swede said. "Can't offer you a drink though. Can't even offer you coffee. Cold as hell out, ain't it?"

Louie felt in his pocket and pulled out a five-dollar bill. "Here. Go get a drink. I want to come down here."

The Swede looked wise.

"It ain't what you think," Louie said.

The Swede took the bill and bundled himself into his coat: Why don't he hurry! Forgot his muffler, unbuttoned the coat and laced the muffler inside.

"Give me the keys," Louie said.

The Swede gave them to him.

"If I ain't here when you come back I'll leave them in front of the door."

Louie went back to Judy where she was shivering on the corner. He took her along the narrow sidewalk between apartment buildings, their feet crunching in hard snow and slipping on black ice, to the narrow snow-heaped cement steps down.

"We can go down there."

She nodded yes.

They went down the steps, Louie guiding her, his hand gentle on her elbow, past garbage cans filled to overflowing with frozen garbage, ashes and clinkers, feet deep in snow, snow going over the tops of their shoes and inside.

Louie opened the door.

Just the holes of the furnace door glowing red and yellow. Then the bare bulb turned on, and the ash- and soot-covered cement floor, the implements for stoking a furnace. A slight hissing from the water pipes. Old newspapers, stacked in a corner for selling.

And warmth.

Louie kissed her.

And they both stood at the furnace door, side by side, warming their hands, rubbing them together, looking sideways at each other, smiling a little.

Then Louie found a box, put a piece of newspaper on it. "Sit down, honey."

He pulled off her shoes, knelt and rubbed her cold and damp feet between the palms of his hands, the furnace door open, its low coals murmuring, looking, purring as a cat purrs.

And she stoops and kisses the top of his curly head. And he lays his head on her lap. Then again massages her cold feet until they are warm.

"Louie, I love you," she says.

"Honey, I know it. And I love you."

He puts newspapers on the floor so that he can sit down alongside her. He turns out the light. The furnace door is open and they sit on the floor in front of it, their arms around each other. It is like sitting in front of a fireplace. Arms around each other. Holding hands.

"I want to be with you, Louie."

"I want to marry you, Judy."

And the first bit of humor:

"Whoever heard of a Romano with kinky hair!"

"I like your hair."

His fingers went caressing.

Her bee-stung lips smiled fully, richly. And they kissed.

"I want to be with you once again, Louie."

444

"We don't have to do that. I didn't ask you to come down here to do that."

"I want to."

"Your clothes will get dirty."

"I don't care."

Louie turned on the light. Carefully he spread newspapers on the cement floor there in front of the furnace in the little cramped boiler room, all over the floor. Judy sat on a piece of newspaper on the floor watching him silently, sadly, her eyes moving with his every movement.

He started to take his coat off to make a pillow for her head, then first stuffed his hands in the pockets. "This is the coat I had on when I met you—when you talked to me." His hand came out of one of the pockets. "Look!" He grinned, surprised. His hand held a small stone.

Sitting there on the floor she held her hand out to him like a child. "Louie, give me that stone."

He looked at her longingly. He said, "I'll always remember you like that."

"Will you?"

Her eyes filled with tears. She still had her hand stretched out to him. "Give the stone to me, Louie."

He put the rock in the palm of her hand.

And they sat on the floor, as people do at the beach, turned toward each other.

They kissed.

For a long time they kissed. Then he rolled his coat up and gave it to her for a pillow.

He turned out the light. He closed the furnace door but opened the vents. Blue and purple, yellow and orange and green showed in the boiler room. Her cinnamon skin was bronze in it, his skin took on its ruddy tones. The first time she had had to go as a whore to a hotel that winked its eye and asked no questions.

They lay together on the cement floor on top of the newspapers and were happy. "My husband!—My wife!" they said.

And for an hour afterward they sat, arms around each other, fingers entwined, holding each other close, looking past the furnace door at the banked, many-colored coals, and were happier.

116

"Barbara isn't here," Grant said.

"I'm glad," Nick said. "I wanted to talk to you."

Then he had nothing to say. He just wanted to see Grant before he went to the hospital. He was ashamed to face Barbara.

"Why haven't you been over?"

"I don't know."

Nick looked around the apartment from the low chair where he sat facing Grant. "Is your wife here?"

"No."

"I'm a little afraid of her," Nick admitted with his slow, sad smile.

"You don't have to be. She likes you and we have talked about you. We know you have talent and we'd like to pay your tuition at the Art Institute. It's four years and it's hard work, but, you see, we believe in you."

Then he knew he had to tell Grant. His eyes filled. "No," he said, "I can't accept that. Maybe—some day—I can go. But I want to work my way through."

Grant gestured with his hand. "You *must* go. You have talent." And Grant looked at him, almost asking him to go as a favor to him. "I tried to do something for your father once."

It was out.

"My father!"

"Yes." Grant lit a cigarette slowly, remembering.

"Tell me about my father."

Grant sat a long time. Then he said, "Well, I knew him when he was about your age. He—well, he was much like you—sensitive, I mean. He got into some trouble." Grant shrugged. "I tried to help him." Grant gestured. "That's about all there is to tell."

Nick's lips were trembling. "That's more reason why I have to—to—"

It was out.

He knew he had to tell Grant.

Nick stood up. "Can I turn out the light?"

Grant nodded yes.

The room plunged to blackness.

Nick came back and sat across from Grant. He put his trembling arms between his knees and clamped his knees tight against them, his head hanging down in shame. "I'm a dope addict," he said.

Then silence. Both sitting. His arms hurt from the vise his knees made, tightening more.

Grant said, taking a deep breath, "I'm sorry, Nick."

More silence and blackness.

Grant said, finally, "Do you want to talk about it?"

"It's only been a few months," Nick said. "Since I haven't been coming here. I was ashamed. I don't know how I started—yes, I do."

If he was crying, the dark room did not show the tears; and he went on. He told Grant about his mother. He told him all he could remember about his life. "And I'm going for the cure," he said. He stopped. He sat head down.

Grant went through the dark apartment, in the dark poured two glasses of wine. "Here, Nick."

They sat again in the blackness.

"You'll need money," Grant said. "I'll pay for the hospital."

"No—" Nick said. "My friends—my uncles—those men I told you about—they have the money for me already."

"Yes. I know Max and Juan," Grant said quietly.

"Please don't tell Barbara."

Grant promised.

"I want to leave before she comes," Nick said.

Grant said, "I have something to tell you."

And Grant was silent a long time: Words can kill a person. And words, truths, can save a person. Should I try? Will I destroy him completely? Is this fair of you? He seems not to know. Why tell it? He's sensitive. Sensitivity can be strength or weakness. Will you take the responsibility if this does it completely? It could save him. Or kill him. Let it go, let it go. Let the dead past bury itself. Why fool with someone else's life? The two boys, Nick and Nick. You tried once. You failed. Let it go.

Instead Grant said, "Nick, this is going to hurt like hell. Maybe it will help you." He paused. Then he said, "Nick, your father died in the electric chair."

He told Nick, the son, all about it.

"That's why I have to take the cure," Nick said.

If he cried the midnight-dark room did not tell.

117

Someone rang the bell. Forbes fitted his false teeth into his mouth and laid aside the book he had been rereading. "I'll get it, hon," he called to his wife, and got up from his comfortable living-room chair. He went to the front door and opened it.

He was surprised to see, standing there in the darkness, the boy who had been accused of indecent exposure, the boy he'd later saved during a raid—the boy he'd often thought about.

"Mr. Forbes—" Nick said.

"Come in, boy."

Forbes led him to the front room and pointed to a chair.

Nick sat down, drawing his body in close. He looked up at Forbes. "I got your name and address at the police station."

Forbes smiled at him. He was pleased and amused; glad that the kid was here. There were rewards in police work.

"Yes, son?"

"You helped me twice," Nick said. "I came to ask you if you will help me again. I want to go to that place in Kentucky for the cure. I have the money and the application, but they say—they say it's hard to get in there. Will you help me get in?"

"Tell me about yourself," Forbes said.

As with Grant, Nick told him everything he could remember about himself and about his mother too.

When he was finished, Forbes said, "Leave the application here with me."

He walked Nick to the door. At the door he slapped him on the shoulder. "When you come out I want you to report here to me." : That's a hell of a way to put it. You mean you want to help the kid.

118

YOU AIIIIINNNNN'T BEEN BLUUUUUUE
NO NO NO NO NO NO NO NO NO NO NO NO NO
NO . . .

Nick clenched and unclenched his hands. Rags of sweat hung from his body and over the bedsheets.

> That feeeeelin'
> Goes steeeeeeeeeeeealin'
> Dooooooown to my shoooooooooes
> While IIII sit and siiiiiigh . . .

If he just had one shot. Just one fix.

> Gooooo 'loooooong, bluuuuuuues . . .

The iron bars were painted in soothingly soft colors of turquoise and rose. There were iron gates and barbed-wire fences and mounted guards. Iron grilles and locks barred almost everything. If he—

Al-ways get that Mooood In-digo . . .

Oh my God! *Oh my God!* Just one shot! Just one fix!

In the evenin'
When lights are looow . . .

If he only had one fix. If whoever had that phonograph would only stop—stop!—stop!

I'm so lonesome I could ccccry . . .

The fishhook cramps came again.

Yoooouuu ain't—been bluuueee
Noo—Noo—Noo—
Till you've had thaaaat
Moooood In-di-go . . .

If he just had one shot.

That feeeeelin'
Goes steeeeeealin'
Dooooooown to my shooooooes
While III sit and siiiiiiigh . . .

Just one fix.

Goooo 'looooooong, bluuuuuuuues . . .

Oh, God, I can't take it!

I'm so lonesome I could ccccry . . .

His eyes cried and his nose ran. He could not remain still on the bed but twisted from side to side, continually. Yawning and sneezing came. Twisting back and forth on the wet sheet, he was doubled into a knot. The cramps! The cramps! His hands trembled and became an uncontrollable shake with a will of their own and as if they did not belong to his body. His legs too.

I'm just a soul who's bluer than blue can be . . .

Goose pimples swept over his body and were as hard as stones. He was cold. Then he was hot. And cold again. His teeth chattered together.

One day.

And one night.

You can't sleep. You can't eat. If you could only sleep and put a bit of the torture out of the way. You can't! You can't! Cramps. Vomiting. Twisting back and forth.

Two days.

You can't sleep. Your body doesn't stop trembling. Your arms and legs jerk and twist. Your features are contorted in a skull-head grimace. You have dry heaves until your heart is pounding so hard against your ribs you're sure it's going to stop. And you wish it would.

Three days.

Your eyes and nose continue to run. The shakes. My God, *the shakes!*

You have diarrhea. The diarrhea is bloody. Your whole body is crying out, screaming for the drug—or just to be allowed to lie down, still, and die.

Three days and three nights.

Nick tries to sit up on the bed. He tries to speak to himself. Tell himself of his agony, his body's hunger for the drug. His throat sounds like the gurgling in a water pipe.

Convulsions come.

Four days.

> *When I get that Mood In-di-go*
> *I could lay me down and die*
> *YOU AIIINN'T BEEN BLUUEEE*

Five days.

His eyes emptied.

He sat up shakily, on the edge of the bed. He couldn't stand it any longer. He was a voluntary patient. He could leave whenever he wanted. He stood up. He stood there like a scarecrow, weaving on his feet. Just one fix and he'd be all right. This torture was too much. Just one fix and in less than five minutes he'd be feeling fine, nodding down in sleep. At peace.

He looked at his arm. Along the vein it was purple. The sick purple of a tattoo. Just one fix.

He dressed with trembling fingers.

My father.

My father died in the electric chair.

One fix. Just one fix.

> *That feeeeelin'*
> *Goes steeeeeealin'*
> *Dooooooown to my shooooooes*
> *While III sit and . . .*

450

He tried to lace his shoes but couldn't. He'd have to leave them that way.

Dressed now. Now to get away from here, somewhere where he could get a fix.

NO NO NO NO NO NO NO NO NO NO NO NO . . .

> *Not I, not anyone can travel that road for you*
> *You must travel it for yourself*

That was Judge Sullivan, yes, he remembered, and the words came back down the long corridor of time as if now, again, Judge recited them aloud.

And he said, "That's Walt Whitman, boy!" to me, "God, how that man could write!" and I was little and he held me in his arms, the red wine spilling out of the cracked white cup. His mustache was red with the wine . . .

Nick stood and walked waveringly toward the door. Just one fix.

Not I, not anyone.

Nick sat down on the edge of the bed, put his hands over his face and began to cry.

Not I, not anyone.

My father. I must be better than him. My mother used to tell me that.

Nick undressed.

Ten days.

Shaking off his painful agony.

In the night, in the dark, Nick. His eyes washed with remorse. Staring in fear. Wild with panic.

The days passed.

"Wanting is the beginning of getting." Judge said that.

"Some day we are going to be proud of you." That was Max and Phil and Norm.

He put his hands over his ears and tried not to hear.

The days passed.

And then he wanted to hear.

Wanting is the beginning of getting some day we are going to be proud of you, you must be better than your father she called me funny-face and we painted in the woods together Louie likes me likes me I know remember and Juan too not I not anyone can travel that road for you a Christmas tree and a train the sawed-off man on his roller-skate framework going down the sidewalk fast.

YOU AIIIIINNNNN'T BEEN BLUUUUUUE
NO NO NO NO NO NO NO NO NO NO NO NO NO NO
You ain't been bluuuuue . . .

blue, bluer than his blue crayon and Judge gave him some seeds to plant and told him to plant them under the porch where the sun wouldn't get at them did that woman say they were the best lays she had ever had funny face funny face not I not anyone and his mother was crying and holding him and the sky was blue, bluer than his blue the dandelions each had a little silver head of age and his mother knelt down before them and drew him down with her look honey blink and blow blow and blink and the little silver parts were on his nose tickling it and dancing against his closed eyelids and next year they would all be shining little yellow faces and his mother said the dandelion is so delicate that you always get some back on your nose if you get some back the dream comes true blow and blink a wish and a dream and the dream is more important than the wish not I not anyone the dream is more important than the wish not I not anyone . . .

The days passed.

Another.

Another.

The Christmas tree and Judge, Max, Phil, Norm. He was remembering it now. All of it. He was laughing and he was crying. And he had to go through with the cure. For them. He had to.

Not I, not anyone.

And the days needled themselves through the eye of time.

He was placed in an open ward.

He asked for drawing paper.

Inside of him they had asked for life and now those drawings came from his mind, came out of his memory, his eye, his emotions, out of the ends of his fingers onto paper.

And finally he was released from the hospital. Released as cured.

It was up to him now.

The doorbell rang and Sergeant Forbes answered it.

"I got out today," Nick said, "and I came over like you told me to."

"Come in, boy!" Forbes said, and held out his hand.

He took Nick into the front room and sat talking with him. His wife brought them coffee and slices of cake and left them again.

Forbes said, "I want you to come and see me every night for a couple of weeks."

"Yes, sir."

Nick reported to Forbes. A week. Two weeks. Three weeks.

Forbes found himself genuinely liking the boy. He reminded him of his own son—his stepsons. And Forbes talked to him until he knew everything about him he could possibly know. And the kid hadn't touched dope. This he knew.

And one night in the third week Forbes said, "You say your mother is prostituting herself in order to get dope?"

Nick colored, lowered his head and nodded yes.

"I want to talk to her," Forbes said.

Nick looked frightened. "You're not going to bother her?"

Forbes smiled and rubbed the palm of his hand over his graying crew cut. "No, boy! Of course not!" And, calling to his wife, "Hon, bring us some more coffee and a piece of that pie you made."

Over the coffee Forbes said, "And there's something I want you to know about your mother. She's a good woman and she has been a good mother." He smiled at Nick, rather sadly. "Drug use of itself doesn't make of a good person a vicious, evil, immoral, vile or wicked person."

He smiled again and signaled for Nick to finish the coffee and pie.

When they had finished, Forbes said to Nick, "You can sleep here. Curl up on the sofa."

Forbes parked his car in front of Headquarters at Eleventh and State and told Nick to wait for him.

He entered the building and went upstairs: I'm going to break the law.

He went into the room. There was an immense bottom and bottomless desk drawer there that was always open. Morphine, heroin, and almost any other narcotic was easily available to any policeman working on it.

Forbes put his hand inside.

I'm breaking the law.

At Nick's house, after Nick had introduced Forbes to his mother and she had gotten over her fright, Forbes said to Nick, "Take a walk, son. For about ten minutes. Then come back."

The door closed. Nellie immediately came and stood alongside Forbes, her hands clenched together in front of her, her head turned down against her collarbone, her eyes searching his imploringly.

"Is he cured? Will he stay cured?"

"Yes," Forbes said: God knows I hope so.

"Thank God!" Nellie said.

"Look," he said, trying to make his voice gruff, "I'm going to give you enough to keep you from getting sick. Just enough. No more. As long as the kid stays off, you'll get yours *daily*. I'll be here every day."

He handed her her fix.

Police work as it should be done, he thought. Prevention.

Daily Nellie got her fix from the policeman. And a month later Forbes sat in his front room with Nick. He told Nick that he had been supplying his mother with drugs.

From his pocket, then, Forbes pulled one of the deadly capsules. He put it on the cocktail table between them and shivered in his fear. Then he looked up from the capsule to Nick. Again he shivered in fear.

"I think you're cured," he said. "From now on"—and he was frightened by his own words; but went on—"I'm going to give you a week's supply at a time for your mother. Give her just enough at a time." He stood up. He put his hands on Nick's shoulders. He could feel himself tremble again, and said, "This could be the end of you, Nick. But you have to trust yourself. I have to trust you. I believe in you." And, clearing his throat, "My wife isn't here. Let's go out in the kitchen and make ourselves some coffee."

They had the coffee in the kitchen. And Forbes, looking at Nick, believing in him, though he knew he would still check for a while, knew that he, Forbes, had found himself and ennobled himself in his own eyes, that all of his early training and liberal thinking had led him, a policeman, away from the law as it existed, and which he recognized as being basically wrong, and had led him into the camp of "the people" where he had always belonged.

At the door he said, "Okay, kid, here it is." He put the deadly drug, with fear, into Nick's hands. "And here are some books," he said gruffly. "You won't like them at first."

Smoke from her cigarette swirled slowly around the room's single bulb. It played purple-blue through the edges of her long blond hair, and her deep-set eyes looked beyond it, watching him gratefully.

Nick sterilized the needle. He tied up his mother's arm. When the vein was ready he inserted the needle. Her blue-gray eyes watched him, never once leaving his face. She was like a dog being fed or petted. Like a child given a piece of candy.

"Thanks, Son," she said.

"That's all right, Mother."

He cleaned and put the kit in its hiding place. He put the key in his pocket.

There had been temptation, temptation, temptation for him at first. The big bang. When you first take the stuff. The big bang when you take it again after the cure.

Temptation.

And then none.

Repulsion.

And love and pity for his mother.

He locked the needle away, and he walked under the clear, cold autumn sky.

He went where he had gone every night since he had been released from the hospital.

He stood under a tree.

He counted seven oblongs of light up and three across. He looked up.

He stood there.

If he could just see her enter or leave the building.

Every night he did this.

8 *let no man write their epitaph*

119

It was an unusual night. Louie Romano was having a good time on the kitchen floor. For once there were no grownups around to yell at him and make him stop doing things. Not even Ang. He had his legs sprawled out, and between them a hammer, a pot, an old alarm clock. He had the pot turned over with its bottom up. With the hammer he beat on the pot. Then he tapped the top of the alarm clock. Then put the hammer down and rattled the marbles together. He did this in a thoughtful routine.

Outside the prison a taxi had drawn up.

A girl sat inside. The driver looked over his shoulder at the girl. "Well, here we are." She didn't answer. Her face was close to the window. She looked up at the jail, at the wall of bars and dim light behind them. "Do you want to get out here?" the taxi driver asked. "You wait here. Just wait here. Just let me sit here," the girl said.

The warden said, "Now this isn't just a show down here today and you have to keep quiet. I don't want any noise and I don't want anybody to yell at Romano. Anybody who does will be taken out of the execution chamber immediately. The chief bailiff is here to see that my words are enforced. One thing more"—he chewed down on his cigar— "I want all of you to button your coats. If any of you want to take out paper or pencils, you had better do it now." And knowing that some of the spectators had come drunk, he said, "Make sure you keep quiet. You've got to have respect for the boy who's going."

He was all caught up. Eighteen steps from this spot they would strap him into the electric chair. Death would be quick and cheap in the little brick and plaster execution chamber. They would kill him with a penny's worth of electricity.

There would come a growling sound like that made by a truck going up a steep hill under a heavy load. Out of the dynamo would race the lightning. It would hit Nick's brain first, knocking him senseless and throwing him, tense and shuddering, against the taut straps. His mouth would gape open, almost breaking the jaws, in a silent scream more horrible than any sound. The tendons in his neck would stick out like water pipes. Across his forehead the veins would pop, large as pencils.

Yellow would creep into the row of bulbs in the control room, and the legal agents of death, without turning to look, would pour more current through Nick. There would be no blinking or dimming of the lights throughout the jail, for the chair will have been switched to special current piped into the jail for the purpose. Into the chair and its occupant the electricity that rapes the heart of its last heartbeat would run, true and hot.

There would be four charges of the chained lightning. Four times the million needles of death would stab him. Most of the current, following the nervous system, would pass along the blood vessels and through the heart. For five seconds 1900 volts of electricity would crash through him. The lightning would still the heart and ravage the reflexes—

Break in the current—

The heart that had stopped immediately at the first touch of the electricity would now beat rapidly and strongly and Nick's arterial pressure would rise fantastically.

Then—900 volts of lightning surging through him.

Steady murder.

Fifty-five seconds with the marker at 900.

The thunderbolt would come through burning hot. His brain

would be heated to 140 degrees Fahrenheit. The current would actually fry him. He would be well cooked.

Third charge—1900 volts for another five seconds.

The great vessels would be full of fluid blood. The lungs deeply overfilled with blood. Already there would be deep fissures and hollows between the layers of the brain.

And the lightning would continue to streak through him.

Break in the current, cutting its flow from 1900 to 900 volts. Current running at the 900 marker to complete the second full minute of frying in the electric chair.

Now a plume of smoke rising from the floor, signaling that the ankle sponge is dry and hot, burning the flesh.

And Nick would be twisted in the chair, thrown roughly against the straps, his head in its black rubber mask twisted grotesquely awry on his swollen neck. His arms would be frozen to stone in a rigor mortis under the cruel chromium clamps. His legs would be locked at the knees, and only breaking could take the sitting position from them. His sexual organ would be swollen in an erection.

And the yellow would be in the row of bulbs in the control room. The growling sound like that made by a truck climbing a hill under a heavy load would sound across the death room. That, and the heavy breathing of the spectators.

Two minutes.

Current off.

Popped eyes staring through the glass at what had been a human being.

And the purple smoke from the charred ankle rising up over the head of the still figure in the chair.

Silence.

Horrible silence.

The old priest then stepping forward and giving the last blessing. Sad mumble of deep-throated words. Zigzag of a cross with a waving arm. Then, as the priest stepped back, one of the guards would unbuckle the top strap from around the chest where hope and pride and life had been; and another guard would rip loose the cheap white cotton undershirt from off the young, virile shoulders, with a loud tearing sound there on the little stage of death, rip it down in shreds from around the broad, husky chest. No demurring from the dead man. A corpse has no pride.

With a towel the guard would then wipe the heavy perspiration from the shoulders and chest. And from under each armpit the sweat would fall, like drops of rain; fall on the black leather of the *chair, drip to the floor. In his pants shorn above the knees, his undershirt in strips of cloth at his belt, wide-eyed, innocent-eyed, glaze-eyed for all to see. Humiliation is nothing to a corpse.*

The chair would show its work and the doctors would come from their seats at elbow's reach from the dead man. First would come the jail physician, his stethoscope dangling from his neck. He would lay the stethoscope on Nick's chest, then step back while the other doctors came forward. Not until every doctor examines him and the jail physician has gone back for another search for a vagrant heart-beat, would Society be satisfied.

The mute man waits. Waits on his throne, his black rubber the spotlight, a huddle like that on a football field, almost comical in their sedate clothing and with their furrowed brows and necks craning together, were it not a serious business, this, of making certain that Society had struck back and killed in turn.

The mute man waits. Waits on his throne, his black rubber crown slipped over his face. Waits with his arms regally upon the rests of the chair but no scepter in his hand. Waits in coldness and disgrace. Under the spotlight a blind-eyed boy on a little stage behind a frame of glass.

Then, no longer watching the dead statue in the chair, the jail physician would announce, slowly and officially, "This man is dead."

Avenged and closed.

No stretcher would be brought. The warden would give the sign to four of his men. They would take the dead body by the legs and arms and quickly walk toward the little door while the audience watched. A corpse has no voice.

The newspaper men would jump out quickly and go to the warden's office to phone their newspapers. The crowd would shuffle out. The metal screen would be pulled down over the little stage. The lights would blink out and, in the dark, would be only shadows of what had happened that night.

And really there was nothing unusual about it.

In the autopsy room on a slab they would dump the body. Rigor mortis would have set in by then with rigid teeth. Where the electricity had hit hardest, at ankles and wrists, the skin would be black and blue as from blows. Inside the body the brain cells have been destroyed; and all through the body the passage of the current shows its work. There is vasculation around the vessels. The small meshwork of fine veins has bled internally. The capillaries are broken. There are red dots in the skin tissue.

For three hours they would hold the body. Cold and white

Nick would lie in death. His arms and legs would need breaking to fit him properly to the casket. His white flesh would lie, face up, on the slab. His sexual organ would point straight up. A corpse has no vanity.

The dead eyes would be open and staring at the ceiling. The eyes would be congested with an unnatural accumulation of bright red blood. The pupils dilated, icy with highlight. The chair has killed more viciously than any killer. Without pride, without life, he would lie, staring with a fixed concentration at the ceiling while all about him his ruined body is frozen on the slab.

Even so, with clothes drawn over the discolored body, with the long-lashed lids drawn down over the innocent eyes, with the curly brown-black hair combed back in waxlike ringlets, he would have a good-looking corpse. There would be a touch of a smile at the edge of his lips as if, even in death, he laughed, was one ahead of them. Carried the laugh with him.

A corpse laughs, whitely, at all outrages.

On the cold slab, this night, Nick will stare through bright, blind eyes at the ceiling. His heart will be sucked of all its blood. His heart will be empty. Empty of defeat and longing. No beat left. No unfulfilled desire. No heavy defeat. Dry, like a sponge. Heavy, in the chest, like a rock.

In the morning his mother will call for the body.

It is night.

In the big, lonely, lonesome city a telephone rings.

Louie walks in the night looking for her.

It rings again.

Louie walks, desolate.

She gave me that and she disappeared. That's why she wanted to be with me again. She knew she was going to disappear.

It rings again.

She loved me. I know she loved me.

He walked into the tearoom and up to the girl behind the cash register.

"Can you tell me why Judy hasn't been here?"

"She doesn't work here any more," the blond girl told him icily.

"Can you give me her address?"

"We are not allowed to give such information." Severely.

Louie walked out.

Two nights. And that was all. Two nights. And it was like a marriage—this one girl he had loved.

And a telephone rings in the city.
It is answered.
The person calling hangs up without speaking.

There are many, many, many nights.
Louie wanders. He goes into the colored night club where he and Judy had gone. I will find you. I have to find you.
Your people are my people. I will live among them until I find you.
He puts a coin into the juke box. The juke box says:

> It's quarter to three
> There's no one in the place
> Except you and me
> So, set 'em up, Joe
> I've got a little story
> You oughta know . . .

I'll stay here till I find you, Judy.
Louie stood against the juke box, looking down at the disk whirling around, glass held in his hand.

> We're drinking, my friend
> To the end
> Of a brief ep-i-sode . . .

A Negro came over and slapped him across the back. "Don't you remember me, man? I'm the guy who insulted you."
Louie looked up. "Have you seen her?"
"You got the same job, man, with the white folks?"
"Yeah—same job. Have you seen her?"

> Make it one for my baby
> And one more for the road . . .

This is the Art Institute. Nick went up the steps between the two lions. He had had to wash the shirt and let it dry before he could go out because it was the only shirt he had.
He went up between the two lions, with his paint box.

> So drop another nickel
> In the machine
> I'm feelin' so bad
> I wish you'd make the music
> Dreamy and sad . . .

Louie leaned with his elbows against the bar. It was the loneliest song in the world.

And when I'm gloomy
You simply gotta listen to me
Until it's talked away . . .

Louie went to the toilet. He stood there, one hand against the wall, staring at the small sign over the trough without seeing it.
He put his head against the cold tile of the toilet wall.
Judy, I'm right back where you found me.
He went back to the bar.

So, thanks for the cheer
I hope you didn't mind my bending your ear . . .

"Come on, man, we're closing, man," the Negro bartender told Louie.
And a telephone rings.
And Louie puts a quarter into the juke box in a bar near his house.

It's a quarter to three
There's no one in the place
Except you and me
So, set 'em up, Joe . . .

Louie sat at the bar, went over every detail of his romance with Judy.

I've got a little story
You oughta know
We're drinking, my friend . . .

Again the telephone rings.
Louie puts in a quarter and pushes the button three times. Louie plays the song over and over.

Make it one for my baby
And one more for the
Loooooong
Loooooone-ly
Looooone-some road . . .

Judy sits at a table in the back of a little bar. Between her hands she holds the stone, pressing her palms into it. Tears fill her eyes. She looks down at the stone, again presses it between the palms of her hands.
Her eyes are brimming.
Is it better to leave him now? Will I hurt him less now or if I

marry him? And which will hurt me more? I have to think, I have to think . . . Oh, Louie!

She lifts her palms and presses her lips down against the stone.

> *It's a quarter to three*
> *There's no one in the place*
> *Except you and me . . .*

Louie sits at the bar looking dull-eyed at the bartender who is stacking chairs on the tables, piling stools on the bar.

> *So, set 'em up, Joe*
> *I've got a little story . . .*

The bartender bangs the chairs and stools angrily. He never saw a guy so hot for one song. A whole two hours of the same goddamn song. Comes in, starts putting quarter after quarter in the box and pushing the same button over and over. 'Nough to make a guy crazy. And nobody else comes in the place tonight. I'm stuck with the loon. Bang! Bang! A couple more stools stacked on the bar. And the guy don't even know when you're going to close the goddamn place.

Bang! Bang! the bar stools said, angry, too, as they marched along the bar and down toward Louie.

> *Well, that's how it goes*
> *And, Joe, I know you're getting anxious to close . . .*

And the bartender, mumbling loud enough for Louie to hear, "My name ain't Joe, but I am."

He snaps out the neon light in the window.

"Okay, buddy," Louie says, nodding his head and listening to the words of the song—

> *So make it one for my baby*
> *And one more for the*
> *Looooong*
> *Loooone-ly*
> *Loooone-some road . . .*

And a phone rings in the city.

"Grant," Wanda says, "will you answer that? For over a week it has been ringing, and every time we answer, someone hangs up."

"Hello," Grant said into the phone.

"Grant?" the voice said.

"Yes."

"This is Nick."

"Hello, Nick!"

"I'm out."

"Why don't you come over?"

"How's Barbara?"

"She's fine."

Nick looked at the telephone receiver. He put it back to his ear and spoke slowly.

"Is she married?"

Grant smiled.

"No."

Nick said, "I think I'm cured. I've been out for four months now."

"Why don't you come over to see us, Nick?" Grant asked.

Again Nick looked at the telephone receiver, then put it back to his ear. "No. I have to be sure first. Every day I give my mother her shot." His eyes, full of tears, were staring at the wall of the tight little telephone booth. "She's my mother. She's been through hell. I—I—"

There was a long silence. Then Nick said, "If I don't touch any for a year, can I come over?"

"Yes, Nick."

"Good-bye, Grant."

"Good-bye, Nick."

> *A tree falls.*
> *A leaf flutters down.*
> *No life is lived in vain.*
> *No death goes unrecorded.*
> *No voice is lost to an ear.*
>
> *Nellie? Nick the father? Nick the son?*
> *Let no man write their epitaph.*

WILLARD MOTLEY was born in Chicago in 1912, where he attended grammar and high school. While he was still a child he contributed to the children's pages of various newspapers. In high school he acquired a lasting interest in sports, and wrote dozens of short stories with a sports background. His first cross-continent trip was to New York by bicycle; shortly afterward he traveled to California by jalopy, working at a variety of jobs, including farm worker, ranch hand, waiter, shipping clerk, cook and coal hiker. His trip West resulted in several articles which appeared in such magazines as *Commonweal*. When he returned to Chicago, he worked with the housing division of the Federal Writers Project as a photographer, radio script writer and interviewer on slum conditions. Here he had his desired opportunity to observe and know the life of the honkytonks, poolrooms and flophouses of the slums of Chicago.

LET NO MAN WRITE MY EPITAPH is a sequel to Mr. Motley's best-selling novel, *Knock on Any Door*, which was published in 1947. *Knock on Any Door* brought him immediate acclaim and caused the New York *Times* to say, "An extraordinary and powerful new naturalistic talent herewith makes its debut in American letters." It is the story of a Chicago boy whose tendencies to decency are beaten down by the life of the slums; it was later made into a motion picture. *We Fished All Night* was published in 1951; it dealt with the postwar problems of three young men in Chicago. After completing this book, Mr. Motley moved to Mexico, where LET NO MAN WRITE MY EPITAPH was written.